Contents

War In The West
- Chapter 1 1
- Chapter 2 15
- Chapter 3 30
- Chapter 4 43
- Chapter 5 56
- Chapter 6 66
- Chapter 7 76
- Chapter 8 85
- Chapter 9 96
- Chapter 10 107
- Chapter 11 117
- Chapter 12 129
- Chapter 13 136
- Chapter 14 145
- Chapter 15 156
- Chapter 16 165
- Chapter 17 175
- Chapter 18 185
- Chapter 19 195
- Chapter 20 204
- Chapter 21 217
- Epilogue 229
- Glossary 231
- Historical Background and References 232
- Other books by Griff Hosker 234

War In The West

Book 10

in the

Border Knight Series

By

Griff Hosker

War in the West

Published by Sword Books Ltd 2020

Copyright ©Griff Hosker First Edition

The author has asserted their moral right under the Copyright, Designs and Patents Act, 1988, to be identified as the author of this work.
All Rights reserved. No part of this publication may be reproduced, copied, stored in a retrieval system, or transmitted, in any form or by any means, without the prior written consent of the copyright holder, nor be otherwise circulated in any form of binding or cover other than that in which it is published and without a similar condition being imposed on the subsequent purchaser.
A CIP catalogue record for this title is available from the British Library.

Dedication

To Rich, Steve, Dave, Alison, Roger, Phil and all the other readers who have been on this journey with me since the beginning.

Part One

Sir William

Chapter 1

I was used to warriors raiding my land for I had been Lord of Elsdon where I had fought the Scots who had sought to wrest that land from us. Now I was Lord of Hartlepool and I thought I knew the land and that it was free from raiders. Not long after I took over the manor I discovered that I was wrong. In my defence, my eye had been taken west to Wales. The King had commissioned me to help Sir Robert Pounderling to strengthen the border along the Clwyd Valley and when I should have been looking to my people I was doing what my family had always done and I was serving the King. The Prince of the Welsh, Dafydd, had been defeated in a battle but was raising more men and the King had asked me to help him. I would be leaving for Wales in the Spring. Thus it was that I was poring over lists of supplies we would need instead of riding my land and looking for enemies.

The Bishop of Durham had given me the manor as a reward for services I had done him. Relations between the Bishops of Durham and my family had not always been the best and my father had the blood of one Bishop on his hands. Times had changed and the Palatinate knew the value of the knights of the Tees led by the redoubtable Sir Thomas of Stockton. It was a good manor for the port was an increasingly important one and the Bishop used it to export wool and to import wines. I had little to do with the mundane, day to day running of it. Brother John had been an incompetent priest responsible for running the port. I had managed to rid myself of him, and he had been replaced by a clerk, Roger of Fissebourne, and he knew his business. He was as dull a man as you could wish to meet but he did his job well and actually seemed to enjoy the totting up of columns of squiggles. I was a warrior and a man of action and I was happy to leave that to him.

War in the West

He came to me one morning not long after day had dawned. I had risen early and was breakfasting as I did my own clerical work and studied the lists of men I would take to Wales.

"My lord, I am sorry to have disturbed you so early…"

I wiped my mouth and waved him to a seat, "Join me."

He was a small birdlike man. He reminded me of the sanderling which puts its head down and scurries along seemingly oblivious of all else. "There is trouble."

I had learned to listen to my people. Elsdon had taught me that and they had often given me intelligence which had saved lives. I gave him my full attention.

"The fishermen who fish the mouth of the river brought news of ships."

I drank some of the ale which had been served with my fresh bread and cheese. "There are always ships on the river. They sail to my father's manor at Stockton."

"These were not ships carrying cargo. The fishermen said they were hunters of slaves and they rowed."

"Vikings!"

"It was dark, and they could not see those on board, but they recognised the ships, there were two of them; one was a snekke and one a drekar. The drekar had a crow on the prow."

I had also learned to be decisive. "Have we any ships in port?" The Bishop used cogs to carry his cargo and I had the authority to commandeer such vessels.

"None, lord, but *'The Heron'*, Captain Kingston's ship, is due in port within the next days. She has been to Frisia."

"When she docks let me know and do not let her leave nor any other ship which docks in the next few days. These pirates must be hunted. You have done well."

The man beamed, "Thank you, my lord."

I had learned in Elsdon that often men will work twice as hard if they are praised and complimented. It cost nothing and it bred loyalty. My steward was Paul son of Michael. As soon as he had escorted Roger out of my hall he hurried back and he was followed closely by Geoffrey of Lyons, my squire. "Geoffrey, saddle our horses, we ride abroad."

"We need men with us, lord?"

"A dozen, archers and men at arms equally."

He hurried off. I could rely on him. "Paul, I need a rider to take a message to my father. By the time you return it will be written."

As he left me, I stood and went to fetch parchment, ink and quill. It was unlikely that the raiders would be a danger to my father. It took a couple of days to sail up to Stockton and riders could cut off any ship which attacked the villages along the river before they made it to sea again. However, he needed to be warned. I was succinct and had the letter sealed when my steward brought in Rafe, one of those who worked in the stables. Paul had made a good choice for Rafe was an excellent horseman. Too slight to be a man at arms and without the training to be an archer, he would become a good horse master in time. "Ride to Stockton and deliver this to my father. Await a reply and tell him that I will ride to Snook Point at the mouth of the river to look for signs."

"Yes lord."

I reached the stables and found that my men were ready. Geoffrey had included Erik Red Hair with the men. He was a good choice for he was a Viking and whilst not a pirate himself, he would have an insight into such raiders. Ged Strongbow led my archers. None of us wore mail but Geoffrey had fetched me a brigandine and mail coif. I donned my arming cap and coif and then fastened my leather brigandine. I was a knight and always had my sword. I mounted my hackney, Destiny, and then fastened my cloak around my neck.

"We ride to Snook Point. Fishermen have reported raiders. We will use the beach and ride close to the dunes. The tide is on the way out and we can use the hard sand."

Erik said, "Is it one ship or two, lord?"

I dug my heels into Destiny's flanks as we headed for the gate in the town wall. "The fishermen said a snekke and a drekar."

"Then we do not have enough men, lord."

"We have enough men to disturb them and to ascertain the veracity of their report. It was dark when they saw them."

Erik knew the type of ships and, as we rode the few miles and passed Seaton Carew, he told me of the difference. "A snekke might have just four oars a side while a drekar can have up to thirty. It is unlikely to be such a large drekar but the crews of the two ships might be as many as fifty or sixty men."

Tom of Rydal and Alan Longsword were my most experienced men at arms and they rode at my side. Alan shook his head, "There is nothing for them here, lord. Snook Point just has seals and the few men who hunt them. Perhaps they come just to hunt seals. This is the time of year when they bask on the sands of the estuary and are easy to hunt."

Erik laughed, "You do not come with a snekke and a drekar to hunt seals!

I waved an irritated hand, "It is idle speculation. There is Greenabella, the home of Peter Seal and his family. They will tell us what they have seen."

The land was still in the grip of winter and few men stepped far from their home and their fires, but fishermen and sealers would have to go out just to feed their families.

Peter Seal had a large family and they lived in the upturned hull of a large ship which had foundered on the rocks of Long Scar when Peter's father had been alive. They had made it into a most comfortable house. Six men and their families lived there, and they made a living hunting the seals and rendering their flesh into oil. The seal skin boots their wives made were highly prized. There was always a column of smoke from the hall as they had to keep the fires burning to render the flesh as well as to keep them warm. However, as we neared the hall, I realised that this was a different fire. The hall was burning!

I drew my sword and my men emulated me as we left the sands to cross the dunes to see what had happened. It was all too clear even before we reached the burning home; the bodies of the men lay where they had fallen. They had fought hard and I saw many footprints around them. While my archers nocked their arrows, I waved Tom of Rydal and Geoffrey to search the hall. I rode with Alan Longsword and Erik Red Hair. We followed the trail down to the sea. I saw, for myself, the blood which told me of the fight the Seal family had put up. The ground was hard. The salt prevented a frost but the cold had kept it firm and we saw the seal skin boot prints and they gave us rough numbers of the enemy.

Erik said, "Slavers!"

Denmark, Frisia and Norway still had a slave trade and although it was not as bad as it had been before the time of the Conqueror, pirates still preyed upon isolated communities. The footprints stopped at what had been the high tide mark. Erik dismounted and examined the sand. He scrabbled around and picked something up. He flourished it and held it to me. It was a brooch from a cloak, "This is Viking. Norwegian. It proves they are slavers."

I nodded. I had failed these people. It had happened before along the border and I had sworn it would not happen again, but it had. "And where will they be now?"

Erik slipped the brooch into his leather pouch and remounted his horse, "This is not over. They will need more slaves than the ones they took here. I am just surprised that they risked fighting six sealers! They are tough men and, from the blood we saw, they hurt the raiders. There are easier targets."

His words should have been a warning, but I was still distracted by this imminent war in the west. "How did they do this? What is their method?"

"They use a snekke to send in their scouts. They may have Ulfheonar, shapeshifters who are the best of warriors and can move unseen. They would have landed first and silenced the dogs. By the time the drekar landed their men then the warriors from the snekke would be in position and they would have slain the men first."

"And then?"

Erik pointed to the river, "There are many mudflats and streams where their ships can hide. They will step their masts and be hidden. Even if we could find them then the mud would protect them. They are only vulnerable to a ship, another drekar which is bigger."

"And we have none. This is cold comfort you offer me, Erik Red Hair!"

He laughed, "I am a Viking and we speak the truth. That is what you wished to hear is it not, my lord?"

"Aye, it is. We will ride back and warn all those who live in these isolated places of the danger. They can come into Hartlepool until we have caught them."

"How will you do that, Sir William?" Alan was like a rock. He, like me, would be working out how to stop these pirates.

"We take a ship and sail into the river. We may not have a drekar, but we have longbows. We take them and rescue the captives." I sounded more confident than I actually was for I had never fought from the deck of a ship.

By the time we had visited all the farms and homes which lay close to the sea, it was past noon. None had taken me up on my offer. They were a hardy people, and they were proud and had stiff necks. They had been warned and all of them began to build a beacon so that they could summon help. As we rode back, I told my men what I planned. I wanted all of my men ready to move as soon as there was a ship for us.

My wife was waiting for me with Dick, my son. I saw from his angry young face that he was less than happy at being left at home. Even before I had time to greet my wife he burst out, "You did not wait for me!"

"And if you are a slugabed then whose fault is that?" I glared at him for he needed to be trained as a squire soon and this was the behaviour of a child, we had no time for such luxuries; we lived on the borders. "Now be silent while I speak with your mother."

My wife had a good heart. She was holding Matthew, my youngest, but she stroked Dick's hair, "Don't worry, your father will take you next time."

Of course, my wife had no idea what we had been doing and when she discovered that we would be hunting pirates then she might be less keen for him to come. "Slavers have taken the Seal family." Her eyes showed the terror in her heart. I invited those at risk to shelter here but I suspect that few will take us up on the offer. I shall go to the port to see if there is a ship we can use. I would not take a fishing boat for they are too small. When we go, I know not how long we shall be away. We have to catch them and return the captives."

"You are right. Dick, you will stay with me while your father seeks a ship."

"But you said that I could go with him!"

I took him from the protection of his mother and held him at arm's length so that I could look into his eyes, "That depends. Can you be as all the others I take and obey orders?"

I watched him bite his lip, "Of course."

"Good, now stay with your mother while I find us a ship."

I took Geoffrey with me and we went to the Slake; it was the name the locals had for the harbour. I saw that the tide was rising, and the fishing ships were preparing to go to sea again. Although it was more productive, they would not risk a night time fish again. They would know how lucky they had been not to be taken by the raiders! I stood on the quay with Roger. I saw the sails of a ship in the distance. I looked at Roger who nodded, "That is ***The Heron'***, Sir William." He smiled, "You get to know the ships who use the port regularly. He will take an hour or so to reach us."

I nodded. I had no intention of leaving for this would be my thinking time. I walked with Geoffrey to the end of the mole. I could see down the coast towards the river and the hills of Eston beyond. My father would have had word already and a message would have gone across the river to the lords who lived along the south bank of the river to warn them of raiders. Although not a unique event, I had not heard of a slaving raid for many years and I wondered what had prompted it. Perhaps the King of Scotland had been successful in his war against the Viking Kingdoms and reclaimed that land for Scotland. That might well make some Norse choose to resort to other ways of making money. Whatever the reason we would not have an easy task and I did not relish fighting from the deck of a ship, even in an estuary.

Geoffrey seemed to read my thoughts, "It will not be easy tracking down raiders in those inlets and estuaries, lord."

"Aye, you are right, but we have one advantage. They cannot raid with prisoners on their ships. They will need a camp and that is what we shall look for. It may be that they have what they wanted. I do not know if they have already raided the settlements on the south bank. If they have then the Seal family are doomed to a life of slavery."

He was silent and then he said, "It is barbaric!"

"And yet the men who do this are great warriors. It is a contradiction but, of course, they are not knights who have sworn an oath."

He gave me a sharp look, "My brother broke his oath!"

"To save you. Things are never black and white, Geoffrey. They are shades of grey and what seem to be clear waters are often muddied." He often brooded on his brother's actions for he had broken his oath for a good reason. His brother! "Come, Captain Kingston will soon tie up."

We walked back around the stone breakwater. Even though we had only stood there a short time I could taste the salt on my beard, and I was glad we had worn our cloaks. The east coast was a cold one. I saw Roger of Fissebourne speaking with William Kingston and knew he was telling him what had happened. His ship was a valuable one. He now used Hartlepool more than Stockton as he could save a whole day and a carter could make the journey to Stockton in half a day. There had been a time when his ship was not welcome in the port, but my father had changed all that. He had wrested his own destiny from the hands of others and few men could say that.

William was waiting for me and he bowed, "I know what you wish of me and I will do all that I can for I would not have any family enslaved but you should know that a drekar or a snekke has a shallower draught compared with my cog. They can sail up channels which would ground us, and I will not risk my ship. They are also made for war and I am not. I fear this will end in failure."

While I had stood with Geoffrey, I had been examining the Slake. "And you need not." I had spied some old fishing boats. They were called cobles and had a crew of anything from four men to ten. "We will tow some of these old fishing boats. I intend to hunt these pirates the way we hunt wolves. We will block up their exits and then beard them. All we have to do is to find where they are camped."

He nodded and looked at the sky, "Then if you believe that they will camp, we should use the high tide tonight to get into position before dawn. My cargo can be unloaded quickly."

"Good, I will fetch my men. Geoffrey, get some idlers from the quay to drag two of those cobles to *'The Heron'*."

"Aye lord."

My men were all assembled. They knew what to expect and none wore mail. The odds were that, if we had to fight, then it would be in water or mud and mail would hamper a man. Like me they wore brigandines, arming caps and coifs for the men at arms and just brigandines and caps for the archers. Nor did my archers bother with bodkins. It was a waste of the best arrow we had. Few carried shields and none carried pole weapons. A forecastle or aft castle was no place to wield such a weapon. I took a short sword and a hand axe. Dick was waiting expectantly.

"You come if you swear to obey every order we give and not to move from your allocated station."

"I swear!"

"Then fetch your leather cap, long dagger and leather jerkin."

I saw Mary, my wife, biting back any words to upset her son but she did not want him to go. Grabbing his gear, he ran without a second glance down the slope towards the harbour. I shook my head, "I will speak with him."

Mary smiled and a tear trickled down her cheek, "He is excited, that is all."

"Nonetheless he should learn that he must behave like the son of a knight and not a wild child who has not been raised well."

I had twelve men at arms and fifteen archers aboard the cog. We placed half of the archers in the bow castle and the other half would use the mast and the sterncastle once we were underway. Erik Red Hair stood close by Geoffrey and me as we left the Slake.

"Lord, something about this does not feel right."

"You mean our hunting them? You think they are fled?"

"You misunderstand me, lord. I am a Viking and I know the way pirates work. There are easier places to raid than this river," he pointed to the hamlet of Stranton we were passing, "there or Seaton Carew would have yielded more captives and would have been easier than a large family of sealers. Further north there are small fishing villages with little or no protection. South of here is Hwitebi and although not as rich as it once was it still has an attraction to a raider." He tapped the side of his head, "There is something in here which makes me question this raid. Why here and why now?"

"It is true, Erik Red Hair, that this is a rare occurrence. Perhaps they are desperate. Can you not divine some reason for this attack here and now?"

He looked despondent, "No, lord, and that worries me for it suggests a cunning plan. Vikings like to be clever and to come up with devices and tricks. We get as much pleasure from that as we do from a victory. I cannot see this band returning across the water and boasting of killing a handful of sealers and taking their women and children!"

The Viking set in motion thoughts and ideas but like the Norse giant, I could not define a purpose and that made me uneasy. We would have to do the best that we could and hope to outwit them. The high tide would enable us to get into the larger channels. I hoped that, if the raiders were still there then they would have fires. Sheep had been taken as well as beer. Vikings liked to celebrate, and I suspected they had been raiding again. Perhaps they were using this high tide to raid and that gave me the hope that they might have left their captives with a few guards.

Once we neared the estuary and while the tide was running in our favour, I had men placed in the two cobles. These light fishing boats were propelled by oars and had an even shallower draft than a snekke. I put Alan in command of one and Erik the other. With four men in each coble, I had more flexibility. Once the men were aboard the two fishing boats acted like sea anchors and slowed our progress. That was not a problem as we had all night if needs be. I had a man in the small castle which was atop the mainmast and he peered into the dark.

I stood with Captain William who pointed to a secondary channel. "That is Greatham Fleet and is the largest channel apart from the river. I can navigate that for some little way, and it will take us into the heart of the marshes."

"I do not expect you to risk your ship, Captain William. As soon as it becomes too dangerous then tell me and we will lower the sail and stop."

"No, Sir William, we will stop, turn around and then reef the sail. I wish to be able to move out of the Fleet when the tide turns."

I could have commanded him but that was not my way. It was Andrew the Walker who was at the top of the mast and he shouted, "South and west, I spy a fire and I can see people moving."

I turned and shouted to the men in the two cobles, "Erik, Alan, there is a fire to the south and west. Untie yourselves and have the oars ready, away on my command."

William shouted up, "Can you see the drekar?"

"No, Captain, I… wait. I see a drekar and it is coming this way." There was a pause, "And it has a crow on the prow. It is the raider!"

"And the snekke?"

"No, my lord."

When Erik's voice came from behind and below me, I knew that this was a trap and knew that this was all a device to get me. "My lord, there is a second drekar, coming from astern! This one has a serpent at the prow! There is more than one drekar!"

It was dark and there was no way of knowing just how many men we faced but I had to assume I was outnumbered. We had always been limited in the numbers of warriors I could bring by the size of my ship. I could have speculated the purpose of this and who was behind it but that would have been pointless, and I could indulge myself in self-recrimination when I was safely back in my home. "Dick, you stay between the Captain and me. Captain, turn, when you can, and we will try to get into deep water."

"Aye, lord, but it will not be easy! Stand by to come about!" His voice sounded calm but resigned.

With little light, the archers would have to loose at closer range. Of course, every arrow would cause a wound but my men would get off fewer arrows as we would have to wait until they were close and we could see them.

Erik shouted, "My lord, we will take this second drekar!"

It sounded to me like the words of a berserker for there would be at least five times the number of pirates on the drekar but that was the attitude of my men. You were only finished when someone tore your weapon from your dead hand.

"May God be with you!"

I heard the arrows as they were sent from the bow castle and from the bow of Andrew the Walker. In many ways he was almost like a secret weapon for none could assail him and he had the best view of all of our enemies. I drew my sword and my hand axe. I felt the ship move a little faster as the cobles were untied, and Captain William began to turn the cog. The tide was at its height and would soon begin to recede. That too would help us, but we had to fight off the drekar whose mast I now saw looming up ahead of us. The one advantage we had was our high side. A drekar had a lower freeboard and they would have to clamber up the side. In addition, they would have to choose one side or another to attack. My use of the cobles had thwarted their attempt to attack from both sides at once.

I saw now that one drekar, the one with the crow, would be attacking from our lee and so I said, "Dick, stay here and guard the Captain. Geoffrey, come with me." The ship's crew were all busy sailing the ship and the captain would be undefended. Dick nodded grimly and gripped his long dagger. His leather jerkin looked inadequate for the task. As we hurried to the waist, the lowest point in the drekar I said, "We do whatever we can to stop them boarding. If they board us, then we are doomed."

The pirates held shields above them and few had been seriously hurt by our arrows but they could not board with shields in their hands. My archers were good and even though there were willow boards taking most of the arrows my skilful longbowmen found gaps and the pirates, none of whom wore mail, began to shout and roar as barbed war arrows insinuated themselves into flesh. I could now see that there were thirty or so pirates aboard the drekar approaching us. If this had been one ship then we could have defeated them. They had trapped me with two ships and the odds were now heavily in their favour.

The Captain had turned his cog and we began to edge back down the Greatham Fleet towards deeper and more open waters where our sail might save us. I glanced ahead and saw that Erik Red Hair had divided his attack and his two cobles were at the steering board of the pirate. The drekar which was closing with us still had way and was gaining as they had men rowing, but as my archers ran from the bow castle to join us at the waist, their arrows hit shield men and the oarsmen became targets and the rowing was more ragged. They would catch up with us and soon the serpent drekar would clatter into our bow and we would all become slaves!

Harry Longbow led my archers. He stood on one side of me and he sent an arrow at the drekar as it approached. It was a well-flighted arrow and I saw it clang off the helmet of one pirate and ricochet into the arm of his companion.

"Well hit!"

"Lucky, lord, and soon they will be close enough to board."

"And we keep them from us for as long as possible. Our men at arms are sacrificing themselves to buy us time." I truly believed that the men in the cobles were lost to us as they tried to take the serpent drekar which was heading towards our bow although all those vessels were hidden in the dark. The crow drekar was close enough for us to smell them!

I heard a foreign voice shout something and although the words had no meaning for me, they must have inspired the crew for they surged to within half a length of our side. The manoeuvre combined with Captain William's need to avoid grounding brought us close enough together for crude grappling hooks to be thrown over the side. The two wooden hulls grated and ground together and made both vessels slow. Half of those who threw the hooks were hit by arrows but there were just two of us able to use our weapons to sever them and men began to walk up the sides.

Andrew the Walker suddenly shouted, "The serpent drekar is sinking!"

Those five words gave us all the hope to renew our efforts. We had a chance and *'The Heron'* was not doomed! A Viking hand grabbed the gunwale and I brought down the hand axe to sever the fingers. Despite the pain it must have caused, the Viking using his axe to hold on to the gunwale and a second pirate used the man's back to climb aboard. I swung my sword at the climbing pirate and my blade hacked into mail links. It must have been an old byrnie and the links broke but these were fanatically brave men and even though my sword came away bloody he leapt through the air, screaming curses at me.

I had quick reflexes and I stepped to the side, almost tripping over Geoffrey as I did so. The flying pirate fell at my feet and I stabbed down into the gap between his head and his byrnie. It was a quick death. Geoffrey rammed his sword into the mouth of the fingerless pirate who crashed back into the drekar. Four Vikings had managed to get aboard our vessel. The archers were still trying to thin out the crew who were attempting to board us and that left Geoffrey and me to deal with four men. I had taught Geoffrey that the best form of defence was attack and as we both held two weapons, we ran at the four men. They held axes and short swords. It was the swords which held the most danger as an axe needed to be swung and the pitching deck of a rolling cog was not as stable as a low drekar. I blocked the blow of a sword with my hand axe as I slashed at the middle of the swordsman. His sword also hit me, but it came at my coif and arming cap. The blow made my ears ring, but my sword came away bloody. As he fell to the deck he tried to hold in his guts. I stepped closer to the axeman and, as he pulled back the axe for a killing blow, I hooked my left leg around the back of his and punched at his face with my axe head. As he tumbled, I thrust my sword tip into his throat.

"Lord!"

Geoffrey was struggling to fight his two foes. He had improved since he had come to me in the Holy Land, but the pirates knew their business. The arrow sent from above by Andrew the Walker hit one pirate between the shoulder blades and drove the deadly barb deep into flesh. The other raised his sword to end my squire's life. Geoffrey held up his two weapons and I swung my sword to take off the pirate's head in one blow. My archers had kept the rest from attacking us and the drekar, with barely a handful of crew, took advantage of the current to head down the Fleet to sea. I looked around the deck and saw only the dead, the crew and my archers. I spied a grinning Dick who waved his long dagger above his head. I ran to the steerboard side and of the other drekar, there was no sign. The two cobles were there, and Erik Red Hair raised his axe, "The serpent drekar is sunk, Sir William, and the crew are drowned!" He held his axe high in the air. "Our axes did for them! They had a piss poor drekar and the keep had the weed!" It was a strange thing, but most sailors could not swim. I think that had I been one who plied the seas for my trade I would have learned.

"Bring your coble here and I will join you. We will search for the captives."

He nodded as I sheathed my sword, "Brendan of the Hook is dead. I am sorry."

If he was the only loss, then I had been incredibly lucky. "Captain, can you anchor in safe water and await us?"

"Aye and we can swill my decks. Your son is a game 'un, lord. He faced off two pirates. He could not know that your archers would slay them, and he obeyed your orders. He has the Warlord's blood in his veins."

I nodded and shouted, "There, Dick, now you see the reward for obeying orders! Men think better of you and you are safe! You live." I turned to Geoffrey, "Come, this night's work is not over."

As I lowered myself over the curved hull of the cog, I began to feel the cold. A mist was already forming on the Fleet. Erik held the coble against the cog as I dropped to the bottom of the fishing boat. The body of Brendan lay on the bottom covered by a blanket. We would bury him with honour at St Hilda's. He had been a pious Irishman. Erik had a troubled look on his face as he, Geoffrey, and my other two men at arms stroked the oars. I wondered if he had found it hard to kill fellow Norsemen. Alan brought the other coble behind us. We headed up the Fleet looking for the snekke and the camp. What I feared was that they had slain their captives to trap me. It made perfect sense. I was more valuable for ransom than any number seal hunters would be.

As I was seated in the stern, I had a better view ahead and I looked for signs of the snekke. We passed one body floating in the water but when I turned it, I saw that it was a Viking who had been hit with an arrow. That gave me an indication of where the battle had begun. This part of the estuary was strange looking in daylight but in darkness, it did not look like England. There were patches of mud which looked like beached whales and other tufty areas where the grass had begun to grow. I saw a glow ahead and knew that must have been the fire Andrew the Walker had seen and then I saw the mast of the snekke sticking up beyond a tussocky island.

"Head to the south. I can see the snekke beyond the island." With **'The Heron'** effectively blocking the channel she could not escape. Unlike many lords, I was not precious about either my dignity or my clothes. I jumped over the side and the water came up to my chest. I grabbed the rope which Erik handed to me and I slurped my way through the mud to the bank. I grabbed the grass and found it held remarkably firmly. When I dragged myself up onto the mud I half rolled like a baby when it is learning to walk. I believe the roll saved my life for a pirate rose from the grass and rammed his spear down where I had been just a heartbeat before. I dragged out my hand axe as it was the closest weapon to hand and the easiest to draw, I pulled it as the spear came down. I rose and, half crouching, I hacked at his knee. He collapsed to the ground trying to stem the flood of blood which poured from it and then, amazingly, stood. I knew not how he did it. These Vikings were frightening enemies. My men had all leapt from the two boats and the other five pirates who ran at us found ten men facing them and not the one they had seen drag himself ashore.

I drew my sword and shouted to the wounded pirate to surrender. I wanted to know why they had tried to trap me. Perhaps he did not understand my words or wished a warrior's death but whatever the reason he lunged at me with his spear. Despite what minstrels may sing a man who fights another wielding a deadly weapon fights to win. I suspect that the wound to the knee would have been fatal, left unattended, but as I used my left gauntlet to fend off the spear he ran on to the sword. There was hatred in his eyes as he spurted blood from his mouth. The others had all died too. There would be no prisoners.

"Find the captives!"

Alan and Geoffrey led my men to search the grass-covered mudflat to seek the women and children, but Erik Red Hair remained where he was. I could see, in his eyes, that he had something to say. "Speak Erik. Do the deaths of your countrymen sit heavily with you?"

He shook his head and gave a sardonic laugh, "They were not warriors they were pirates and piss poor ones at that. They are the scum of the seas. No, lord, when I hacked into the hull of the drekar we caught one man in the water. I offered him death by a sword. He took it and told me that they were paid to come here." I nodded. As I had thought, they sought ransom. "They were sent to lure you into a trap and to kill you! The Welsh want you dead! They were paid by someone who lives within sight of Wyddfa. You were the target!"

Chapter 2

The women and children were found and we boarded them on the ship. They were a resilient family. Although they had lost their men they were grimly determined to begin again and continue the life of seal hunters.

I kept the news that I was the target to myself as we loaded the snekke along with the cobles and, with dawn breaking, sailed to the beach whence the sealers had been taken. They were hardy folk and insisted on resuming their life despite the death of their menfolk. I gave them all that we had found on the dead pirates as well as the snekke which was a handy little vessel and promised to send sheep and a milk cow. It was more than they had lost but I felt guilty. They had lost their menfolk and their home; that was down to me! Even as we pulled away from the beach, they were beginning to salvage what they could from their home. We also found others who had been taken closer down the river towards Stockton. That confirmed that they had been seeking me and had thought to draw me earlier than they had. We did not reach Hartlepool until noon and I saw my father and nephew, Henry Samuel, waiting for me with Roger of Fissebourne.

I turned to the sea captain who had risked his ship and his life for me, "Thank you, William. You and your family have ever served mine well and I am sorry that your men came close to losing their lives."

"We have worse dangers at sea, and I could not have slept knowing that those raiders had English captives as slaves!"

My father examined Dick and me as we stepped down the gangplank. He was looking for injuries. I smiled and shook my head, "We are whole, father, but we were lucky."

"It does no harm to check!"

"Dick, go with the men and Geoffrey to the hall and warn your mother that my father will be dining with us."

"She knows I am here, son."

"I know but she may not know that you are staying."

"And am I?"

I nodded, firmly, "You are." When the others had left us, I turned to Roger of Fissebourne. "The threat is gone although some of the pirates, not many, escaped in a drekar. The captives have been recovered and taken home. All is well but you need to tell captains to watch out for these pirates. There were three ships! One we sank and another we captured." I saw the look of horror on the face of the official. "We were lucky."

I took my father up the slope from the harbour to the church of St Hilda. I needed to speak to him and in the lee of the church, it would be quieter. God's house would protect us from the savage east wind. The pirates would have a hard journey home. They would have to row and there were but a handful to do the job. God had punished them. My father was a little out of breath when we reached the church and it meant I told my story without interruption.

When I had finished, he said, "Did Erik have a name?"

I shook my head, "Not the Welsh Prince but one of those related to him. That is the part I do not understand. Had it been the Prince it would have made sense but these Welsh fight each other for the crown as much as they fight us for their land. It is why I wish this kept quiet. Until we have a name then all men are suspect."

He nodded, "And you lead our men there soon! I will write to the King and warn him."

"My men believe the trap was to take me for ransom. I shall not tell them of this plot until I have to. They will be pulling knives at shadows otherwise."

He took my arm, "Come, I am too old to be so cold. Let us go back to your hall and a warm fire. You are right. I will have to stay but we can find a quiet corner of your house where Mary will not hear of the threat. I take it only Erik knows?" I nodded, "Then keep it that way." As we walked, he said, "I know not why the King goes to war with the Welsh. He is no general and his Marcher Lords could keep the Welsh in check."

My father had not been on campaign with me and I explained, "It is North Wales where the King seeks to increase his power and subjugate the wild Welsh who live there. Gwynedd has little to offer to lords who wish to be rich, but it is the last stronghold of Welsh Independence. The southern lords are too closely related to the Marcher Lords and it is not in their interests to be independent. But you are right, King Henry is no general."

"And that is why they sought to end your life. With you gone it would be Sir Robert Pounderling who led the army and from what you say he is not good enough either. I have trained you too well!"

Back in my hall, he played with my three children, but I knew that my father was keen to speak with me at length. After the children, including a most disgruntled Dick, had been whisked off to bed, I sat with my father and we discussed the forthcoming campaign. He had fought in Wales and knew the problems that we faced.

"It is not like the Holy Land; we can win there but I am unsure of the value of such a victory. It is a poor land. However, if the King wishes to hold it then he needs to build castles and I do not think that Parliament will back him. Use your men at arms to threaten the Welsh and then play them at their own game, use archers. When I write to the King, I will ask him to find hobelars for you. They can make a difference and you should take only mounted archers. If you can move faster than the Welsh, then you will win. Starve them out."

"And who are the ones who sought my life?"

He laughed, "It could be any number of men. Prince Dafydd is a good leader but he is childless. His nephews Llewellyn and Owain each seeks to be the Prince and that division suits the Prince. Llewellyn also has the support of the people of Gwynedd. However, it is not as simple as that. There are other branches of the family who could have a claim to the crown that Prince Dafydd wears." He shrugged, "They are complicated for they are still petty kingdoms. There is another uncle, Maredudd. He seems feeble-minded but one never knows." I nodded. I had seen such men at the court of King Alexander of Scotland and often they played a part to insinuate themselves close to power. They were not warriors but that did not make them any less dangerous. "You will be taking my archers and men at arms?"

I shook my head, "I will need your archers but your men at arms will have to watch my manor too. Sir Geoffrey of Elton, Henry Samuel, Sir Gerard, Sir Mark, Sir Robert of Redmarshal and Sir Richard of Hartburn will all be coming with me and that leaves the valley requiring a strong hand."

"I will have Sir Fótr."

"And that is not enough."

He nodded, "I will send my letter to the King as soon as I reach Stockton and the muster?"

"April, at Chester."

By then we had consumed the better part of a large jug of wine and the two of us reflected on the family without Alfred. He had been the one who should have taken over from my father, but a treacherous knight had ended that dream. "Will Henry Samuel be the logical successor, father?"

He shook his head, "You have not seen how they all view you. When you withstood the forces of France and Scotland on the border few, save perhaps me, would have realised that you could succeed. It is you who will be Earl of Cleveland and Lord of Stockton. King John stopped that but I will ensure that his son makes good his promise to me! When you are the Earl then you can make the decisions for I shall be in my grave."

"And that is many years hence."

"I have been wounded and hurt too many times to expect a long and peaceful old age. I just take each day as it comes!"

I smiled. I wanted my father to live a long time for I knew of no other who had done as much for England and had so little reward from an ungrateful royal family. I spoke out for there was something which had been on my mind since I had sailed into the estuary. "Father, when we suspected a trap I thought that it might be to capture me for ransom." He nodded showing that although we had drunk well his thought processes still functioned. "Know that I will never ask for ransom. If a demand comes for ransom know that it is because I was tricked, and I will affect my own escape."

He put his goblet down, "That is a bold thing to say, my son. We have the money."

"And that money should stay in the family. I am resourceful as are you. I do not believe that I will be defeated in combat and captured; that is not arrogance it is just that I have yet to meet someone with more skills. Promise me that you will not send ransom."

I found my father's eyes boring into me and when he seemed satisfied, he nodded. "I confess that I, too, would not have sent for ransom but when I was younger there was no fortune."

"There was Aunt Ruth."

He picked up his wine and sipped it, "Aye, Aunt Ruth and she would have paid. I should have had this conversation with her. Becoming rich and powerful has many drawbacks. When we were poor none would have thought to ransom us."

"Will my nephew be coming with us?"

Alfred, my brother's namesake, had been his father's squire. He had been undergoing preparations for his knighthood. My father shook his head, "Your mother has a soft spot for Alfred, and I think that she would see him knighted and here safe. I know that my grandson will be unhappy to be missing out on a war with the knights of the valley." He smiled, "I am an old married man and I do anything for an easy life! There will be a time for him to go to war but this is not it."

He left the next day with his escort of men and I began to prepare for the war in the west. There was much to do these days. I had coursers, palfreys and hackneys. I would not need them all. I decided that I would take Lion as my courser and Destiny as my hackney. Geoffrey had two good palfreys and he would take both. My men at arms were armed and armoured more like knights than the normal retinue of a knight although there were fewer of them. They also rode to war on horses which were specially bred for me by Walter of Elton who had a horse farm. They were a cross between a hackney and a courser. When a horse breeder bred horses not all turned out as he would have wished. Knights were quite specific about the horse they rode. My men at arms just needed a horse which could carry a mailed man. My Viking, Erik, had needed a larger horse than most and his was almost a courser. None of the men at arms I led would have a spare but the four servants who rode with us would have the sumpters which carried spare war gear and their own horses. If a man at arms needed a replacement, we had them.

My men at arms all wore mail as did I. Their helmets were the same too. None had a visor on their round helmets. Erik liked the Norse helmet with a nasal, but the rest wore open-faced ones and each had a good coif which gave protection for their necks. A couple of men had acquired greaves for their legs and none of them wore the metal sabatons. They were new and very expensive. That was how you recognised a knight. You looked at his feet for the sabatons and the spurs. Three of my men liked axes. Erik's was a longer one than the rest and reflected his Norse background. They all had a good sword. Our shields were identical and were shorter than the ones which had been carried by my father at Arsuf and yet still protected our legs. Like me none of my men used lances. We all preferred a long spear. Although a lance would give a longer reach they had a tendency to shatter added to which a spear could be thrown! I had changed my livery from the one I had worn at Elsdon. Hartlepool used the symbol of the hart or the stag and I had a stag between red bars on a pale blue background. My father had a gryphon on a pale blue background, and I would wear that when I was Earl of Stockton.

My archers all rode a sumpter. None would fight from the back of a horse. I had seen the barbarians in the Holy Land and admired them but their bows were completely different from a longbow. When they fought our four servants would hold their horses. Each archer had hose and buskins. They also wore a brigandine of leather and on their heads, they wore a hooded cap in which they kept their bowstrings. They all had a short sword and either a hand hatchet or a hand billhook. Some liked to have a bodkin blade. When they fought, they were the masters of finding ways to kill knights who wore armour! Although the bag of arrows they carried to war only held twenty-four arrows we would have sumpters carrying replacements. My archers could get through a great number of arrows. Many of the arrows we took to war would be blanks and my men would have a bag with spare arrowheads which could be fitted quickly. Bodkin arrows were expensive to make and not to be wasted.

The four servants we took were all tough men and yet none had been warriors. Each of them had come to either me or my father through different routes. They could use weapons but were not as strong as either my men at arms or my archers. They were all hardworking and, most importantly, loyal to my family. Leofric, Edward, Edgar and Oswald would cook for us and could also help my men at arms to don mail. They would help to build marching camps. My father had taught us the wisdom of employing such men and if other lords did not choose to do so then that was their loss. When I had been in Wales, I had seen other lords' servants who knew how to keep clean a tunic and how to cook fine food. My servants could scavenge for food, ale and hunt. If the camp was attacked, then they could defend it.

In many ways, Geoffrey and Dick would also be classed as servants. They would help me to dress, groom my horses, sharpen my weapons and prepare my food. The difference would be that both would be dressed for war and, in Geoffrey's case, they would also ride to war. He had a small shield and his brother's sword, the family sword. His brother had been a knight, but he had lost his life when he forgot that he was a knight. Geoffrey also wore a short hauberk of mail. I knew that my wife would fret about Dick. He would wear a leather cap and leather brigandine neither of which should be needed for he would be nowhere near the fighting but camps could be attacked and this campaign would see my son learn lessons which would prepare him for the day he took over Geoffrey's duties.

After speaking with the reeve and Roger of Fissebourne I was ready to ride to war and we left on the long journey south heading first to Stockton where the rest of the retinue of the Earl of Cleveland awaited us.

I was a grown man and a counsellor to the King but to my mother, I was still her only living son and I saw Dick smiling as my mother made a great fuss of me when we arrived at Stockton Castle. It was like being a child again, but I knew why she fussed so. She had her daughters and they were close but my elder brother had been killed and that made me even more special. It was the bond between a mother and a son. I accepted it for I, too, missed Alfred.

My father had had to seek permission to rebuild the castle after King John and the Bishop of Durham had taken away its defences. The result was that while it was not as imposing as in the days of the Warlord it was cunningly built. The low curtain wall had been joined to the town wall and there was a higher internal wall with a mixture of towers. There were four square towers at the corners of the keep and rounder ones along the curtain wall. The accommodation buildings were all contained in the inner bailey while the outer bailey just held the bread ovens and the workshops for the weaponsmith.

All of the knights who awaited me lived within a few miles of the castle and were only at the castle for the feast thrown by my parents. It was a rare chance for the family to get together. Knights like Sir Gerard and Sir Mark were not family but most of the rest were. My mother had been a great lady whose hand had been sought by great and powerful lords. She knew how to throw a feast, and everything had to be done just so. Geoffrey and Dick were tested as they served food under the watchful gaze of the matriarch of the family. There were no children and no wives at the feast. It was a martial gathering. The conversation buzzed around the subject of war.

Sir Gerard had come to me as a spoiled young noble that his kinsman, the Bishop of Durham wished to be turned into a warrior. We had succeeded and now he was desperate to come to war again. The others had all fought alongside my father, some in the Holy Land and some in the border wars but Sir Gerard had just one campaign to his name and he was quite bellicose in his words. It took Sir Mark, the son of a tanner whose brother Matthew had died when we had rescued Geffrey of Lyons, to teach to him the reality of war.

"It is one thing to fight an individual Welshman on an open battlefield, but we will not have that luxury. It will be as it was when my brother died. We will be fighting in a land which is familiar to the Welshman. They will be defending their own land and they will use every rock and blade of grass to their advantage. We have good archers, but the Welsh are our equals and, some might say, in their own land, better. One to one I would back any knight in this room to defeat any Welsh knight." He smiled, "And Sir William, two, but that will not be the case. They have castles into which they can scurry and taking a castle by storm is not for the fainthearted. King Henry wants Wales and he will use his best weapon to do so, the knights and men of Cleveland but, as with any weapon which is used hard, it will become blunted and, sometimes, damaged beyond repair."

Henry Samuel smiled. He was the joker in the hall, and he lightened the mood, "Well Mark, you have become quite the philosopher since you were married."

Sir Mark looked up to my nephew and he blushed, "Aye, Sarah has given me a new slant on life." He turned to Sir Gerard, "I am sorry if I have offended you."

Sir Gerard had changed beyond all recognition and he shook his head, "I know I am privileged to be with this lance of knights and warriors. I am happy to learn. I feel as though I am less skilled than your squire, Edward!"

My father spoke, "I am pleased with all of you, Sir Gerard, and I know that my lessons as a sword for hire have, in some way, helped to form you into the knights that you have become. When I am no longer here it is good to know that I have helped to mould you."

My mother laughed, "Thomas! You have become a maudlin old soul! Is this any way to send young men off to war? You will be here when they return, and they will be successful for they are not like the pampered knights of the court! You are the knights King Henry chooses to use when he needs to get things done. The fact that none of you are rewarded as you should be is another matter." She looked at me and patted my hand, "William, you need to take this King in hand! Do not be walked upon!"

I watched my father shake his head and I smiled, "I shall do so, mother, for even King Henry would not face you!"

All laughed. King Henry was just a couple of years older than me and I knew I had far more battle experience than he did. There was a lack of good warriors in England at the moment and with the unrest being fermented by the Poitevins, Lusignans and Simon de Montfort, the good warriors would soon be tested.

My nephew, Alfred, sidled up to speak quietly with me, "Uncle, my father has told me that I am not to come with you to war." He waved a hand at the hall, "I am to stay here in Stockton until I am knighted."

I smiled as I had been expecting this, "And where else would you wish to be knighted? You will spend your vigil with the tomb of the Warlord close by and the spirits of our dead."

"But I would fight with the family!"

"And you will, just not this campaign."

"My cousin Dick goes to war and he is a boy!"

I wagged a finger before him, "And did you not go to war with your own father much upon his age?" He nodded. "The difference, Alfred, is that when you next go to war you will wear spurs and you will lead men. That takes preparation. Let my father do this for you. By the time we return you will be a knight and he will have passed on his wisdom to you. When you do go to war you will be all the better for my father's words!"

He seemed satisfied and rejoined the other squires. I remembered my own knighthood. I had not spoken falsely, the vigil changed a young man to a warrior and the Warlord's church was a special place.

The evening ended with all in high spirits and then my father and I were left alone. My mother liked to retire early these days. My father said that she prayed a great deal. "I am not happy that you have been targeted, my son. You have taken on my mantle and with it, the animosity and enmity of more than half the Kingdom. I feel as though we are besieged here in the north and I trust no one south of the Humber."

"Father, I am no fool and you have raised me well. I will watch my back and I have good knights around me. Even more importantly I have the best men at arms and archers in England, nay, Wales too!"

"I do not doubt your ability to slay any knight who dares to beard you but there are many enemies who have other ploys. I am pleased you have the Viking with you. They are the best of bodyguards. When I fought alongside Birger Brosa, I saw how good they were. He would die defending you."

"And I would have him live!"

He laughed, "Then you do not understand Vikings. They wear crosses but scratch the skin and you will see a warrior who wishes to die with a sword in his hand and go to Valhalla." He added, "Did not Erik obtain the information you needed by facilitating a journey to Valhalla?"

He was right, of course, and Alan Longsword was not getting any younger. Geoffrey was too young. If I was to return from Wales, I would need my Viking to watch my back!"

The next morning I rose while it was still dark for I wanted to be well prepared. As Geoffrey, Dick and I prepared our horses David of Wales, my father's Captain of archers, came to see me. I was shocked at his appearance; he looked older and thinner.

"Sir William, I am sorry that I did not see you last night and that I have not been asked to come with you."

"You have done enough, David of Wales and should enjoy your old age."

"I have been an archer all of my life and it is hard not to ride to war." I nodded, "You have good archers with you but Idraf of Towyn will be especially useful." He smiled. "I helped to train the boy that is now a man and know his qualities. This is his land to which you go and he can lead men! Of course, it is your retinue now and..."

I put my arm around the old man, and I could feel bones. "Old friend only a fool ignores advice from one such as you. My archers will happily serve under Idraf."

"I wish that I was coming to the land of my birth but it is not meant to be. Take care, lord."

It took some time to cross the river. The ferry which serviced the castle and town could only take ten horses at a time. The crossing was short, but it still took time. The rest of my knights and men would be awaiting me at East Harlsey which was just thirteen miles down the road. This first day would be our shortest, but I hoped to make almost forty miles a day thereafter. I knew it was optimistic, but we rode good horses and we had a few spares. I was not going to use the high passes which lay close to my home but use the faster road which headed south and then take the slightly lower pass from Hudersfeld to Manchester. From the manor of the Gresle family to Chester was the journey of less than a day. Chester was one of the homes of Simon de Montfort and he had recently begun to criticise the King. King Henry was not a great leader on the battlefield, but he knew how to plot, and Simon de Montfort was now his Lieutenant in Gascony and Aquitaine which would leave the castle empty for us to use.

It was as we followed the river from Manchester west that Henry Samuel showed that he had listened when we had dined with Lord Gresle before leaving Manchester. "What I cannot understand, Uncle, is why the King does not use the Earl of Chester to fight this war. He has taken us from the northeast when the Earl has archers who are the equal of ours and a more vested interest in subjugating the Welsh."

I had spoken of this with my father for I had not understood it either until the wise old patriarch of our family had cut through the Gordian knot tied by the King. "De Montfort is a threat to the King. He was a former ally and was close to the King's brother. The disaster at Taillebourg has not only driven a wedge between the two men it has allowed de Montfort to foster rebellion. He is also close to the Welsh. By sending him to Aquitaine he makes the Frenchman become the focus for the opposition to English rule. Simon de Montfort is an arrogant man and has a high-handed manner of dealing with people. That is why it is not de Montfort and to answer your question, why us? That is much easier to understand. Trust. He knows that he can trust us. He would not have his crown but for my father. We have no desire for lands in Wales and so when we succeed, he will not have to reward us with land. We will be one of the smaller battles in King Henry's army, but we will be the one he uses to achieve his ends."

Henry Samuel nodded, reflectively, "And it is not a glorious war. The lords who live closer to the King in London and the Midlands would not thank him for asking them to fight the Welsh."

"And I would not wish those to be fighting alongside us. Better to have fewer men upon whom you can rely than vast armies which will disappear when there is the first hint of trouble."

The King's plots thickened for when we reached Chester a pursuivant awaited us there. Dressed in the King's livery he was not a knight and he was guarded by two men at arms, but he thought he was superior to knights and he spoke to us as though we were his to command. I did not like either his attitude or his manner. Gilbert d'Etoile was a Frenchman who had ingratiated himself into King Henry's favour.

"Sir William, I am directed to ask you and your men to ride to Shrewsbury where the King awaits you. I would not delay. I have waited here these three days for you and your retinue!"

"And had you had the wit to ride north you could have met us on the road and, even now we would be in Shrewsbury!" I think he was used to dealing with men who were impressed by his fine livery. He recoiled at my words and seeing that the knights who followed me were of the same mind he beat a diplomatic retreat. In his haste to be away from me he tripped over his own feet and was only saved from an ungracious tumble by the two men at arms both of whom grinned. I saw, in that instant, that they did not enjoy this duty!

I turned to my knights. "We leave at dawn. Let us see if this painted popinjay can keep the pace of the men of the north. It is a hard forty miles of rough road we travel. The King, it seems, plays games."

I spoke with the castellan while we ate for I would use this annoying diversion to my advantage if I could. I asked about the lords who lived to the west of the road and discovered that Maredudd of Llangollen was a relative of Llewellyn ap Gruffyd and was known for his flexible attitude towards England.

Robert of Chester was an older knight and he understood the politics of this land better than most. "When Sir Robert took Twthill along with yourself, Sir William, Lord Maredudd who is lord of the Clwyd Valley chose the line of least resistance and did not send men to fight. Since then he has allied himself with his uncle Dafydd ap Llewellyn for King Henry has not prosecuted the war as vigorously as he expected. While the two brothers, Owain and Llewellyn squabble like dogs over a piece of meat, Wales is a divided land. This may be a good time to take on the men of Gwynedd."

I smiled, "I hope you were not so open with the popinjay!"

He laughed, "There are many differences, my lord, between you and that Frenchman, the most important of which is that you are a warrior and a man of his word. Besides, your family is known for its discretion!"

As we rode south, I sent Idraf of Towyn and Ged Strongbow to scout out Llangollen. I had heard little of this Lord Maredudd and my father had told me to find out as much as I could about the men we would have to fight. The two archers were swift and would be able to join us the next day.

My men found the discomfort of the pursuivant amusing. We were immune to the rigours of hard riding. The pursuivant was not and after a fifteen-mile stretch without a break, he was almost weeping for us to stop. As it happened, I was ready to make water myself and we were close to the village of Threapwood when I acceded to his request. From his reaction, you would have thought I had conferred a knighthood upon him. It told me much about the men who now surrounded King Henry. They were not warriors and that worried me!

Shrewsbury Castle was a bastion in the west. It dominated the borderlands much as Alnwick and Warkworth did in the north. I saw the tents in the lee of the castle where the men who would fight for the King were gathered. The pursuivant scurried off to report to the King as soon as we entered the town. I was not worried by his tittle-tattle. At the moment I was too important in the King's plans and I would be forgiven anything… for a while!

"Henry Samuel, I will report to the King and you can make our camp!"

I knew I could rely on my nephew to find us a good site with water, grazing and access to a good alewife. King Henry was a pious man and he was surrounded by priests and bishops. There were warriors with him, men like his brother Richard of Cornwall and de Clare but they were in the minority. The better warriors were with de Montfort in Aquitaine and had I been King then I would have worried about the influence the ambitious Frenchman had. I saw the pursuivant reporting to the King when I entered. I did not rush and when Richard of Cornwall sought me out, I had an excuse to delay my meeting with the King. I was not concerned about the meeting, but I wanted the pursuivant to know that I cared not if he misreported me.

"Well, Sir William, my brother sends for you again? It seems he does not trust the men of the west."

I knew that the worst thing I could do was to either agree or disagree with him. This was the political swamp that was the court when men would seek favour by informing on their friends or twisting words. "I am happy to serve King Henry where'er he chooses and besides the north is quiet now."

"Aye, once more you and your father have shown the Scots who rules in that part of the world. Tell me, do you have much to do with the Percy family? I have heard, through friends, that they are ambitious and see themselves as the lords of the north."

"I shook my head, "They are valiant warriors, but the family is new to the north. I am just pleased that they guard the borders aggressively for the Scots will take advantage of any perceived weakness."

"As do the Welsh." He nodded, "My brother, it seems, is ready for you."

The King was waving an imperious hand and I gave the Earl a slight bow and headed for my royal audience. "I hear you have been upsetting my officials, Baron."

"Your Majesty, if I was a little short with him it was because I did not appreciate the way he spoke with me. If I have offended Your Majesty, then I will happily take myself back to my manor where I can reflect on my words."

"Do not try my patience. You know that I need you as I needed your father but some of your actions border on the insolent." I had said enough and so I nodded. "I am pleased you have brought all of the men I asked. You should know that I intend to strike towards Anglesey. It is the bread-basket of Gwynedd and if we hold that island then we hold the whole of Wales." Someone had been advising the King well, but I knew it would not be an easy victory as the narrow passes which led to the straits were easily blocked. I said nothing for it was clear that the King had more to say. I suddenly noticed that we were alone. He had dismissed his clerks and clerics and his bodyguards kept all out of earshot. He lowered his voice. "I have a special task for you and your squire. Choose another to lead your men, but I want you to go to a place called Llanrwst," he shook his head, "the Welsh language is impossible. It is the place with the church of Saint Grwst and is less than fifteen miles from the mouth of the River Conwy. There is a lord there, Iago ap Nefydd Hardd, whose family ruled this land more than a hundred years ago. He has let it be known that he is willing to be King and to support me, but he wants to speak with someone he can trust. He is not a man of war and, indeed, is a rich man but we can use his name."

I shook my head, "I do not know the man and I have never even heard his name."

The King smiled, "But he knows your father's Captain of Archers, David of Wales. They knew each other as boys and he feels he can trust your family. You will go alone and speak to this man. You can speak with my full authority and promise him whatever he wishes just so long as he delivers me Wales when we have rid Wales of his rivals."

Something about this did not feel right. "I do not know this man and David of Wales is in Stockton."

The King waved a hand as though this was of no importance, "I did not want news of this possible alliance to spread. If the man is a fraud or you think he cannot deliver, then you join us in our attack, and we have lost nothing." He gave me a sly look, "But if you succeed then think how many lives we might save. There is a small risk, that I accept but the army will be less than twenty miles from you and, if I know your men, then they will be able to extricate you from any predicament in which you find yourself."

I suppose that I should have mentioned the possible attempt to abduct me, but I did not, and I paid the price. Instead of speaking honestly, I sighed and said, "And when do I leave?"

"As soon as you can. You have ridden hard to get here but it cannot be later than two days for the army moves along the same road which you will take for part of the way!"

I left the King and headed back to my men. I had much to occupy my mind. I did not wish to leave my men nor did I want to put my son in such danger. However, there was a chance to avoid conflict and affect a peaceful conclusion to this attempt by King Henry to take Wales. That was worth a two-day ride through potentially hostile land. I needed to speak with Idraf who might know this Iago ap Nefydd Hardd. He would not be back for some hours. He would have a hard ride to scout out Lord Maredudd. I looked to the west. The mountains of Wales were always there like a natural wall. The Welsh could hide behind it. My job was to be the one to winkle a way in. It would not be easy, but I knew that I, of all the knights in King Henry's army, had the best chance to achieve that which he wanted, a successful outcome to this campaign.

War in the West

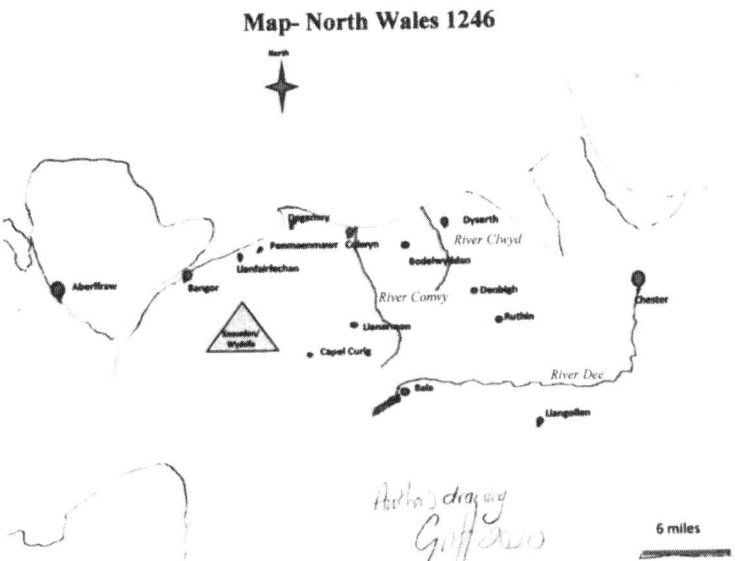

Chapter 3

I spoke first with Sir Richard. I told him what I had been asked to do. It was not that I did not trust the others but when you spoke to more than one man you risked muddying the waters. "When I leave I intend to ask Henry Samuel and not you to lead the men." He said nothing. "I do this for two reasons, firstly, Henry Samuel needs the experience of leading and secondly you will not allow him to do anything foolish. The men we brought from my father need someone from my family to lead them. More than half are my father's men."

Richard smiled, "I am not precious about this and I am more than happy to be a mentor to Henry Samuel. He is a good knight and has a clever mind but Sir Geoffrey may be offended. He is older than all of us."

"And that is another reason for you to be the one who advises Henry Samuel. Sir Mark and Sir Robert of Redmarshal will support Henry Samuel as will Sir Gerard for they are of an age. You need to be the one who sways Sir Geoffrey."

"Then I will give as sage advice as I can, but you take care. I am unhappy about this clandestine meeting."

I clasped his arm, "Thank you, my friend." After finding Henry Samuel we headed for the river.

"Something troubles you, Uncle?"

I decided to be honest with Henry Samuel for I knew that I could trust him. I told him of the Viking raid. He had heard the story I had told my mother and the others at the feast but the details of Erik's intelligence I had kept to myself. He kept silent as I told him all that Erik had learned and his misgivings. I then told him of my mission.

At that point, he was unable to remain silent, "Uncle! It is clearly a trap! You cannot go alone."

"I will have Geoffrey with me, and the King is right, you and the rest of our men will be close enough that if I stray and I am captured then you could rescue me. I go to visit a hall and not a castle. Like you, I think that this is a trap, but I cannot yet fathom how it is going to succeed. The man does not have an army and is a merchant. If this Iago ap Nefydd Hardd wishes me harm then I would say that I do not know him and while I might be seen as a threat to the two other branches of the royal family this one has a connection which is so tenuous that I cannot see it succeeding."

"Then why go?"

"For the same reason your grandfather took us on crusade; because we have learned to stay on the right side of the royal family, for a whole host of reasons!" I smiled. "It is good that I have spoken with you. When Idraf returns I will have a better idea of what this is about."

It was late when Idraf and Ged returned. Before I told him what I would be about he gave me the intelligence he had gathered, "This Lord Maredudd is a cunning plotter, lord, and I would not trust him an inch. His people do not like him and while that is not always unusual it is in this case for Maredudd is from the family of Llewellyn the Great and the Welsh still see his family as the hope of a powerful land. He does not have a castle but a large hall with a curtain wall around it. He has armed guards."

I had to smile when Idraf spoke of the Welsh as though they were a different entity to himself. He had served our family for so long that I suppose that was inevitable.

"And what do you know of Iago ap Nefydd Hardd?"

That made Idraf frown. He shook his head, "I know the family, vaguely, although David of Wales might have known them better for, as a young man, he served with Iago's father and, I think, might have known Iago when he was Dick's age. He might even have trained him!" He shook his head, "This is pure speculation, lord. All that I know for certain is that David of Wales comes from around here and I have heard him speak of Nefydd Hardd. The son that folk spoke of was a studious man and not a warrior. The whole family lacks any ambition. It is four generations since the family had any power. Why do you ask, lord? He is as different from Maredudd as the day is to night."

There seemed to me to be too many '*mights*' and '*possibly*' for me to give too much credence to this.

"I am to meet with him on the King's behalf." I could say no more but Idraf seemed relieved, "Then all will be well. You could go with just Dick at your side and be safe. He is a man who is surrounded by books. I doubt that there will be a weapon in the hall. They have many farms and produce great quantities of wool; the family has money which they keep because they do not spend it on warriors. Lord Iago spends it all on books. I confess, my lord, that the last time I heard of the man was ten years since and he may have changed but, knowing the family, I doubt it. He was more like a monk than a lord."

Idraf's words put me at my ease. I decided that I would take Dick with me along with Geoffrey. My son might be unhappy at missing a battle, but I wanted him where I could keep my eye on him. I returned to my knights and told them that I would be leaving them under the command of my nephew. "I will not take my courser for the roads may be rough and I will ride Destiny and take just Geoffrey and Dick with me as I wish to travel quickly. When my business is concluded then I will join you and the rest of the army."

Sir Richard, who had served with me on the border when he had been Lord of Otterburn, said, "I like this not, William. We will be riding the same road as you. This Welsh lord could just as easily meet with the King when we travel that way."

"From what Idraf has told me Iago is a studious man and this plotting is out of character. He might be fearful. The fact that David of Wales knows him may be the only reason that he is willing to speak to me. I think if my father was with this host then it would be he who would be speaking to him." They nodded at the sense of that. "Besides, I can do the journey in two days. It will take the army four to wend its way close to there. That is another reason for just three of us riding that way. We will attract less attention; the three of us will go as buyers of wool for it is known that they are known in that part of the world as the producers of sheep and wool."

I wanted to leave early and so I had Geoffrey and Dick prepare everything that we would need. I was unsure of accommodation and so we took a sumpter with a tent. My squire and page wore their brigandines while I wore a simple tunic. None of us would wear helmets and my mail would be with the four servants. We would have our weapons for none travelled these roads unarmed. Idraf gave us some simple phrases which we could use to purchase a bed or food. My last visit, before I retired, was to the King's chamber. He was still awake for one thing you could not say about the King was that he was lazy. He was the first to rise and the last to sleep. He was surrounded by papers and parchments.

"So, Sir William, you have spoken to your man and you are ready?"

"Yes, Your Majesty, and by the time you pass through the village all should be concluded, and I may well be able to rejoin the army."

"And that is my dearest wish too but as much as I might want you at my side, I would prefer that you concluded an alliance so that I can outwit this Prince Dafydd! It may be that we do not pass through the village. De Clare and my brother have spoken to me and they are of the opinion that we should keep our sword in Prince Dafydd's back."

When I returned to the camp most of the men at arms and archers were preparing for bed. It worried me that some of the other knights were carousing and seemed to regard this campaign as a foregone conclusion. In contrast, my knights were studying maps which my father had provided and my men at arms and archers were quite concerned for my welfare. Alan Longsword and Erik Red Hair were particularly concerned. It became clear that Erik had confided in Alan.

"Lord, this sounds like a trap! They tried in the river but there you had men with you. Here you just have a boy and a single warrior!"

"Erik!"

"Lord, I only spoke with Alan for we both watch your back and I agree with him. I know not the Welsh, but I do not trust them!"

"I thank you for your concern, but this is a calculated risk. There are no forts on the road we take, and the Welsh are waiting by the coast. It is why the King goes to battle with them. Idraf has told me that Iago is a studious man without warriors. We will travel quietly and avoid attracting attention. I would have my men guard my nephew. I would not wish anything untoward to happen to Henry Samuel."

Alan Longsword nodded, "He will be safe, lord, and I wish that we were watching you for that would guarantee that you were safe too!"

We left well before dawn. If we had been in my hall it would have taken the earth moving to rouse Dick, but the thought of an adventure had my son up and ready before me. I had studied the maps and knew that the less direct route was the one which had the worst road. The King and the Army would be taking the valley road which had been built by the Romans and still had cobbles but the three of us could take the road which lay, first to the west of the Roman road and then, after we had crossed over, to the east. We would make good time but, most importantly, we would be, largely unseen and could avoid Llangollen and the manor of Lord Maredudd. We were heading for the village of Llanarmon. Idraf had told us that it was small and was a stop for those who wished to avoid the main road. It would suit us. If we could find a roof, then all well and good but if we had to camp then we could.

My father had taught me that when you were in a foreign land then you always tried to speak the local language. His philosophy was that if you butchered their words then they would speak your language. It had worked for him in the Baltic and for me in the Holy Land. Each place we stopped for water and to graze our animals we spoke to the locals. Sometimes we were ignored or simply shunned, and I took no offence but more often than not they spoke to us. This close to the English border the locals had a fair knowledge of our language. The ones who did speak to us looked to be unhappy folk. On my father's manor travellers were greeted by smiles and happy villeins.

It was late afternoon when we reached Llanarmon and, as we rode into the village, I thought that Idraf had been a little generous in his description. There were just four houses although there were another four farms within four hundred paces of it. One house had a second story to it and a water trough. As soon as we reined in a pair of men came around from the rear of the dwelling. They had with them two sheepdogs which growled at us. One of the men was a huge glowering sort of man and the other looked to be of an age with me. He was the one who silenced the dogs. I dismounted and began to speak. I had learned that the best kind of lie to use was one which had the basis for truth. I had practised with Idraf and began my talk in Welsh, "I am William of Hartlepool and I am heading for Llanrwst to buy wool. Is there a barn which we could use for the night?"

As I had anticipated my polite tone and my butchered Welsh encouraged the better dressed of the two to speak to me in English albeit with a sing song modulation. "I am Davy ap Hywel and I am the head man of this village. You are a long way from home to seek our wool. Is there not a source closer to home on the uplands of Yorkshire?"

I nodded, "Aye, there is but the Welsh wool fetches a higher price and the sea voyage from Hartlepool to Wales is a perilous one for the seas are full of pirates not to mention natural hazards. The Saxon Sea is benign in comparison with Cornwall!"

He smiled, "You have the right of it." He looked at my boots which were well made, my richly decorated scabbard which suggested a fine sword and said, "You may use the barn, but you look rich enough to pay for the privilege."

I nodded and took out five silver coins, "And I would not ask for charity. Will this cover the cost of your roof?"

"Aye and a meal at our table." He smiled. "We see little silver and gold here. A copper coin every now and then is our reward. We mainly barter."

"And taxes?"

His face darkened, "We avoid paying those for the lords we have hereabouts take the coin and do little to reward us."

"Ah, we do not have that problem as it is the Bishop of Durham who taxes us."

"Being a man of God does not stop them from robbing too."

"You are right, but the Bishop is a good man."

"Take your horses to the barn and I will tell my wife we have guests." He then spoke Welsh to the glowering man, but I heard the name Idwal and knew it to be his name. The Welshman gestured and we followed.

Geoffrey knew better than to speak in front of someone we did not know and when Dick began, "It is far to…?" My squire gently cuffed him to silence him. When Dick looked up in shock Geoffrey smiled and put his finger to his lips.

Idwal took us to the barn and I saw that they had just one horse inside and a milk cow. There were other animals, but they scratted around the cobbled yard at the rear of the house. The Welshman pointed to the well and I said, in Welsh, "Thank you!" I did not understand his reply, but I smiled. I did not mind if he insulted me.

While Geoffrey and Dick unsaddled the horses, I took off my cloak and then I hauled a pail up from the well. The horses had already drunk from the trough and so I used the water to wash the dust from the road from me and I used the wooden beaker which hung from the well to soothe my parched throat. I handed the bucket to Dick and Geoffrey and then began banging my dirty clothes. It would not make them clean, but I would not bring as much dirt into the house. While we were alone, I went close to Dick, "Say nothing at all save please and thank you. If you have to play the village idiot."

He was a quick learner and he nodded, "Sorry, father, Geoffrey. I was excited!"

Geoffrey nodded, "It is for us all, but that excitement is tinged with danger. We have been lucky thus far. Let us hope it continues."

Davy ap Hywel had a pretty wife and two sons. His wife had the most beautiful hair which in the dim light of the farm appeared to look like chestnut and she had a beauty which was astonishing although my judgement may have been coloured by the dour, glowering women of Wales we had seen up to that point. The boys looked to be four or five years of age and I do not think they had seen many strangers although the glowering giant that was Idwal made us look positively benign. I think that their mother must have been very young when she bore the eldest. He also had his unmarried sister, Eirwen, living with them. During the evening we discovered that Davy's parents had died and he had taken on the role of protector for his sister. She was a pretty young thing and I took her to be no more than sixteen or seventeen summers. As an unmarried girl, she kept away from Geoffrey and myself. I do not think I heard her utter a word that first meeting, but she looked to have the measure of Davy's two lively sons. She kept them well behaved while they ate. The food was, as I had expected, simple fare. It was a stew. The main taste was mutton because I think they had used sheep's bones for the base. It had had some rabbit too although as there were no small bones, I guessed that had been a different meal. The stew consisted largely of beans and greens. Our unexpected arrival had merely made the stew thinner as Davy's wife, Myfanwy, had merely added three portions of water to the evening meal. The ale was good. In these isolated communities you made sure that the ale you drank was the best it could be as it was one of life's few pleasures.

There was little talk while we ate. That was the way of these places and when we did speak it was in English which largely excluded Myfanwy and Eirwen who, it appeared, could speak but a few words. Davy, because he thought I was a trader, was interested in the contrast between life in Hartlepool and life in Wales. It became clear that the lord of the manor, Maredudd, was not a good one and it confirmed my initial opinion that anyone who changed sides so often was not a man to be trusted. I heard the envy in Davy's voice when I spoke of the variety of trades and people in Hartlepool.

He shook his head and rattled something off in Welsh. Myfanwy shook her head and smiled. She answered her husband, who translated for her, "Myfanwy says it would be good to have other young mothers to speak to. Here she is the youngest." He smiled, but it was a sad smile. "Her own mother died young and she was brought up by her grandfather, Dai. Her father died in the wars between Lord Maredudd and Gruffyd ap Gruffyd. Dai was a sad man who believed that he was cursed and he lived alone too. Myfanwy loves company for she was denied it until she met and married me."

"Then you have a good life. It seems peaceful."

He laughed, "And that is an illusion. When war comes then men raid us and take our sheep. It matters not which side, Welsh or English. Unless you are a lord who can protect your animals then you are used and abused by all. Are you raided in Hartlepool?"

Once again the fragment of truth came in handy. "Viking slavers recently tried to take a family away, but the local lord recaptured them. Their men died."

"But they did not live in the town?"

"No, it has a wall!"

"When my sons are older, I will show them how to use the bow and we will defend our land. The coins you gave to me will buy metal to make arrowheads. The next men who raid, English or Welsh, will not take what is ours so easily."

That night, as I tried to sleep, I found it hard to achieve as I was filled with all sorts of recriminations and guilt. I had raided men like

Davy and thought naught about it. I had assumed that they were like my father's tenants and were well looked after. I was wrong. I was now seeing life from a different perspective and it was uncomfortable. The farmer and his wife insisted upon providing us with breakfast. Myfanwy made us small oatcakes which she cooked on the fire. I gave her another four silver coins before we left. I determined, when all of this was over, to do something for the family. I felt as though I had deceived them. I had not really but I did not like the feeling, and the sour taste it left in my mouth. Geoffrey and Dick knew there was something wrong but were wise enough to remain silent.

After we had crossed the Roman Road I began to prepare for my meeting. I had met with kings before now; indeed, King Alexander and his wife had almost arranged my marriage to Mary, but this was different for the King was using my judgement. If I thought that he was being tricked, then I had to spot it quickly. I knew that I was out of my depth as I was a warrior and not a plotter. Llanrwst was an important town although it had no castle for it was the centre of a huge sheep market and that, I suspected was where Iago ap Nefydd Hardd and his family had made their money and it explained why he was not a warrior. He could indulge himself in his monkish pursuits. One item of information which had come up when we had eaten with Davy and Myfanwy was that the Lord Iago ap Nefydd Hardd had married less than a year ago and that gave me an insight into the apparent change in the man. Perhaps he had a wife who sought power.

When we rode into the town, towards sunset, I saw the most prosperous place since we had left England. The people were all well dressed and there looked to be plenty of businesses. It reminded me of Stockton without the town wall. The town had a green and I reined in and spoke, in English, to the first person I saw, "I am looking for the home of Iago ap Nefydd Hardd."

He gave me a blank look and I contemplated trying Welsh. I had spoken English as I assumed that Iago ap Nefydd Hardd would expect that. I dismounted and looked around for some sort of building which would suggest a member of the royal family. I saw some hundred paces from where we were stood, a wall and behind it was a large building with several chimneys. In my experience that meant money. I handed my reins to Geoffrey, "Come, Dick, lead the sumpter and keep your eyes and ears open." I was aware of eyes watching us. My words had identified us as English and if this was a trap then men would soon pour forth and we would be fighting for our lives. The eyes which stared were curious rather than belligerent and I remembered the words of

Idraf. This was a prosperous place and they would not wish to upset the status quo. I believed that we were safe!

There was a large double door. It was substantial and would have taken axes to demolish it. I saw that there was a rope next to the door and that suggested a bell. This was not a martial home. I pulled it and I heard a bell. Geoffrey smiled, "Interesting, my lord!"

I nodded, "I have yet to see a sword or a weapon! Perhaps this man means what he says!"

The door swung open and a man of about my age stood there. The fact that he spoke English to us told me that he knew who we were already, and he was playing games with us. I did not like that, but I remembered that we were here on the King's business. Personal matters were irrelevant. I had seen that when I had followed my father on the Baron's Crusade! The man looked to be a warrior, but I did not like his eyes. They were cold.

"Yes, my lord, what can I do for you?"

"I am Sir William of Hartlepool, son of Sir Thomas of Stockton and I am here to meet with Lord Iago ap Nefydd Hardd."

There was a pause of a heartbeat and then he smiled but not with his eyes, "Follow me, my lord." He snapped his fingers and four men appeared from the shadows. These were not warriors but looked to me to be bodyguards of some kind, "I am Lord Iago ap Nefydd Hardd's steward, Rhodri. These men will take your animals to the stables. They will be cared for." As the men whisked away our horses, he snapped his fingers again and a liveried servant appeared and held his arms out. "If you would give Siesyll your cloaks we will have them cleaned. You are expected and there are rooms readied for you. There is, if you wish it, a bath." The man seemed confident and I did not like him from the moment I first saw him. He said he was a steward but the sword at his waist was the sword of a warrior. This man was playing a part. Of course, at the time, I dismissed these worries but I had time enough, later, to reflect on them.

The fact that we were all taken aback caused confusion and I now know that was intended. At the time I just thought that this was a lord who was desperate to impress King Henry. The building was built in stone and had few defensive features. I noticed such things. There were three floors to it, and I guessed that it might have been designed originally as a keep but changed to a hall before it was completed. They even had glass in the windows! The crenulations on the top floor looked to be purely for decoration. The door was well made and had a dragon knocker. It was opened before we reached it. Inside there were two liveried servants.

"Madog and I will take you to your room, Sir William, and Dafydd will take your squire and page to theirs."

"Are they not close to each other?"

"Your squire and page are in the room above yours, Sir William. This is not a castle and your chamber is next to Lord Iago ap Nefydd Hardd. He is showing you great honour by giving you the room."

I did not like this for I wanted Dick close to me, but I could see no fault in the explanation. It was just that I did not like this smooth steward who seemed to have an answer for every question before I had asked it.

"Have you worked for Lord Iago ap Nefydd Hardd for long?"

He shook his head, "I came here when he married. I served the father of his bride, Lady Angharad."

He said no more, and I saw now that this marriage had changed the life of the young man. I nodded to Geoffrey as he was led up the second flight of stairs. He would know to keep his wits about him. The room into which I was led was sumptuous. There was a fireplace and the bed looked to be expensive. There was even a wooden piece of furniture and was intended to hang clothes within. A well-made walnut table had a crafted jug and basin. There were rose petals on the bed. They either thought I was more important than I was or there was something afoot. I decided to keep my wits about me.

"Do you wish to bathe, sir?"

The fact that he seemed so keen to have me bathe made me decide not to. "No, thank you, Rhodri. I am here at King Henry's request and it is more important that I speak with Lord Iago ap Nefydd Hardd sooner rather than later." Even as I said it, I knew my words sounded feeble and I cursed King Henry. His pursuivant would have been a better choice except that the link was with David of Wales.

The steward smiled an oily smile and said, "His lordship will eat in an hour. Is that time enough?"

"Of course." When the door closed, I examined the room. There was just one way in and out. The glass-covered window allowed light in, but a man could not escape. I was in a virtual prison. I stripped off and used the basin of water to bathe. It helped to clear my mind. Something was not right but I could not see it. Perhaps I was too close. I did not think that there would be discussions over the food, and I would not drink too much. I would use the night to devise a strategy. This would be my scouting expedition. The discreet knock on the door told me that it was time to eat. As I descended the stairs behind Madog I examined my surroundings. The door had no lock upon it. Unless they mounted a guard outside then I could escape if this was a trap. I did not know what it actually was, but my sixth sense kept warning me of danger and I always heeded such warnings.

The hall to which I was taken was sumptuously decorated with fine tapestries and furniture which was exquisitely carved. Lord Iago ap Nefydd Hardd and his wife Angharad had excellent taste. I saw that I was alone in the room, and before I could even ask the servant where Geoffrey and Dick were, he had disappeared. I was increasingly anxious about this situation. I had the feeling that we were like pieces on a chessboard and we were being moved into position. Rhodri entered and I saw that he was dressed in his finery. It was even more manipulation.

He announced grandly, "Lord Iago ap Nefydd Hardd and Lady Angharad."

I was not sure what I was expecting but it was not this. Lord Iago ap Nefydd Hardd was only slightly older than I was and had grey hair. He had a distracted look about him. His wife, in contrast, was a stunning young woman who could have been of an age with Henry Samuel. Her jet-black hair was plaited and twisted into a complicated shape and her dress showed that it had not been made in Wales. When she looked at me her eyes were so dark as to be almost black and it was as if she sought your soul as she bored into you. She was one of the most beautiful women I had ever seen in my life yet there was something about her which terrified me. She held out her hand for me to kiss.

"Sir William, my husband has been looking forward to this meeting for a long time. Your arrival heralds a new dawn in this family's fortunes."

I gave a slight bow, "King Henry is keen to begin discussions about an alliance but before we begin can I ask where my squire and my page are? The page is my son."

There was just a hint of irritation in the lady's eyes before she recovered herself, "I did not know. Rhodri, have the page's belongings moved to his father's room."

The steward, too, looked as though he was caught off guard. "Yes, my lady." He scurried away.

"And will they be joining us?"

She laughed and led me to the table which I now saw was set for just three people. "This is a meeting of two nations, Sir William. Your son and squire will dine with Rhodri and the servants. Believe me, they will be as safe as you are, and you will see your son when you return to your room."

As I was seated between the two of them, I noticed that Lord Iago ap Nefydd Hardd had not said a word. The whole conversation had been with Lady Angharad. "Lord Iago, you have a fine home."

He nodded, nervously, "I like it and you must see my library. I am proud of it."

Once again Lady Angharad's mask slipped and she said, somewhat irritably, "My lord, this meeting is more important than some dusty old books!"

"Sorry, my love." Lord Iago gave his wife such a look that it bordered on adulation; he was obviously besotted with the young beauty. This meeting had been engineered by her. She was the force behind the man, and it explained the change in the lord. Idraf had wondered at the change for he had thought Lord Iago to be a man of books and not of politics.

As the food was brought in, I decided to continue to speak to Lord Iago as it so obviously irritated his wife. "And how is it that you know David of Wales?"

His face was blank as he said, "David of Wales?"

Lady Angharad's voice rose an octave as she said, "You know, my lord, you knew him as Dafydd ap Caradog."

Again, there was a moment's hesitation and then he said, as though remembering lines he had learned, "We were neighbours when I grew up and we played together. I hear he became a great archer."

He did not know David of Wales. David was too old to have played with Lord Iago. This was either a trap or a ploy to get me away from King Henry! Thus far I had not seen any armed men. In fact, the only swords I had seen, apart from Rhodri, were worn by me, Geoffrey and Dick.

Lady Angharad put her soft hand on the back of mine, "Tonight we will eat well and then tomorrow we can discuss how my husband can gain the crown he so rightly deserves."

I smiled but it was not with my eyes, "My lady, I am here not to hold discussions but to establish your husband's credentials. The King was informed that I had to initiate them as Lord Iago would trust me due to his friendship with David of Wales. I am here as evidence of good faith but that is as far as it goes. Tomorrow I will sit with Lord Iago and we will talk of his claim to the crown of Gwynedd."

Lord Iago burst out, "Oh, I have many documents which will provide clear evidence of my blood. I told you, Sir William, I had an extensive library. We could go now if you wish! I prefer devouring books than eating food."

Lady Angharad's voice was shrill as she almost screeched at her husband, "My lord, we have food and wine which has taken the servants hours to prepare. We will eat! Rhodri!" She clapped her hands and then tried to recover her composure. She shook her head, "My husband does love his books!"

This was like combat. When a knight fought a new opponent, he sought weaknesses. I now saw the weaknesses in Lady Angharad. She had created this situation and she liked to control everything. She could not handle deviations from her plan and so I came at her from a different direction.

"So, my lady, how did you and Lord Iago meet?"

"What?" Once more I had caught her off balance and she was not as assured.

"Well, with all due respect, the two of you are as different as any two people I have ever met and I cannot believe that Lord Iago would have left his library to seek a bride." I did not need to turn to know that Lord Iago agreed with me. "Where does your family come from?"

Rhodri brought in the jug with wine and the goblets. He poured some in my goblet, "As Lord Iago's guest would you taste the wine and tell me if it is to your taste. I can always open another if it is not."

Rhodri was Lady Angharad's accomplice and he was helping her out by giving her thinking time. I quaffed the wine in one. It was a little sweet for my taste, but I nodded, "It is fine wine. Now, my lady, you were going to tell me where your family came from."

She smiled and this time I felt a chill down my spine for it was a smile of triumph, "My family lives to the east of here. I am the daughter of Lord Maredudd of Llangollen and you, Sir William of Hartlepool, will never see your family again!"

The wine had been poisoned! I saw now that Rhodri had not poured the other two goblets and I tried to rise. My legs would not obey me, and I began to feel woozy. "My son…"

The last thing I saw and heard before blackness overcame me was her maniacal laugh and the look of triumph on her face.

Henry Samuel

Chapter 4

To say that I was less than happy when my uncle rode off was an understatement. My grandfather would not have allowed his son to ride alone on such a ridiculous quest. We did not need a puppet on the Welsh throne and far better to defeat the Welsh in battle than playing these conspiratorial games. I had spoken with the Welsh archers and they had confirmed what I knew in my heart, that the only way the Welsh would be beaten was by subjugation. If anything, the King should have been fostering enmity between the Welsh factions who were always happy to fight each other. However, I now led the men of Cleveland and I had to put my fears and doubts from my mind. I owed it to my uncle and grandfather.

We were given the dubious honour of guarding the baggage train. Since King Henry's father, John, had lost the crown jewels crossing The Wash, the replacements were always guarded by the best knights who were available. It was an honour, but it did not sit well. I would have preferred to be in the van and scouting ahead; that task was given to a Marcher Lord, Roger de Clare. I did not think that the Welsh would be so foolish as to attack such a well-guarded column. We headed along the Roman Road and, while we were alert to danger, we were able to observe the land and to talk. I rode with Sir Richard and Sir Gerard. Sir Richard and my uncle had been the sentinels of the north, I had served with them both and Sir Gerard was so desperate to emulate our deeds that he hung on our every word. Sir Richard gave me advice as we rode. Not all of it was about military matters. He knew my character and told me how to curb some of my reckless traits. He also gave me moral support and that was the most important of all.

"This will be a short campaign, Henry Samuel, for the Welsh have few knights who can face us."

"Sir Richard, that may be true, but my uncle was concerned that they would use their archers in the high passes."

Sir Gerard leaned forward in his saddle, "Then how would your uncle use knights?"

"He would dismount them and use them with archers. Our archers keep down the heads of the Welsh archers and the knights winkle them out of their eyries."

"That does not sound glorious!"

Sir Richard laughed, "You will learn, Sir Gerard, that there is little that is glorious about war. Fighting on foot may not seem glamourous but it allows a knight to show his skills for there is less chance of tumbling from a saddle because of a rogue rock or some slippery soil." He patted his horse's neck, "And it is less dangerous for an expensive mount."

I let Sir Richard explain to the novice knight how to fight on foot and wondered how my uncle and cousin fared. He had left a day before the army and would, in all likelihood, be with Lord Iago even as we would be preparing our camp. When we reached Llanrwst he would probably be waiting for us and yet there was a nagging doubt at the back of my mind. We made less than twenty-five miles that first day and as it was we who were with the baggage we had the worst of the camp. Luckily, the archers and men at arms we had brought knew how to make the best of a bad job in addition to which they were excellent scavengers and our archers brought two sheep for us to butcher and to eat.

The scouts sent by de Clare had told us that the Welsh were gathered inland and were using the rocky passes close to the water called Llyn Brenig. It was east of where we were. and we would have to fight them there. We did not follow the same route as my uncle and passed some fifteen miles to the east of the small town. It was two days into our chevauchée when men returned from their scouting expedition to Llanrwst. The King summoned me and I spurred my horse to speak with him. The King looked annoyed, "Your uncle, it seems, has let me down. He did not arrive and Lord Iago ap Nefydd Hardd and his wife have been taken by men I believe to be Prince Dafydd's!"

I could not believe that my uncle would do such a thing deliberately. The King was missing the point for this was unlike my uncle who was resourceful and clever. "Something must have happened to him. The three of them should have been at Llanrwst three days ago!"

The King waved an irritated hand, "Then their bones will be bleached on the hillside. He has failed me and now you command."

I became angry and that was a mistake, "I will take my men and we will hunt for them. I will begin at Llanrwst and tear the buildings down brick by brick!"

The King roared, "You will not! I command here and any further outburst will see you in the Tower!" He meant it and I saw that I had made an error of judgement. I should have said nothing and then ridden to the hall myself. The King was not with the baggage and would not have known!

I nodded and rode back to my men. As I approached, I waved over Idraf, "Idraf, Sir William, Geoffrey and Dick are missing! The King will not allow me to seek them. Take some archers and ride to Llanrwst and ask around. See if you can find any truth in the story that he never arrived. When that is done take five archers and find him. The King says that he did not arrive. I do not believe that. Do not return until you have information."

"I swear that I shall do so for I feel responsible. It was I who told Sir William that the lord of Llanrwst was harmless."

We camped by a small stream and I gathered our knights and senior men at arms around me and told them the news. Like me, they were incensed but all were realists. We could not go against the King. "We will need to disguise the fact that we will be six archers light."

It was dark when Idraf returned. He shook his head, "The people there have been terrified, and they all stick to the same story that no visitors arrived, but they were lying. My men who questioned them heard the same story, word for word. It was as though they had been taught it! However, what they could not disguise was the fact that when those in the house left it was in the middle of the night. The villagers report armed men coming from the mountain above the River Conwy in the early evening and they suggested that they were Prince Dafydd's men and that when they awoke the house was closed up as though all had left. When the village awoke the house was empty. None have been in since it was abandoned. I also learned that while most of the horses and a wagon headed towards the mouth of the River Conwy and the coast, a second wagon headed back down the road to the east." He smiled, grimly, "Whoever told them the story they were to retell forgot to add that they should remain silent about all else."

I looked at the Welsh archer. He was not only one of our best scouts he was also a clever man and I used his mind, "Idraf, where do you think my uncle is?"

"I would have said across the Conwy with the Welsh Prince but, at the back of my mind is a question. "Why send a wagon east? I think I have the answer for Lady Angharad's father lives to the east of here."

"You would go east?"

He shook his head, "First, we need to scout out the Welsh who wait along the River Conwy. Lord Iago might not stand out but from what the villagers told me Lady Angharad is a beauty and will stand out. Had we more men who could pass for Welsh we might try two searches but…"

I nodded, "And David of Wales is not here. I now wonder at the message my uncle received." I was thinking of the plot which had nearly seen him taken at sea. "Do your best and we will be with the army!"

The road west was taking us towards high ground and passes which I knew would be filled with Welsh archers. We had the River Conwy to our left and mountains to our right and ahead of us. The road twisted and turned as it climbed and I feared the worst. I wished my uncle was here to guide the King for our liege lord was not as clever as my uncle when it came to war. I looked around at the men who were with me. We were the best in the army and yet we guarded the baggage. It was a waste of the best men in the army.

It took a whole day to get close to the Welsh although as we were at the back of the column the whispers we heard had been passed on by so many that it was hard to test their veracity. All we knew was that the vanguard was in contact with the Welsh. It was as we began to climb up towards the narrow pass which led to the coast that the King made his first mistake. He did not have mounted archers as scouts and the knights and men at arms who led the vanguard rode into an ambush. Many horses and men were killed and the King compounded his error by trying to force his way through with sheer weight of numbers. The pass was far too narrow for that. Prince Dafydd had chosen his ambush well. It was a disaster for we lost knights whom we could not replace.

It was Gilbert d'Etoile who rode back to summon me. He was no longer the smartly dressed and officious courtier who had annoyed my uncle and his attitude had changed somewhat. "My lord, King Henry asks that you join him at the van and that your men begin to make a camp here."

"There is trouble?"

He nodded, "We have been ambushed."

We had the healers with us as well as the priests. "Richard, make an armed camp and warn the healers that there will be wounded arriving." I turned to my squire, John, "Come with me."

The two of us made our way through a road which was now crowded. The King had just stopped the army and men were waiting for orders. Already the wounded were being brought back. I could hear the battle as I neared the pass. The King's standard fluttered and I heard the Welsh arrows as they clattered onto shields and mail. Bodyguards held their shields protectively over the King. Even as we were approaching, I held my shield up and John used his to protect my left side. I saw de Clare and Richard of Cornwall trying to rally the men ahead of us.

The King turned and he looked almost angry, "Where is your uncle when I need him?"

It was such a ridiculous statement that I ignored it. The King had sent my uncle on a foolish errand and now the King was blaming him. "Your Majesty, you must withdraw out of the range of these arrows." Even as I spoke a bodkin arrow plunged into the helmeted head of Sir Walter of Ludlow who fell dead at the King's feet. "We are losing too many men!"

"But they are just archers and there cannot be many of them!"

"Then let us withdraw, King Henry, and assess the situation." I pointed at the sky. It was late afternoon. "The day is almost done. You wished to find the Welsh; well you have them now!"

"I like not this retreating!" I nodded in agreement. "Fall back out of bow range!"

Arrows struck my shield and John's as we backed our horses through the press of men. The Welsh were using bodkins and men were dying. King Henry had been defeated for we had lost at least thirty men at arms and knights not to mention many dozens of other men who had no armour. We stopped where the ground widened out; it was out of range of the deadly Welsh missiles and as those who had been before us filtered through, I examined the position. It was not a particularly high pass but it was narrow. The approach to the two sides was rough and there were many rocks behind which a small number of archers could inflict great damage on a slow-moving enemy. This was not the place for horses. I saw that many horses lay dead and others were wounded.

The King, surrounded by the esquires who were his bodyguard, approached me. I saw that Richard of Cornwall was there too. I knew him to be a brave man, but he did not have a great mind when it came to strategy. My grandfather and Simon de Montfort had been the ones who had led our army to success in the Baron's Crusade. One was in Aquitaine and the other no longer went to war. My uncle was the next best choice and the Welsh had managed to neutralise him. I still did not know how but it was clear to me that they had tricked the King. Now it was left to me. My wars in the north as well as the Holy Land had given me a reputation. I was also from the Warlord's family and we did not lose! The King looked expectantly at me.

Removing my helmet and slipping my coif from my head I said, "We would be best to camp, King Henry, and then attack at dawn using dismounted men at arms and knights supported by archers."

"And that would work?" His voice had a pleading quality to it.

I shrugged, "There are no certainties in war, King Henry, but I will lead the attack and prosecute it to the best of my ability. The Welsh just mean to slow us up so that they can all cross the River Conwy having hurt us and showed their people that the English are beatable."

I knew, even as I said it, that it was a criticism of the King, but it was his lack of experience which had caused it. A lack of good scouts had allowed us to walk into an ambush.

"Will you need others to help you, Sir Henry?"

I shook my head, "The ones who suffered today will be in no condition to fight tomorrow. Better that I take men who are not defeated and have confidence."

"Then I leave it in your hands."

I rode back with John to our camp and I gathered the knights and my captains for a council of war. In the absence of Idraf, it would be Harry Longbow who would command the archers. "Tomorrow we attack the left flank of the pass. I examined it while we fell back, and it will suit us. The Welsh will think that the ground has too many rocks, but they can be used to our advantage. We move from stone to stone and rock to rock. We use cover. John here protected me with his shield. Each knight will advance with his squire. The squires are not required to fight but to carry a shield to protect their lord. The men at arms, Alan Longsword, will advance in pairs. With each knight and each pair of men at arms, there will be an archer. Those archers will be close support to the advancing men. Harry, the rest will form a solid block and shower the Welsh with arrows; you will make them suffer! Have Adam Green Arrow lead the others."

"Lord, we have six archers who are not here."

I pointed to the livery on Garth Red Arrow's tunic, "And they seek the lord of these archers, Sir William. Had we but six archers to attack this pass then I would still do so for it is what my uncle would do." He nodded. "I do not want to lose a single man. There is no rush up this pass. We get rid of the Welsh as we should have done today, carefully. We will be in position an hour before the sun rises and I intend to attack as the sun peers over the sky behind us. Let the August sun shine into their eyes. I want every helmet and sword polished so that they blind the Welsh. Let us use nature to defeat the Welsh. Once they are driven from the pass then we use our swords to push them into the river."

Sir Richard said, "But the river is many miles to the west of the pass."

"And that is why we will tether our horses at the bottom of the pass so that when they are driven from the heights and our archers cause great mischief amongst them, we will mount our horses and pursue them. The more we hurt the easier it will be to win this war."

John, my squire, was the son of Johannes who had been one my grandfather's sergeants. Johannes was dead but he had trained his son well. I was not sure if John wished to be a knight and he reminded me of Ridley the Giant who had also chosen to be a sergeant rather than a knight. However, John was probably the best squire we had for he was solid, dependable and incredibly strong. I knew that he would be able to carry the kite shield easily and give me better protection than any other knight. It was for that reason that I chose to be the point of the arrow which would ascend the slope before the pass. I asked Harry to come and speak with me when he had told the other archers my plans.

"I would have you and Garth Red Arrow with John and me tomorrow. We can protect two of you with our shields and I wish to punch a hole in their lines."

"Aye, my lord. I meant nothing when I said we had archers missing it is just that I would prefer Idraf to lead as this is his land."

"And I know that too. I did not take offence and I know that we are worried about my uncle, Geoffrey and Dick."

"Do you think they are dead, as the King believes?"

I shook my head, "I can see little argument to say that they do live but," I tapped my heart, "in here I believe that they live and until I see the bodies then I will do everything in my power to save the three of them."

Harry smiled, "I thought that I was foolish to believe but like you, I cannot believe that Sir William is dead."

John polished my helmet until it gleamed and then he did the same with my mail. He sharpened my sword and my dagger. I knew that some of the men at arms would take axes and pole weapons, but I would use the weapon I felt most comfortable using. That night, before I retired, I held my sharpened sword like a cross as I knelt and prayed for my uncle and cousin, not to mention Geoffrey. I knew that something bad had happened to them, but I could not fathom what it was, and I needed God's help!

It was dark when I rose, and John helped me to don my mail. While he put on his short hauberk, I ate some food. No matter how hungry I was I could never eat well before we fought, and I had learned just to eat enough to take the edge off the hunger pangs. I drank some ale but not too much and then we left for the line of sentries which marked the start line.

They were not my men and so I spoke with them, "Did you hear movement in the night?"

The Sergeant at Arms was an older warrior and he smiled in the dark, "You mean have they left, my lord? No, they are still there. We put down traps in case they tried to slit a few throats in the night, but they just stayed in their nooks and crannies. Why should they move? They had the beating of us yesterday and, with all due respect, I cannot see it being much different today."

"You mean my youth?" He said nothing but looked to the ground. "Like you, Sergeant, I wish that either my grandfather or uncle was leading this attack, but it has fallen to me to uphold the family honour." I smiled, "Let us see what the blood of the warlord can achieve, eh?"

He grinned, "Aye, my lord, that is the spirit. Are you bringing your horses up now?"

"Sergeant, we attack on foot. Let us see what they make of that!"

My two archers ghosted up. I saw that they had war arrows in their quivers but in their belts, they both had half a dozen bodkins. David of Wales had trained them well and they knew their business. There would be no trumpet to herald the attack. My knights and men at arms would watch my sword and when it swept down then they would advance. I peered up into the dark trying to make out my route. I saw a large rock which lay some forty paces from me. In the dark, it looked like a shadow, but it would afford me some protection. Attacking up the slope meant that the Welsh would rain arrows down on us and our two shields, held upright, would be able to shelter us from the worst effects. When de Clare's men had attacked mounted on horses some Welsh archers had been able to use a flatter trajectory. They could not do that with us!

I glanced behind me and saw the corona of light behind the mountains. The sun would suddenly flare up as dawn broke and I wanted to be closer to the Welsh when that happened. I raised my sword and when the action was repeated down the line, I began to walk the forty paces to the first rock. The Welsh would hear the jingle of mail, but I hoped that they would think we were mounting our horses. They could not see us clearly. They might see shadows but that would be all. With my shield held horizontally above me and John's slightly above and before we moved off. Harry and Garth each had a war arrow nocked but they had not drawn back. They would do so and release in one movement when the time was right. Above us in the rocks, I heard Welsh voices sound the alarm and that was not unexpected. We reached the first large rock which came up to our chests. It was covered in a mossy sort of grass. The ground had dew upon it but it was not excessive, and none of us had appeared to slip. I glanced behind me and saw that the sun would burst forth in the next moments. I raised my sword again.

All the planning for this attack had assumed that things would go right for us, but I knew that sometimes they did not. I prayed that we would not lose too many men and I focussed on a route up the rock-strewn slope. God was with us that day for as the sun suddenly erupted from behind us a shaft of sunlight shone off my sword as I twisted it to signal the advance. It was as though the sword was on fire and as we moved the light reflected off helmets and mail so that we shone. The Welsh were taken by surprise, but that surprise lasted but a heartbeat and arrows showered down upon us.

Then I heard Adam Green Arrow's voice as he shouted, "Let fly!" The releasing arrows sounded like a flock of birds taking flight. Garth and Harry did not draw for we had no targets.

As we moved to the next line of rocks, arrows began to hit our shields and our mail. We had confused them and there was a mixture of bodkin and war arrows sent in our direction. One war arrow hit my left shoulder, but it did not penetrate. I would have a purple bruise, and when I pulled out the arrow, I saw that the skin was unbroken for there was no blood. It was a steep slope and while that made it hard to climb it also made it equally hard for the Welsh to hit us. They had expected us to attack up the road again. The sun had now risen and was shining in the eyes of the Welsh who struggled to hit us. John and I were tight together and although arrows were sticking from the shields none had penetrated. I could hear horns from the Welsh and that told me that we had taken them by surprise for they were summoning reinforcements. They might have been waiting for the sounds of horses or looking for men forming up on the road. The attack from a single flank had caused them problems.

The two shields we held obscured our view a little and I was aware of Garth and Harry drawing back their nocked arrows and sending them over our shoulders. The spearman, swordsman and man at arms who raced down the slope towards us did not expect such quick reactions. The spearman and the swordsmen both fell with arrows embedded in a chest and face respectively. The man at arms had two bodies to negotiate and I took full advantage. Angling my shield to take the force of the thrusting spear I dropped to one knee. The man at arms had a short hauberk and I hacked my sword across his unprotected knee. He was not wearing, as a knight would, chausse and my sword sliced through flesh to shatter his kneecap and half chopped his knee in two.

Rising I shouted, "For Sir William and Stockton!"

The battle cry worked and the knights and men at arms I led responded with a roar which must have disheartened the Welsh. As I stepped over the men slain by our archers, I saw that the top of the rise was just forty paces from us but there was now a wall of shields. That gave me hope for it meant our archers were winning the battle.

Garth shouted, "Ware left, lord!"

A knight and three men at arms were racing towards me. Garth sent a bodkin into the chest of a man at arms as Harry's arrow drove into his companion's shoulder.

"John, behind me!" This was no place for a squire no matter how experienced. I would face the Welsh knight and the man at arms alone.

The knight's axe swung at me and it was a long strike, coming from behind his back. Had John not been attempting to get behind me I might have stepped back but I could not and I braced myself for the blow as the other man at arms was hit in the leg by a bodkin arrow and one hit the knight's upper left arm. The axe when it struck shivered my arm, but the willow boards of my shield held. I lunged with the tip of my sword at his left shoulder. He was not expecting the blow and the arrow from Harry had weakened him enough so that he was slow to make the shield rise. The end of my sword found a mail link and widening it drove into flesh. Before he could use his axe again, I smashed my shield into his right side. It made him begin to topple. All around the two of us were sets of mailed men but mine were better and with archers accompanying every pair of men we were winning the battle. As the knight stumbled, I used my right hand to prick against his cheek above his coif. It was just a finger from his eye. I saw the man at arms fall with an arrow so deeply embedded in his skull that it was sticking out of the back of his helmet.

"Yield or die! I care not which it is!" To emphasise my words, I pushed into the flesh and blood spurted.

"I yield! I yield!"

"John, take this knight to our camp. He has surrendered."

I turned my attention to the Welsh and, after ensuring that I still had the two archers I ran to join Sir Richard, Sir Robert and Sir Gerard who had taken over the point of attack. The Welsh were now a ragged line as the archers who had climbed with us were able to hit men at arms and knights at such close range that their mail availed them little. Then I heard a trumpet and knew that King Henry had decided to enter the fray and was leading horsemen to aid us. Welsh horns sounded the retreat. They had gambled and almost won. Had they left after the initial ambush then they might have regarded this as a victory. If the King was clever then we could reverse the outcome.

With a roar, some of the Welsh who faced us decided to salvage their honour by knocking us from the hill. I saw Sir Robert stumble as a spear struck his side. This was where our training came in. I stepped between Sir Richard and Sir Gerard. Their two squires pressed their shields into our backs and the four archers we had with us stood behind the squires. With our shields locked together and support from behind, we were like a metal wall. The Welshmen who ran at us had spears held before them. With metal heads the length of a small sword and an eight feet long haft they were a dangerous weapon, but our shields were locked and only our eyes peered over the top of them. We held our swords between our shields. As the six spears crashed, smashed and, in two cases splintered against the shields we thrust up with our swords. While we had seen the approach of the spears the three swords were unseen. Mine tore into the mail and then the aketon of a man at arms before piercing his ribcage. He had helped to kill himself by driving on at me. I drew the sword out sideways as four arrows flew alarmingly close to our heads to drive into the faces of four more Welshmen. I pulled back my arm and thrust again, but it was unnecessary for we had broken them and the three survivors of their attack tried to flee. The four archers we had brought with us ended that hope.

"Fetch your master's horses and mine. I think the battle here is ended but there is much work to be done."

As the two squires raced off, I looked along the line. None of our knights had died for they were all standing although Sir Robert was wounded. My plan, strange though it had sounded to me had worked. The King's intervention had helped but I believe it would have succeeded in any case.

Garth shouted, "Archers, let us clear the battlefield!" This was one of the more gruesome tasks. Knights could be ransomed but any man who was too badly wounded to escape the battle would have his throat cut by my archers. It was a merciful end and my men knew that it was their fate if they lost. The archers would also strip the dead of mail, weapons and any coins that they could find!

It seemed an age, but the squires brought our horses. John was with the other two and he had my horse, Guy, "I left the knight with Leofric and the others. He will be safe."

As I mounted Guy, I knew that I would extract information from my prisoner when I had the chance. He might know something of the whereabouts of my uncle, his squire and my cousin. I hung my shield from my cantle where it would protect my left leg. None of the squires had thought to bring spears and that was disappointing because hunting running men with a spear was much easier. To use a sword successfully when running down fleeing men a knight had to lean down from his saddle. A misplaced hoof could result in a fall and such accidents could be fatal. I saw that the King and the men he and his brother led had attacked the Welsh camp. He would be looking for Prince Dafydd and treasure. The camp did not look to be a large one and it confirmed my suspicion that this was a holding action. The fact that they had had such great success would have emboldened the Welsh. I led my men down the slopes to the side of the road. My aim was to get to the river as soon as I could to prevent men from escaping. My uncle and grandfather had taught me that a leader had to be ruthless in battle. If he was not, then the ones who escaped would come back and would have to be fought a second time. Fight well once and a second battle might not be needed.

The first men we encountered were the ordinary warriors. They wore no armour, and many did not even possess a helmet, but they were fleet of foot. They and the Welsh archers were using every trick that they could. The rocks and bushes we had used on the other side of the pass now provided the Welsh with the same degree of cover. It was like hunting wild pigs; a rider had to avoid obstacles and yet remain aware that his prey could turn and fight. Neither the spearmen nor the archers had discarded their weapons. Guy's hooves thundered for he was a large courser and I saw the spearman I was chasing glance over his shoulder. He was running like a mountain goat and springing from rock to rock. I had to either jump them or twist around them. Jumping in an unknown land was not an option and so I twisted and turned around them. The ground began to flatten out as we neared stone-walled fields filled with sheep. Here I would have to jump or ride to find an opening. The spearman I was hunting leapt the wall by using his left hand to pivot and he disappeared over the other side. I knew that he would be waiting with his spear to gut Guy as he leapt the stone wall. The line of knights and men at arms who pursued the fleeing Welsh was spread out. If my horse fell, then the Welshman would have the opportunity to escape. Instead of jumping where the Welshman had skipped over, I went ten feet to the left. I landed on turf; the sheep which had sheltered there had already flocked with the other Welsh to the far side of the field. The Welshman was six feet from me, and I saw the curse on his lips as he realised he was doomed. He was brave and came at me as I wheeled Guy around to face him. John leapt the wall diagonally and the rear hooves of his horse smashed open the skull of the Welshman.

Raising my sword in acknowledgement I turned to charge with the rest of my men across the sheep field. Hitherto the Welsh had been able to evade us but now we had flat grazing and an enclosed field. There was nowhere for them to run. It was almost sport as we ran them down.

Even the squires, such as John, were able to practise their skills as they learned how to lean from the saddle and hack across the back of a skull. They discovered that hitting a back or neckbone jars a warrior's hand but a sword hit across the back of an unprotected skull smashed the bone like a boiled egg. We chased and harried for five miles as we ran towards the River Conwy. A man is slowed when he kills, and each dead Welshman allowed more to escape. I was aware that none of the men we hunted wore mail of any description. Their best warriors had already escaped. As we neared the river, I saw the last of their knights and men at arms being ferried across the river in the boats which they must have moored there. The last remnants of the archers and spearmen simply jumped into the icy river and swam. A few would drown but most would survive. Whoever led the Welsh army now organised archers and I saw arrows nocked. I waved back my horsemen so that we were safe from arrows and we awaited the King.

Sir Gerard took off his helmet as he and Sir Richard reined in next to me, "A great victory, eh Sir Richard?"

Sir Richard shook his head, and waved his sword towards the Welsh knights before sheathing it, "How many knights and men at arms did we slay today?"

I saw him calculating, "Forty, fifty?"

Sir Richard laughed, "More like ten or fifteen. Henry Samuel here captured a knight and I saw no others who fell. The ones we hewed were not important. When de Clare's men walked into that ambush, we lost more than sixty men at arms and knights. We lost the battle; all we have done is minimise the gains the Welsh might have made."

I nodded, "Aye and my uncle is still to be found. Even had we slaughtered many hundreds more this would still not be a victory. That will only come when I see my missing family!"

Sir William

Chapter 5

I was awake but the world was still black, and I realised that I had been hooded and my arms and legs bound. I forced myself not to panic and to look on the positives. I was not dead, but I was a prisoner. I had told my father that I would not be ransomed, and I prepared myself to be treated harshly. I tried to shout but realised that I was gagged. My captors, Lord Iago and Lady Angharad wanted me silent. I was also in a wagon of some type for I felt the wheels each time they went over a stone or a rock. Why was I still alive? It had to be a risk transporting me for King Henry was in the field with an army. My men, when they found I had been taken, would be seeking me. Then I realised that I did not know where Geoffrey and Dick were. Perhaps they were tied and bound in the wagon with me. Speculation was idle and I tried to work out how I could escape. First, I tried the bonds which held my hands and I pulled and stretched them. Amazingly there was some give in them, and I pulled even harder. The effort was a mistake for I was not alone, and a Welsh voice shouted something. They must have used a cudgel or some other club for there was a crack and I drifted into unconsciousness.

Water was thrown into my face and it woke me. I coughed as my eyes became accustomed to the light. "You are a hard man, Sir William. Idris here hit you hard enough to kill you and yet you survive." I opened my eyes and stared into a face I did not recognise. It was a man and, by the mail he wore, a warrior, an older, grey-haired warrior. I realised that not only the hood had been taken from me but the gag removed, and my hands were now tied behind me.

"Who are you and what do you want with me? I was a King's emissary and there will be repercussions."

The man laughed, "I think not. I am Maredudd of Llangollen and I believe you have met my daughter, Angharad. She has great skill in potions. You slept for a whole day and a night and now you are my guest. You were brought far from the place your people might look for you. Not that it is likely that they will try to rescue you for they think that you are a murderer, an outlaw." I looked around me and saw that I was in a room without natural light. Two brands were burning in sconces and I saw two men who wore mail and looked as though they knew their business. They had tattoos and beards. I had seen the type before. They were the kind of men lords hired to do unsavoury work!

"And where are my son and squire?"

He smiled and it was not a pleasant smile, "I confess that we did not realise you had brought your son for some time. My daughter, thankfully, is quick-witted and she used them to our advantage. Even now they are with Prince Dafydd and his army. They will be the evidence that you murdered Lord Iago ap Nefydd Hardd before my daughter's men managed to kill you. So, you see, you are unnecessary but I am a careful man. Until my plans are fully realised, I need you alive as something to bargain with. Of course, your condition is immaterial."

"Lord Iago ap Nefydd Hardd was alive when last I saw him."

"Of course, he was. My daughter endured more than a year of marriage to that simple-minded fool and now she has inherited the fortune of the richest landowner in Gwynedd. In her widow's weeds, she will garner great sympathy from Prince Dafydd, and your son and squire will confirm that you were sent by King Henry and that you were alone when my son in law died. They would have seen the body with your dagger dripping with blood. Even if they do not believe you did it, they will report the evidence of their eyes and in the absence of your body then all will assume that you have fled."

It was then I began to feel better. My son and squire were not only alive, it was in the interests of all to keep them alive. The implausibility of the story also helped me. King Henry would not believe that I had killed Lord Iago ap Nefydd Hardd and my men would not rest until they found me. Idraf had scouted out this hall already. Surely, he would return. All I had to do was to stay alive and try to find a way out.

Lord Maredudd laughed, "I admire you, Sir William. Men said that you were the one English knight we should fear and I believe they were right. Even now you think to plan an escape. There is none. These two men will be your constant companions until I decide I no longer need you and then they will be your executioners. You will be given the minimum of food and water for I know not how long I need to keep you alive, but this is your resting place. This cellar is the last place you will see on this earth."

I nodded, "After I have killed you and recovered my son and squire, I will hunt down the bitch you spawned and end her life too."

He backhanded me across the mouth and as he was wearing rings, he ripped open my cheek. Added to the blood and bruising from the cudgel I was rapidly becoming a mess. The chair fell over and the two guards righted it. "You still do not realise the position you are in. You are a dead man! Make your peace with God!"

When he left, I began to plan my escape. I watched him leave and saw that the door was not barred either on the inside or the outside. It explained why the two guards would be my companions. Only one would sleep at a time. The two of them had but a single bed. There was a table and two chairs. They had, upon the table, a jug of what smelled like beer and there was also a large platter of bread and cheese on the table. That would not be for me, of that I was certain. My legs were not tied to the chair and that would help me when I did escape. There was a timescale to any hope I had of rejoining my men. I needed to escape sooner rather than later. The longer I was in the cellar then the more likely it was that I would be too weak to escape. Also, their plans might come to fruition quickly in which case they would execute me. I had to get out while I was still fit.

The two men were playing some sort of wooden board game and I did not interrupt them. I deduced that, unless they intended to feed me and to deal with my calls of nature then they would have to untie me at some point. At first, they would be wary that I would try something and would be watching me. I had to lull them and take advantage when there was just one on watch. They were both tough-looking men, but I knew that one would be stronger and meaner than the other. I just had to work out which one. I began my plan by working out what time of day it was. Maredudd had said I had slept for a whole day and night and that suggested that I had arrived late at night but that seemed unlikely as Lord Maredudd would not have bothered himself with me at a late hour. I felt the need to make water. I had had little to eat and there would be little for me to pass until they fed me. I waited for a suitable length of time and then put my plan into action.

"I need to pee!"

The one who laughed told me that he thought himself the tougher of the two. "Piss in your breeks!"

I nodded, "Very well, but you will have to live with the smell, too!"

The other rose, "He is right, Coel. You watch him and I will untie his bonds." He turned to me as Coel unsheathed a hand and a half sword. He held it at my throat. "Try no tricks or we will cut you!"

I now knew the name of one of them. I nodded and played at the frightened prisoner, "I just need to pee. How can I escape there are two of you and I am unarmed?"

"Just remember that and your last days on this earth might be slightly more pleasant!" He undid my bonds but made certain that he was far enough away from me so that if I lurched towards him, he could back off safely away and Coel could cut me! He pointed to the large jug in the corner. "In there and we are watching you." The jug was in the opposite corner from the door. It was half the size of a man and as I could not see them taking it out, I knew that others would come to remove it. Anyone else who came into the cellar could help with my escape. Coel followed me with his sword pricking my back. I found that I was desperate to make water and the pungent smell told me that my body had stored it up longer than it should have. I fastened up my breeks and sat down and was surprised when they did not retie my hands. That meant there were others in the building and any escape would have to take account of that. I played docile. Once I was back in the chair they resumed their game. A short while later Coel used the pot. Time passed and then there was a knock on the door. As it was not locked it showed that they were taking no chances.

Coel went to the door and opened it a crack, "Rhys, food!" Food was one of the words Idraf had taught me. I now knew the other's name. The two men had finished off the bread and cheese. The aroma drifting from the food told me that this was hot food. They had bowls of stew and from the smell, I deduced that there was some mutton in it. There was also more beer. The two servants placed another bowl and a beaker on the table. Coel said as he pointed, "The piss pot needs emptying!" I did not understand their words but was able to deduce them from their actions and inflexion.

The two men grumbled but carried it out. Coel and Rhys did not attempt to feed me. They were both noisy eaters and after wolfing down their stew they used the bread to mop up every last morsel. It was only when they had finished their ale that they brought my bowl of thin, watered-down stew and three-day-old bread. I knew that I had to eat everything for I would begin to grow weaker and I needed my strength. The two of them laughed as I tried to bite the bread; it was like biting into a tree but with less flavour. I soaked the bread in the watery stew and it gradually absorbed it all. The bread became softer and I ate it slowly. The two men became bored with me and took out some dice.

As I sucked and ate the bread, I sought weapons. Both men had knives and swords as well as a club, but they were all beyond my reach as the swords were hanging up and the cudgels lay on the table where they could easily reach them. My best opportunity lay with the knives in their belts. I studied their exact position. I would need to be able to grab one without even looking and I would need to kill silently. As I licked the inside of the bowl, I mentally practised the actions I would need. I would have to be behind whichever was awake and I would have to take his dagger while ensuring he was silent. Only then would I be able to drive the blade into the man. I had two choices, the ear, or the throat. The problem with the throat was that they both wore brigandines with high collars. I could do it, but I could not guarantee death. A dagger driven into the brain would work. As I sipped the small beaker of water I worked out when I would do it. One would need to be asleep and soundly too. The other would have to be in the corner making water.

There was a knock on the door and Rhys opened it this time. The emptied jug was with them and after replacing it they took out the pots. Coel said something in Welsh which I worked out was a request for more ale. That suited me. Coel went to the pot to make water. He was noisy and it sounded like a horse. That gave me confidence. The noise might allow me to get close to them. My buskins had been removed which meant I was barefoot. I suppose they thought it would be less likely that I would try to escape.

"Where do I sleep?" I asked the question of Rhys who seemed the marginally more reasonable of the two.

He pointed to the corner on the opposite side to the piss pot and across from the door. It was as far from the door as they could manage but that did not worry me. I had murder on my mind. The door would be the last place that I would go!

Coel had finished and I saw that Rhys was ready to take his turn. I rose slowly and Rhys stopped unfastening his breeks as he watched me. I feigned indifference to their looks and I lay myself in the corner and rolled myself into a ball. When he was satisfied that I was occupied Rhys carried on. I closed my eyes. I would catch some sleep but I knew that it would not be a deep one. When I woke I would seek an opportunity to escape. I guessed that it was nightfall when Rhys after he had finished at the pot, lay down on the bed. I fell asleep far quicker than I had expected. Perhaps it was exhaustion, lack of food or, more likely, that there was still some of Lady Angharad's potion in my body.

When I woke it was to the sound of snores. One of the brands in the sconces had gone out and the room was dimly lit. I looked from under hooded eyes and saw that it was Rhys who was sleeping. Coel was drinking and I worked out that the servants had brought more ale. The snores from Rhys were so loud that Coel shouted something in Welsh. His voice sounded a little slurred. I watched him as he stood. He was contemplating making water but before he did so he came over to me. My eyes had been just slits, and I kept my breathing deep and regular. I could smell the ale on him. In addition, he had the pungent smell of a man who rarely bathes. I had seen, when he had been seated, that his dagger was tucked in the left front of his belt. It meant he could draw it quickly. When I heard his feet move, I opened my eyes and saw that his back was to me. He was heading for the pot and I rose. It was almost my undoing. My left leg almost gave way for I had not used it much in the last few days. Rhys' snores came to my aid and on bare feet, I padded across the stone floor of the cellar. I saw that Coel was using both hands to clumsily unfasten his breeks but that his head was down as he looked at the leather thongs. It would have to be his ear. I was committed now and there would not be a second chance. I would either succeed or the two men would beat me to death. As his head came up and I heard the sound of water hitting the jug, Coel gave a satisfied sigh and I used that moment to reach with my left hand and pull back his head as I reached around to grab the dagger with my right.

    Coel bit into my hand but that bite stopped him from shouting and as his hand came up to grab my left one, I drove the dagger with all the force I could muster into the man's ear. I drove it in until the tip came out of the other side. He began to fall but, luckily, I had the strength in my left arm to support him so that he slowly sank to the floor. Once he was there, I took two strides to get to the bed. I must have made a slight noise, or Rhys might have been ready to wake. Whatever the reason I saw his eyes open. I leapt on him and clamped my bloody left hand across his mouth. This time I ripped the knife across his throat. Blood spurted and he thrashed but when he stopped then I knew that he was dead.

    I had no idea of the time but knew that whatever I had I could not waste! I took the better of the swords, it was Rhys', its belt and scabbard. I took a cloak from the corner and going to the door I opened it a fraction. I saw a dim light at the top of a short flight of stone stairs. There was silence and I guessed that it was still night. I fastened the cloak around my neck. It would disguise me a little. I went back and took Coel's boots from him. He looked to have the bigger feet. They were tight but they fitted. I slipped Rhys' dagger into that boot and the bloody one of Coel in my belt. I left the cellar and headed for the stairs. As I had expected they came out into the kitchen, however, as I waited outside the door, I could hear no noises and I risked slipping in. I now had a sword and I could fight. The light from the cooking fire still glowed and illuminated the kitchen sufficiently for me to see the door leading to the outside. I had no idea of the layout of this place. Was it a castle? Was it a hall? As I headed for the door, I spied a ham which had been sliced into but there was still enough for me to gain some sustenance. I tucked it inside my tunic. I sought and found the waterskin which hung from a nail behind the door. Shaking it I discovered there was enough in it until I could replenish it. I smelled and then saw the dough which was proving close to the coals of the kitchen oven. I opened the door to the kitchen and peered outside. There was a wall and it was one with a fighting platform. I could see no gate, but I could hear, muffled from the other side of the building, voices which suggested men guarding a gate. Time was not on my side as I could see from the sky that morning was a few hours away. Servants would be arriving at the kitchen to prepare food and that meant someone would see to Coel and Rhys. I was under no illusions; I would be hunted, and I needed to be as far away from this place as I could.

I stepped out and hurried across the cobbles towards the wall. There was no gate on this side nor were there stairs but there was a bread oven close to the wall. I hurried to it. I could hear horses as they sensed me and neighed, but I could not see the stable. The oven was warm to the touch, but it had yet to be lit. That added urgency to my actions for they would soon come to spark it into life. I had seen the proving dough. I clambered on the bread oven and leapt to the fighting platform. To me, it sounded noisy as I landed, and I stayed still to listen for the sounds of alarm. There were none. I peered over the top of the wall and saw that while there was a ditch it was not well maintained, and shrubs and weeds had sprouted in its bottom. I looked out into the darkness and I turned to look back at the hall from which I had escaped. The sky was lighter behind it and that told me that I faced west. As that was the direction I intended to take I began to clamber over the wall. I hung from the crenulations and then dropped. The borrowed boots saved me from injury, and I scrambled out of the ditch and headed across the fields to the west.

I had seen from the walls that there were no houses on this side of the hall and the land was largely wooded with hills and mounds. I guessed that Lord Maredudd used it for hunting or perhaps, grazing. I headed for the woods knowing that I would be less exposed, and it would give me the chance to think of a way to escape from my predicament. They would hunt me, and they would be mounted. They might even have dogs. The borrowed boots might throw them off the scent, but I needed to do all that I could to put distance between me and my hunters. As I made my way through the wood, I took out the ham bone and bit into it. There was enough meat on the bone to keep me going for a day or two and if I had not found sanctuary by then I would be dead. I knew that the River Dee flowed from the mountains past Llangollen and Lord Maredudd gave that as his title. I guessed that was where I was. I could use the river to refill my waterskin and to use it to mask my scent. As I made my way through the well-spaced trees, which told me that they were controlled, I saw that the land dipped a little to my right and I could see shadows to the north of me which suggested higher pieces of ground. I headed in that direction and found a small stream. I jumped into it and the water came up to my knees. It mattered not. It would mask my smell and lead me to the river.

Already the sky was becoming lighter and I did not wish to be exposed when daylight came. Despite my hurts, I forced myself on. I heard the river before I saw it. Here it was a young river and vigorous. I left the stream and headed towards the noise. I found some scrubby elder bushes and squatted there. I drank from the skin and then knelt down to refill it from the bubbling, frothy river. As I did, I saw that there were flat rocks which lay just below the surface. I put the stopper back in the skin and stepped on the first one. I began to make my way upstream using the stones as my route. Although many of the stones were below the surface the speed of the river had scoured them of weed and I did not slip. I made fifty paces before they stopped, and I had to step into the water. It came up to above my knees and filled my boots. I waded for another twenty paces and realised that the going was too slow. I headed for the shore and sought a rocky exit. I found one and sat to empty my boots of water. I had bought myself some time.

I hurried along the riverbank using rocks whenever I could. The wet footprints would soon dry and if they had no dogs then I would escape. However, I worked on the assumption that they would have dogs and that added urgency to my feet. I had to head to the army of King Henry and that lay forty or fifty miles to the north and west of me. The closer I could get to the Roman Road the better my chance of survival for there would be riders from the army using that road. As I headed along the riverbank I was aware that I was not taking the most direct route as the river looped and twisted. By my estimate, I was four miles or so from my cellar when I smelled woodsmoke from a dwelling. Whoever lived close they would be unlikely to be friendly. The odds on finding another Davy ap Hywel were not good. I turned south and clambered up through the trees. The sky was definitely lighter and that helped me to find a safe path through the undergrowth. When I reached the top, I saw the Roman Road. That it was the road was obvious from its curved shape and the ditch which ran along the side. It was confirmed when I saw the mile markers.

I now had a dilemma. I had wanted to find the road but not this close to Lord Maredudd. One thing I had learned serving as the sentinel of the north was to think and act quickly. The sun would be fully up in less than half an hour. The road would become busy then. I had half an hour to get me as far down the road as I could and then I would find somewhere to hide up until nightfall.

As I hurried down the road, I used my sense of smell and hearing to warn me of danger. Annoyingly there were dwellings on the road and in that half an hour available to me I covered little more than a mile and a half as I had to keep leaving the road to avoid alerting dogs and to keep away from the houses I passed. A sudden shaft of sunlight from the east told me that I had to leave the road for a new day was about to begin. The river and the last house I had passed were to my right and that meant I had to go to the left and climb the small slope through the trees. The first sunray heralded many more and soon the wood was filled with dappled light and I felt exposed. Once again it was a small, seemingly insignificant stream which saved me. I stepped into it and began to climb. It was when I was just twenty paces up the stream that I realised I needed to make water, and this was as good a place as any for the stream would take away the smell. When I had finished, I struggled wearily up the stream. It was when I stumbled that I realised I was tired and tired men make mistakes. There was a sudden scurrying and I saw a fox leap from its hiding place just ten feet from me. I doubted that it was a den and when I reached the place, I saw a half-eaten rabbit to the side of the stream. I picked up the rabbit and walked back down the stream to place it halfway from where I entered the stream. If they had dogs then the rabbit and the smell of the fox would interest them and if they continued up the stream then the smell of the fox I had forced to flee would mask any smell I might have left.

The sun was rising higher and I forced myself to stop and seek shelter. I spied an unlikely refuge. There was a huge blackberry bush and it overhung the small stream I was using. I made my way to it and after covering my head and hands with the cloak I rolled myself under it. Even though it was a thick cloak I was still stabbed and scratched but once in the centre there was less growth and I was hidden by the leaves, fruits and thorns. I could not see clearly, and I doubted that any would be able to see in. I pulled the cowl of the cloak tightly about me and I slept.

I was awoken by the sound of Welsh voices and they sounded close. I was alert immediately. I was in darkness for the cowl of the cloak was over my face. I slowly lifted it and I saw through the brambles and the leaves, four men walking up the stream. From the light, it was afternoon for the sun was in the west, but I had no idea if it was early or later afternoon. The men had two dogs with them. That they had followed me so quickly was worrying although I had no idea of the exact time of day. I could have slept for hours. I peered at them looking for clues. The dogs were just sniffing, and I did not think that they had my scent. The Welshmen were obviously annoyed, and I heard an argument. Of course, as it was in Welsh, they could have been simply passing the time of day for Welsh always sounds aggressive to me. One of the dog handlers pointed to the sky and said something. It was then I realised that the sun was setting; I had slept a long time and it was late afternoon. After a further heated debate, the two dog handlers took their dogs and headed downstream. When the other two walked just a little way from the stream and began to build a fire I knew that they were making a camp. My attempt to escape had only been partially successful. I was trapped under a blackberry bush and when dawn came, they would renew their hunt.

Henry Samuel

Chapter 6

By the time the King and his brother arrived with the bulk of the knights, the sun had passed its zenith and the Welsh had disappeared from the east bank of the Conwy. The river had taken away the bodies of those who had drowned, and they would now be at the sea.

"You have done well, Baron, and your plan exceeded all of my expectations. You have your grandfather's mind and courage! Well done!"

"The Welsh are fled, Your Majesty, but they still have their knights. The bodies you see are of their spearmen and some of their archers."

He frowned, "And there is no bridge here." He turned to Sir Robert Pounderling. "You know this land better than I do. Is there somewhere we could use to hold the Welsh and protect your castle?"

I had fought alongside Sir Robert when we had campaigned in the Clwyd Valley. He was a stout if unimaginative man. He nodded, "Further up the river on the coast is an old castle, Deganwy. It is unoccupied for I have seen it from the sea. It is mounted upon a hill. It might need some work, but it would control the mouth of the river and with ships, we could ferry men across the river. It would be a starting point. We would need to build new walls and a keep but it has a good position,"

"Is it far?"

I saw Sir Robert rub his chin. "I would say no more than fourteen miles or so."

The King looked at the sky, "Then as the Welsh are all to the west of the river we will ride there. Lead on Sir Robert." He looked at me, "You can fetch the baggage on the morrow, Baron." With that, I was dismissed.

Sir Robert turned to me as he mounted his horse, "That was well done, Sir Henry, and your grandfather would be proud of you. I confess that Dyserth is a stronger castle because of your grandfather and uncle." He nodded to his servants. "I will leave these with the baggage train knowing that you will watch over my men. There will be more riders joining us soon."

I did not mind being detached from the army. It would give me the chance to question my captive. I think that the success of his attack had encouraged the King and given him confidence and he was happy to let me watch his treasure. As we rode back along the road, we saw the archers I had left and they were still stripping the dead. Their bodies would be left for either their families to collect them or for the carrion to benefit. It was not only our servants who had been left with the baggage. Other servants, the healers and the priests were all there too. Two disconsolate looking Welsh men at arms were there with the knight. Without the hope of ransom, the two men would fear the worst.

Leofric and our other servants were guarding all three of them and the two men at arms had been stripped of their armour. Leofric smiled when he saw we were all whole, "Your captive is Rhodri of Abergele, lord. he is not happy!"

I dismounted and handed my reins to John, "He will be even less happy when I have done with him."

Sir Richard said quietly, "Henry Samuel, he has given his word and cannot be harmed."

I turned to Sir Richard, "My friend, my uncle and cousin are missing. I will discover what this man knows and if he is innocent then he need fear nothing." I was aware that the man was listening and his face showed understanding. He spoke our language. "Sir Rhodri, I seek a man, a squire and a boy of ten summers. Have you seen or heard of them?"

I had asked the question so quickly that he had not had the opportunity to compose himself and I saw the flash of guilt upon his face. When he spoke then I knew it was a lie. "I know nothing."

I put my face close to him, "You lie! Erik Red Hair!"

My Viking stepped forward. His tunic was bespattered with blood and gore. When he fought it was with a ferocity which terrified friend as well as foe. With his dramatic beard, he looked like something from a bygone era and as he neared us, I saw Sir Rhodri recoil.

"Yes, my lord?"

I turned back to the Welsh knight, "I will ask you again, what do you know of an Englishman, his French squire and his son?"

He looked from me to Erik. I had not threatened him, but I did not need to; it was implicit in the presence of my Viking giant. His shoulders slumped and he nodded, "I know nothing of the man but there was a French youth and a young English boy. They were with the widow of Lady Angharad of Llanrwst. I believe the man of which you speak murdered her husband, Lord Iago. That is all that I know for they were with Prince Dafydd."

His words had the ring of truth about them and I believed him. "And when last you saw them, they were well?"

"They were but they left the camp in the night with the Prince and his bodyguards."

I smiled, "Leofric, you can feed him now." I turned to the other two. "What do you two know of this?"

Like all men at arms, these men could speak many languages. They were swords for hire. If they were working for the Welsh, then they were not the best for the Welsh did not pay as well as we did. "We saw the two of them but there was no man."

"Do not try to escape and I may release you when it pleases me. Sir Rhodri, you will pay the ransom?" He nodded, "Then when you are fed take your horse and send the ransom to Chester. It will be ten pounds of silver and four pounds of gold."

He nodded dully. I had estimated his worth well. Abergele was not a rich manor but it could afford the gold and silver I had requested. "Thank you, I will leave when I am fed. Is there a horse?"

"Leofric, find him a sumpter." I went with Richard to join the other knights and men at arms, "Thank you, Erik."

He grinned, "You are welcome, Sir Henry!"

When I sat it was Sir Richard who spoke first, "Sir William would never murder a man." It was such an obvious comment that it did not require an answer.

Sir Mark asked, "What has happened?"

I let Sir Richard explain while I ran through all the facts in my head. Geoffrey and Dick were still alive, and we had a vague idea of their location but where was my uncle? It did not sound to me as though he had been killed; perhaps he was being held and awaiting trial but, if so why separate him from his squire and son? The fact that the widow was with them gave me hope for women had a gentler side of them to warriors and I knew that this would be hard for Dick. They were, however, south of the river and that posed a problem. Where was Idraf? He would still be seeking the three of them, but he would not know that they were not together.

I was aware that the others were looking at me. Sir Robert of Redmarshal said, "Should we cross the river and seek them?"

"That was the first thought which crossed my mind, but I doubt that we will be allowed to. Today we showed the King what we can do, and I do not think that he will let us get too far from his side. We should make the most of this time. What I want is Idraf to come riding over that hill and tell me that he has found them." I spread my arm, "We had better get the baggage moving. I dare say the King will wish his treasure close to hand. We will have the men at arms guard the baggage, the healers and the priests. The knights will be the vanguard and unlike de Clare, we will have our archers as scouts."

It took time to hitch up the wagons and to ensure that the wounded were comfortable. By that time Harry Longbow and the rest of our archers had arrived. I was already mounted and so when they rode in, I said, "I want a screen of ten archers a mile ahead of the main column. The rest of the archers will be a quarter of a mile behind them and along the flanks. We will be passing through rocky passes. Hopefully, they will not be as dangerous as the one where we were ambushed but have them keep their eyes peeled. We may have sent the main Welsh army across the river, but you can bet that there are scouts and bands close by who will be seeking for weaknesses."

He nodded, "Idraf will find them, lord, if they are still alive."

I was aware that he was not privy to the latest information we had, "We know that Master Geoffrey and Master Richard are still alive for they were seen in the Welsh camp but they were whisked away before we attacked. They are south of the river. My hope is that Idraf can find Sir William."

We were about to leave when two hobelars galloped in. "We seek Sir Robert Pounderling."

I waved them over, "He is with the King and heading to Deganwy."

"Thank you, my lord." They were about to ride off but I held the reins of one of the horses.

"What is it?"

"There will be no more men coming from Dyserth as the Welsh have taken Mold and are besieging Dyserth. We need Sir Robert back there."

"It is late. Travel with us and that guarantees your news will reach the King for there may be Welsh warriors waiting to ambush two lonely riders!"

We headed north and west along roads which were little more than heavily used trails and were largely unsuitable for the wagons we were using. We made painfully slow progress. The King had taken the river road and the road we were on joined it just short of the place where my uncle had disappeared. The settlement had emptied when the King had passed through and so I took the opportunity to stop.

"Water the horses. Sir Richard, have the men search for food, who knows the King may have left some for us! John, fetch Erik Red Hair and Alan Longsword. I would examine this place which my uncle did not visit."

When the two men at arms joined us, we rode towards the hall which dominated the settlement. When the King's men had visited the place, they had taken the word of those who lived there that Sir William had never visited although if he had murdered Lord Iago then he obviously had visited. Idraf had been clandestine. I needed to look with my own eyes. I feared the worst, as we neared the impressive wooden gates. Had my uncle been killed? The knight had said that he had murdered Lord Iago but not the consequences of that murder. When we reached the gates, I said, "Erik, break them down."

John said, "Let me try something, my lord." He was a skilful horseman and he jumped upon his saddle and he leapt to the top of the wall. He pulled himself up and disappeared over the top. A few moments later the gates opened, and Alan led John's horse within.

The hall was as impressive as the gates which guarded it. I dismounted and went to the door which was locked. There was no easy way in, and I nodded to Erik. It took just three blows from his axe to hack the lock. Alan used the pommel of his sword to knock the lock away and the door swung open.

"John, search the grounds and look for any evidence of Sir William or the others."

"Aye, lord."

"Alan search the cellars and Erik, the ground floor. I will search the upper floors."

I drew my sword. We had been told that the hall had been abandoned but who knew if that was the truth. I was ready for any treachery. As I searched the well-furnished rooms what I did not find were weapons, however, I found a room which was filled with books and parchments. It confirmed what I had heard that Lord Iago ap Nefydd Hardd was a studious man. My uncle would not kill him, not unless he had to. I dismissed the thought. There was no series of events which would see that happen.

When Erik shouted that John had found something then I feared the worst. We ran outside and found him near the stables. He pointed to the open door, "I found the reins from Sir William's horse. I recognised the leather for Sir Mark's father made them especially for him but that is not what I wish to show you. I have found a rough grave which is hidden from view."

"Is it...?"

He shook his head, "I uncovered it first."

"Who is it?"

"Come and look, my lord, but I think it is Lord Iago."

When we went around the back of the hall, we saw that it was, indeed, a shallow grave. The body had simply been dumped. It had to be Lord Iago. The man had smooth hands and polished nails. He had never done a day's work in his life. His throat had been cut. "It looks like it could be him. Come, let us return to the others and decipher this puzzle."

Alan Longsword said, "Let us assume he escaped, my lord. He could not ride out of here for there is just one gate as we discovered when we came here. If he went over the wall then he would have two choices, head to Shrewsbury or find the King."

"That makes sense, but we can do little until Idraf returns."

I told the others the news when we returned, and I asked the priests and some of the servants to re-inter the dead man. I went with them for the King would wish to know about this murder. A rider came in from the west just after sunset. He was from the King who wanted to know what was amiss.

"Tell the King that the roads were not the best and we had wagons. We will be with him soon after sunrise." If you had asked me when we had gathered in Stockton if I would stand up to a King, then I would have laughed. The position in which I found myself had forced me to change. I would never be the same idealistic young knight I had been.

When we reached Deganwy I saw that little work had been done since it had been built more than a hundred years earlier It was still a largely wooden castle. This, however, was what the King enjoyed. He had improved Westminster as well as Windsor and he had men busy sourcing stone while others were labouring to dig ditches and erect new walls. The King showed his displeasure at my apparent tardiness by keeping me waiting for a whole day before he allowed me to report to him. For me, this was a day wasted, a day when we could have been hunting for my family. I sent the two hobelars to report to Sir Robert. He would be invaluable in giving advice to the King. When I did report to the King, I had to fight to keep my temper. Sir Richard had advised me to do so. He had had dealings with King Henry when he and my brother had defended the northern border.

As soon as he allowed me to I burst out, "King Henry we have learned that my uncle's squire, Geoffrey and my cousin, Richard, have been taken by the Welsh and, I believe, are to the west of the river!"

He waved a hand, "That is sad, but it is your uncle's fault. From what you say he either murdered Lord Iago or fell foul of his men. Your uncle should have taken more care and I cannot jeopardise what we have won by searching for someone who may already be dead."

I could feel the anger rising in me and I remembered not only Sir Richard's words but those of my grandfather. He had endured far worse from King John. I nodded, "You are right, Your Majesty, and I assume that you intend to spend some time rebuilding this castle?"

"Of course, and with a larger stone castle we can control the river and the Welsh." He pointed across the river at the small village called Conwy where the Welsh were camped. There was no sign of the Prince, but it was a strong force and they could use the ferries and boats they controlled to launch attacks on the east shore of the river. "When it is built, we can cross the river and chase those from that shore too!"

"Then you will need Prince Dafydd and his men watching and controlling. There is no sign of the Prince here. Where has he gone?" He frowned, "I have just heard from Sir Robert's men, Your Majesty, that Mold Castle has fallen, and Dyserth Castle is under siege. Sir Robert Pounderling is needed in the northeast." I saw the shock on the King's face. His plans were falling apart. "The best form of defence is to attack. I have a small force of men, but they are the most mobile. If we cross the River Conwy, then we can threaten Prince Dafydd's lines of communication with Anglesey. We can raid for food and allow you the time to build."

He frowned, "And this has nothing to do with your uncle and cousin?"

I shook my head, "I will not lie, King Henry, while I harass the Welsh, I will keep watch for my relatives but I can do both and my chevauchée serves you as well as I. You have enough men to build your walls and the risk is to the men of Stockton. What have you to lose?"

He shook his head, "Your men but you are right, and this makes military sense, but I want you returned by the start of October." He turned to an aide, "And send for Sir Robert Pounderling. He was remiss not to report to me of the loss of Mold. He must regain control of the Clwyd."

As I was heading back to my men, I met with Sir Robert, "I am sorry, Sir Robert, I gave the King the news about Mold and he was less than happy."

"It is my fault. I should have stayed in Dyserth for I knew that there were Welsh abroad, but I obeyed the King's summons."

I nodded, "As did I. You will be blamed for this just as my uncle was blamed for obeying the King's orders!"

"Good luck! If I had the men I would have them search the Clwyd for Sir William. I liked him and I would not have my castle but for him." He looked at the sky, "It will not be until tomorrow that I can leave and I pray that they have yet to assault my castle. It is not yet completed!"

When I reached my men, I set about rattling orders and commands. This time I held a council of war with just my knights for I would speak with my captains of archers and men at arms later. I needed the knights to know what we were about. Sir Geoffrey Fitzurse might not be happy about putting his head above the parapet. What I intended was dangerous; we were poking a stick into the dragon's lair and we might get burned.

"We ride back down the Conwy and cross at Llanrwst. I intend to take the Roman Road to the straits and threaten Anglesey. It may well be that Prince Dafydd is at Aberffraw and while we cannot cross the water, we can raid the land under the mountain! This is the heartland of Gwynedd and is sacred to the people. We will draw them hence and, I hope, fetch Idraf to us. I believe that if he has followed Geoffrey and Dick then he is close to the Welsh army. He is a resourceful man, but he will need help to extricate Geoffrey and Dick."

"And what of your uncle? Have you forgotten him?"

I knew that Sir Geoffrey would not be happy about my plan. "No, Sir Geoffrey, but we know where the two young ones are. We will seek my uncle when we have Geoffrey and Dick."

Sir Richard nodded, "I know Sir William better than any here, save Henry Samuel and he is right. This is what Sir William would wish us to do and besides, I like the idea of tweaking the dragon's tail."

As the others were agreed then Sir Geoffrey had no choice but to go along with it. My orders to the archers and men at arms were easier for they needed no convincing. "Harry and Garth, I want half of the archers to seek Idraf. I know it is asking a great deal for the rest will be spread thinly but I do not think the Welsh will expect us to come from this direction. We take no wagons and live off the land. It is summer and the sheep are on the hills. We take them."

I had no arguments from any and the next day we slipped out of the building site to ride the fourteen miles to the crossing of the Conwy and we began our search.

As we passed through Llanwryst I was tempted to take my anger and frustration out on the villagers who had lied to both the King's men and Idraf but that was not our way and so we passed through and crossed the river. We went slowly at first for the archers were looking for signs that my uncle had escaped his prison and was hiding nearby, perhaps hurt. The wagon which had headed east still confused me but we had to be logical and we used the slow progress to take sheep while we could. It was interesting that there were fewer protests than one might have expected. That worried me for I wondered if it meant that the Prince knew we were abroad in his land. As much as I wanted to be searching for clues, I knew that I was not the man to do that. The archers were and I had to be patient. It allowed me, as we moved at the pace of a walking man, to contemplate the wider picture. The King's plan was in tatters. Perhaps if my uncle had been with the army then we might have repaired the flaws, but I was too young and out of favour. The King was isolated in Deganwy and Flintshire and Denbighshire, which had been won by my uncle, were now in danger of being lost. Perhaps Simon de Montfort was right, and the King should be locked up for his own good. He had lost a war in France which had cost thousands and now he was doing the same in Wales. His only success had been in Scotland and that had been because of my grandfather!

We camped just eight miles from Llanwryst at a farm whose occupants fled as my archers approached. The same had been true when we had passed through Betws-y-Coed and the other small hamlets. While sheep were cooked, and my archers reported I saw a way to take Wales from the Welsh.

"Lord, there is no sign of Sir William nor any pursuit west of the river. My lord, there was no sign of any military activity. This is a peaceful land. I do not think that Idraf has been here and even if he had come here he would have found nothing,"

I did not bother to question further; my archers would have turned over every blade of grass and every rock seeking evidence. I nodded, "Then tomorrow we move as fast as we can. I have seen little evidence of any opposition and we have butchered enough animals so that we can eat well. I intend to ride hard for Bangor and Penryn. There are ferries that are used to cross to Anglesey, and I would destroy them. My intention is to ride around this mountain which looms over us and to cross back over the River Conwy to rejoin the King."

I saw Sir Geoffrey pale, but he said nothing. It was left to my uncle's friend, Sir Richard to speak. "And if we meet the main Welsh army?"

"Then we have a good chance of finding Geoffrey and Dick." I saw the doubt on the faces of Sir Geoffrey and Sir Robert of Redmarshal. Sir Mark and Sir Gerard would go along with whatever plan I conjured. I could not read Sir Richard. I knew my uncle had spoken with him before he had left on his disastrous mission for the King. I wondered what had been said. "I am not being foolish, and I see a way here to defeat the Welsh. A fast-moving column of well-armed men can cause havoc. Garth has told us that he has seen no sign of soldiers. Sir Geoffrey, if you were Prince Dafydd, would you expect men to attack Bangor and the ferries?"

He shook his head. "He may have gone to the Clwyd."

"He may, it is one of many possibilities, but we saw no sign when we were at Llanwryst. I think he will be gathering men from Anglesey." I had learned from my grandfather that if you led then that is what you did. There would be no further debate and the men would follow my orders. I prayed that I had made the right decision. "Garth and Harry, we now revert to the former system. A group of archers well ahead of the rest to watch for an ambush. Half on the flanks and the rest four hundred paces behind the scouts."

"And Idraf?"

"We trust him. It will be easier for him to see us than for us to find him!"

As we ate our meal Sir Richard sat next to me. "This is a good plan, Henry Samuel but it is bold. Are you sure you are not doing this out of anger?"

"There may be an element of that, Richard, but I want to let Geoffrey and Dick know that we are close to them. It may encourage them to escape. The longer they are with the Welsh and the further they are away from the army the less chance they have of escape. My greatest fear is that they are already across the straits and beyond help."

"Then you can forget that fear for although you can do many things you cannot fly across the water. If they are beyond your grasp, then we try to find your uncle."

The words cut me like a sword for he was right. Finding my uncle would be hard for Gwynedd was a large place but we had more chance of finding him than crossing the straits.

Chapter 7

The days were still hot but not quite as long as they had been as we were halfway through August. We reached the heights above Bangor just before noon. There we saw our first soldiers. The two standards told us that they were led by knights but Garth, whose archers had found them first, told us that there were just two hundred men in all, and more than half were just spearmen. They were camped close to the settlement. We spied down on them from a piece of high ground our archers had found. I had my knights with me but we were hidden from the camp.

"Any sign of Geoffrey or Dick?"

"No, lord, and no sign of the woman nor Prince Dafydd. I think they just guard the port."

I turned to Richard, "What think you, Sir Richard?"

"They are either reinforcements for Conwy or here to protect the ferry." He pointed, "They have no sentries set out and few horses. I think they guard the straits. If you were Prince Dafydd and had to bring your men over by boat, you would wish them to land without disputation!"

Garth nodded, "Aye lord, my scouts tell me that they have stakes to the east of the town closer to Penrhyn. They would do that if they feared an attack from the east."

This was a time for decisive action. "Garth, dismount your archers. Leofric and the servants and squires can watch them." I knew that John would be disappointed, but it could not be helped. We could not be afoot this far from home. "Filter down and surround the camp. When I see you in position then we will charge them. They outnumber us but we have a major ally, surprise!"

"Aye, Sir Henry."

I dismounted my hackney and mounted my courser, Guy, "We use spears and we hit them hard. Make them think that we are the whole of King Henry's army." We had few knights but the thirty men at arms I led were the equal of knights. Men like Erik Red Hair would not be happy about using a spear and as soon as it shattered then Erik would use his axe. Others would do the same.

From our elevated position in the shelter of the trees on the gentle slopes of the ground to the southeast of the settlement, I watched the moving shadows as my archers used whatever cover they could find. With nocked arrows, they would silence any who threatened to give them away. I hoped that they would not be civilians, but this was war and there were always casualties. The abduction of Dick had removed any sympathy I had for the Welsh! Garth's distinctive face, I recognised him even at a mile, turned to look at us and I knew that they were in place. I raised my spear, "Remember to hit them hard, make them run!" I spurred my horse and led my men down the road.

We would be heard, and it would take some little time to ride the one mile to Bangor, but I counted on a number of things helping us. Firstly, the direction from which we came. Their first thought would be that it would be allies. In the time it took to ask the question we would have covered half the distance. Secondly, Garth, Harry and the rest of our archers would target the knights and leaders. We were less than four hundred paces from the camp when we heard the horns sounding the alarm and we started to spread into the fields which were alongside the road. The shallow ditches which lined the road were no obstacle. The arrows began to fall as we passed the archers who were using every piece of cover that they could. I began to lower my spear. I held my shield loosely at my side for the odds were I would not need it.

We were in our usual formation with the knights in the centre and the men at arms echeloned to the side. That we had caught them by surprise was obvious and Welsh warriors were still rushing for and stringing bows and seeking their weapons. With just a few knights the spearmen and archers were looking for commands. In addition, our archers were hurting them. Soon the Welsh would break. I saw a pair of spearmen forming up to start a defensive line. It was the right thing to do but two was just too few and I did not even have to raise my weapon, my horse simply bowled them over. The nearest they came to hurting me was when a spearhead glanced off my cuisse. Other spearmen and archers were not so lucky. I saw that Garth's archers had hit many already and there were men who had been skewered by spears. I aimed for the two knights and ignored the spearmen. The knights were trying to organise the men at arms into a shield wall. My courser, Guy, had the bit between his teeth and his long legs were eating up the ground. The knights saw the arrow of armoured men coming towards them and they tried to switch fronts. They were not helped by the fact that Garth and my archers had followed us into the camp and the range was much closer. They could aim at individual men at arms and knights. One man at arms found that even his shield and mail did not stop an arrow sent at a range of fewer than fifty paces.

Of course, we were no longer having it our own way. The Welsh were nocking and releasing arrows, but most were just war arrows. I discovered that when one hit my mail and just stuck there. It did, however, encourage me to ride faster and I pulled my arm back to strike over the shield of the nearest man at arms as I urged on my horse. My men were keeping as close to me as they could. I was a bigger target, but the majority of the target was the horse. Killing my mount would unhorse me but the Welsh archers still aimed at the rider. Another thing in our favour which kept us safer was our speed. The line of men we would hit might slow us down but that would not help the spearmen who had to face the charging mailed men on horses. As I neared the first spearman he thrust up at my shield. It still hung from my left leg and arm and the head slid up the shield, grazing and tearing my surcoat. My unerring aim meant that my ash shafted spear, punched hard, struck him in the nose and the metal head tore into his skull. Sir Richard's spear struck a Welsh knight in the shoulder while Sir Geoffrey's transfixed another in the chest. Sir Robert's had shattered, and he was using his sword. As I pulled my arm back for a second strike, I saw that Erik Red Hair had discarded his broken spear and was laying about himself with his war axe. In theory, the men with the spears should have had the advantage for their weapons were longer but there is something about a wild, bearded man riding a huge horse and swinging one of the deadliest weapons known to man that makes a warrior want to empty his bowels. I knew that the Viking had no fear of death. He and Alan Longsword carved a swathe of death through the Welsh line of spearmen and, inevitably, they broke. By now we outnumbered them. Their knights were either dead or wounded and so the spearmen and archers fled. They ran to the harbour and we pursued them down the narrow streets, driving them before us.

Once in the town, it was more confusing and harder as the streets were narrower. For the Welsh, it became a death trap as groups of riders speared men in the back as they were caught like fish in a trap. Many escaped by simply running into the buildings. Garth and his archers would winkle them out. I shouted, "On, to the seas!"

The streets became steeper as we neared the port. Already some of the burghers had taken ships and pushed off towards the Island of Anglesey which looked close enough to touch. Some of those we had defeated would inevitably escape and they would board the departing boats. We could not pursue them into the straits, but we could stop others from trying to leave. Every man we killed now was one less we would have to kill in the future. My horse, Guy, was travelling so fast down the cobbled street that I almost failed to stop him as his hooves slid and sparked along the quay. I barely stopped him but, as I turned him, I managed to slash at one of the stays on a fishing boat which was just pulling away. It might escape but they would have to repair it before they could return.

"Stop any more ships from leaving! Burn them!"

I dismounted and held the reins in my left hand. Turning I faced the other Welshmen who were trying to escape. Some of our archers had been so fast that they had kept up with us and they ran into the houses to fetch burning brands which they hurled into some of the ships which were still tied up and some which had barely managed to leave the quayside. Fire is the deadly enemy to all ships. Tar is used to protect ropes, and, in high summer, the decks and timbers are bone dry. There were a series of whooshes as flames leapt up masts and ignited sails. Some ships tried to turn and merely fouled other ships. Soon the whole of the harbour was ablaze and spread to some of the wooden jetties. From there it was a small leap to set fire to some of the houses.

We were in almost as much danger as the Welsh and so I mounted my horse and shouted, "Back up the hill to safety. If you can save food, then do so!"

This was what my archers did well, and I saw them race into buildings which were either made of stone or had yet to catch fire. We would eat well that night.

By the time I reached the scene of the battle the servants and squires had arrived and with the horses tethered, they were collecting treasure from the dead. We would have to shift the bodies before we could make our own camp, but the wagons could be used. We would pile the bodies in them and simply roll them down the slope to the fire or the sea; either would do the job.

I was weary and yet I knew that we should move up the coast to Penrhyn where there were more boats. I decided to rest and leave in the morning. After handing my horse over to John I waved over Alan Longsword, "Did we lose many men?"

"A few, my lord, none of the Earl's or Sir William's."

Garth walked up from the port with a blackened face, four of his men and a huge cooked ham. He looked happy, "We eat well tonight, my lord. I didn't think the Welsh ate pig."

"Their lords like it and that must mean that they expect their knights to come back through here soon. Any sign of Idraf?"

The smile left his face. Like the rest of us, he was worried, "No sir, and the lads have been keeping a weather eye open."

I chewed my lip and I thought through the problem. We needed to get to Conwy sooner rather than later and yet we had to deal with Penrhyn. "Sir Richard, tomorrow I want you to lead the attack on Penrhyn. I will go with Erik and a dozen or so archers and the four servants. I intend to ride up the coast road and scout out Conwy myself."

He pointed to the mountains just ahead of us, "You realise that the land narrows at that point so much that it is the perfect place for an ambush!"

"I know and that is why I will scout it out. There will be no soldiers at Penrhyn, and you should be able to burn the boats and capture supplies. Do it quickly and then join us. It is less than fourteen miles to Conwy from here. If we can dislodge the men, there before the reinforcements from Anglesey get here then the King might be able to build his defences."

"Reinforcements are coming?"

"From the supplies we have found it seems likely that they are and that explains why Prince Dafydd went to the island."

John was happier to be riding with me and he was in a better mood. The twelve archers I had were good ones and three of them were Welsh. As we passed Penrhyn I saw that there were still some boats in the small harbour. I wondered why they had not left for they must have known we were coming. I knew from the maps I had studied in Chester that there were just two small places between Bangor and Conwy: Llanfairfechan and Penmaenmawr. Neither would have a garrison but both were in a position to hold us up. For that reason, I had Dywi and Ieuef, two men of Gwynedd as my scouts and they rode just half a mile ahead of us. Sir Richard was right, this was a perfect place to hold up an army. In places, there were just two hundred paces between the sea and the steep rock-strewn slopes. We were approaching Penmaenmawr when the two archers suddenly turned and galloped back towards us.

I knew that their speed meant trouble ahead, "There is danger! Dismount. Leofric, have the servants hold the horses. Archers find some cover."

Ned the Nocker said, "Should we not ride back to the main column, my lord?"

"Let us see the size of the problem first, Ned. Do you not trust your own skill?"

"Aye lord, but I would not have her ladyship's favourite grandson die while I was on watch!"

I laughed, "And that will not happen. If I deem it dangerous then we will mount and ride back. I need your bows! Now find shelter. John, Erik and I will draw their eyes to us."

Erik was actually laughing as he took his axe and stood on my right side. I looked and saw that the slope was not too steep to walk up but the balance would be tricky. There looked to be some sort of trail of path half-way up but it was difficult to make out because of the line of trees which had managed to grow there. There looked to be but one way to attack, down the road and narrow shingle beach.

Dywi and Ieuef reined sharply in and threw themselves from their saddles, "There is a column of men riding from the direction of Conwy, my lord."

"How many Dywi?"

"I saw four mailed horsemen and the rest look like hobelars or lightly armed horsemen. Perhaps thirty or more in total."

They all looked at me and I weighed up the odds. Two to one in their favour but we had archers. "We stand. You two find somewhere to rain arrows on them. Dywi, I leave the command to you."

I donned my helmet and hefted my shield. I had my sword in my hand. John had a spear and a shield. He, too, had a helmet, an open bascinet. "Lock your shield with mine. We will make them come to us." I gave no such command to Erik for he had his shield upon his back and was wielding his axe two handed. He had left a gap so that I could swing my sword.

I saw sunlight glint off metal as the mailed men galloped hard towards us. We would appear as a tempting target. What we were doing was not as foolish as it seemed. If only four men were mailed, then the archers could target bodkin arrows on them. They would be the only ones on large horses. John was the one most at risk as he only had a brigandine. He carried his long spear and a good shield. When this was over, I would find him a hauberk for he fought like a man at arms more often than not. Glancing to the sides I saw that most of the archers had scrambled up the slope to find shelter behind the rocks which had tumbled at some time in the past from the mountain. Three were on the beach where they had some shelter from the road. Those three were the most vulnerable as riders could come down the shingle of the beach. I knew that behind me the four servants, whilst holding the reins of the horses, would also have their short swords ready. They had all been warriors once and knew how to hamstring a horse or stab it in the eye. They were safer than we were for they were partly hidden by a bend in the road. The Welsh might see the rumps of two of the horses but not the men who held them.

"John, hold steady and we will emerge victorious."

"I am not afraid, my lord. I trust the archers and besides, these are just Welshmen!"

Erik laughed, "That is the spirit! They are little men!"

Four hobelars were hurtling down the shingle and that meant they were falling a little way behind the ones on the road as it was slower going than the cobbled road. The mailed men led the others for, with a drainage ditch, they did not have enough room for more. The Welsh would have seen the two scouts racing down the road and assumed that they were the ones on the beach. They might wonder if we had more but in the absence of bodies and horses they might see this as an opportunity to capture a knight. My archers would wait until their bodkins would punch holes in the mail of the four riders at the fore. I wondered if they had left it too late when the four mailed men had approached to within forty paces and no arrows had been sent. In fact, the three archers on the beach loosed their arrows first and they sent them at the hobelars rushing down the beach. The rest of the arrows were all sent at the four mailed men and everyone found a mark. Two stuck horses and as the four men fell and two horses crashed to the ground the hobelars behind were forced to take evasive action. That meant either going onto the beach or into the drainage ditch. Both slowed them up. Four lightly armoured horsemen on palfreys leapt over the dead, dying and wounded. My archers were fast and could nock and release an arrow incredibly quickly, but they only managed to hit one of the flying Welshman, in the arm. John's father had trained him well and he had the spear braced against his right foot while my shield offered him some protection. As the Welsh spear came at me, I swung my sword in a long sweep. I knew that his spear would hit me, and I just had to hope that it would not be a fatal wound. I saw John's spear strike his Welsh opponent in the leg as the other Welshman's spear hit my shield and knocked me back. The action caused a gap between John and I but it aided the swing of my sword. The palfrey's head snapped past my shoulder as my sword hacked deep into the man's leg and sliced along his horse's flank. The horse veered and as it did so, forced the Welshman with the wounded arm to rein in to avoid crashing into the injured horse. The last of the four hobelars had no such obstacle and he came at Erik Red Hair. Erik Red Hair had more skill with a long axe than any man I knew. As the hobelar's spear was rammed towards his undefended left side, Erik Red Hair stepped forward and to the right whilst swinging his axe. His axe not only chopped the man's leg in two, but it also gouged a hole the length of a man's forearm in the palfrey's side. It gave a scream and the dying Welshman was thrown from his horse.

The rest of the lightly armoured Welshmen had managed to negotiate the dead and the dying, not to mention the wounded, and were intent, it seemed on regaining some sort of honour. Their problem was that my archers also felt that they had let me down as they had not managed to hurt the four jumping hobelars. John, Erik Red Hair, and I no longer had cohesion and it was every man for himself. John had the best protection as there was a drop to the ditch and beach on his left side, but Erik Red Hair was exposed. I could tell he did not care for rather than sheltering behind my sword he advanced towards the charging Welshman. He was so big that his mail did not slow him and the hobelars misjudged their thrusts. Now that I no longer had to protect John, I could use my shield offensively and I punched my shield into the first horse which came close. The animal missed its footing and as the rider tried to readjust his strike I lunged with my sword. It slid along the horse's neck without making a mark and as the rider thrust his spear at my head my sword went over the saddle and into his groin. It made him drop his sword. The archers were now pouring their war arrows into the Welshmen. Not all were fatal blows but enough caused wounds to slow them.

Then I heard a roar from behind me and wondered if Sir Richard had brought our men from Penrhyn. When I heard Leofric's voice I knew it was our servants. Amazingly, their sudden appearance frightened the Welshmen who feared reinforcements. The survivors turned and ran. My angry archers did not give them any respite and arrows were sent into unprotected backs. Eighteen bodies lay on the ground before us along with one dead horse and a second which would have to be destroyed. Three horses were wandering along the beach.

Garth shouted, "Search the dead and make sure the bastards are not feigning!"

I turned to Leofric, "The horses?"

He smiled, "We tied them to trees for you appeared to be enjoying yourselves."

I saw that two of the archers from the beach had been cut by spears and would need wounds tending but the others, not to mention John and Erik, appeared unscathed. We had just mounted our horses and were preparing to head along the road when Dywi suddenly shouted and pointed up the slope. Stones were skittering down the side from the trail four hundred paces above us. There were too many for a single animal. Had we been outwitted and had the Welsh occupied us so that they could outflank us?

"Nock arrows!" Garth gave the command even as he dismounted. Erik Red Hair swung his shield around from his back for, like me, I think he believed that they were archers above us for it was unlikely that men on horses would risk the slope.

Sure enough, we saw movement and then saw a line of six horses and riders heading along the trail. I saw that it zig-zagged down towards us. Garth and his archers tracked the men and horses but so long as there were no archers above us then we were safe.

"Who is it, lord?"

"They are too far away to make out, but I do not think they are Welsh or, if they are, they are not a threat. It may be that they come to talk to us."

As they neared us, I saw that two of the horses were ridden double. Whoever it was had lost horses. It was sharp-eyed John who suddenly recognised who they were and shouted, "My lord, it is Idraf and his archers! He has with him, Geoffrey and your cousin, Dick. They are saved and are alive. God be praised!"

I confess that I closed my eyes, gripped the crosspiece of my sword and said a quiet prayer of thanks. Now, all we had to do was to find my uncle!

Sir William

Chapter 8

I knew that the Welshmen would find me eventually and I had to take matters into my own hands. While they were busy making their camp, less than twenty feet from me, I undid the cloak so that I would be able to slip out of it and into the water. The bubbling stream masked any noises I might have made and I kept my face away from them so they would not see the flash of white. I heard them pile dead wood and then heard the sound of a flint as they lit their kindling. I heard them say something else and heard one walk downstream. When I heard him walk back, I guessed he had passed water. If I was going to be seen, then this would be the time. I had hidden well and he rejoined his companion. They began to cook something. The smell made my stomach ache for I was starving. The sun set behind the hills while they cooked and chatted. I cursed the fact that I could only understand one word in ten and that made no sense. The only words I truly recognised in context were Lord and Maredudd. It merely confirmed what I already knew. Lord Maredudd was protecting himself. While I waited for the fire to die a little and for them to go to sleep, I tried to work out what the plot might be.

I knew that Maredudd was related, in some way, to the Gwynedd royal family. Lord Iago had been another branch. Now that Lord Iago had married and had been murdered, his widow would inherit his lands. That made Lady Angharad, and by association, her father the richest family in Wales. Apart from Dafydd, there were Prince Dafydd's nephews, Llewellyn and Owain. So far as I could see Maredudd's family was the fourth in line and it would take some sort of disaster to bring the crown to them. Although I reached no conclusion which made sense the thinking sharpened my mind and helped me to formulate a plan to escape from this predicament. The men who had left with the dogs knew that I was somewhere close by which was why they had left two men to look and listen for me. More men and dogs would return in the morning and I would need to be gone. If I was one of my archer scouts, then I might be able to sneak away without them hearing me. I thought that unlikely. I had to travel over rough ground and through the undergrowth at night. They would hear me. I had to kill them both. It was the cellar all over again except that I was now armed. I had a sword and I had a dagger. Unlike the two hired killers these two men would be little more than hunters.

I listened to their talk until it became silent and I presumed that they were asleep. I suppose they might have been waiting for me to make a move, but I had to believe that although they had a rough idea of where I was they could not know they were as close as they were. I knew that any delay would increase the chances of me being caught. I began to move under the cloak which remained pinned to the bush. I was scratched a little as I made my way to the water, but it was bearable and when my hand found the bubbling water I could have shouted for joy. I eased my way in, ignoring the icy shock. I kept my face down for the light from the fire might pick it out and my tunic was so soiled, bloody and muddy that it would disguise me. Once in the water, I allowed the current to move me and I used my hands to walk along the bottom of the shallow stream. The bramble bush and the camp were to my right. I was heading to the place where the man had made water. It was there I almost had a disaster. A fox was sniffing the urine-soaked earth and had not heard me in the water. As I raised my head to find a place to leave the water it raced off. The Welshmen heard it, and both started. I cursed my luck. However, they must have recognised the beast as it sped off for one said something in Welsh and I understood one of the words, '*Cadno*'. It had been the word Idraf had used to describe Lord Maredudd and I guessed it meant fox. I had to wait in the water now for the two men to go to sleep again. When I heard regular breathing, I hauled myself out of the water. I was shivering and shaking. The cold water and lack of food were having an effect. I crawled away from the stream keeping the two sleeping forms between me and the fire. When I felt confident then I stood and drew the sword I had stolen. I held it in two hands for I could not trust myself to use just one. I had taken just one step when one of the men awoke and shouted. He did not look at me but where the fox had been and that saved my life. I stepped quickly towards him while swinging my sword. He had slept with his hand on his sword hilt and he brought up his own weapon as he tried to stand. He partially blocked my blow, but the sword still hacked into his arm. The other rolled away and drew his sword too. I could not fight two at once and so I brought my sword up and then sliced down on the man I had wounded. He had not been able to regain his feet. This time the block did not come, and I split open his head.

The man I faced drew a dagger too and he grinned evilly at me. It was clear he knew who I was for he spoke in English, "Lord Maredudd just wants your body and there is a gold piece for whoever finds you. I now no longer have to share it!"

As with all such men he could not resist crowing or perhaps it emboldened him. I was a knight although, bedraggled and bloody from the brambles, I looked little like one. I remembered the lessons from Ridley the Giant, and I balanced myself on the balls of my feet. I was bigger than he was, but I was in no condition to fight for any length of time. I kept him with his back to the fire. He had the advantage that he could use both weapons. His sword was as long as mine, but I was still shaking from the cold.

He feinted at me with his dagger and it was so obvious that it gave me confidence. When I feinted with my sword, he lunged at me, somewhat clumsily, with his own. I whipped it away with such force that it left a gap and, holding the sword in two hands I was able to slash at him. It was not my sword, but it was sharp, and it tore across the man's side, drawing blood. It would not harm him overmuch, but it did two things, it enraged him and put fear in his eyes. This was a fight to the death and there were just two of us. Perhaps he was used to having help when he killed. He roared and swung both weapons at me, hoping to ensure that at least one of them found flesh. They would have done had not Ridley the Giant taught me how to pirouette on one leg and spin around. For a large man, Ridley was light on his feet. The Welshman's sword and dagger found fresh air while the sword hacked around into his back, severing his spine. He fell in the fire and his flesh began to burn. I kicked the body from the fire. Burning human flesh would draw any other of Maredudd's men who were nearby.

I sheathed my sword and then stood close to the fire to get some warmth. I saw that there was a stale piece of bread which had been discarded and in the pot which lay next to the fire, there were the dregs of the stew. I wiped it clean with the bread and ate it. I found their ale skin and it was half full. I drank from it and then went to the stream to top it up with water. I knew that I was on borrowed time, but I now had the chance to prepare myself for the long journey north. I realised that my plan had been flawed. The route I had been taking had too much high ground to cover. The best route would be due north. There would be more people but that would afford me more opportunity to forage. I took the better of the two cloaks. I left their swords for mine was better, but one had a sling and a bag of stones. I would take those as I might be able to hunt with them. The only other treasure they had which was worth taking was a small block of cheese and I took that. I did not risk going back under the bramble bush for the other cloak and ham bone. I had chewed most of the meat from it, but I was reluctant to leave it. I had wasted enough time and I set off using the North Star to guide me. I walked for the first four hundred paces along the stream and managed to leave where there were four large stones. The dogs would find my trail in the morning but by then I hoped to be fifteen miles or more away!

Although it was night and dark, I did not make more than ten miles and that was due to the terrain and it was not until I found the small trail which became a road that I picked up speed. That speed was bought at a cost. I passed farms as I headed along the track. Dogs barked as I passed one and I had to run for a while. I intended to use the road until dawn and then use the fields, woods and greenways. I would keep going, even in daylight, but I would try to stay hidden. If I had not slept, I might have avoided the encounter with the two men.

When the sun peered behind me, I looked for a trail which led from the road and the one I found headed not north-west but northeast. I took it for I needed to be hidden. I do not think that I had ever run as far in my life, but the fact was that I was running for my life! I found that my chest hurt, and my calves burned. I had a pain in my side that would not go away but I kept pounding along the trail. I stopped only to either drink the watered ale or to eat a mouthful of the cheese. I made water but my bowels did not need emptying; there was little within my gut! I marvelled at the men who marched rather than rode to war. The trails I used ran uphill and down dale. They twisted and turned and crossed rocks which threatened to trip a man up. I ran until I lost track of time. It was when I was aware that night was falling that I began to look around for somewhere to sleep. If I was to speak honestly, I was so weary that I would have relished meeting someone just so that I could take my anger out on their person.

I found a dell close by the trail. I did not want to have to run as far the next day. I wished to walk out from my dell on the trail and only begin to run when I was hidden from view. A running man attracted more attention and besides, I was not sure that I would be able to run for I had only eaten the cheese all day. After I had made water I searched for a stream and found one. I would not top up the ale skin until the next day. I then searched for food. I found some wild crab apples but therein lay the shits! I found wild brambles, strawberries and autumn raspberries. I collected them in my cloak. I found some nuts and that was all. I took them back to what would be my camp and laid them to the side of the cloak that would be my bed. I knew that once I had eaten, I would simply fall asleep. I took my dagger and cut wild honeysuckle and ivy. The vines were tough, and I tied them between the trees which surrounded me. They would not stop anyone but if someone tried to get close, they would trip them, and I would hear them and sell my life dearly! That done I ate my fruit and the last mouthful of cheese and I drank some of the watered ale. I said my prayers for I needed God and then I did not so much sleep as pass out!

I woke to birdsong which meant dawn was not far away. It was strange but the birds I had heard on the other side of the country from my home were largely the same. The gulls of Hartlepool were absent, this far inland, but the rest seemed to me to be the same and yet the land was so different. I had seen few farms which grew recognisable crops and it seemed to be sheep farming which ruled. Perhaps that explained why Anglesey was so important to Gwynedd. The fruit I had eaten the night before worked and I knew that if Maredudd's men were still hunting me then I had left clear evidence of my presence. It could not be helped. I walked back to the trail and stepped on it. As far as I could tell there was no one in sight but I walked anyway.

The greenway along which I walked and, sometimes, ran had been here before even the Romans came to this part of the land. We had them at home, and they were the grass-covered paths which had suited men who walked rather than rode. For me, they were a Godsend as they had shelter from prying eyes in the form of overhanging trees and bushes. The bushes also yielded fruit for all the bushes were laden. Even the elderberries could be eaten although they were a little sharp. I kept my wits about me and when I heard anyone on the path, I took shelter. I only had to do that twice and both times it was a pair of women, heading, no doubt, for some nearby market. Each time I crossed another path I took the one which headed north. At noon I felt the need to rest. I had run for half a mile along a gentle slope which led down and so I drank more of the watered ale. I spied, in the hedge, a blackthorn tree and, using the sword hacked away a long, straight and sturdy branch to use as a walking staff. A billhook would have cleaned it quicker than the sword I used but when I began my march north, I felt the benefit of the staff. It also made me stand out less.

It was late afternoon when I heard the sound of men and not just a handful but a number. Now my protective covering of undergrowth hampered me for I could not see them. They were getting closer or, perhaps, I was getting closer to them. I moved more cautiously. I knew that I had been moving along the Clwyd valley but I had not recognised any of it for when I had been here with my father I had been with an army and we had used the main roads. I had avoided all of the towns. I know that somewhere close would be the castles of Mold and Dyserth.

That meant the voices I heard could be English patrols, but I needed to be certain. Two hundred paces later I came to an open area and spied the road ahead. As soon as I saw it, I recognised it. The road was the one which ran from St Asaph to Bodelwyddan. I had fought close by. In one way it was a relief. I knew that Sir Robert Pounderling's castle at Dyserth was less than five miles away, but I would have to pass close by the Welsh castle of Rhuddlan. We had destroyed most of it but in the present climate, I was certain that they would have reinvested it. Added to that was the fact that I now saw the men whose voices I had heard, and they were Welsh.

My instinct was to turn and run but even as the thought passed through my mind, I dismissed it. I was growing weaker by the minute and there was no food for me south of here, worse, there were men who were hunting me and I realised that the men who I saw were not Maredudd's men for these were Welsh soldiers and were looking along the road to the west. I found somewhere I could see them more clearly whilst still remaining hidden. The greenway was above the road and I saw that it would join the road five hundred paces to the east of where the men were obviously waiting. The men were just two hundred paces from me and while I could hear that they were talking I could neither make out nor understand their words. There were four men at arms, and they had horses. With them were a dozen Welsh archers. They did not appear to be camping and it begged the question of what they were doing there. I saw that they were waiting where a building had been wrecked. It had probably happened when we had fought there. The building had been burned but the stone walls remained. The four horsemen had their horses tethered there, out of sight. On the opposite side of the road, there had been what looked like an ancient orchard and there were others sheltering, or perhaps hiding, there. If this was my men, then I would say it was an ambush and as they were Welsh then the ones they were ambushing would be English. I put my staff in my left hand and drew my sword. I might be alone and weak, but I could not allow fellow Englishmen to be ambushed and murdered. I moved from the safety of the greenway and headed through the straggly trees down towards the road and the Welsh. And then I sheathed my sword. I had another weapon courtesy of the hunters. I had a sling and some stones. I slipped a round stone into the sling.

It sounds as though I was being foolhardy, but I was not, I had the boles of the trees for cover and the attention of all of the men was to the west. Two Welshmen were stationed a little way down the road, where it rose. It was an ambush for anyone coming down the road would not see the ruined farm and orchard until they reached the crest of the road and by then they would be within range of the archers. Even if the men travelling down the road proceeded with caution the Welsh ambush would probably succeed. The two watchers suddenly ran down the road waving their arms. There were riders, as yet unseen, and they were walking into the trap. They would be heading for St Asaph or perhaps Dyserth and they would be less alert as they were approaching safety. Whoever had conjured this trap was clever. As the Welsh drew weapons and nocked arrows I took the opportunity to move to within a hundred paces of them. They were not talking, and their attention was fixed on the road ahead. If they had turned, they might have seen me, but I moved carefully and used every piece of cover I could. I had left the trees but some of the bushes and weeds had grown so much that they made a screen which masked my movements. There was, however, eighty paces of open ground I would have to cross. I waited.

I heard the hooves on the cobbled road and a shaft of sunlight which suddenly sparkled from behind a cloud in the west shone from metal as the riders crested the rise. They were either men at arms or knights. Had the Welshmen bitten off more than they could chew? Then I saw that it was just a party of five men and only two of them wore mail. It was a knight, squire and servant. Despite my parlous position I had to warn them. I shouted, in English, and as loudly as I could, "Ambush! Ambush! Welsh archers in the ruin!" I whirled the sling and released it. I had not used one for twenty years but you never forgot that skill. The stone cracked into the back of a man at arms and I hurled another which hit a bow.

As I had expected that caused a reaction and I dropped the sling and drew my sword. The knight and his squire drew their swords while two of the Welsh men at arms ran at me. Three archers sent arrows in the direction of my voice. That I was hidden became clear when the arrows flew over my head towards the woods. I determined to sell my life dearly. I had done all that I could to warn the knight, who I assumed to be English and now I would fight two mailed men at arms! Had I been mailed, well-fed and fit then I would have been confident of victory. As it was, the best I could hope was to slow them down until the knight came to my aid. I turned for there was no possibility of them coming through the hedge before me as it was thick. They could have hacked their way through but that would have delayed them even more. They split up to come at me from two sides. I heard cries behind me as men were hit and hurt.

As I had anticipated one reached me some moments before the other. The men at arms had shields and swords. I suppose they must have thought me an easy target with just a stick and a sword. The staff, however, was long and I whipped it across the face of the first man at arms. Of course, he blocked the blow easily with his shield and sword but, in doing so, he was temporarily unsighted. I brought my sword from on high and my blade bit into the mail covering his shoulder. I also cracked a bone there and then I whirled around as I heard the second man at arms advancing. The same trick did not work a second time and the man at arms even managed to hack a foot from the end of the blackthorn. I stepped away from the two men at arms up the slope I had descended. One was impaired and could not use his shield. It was the other I had to damage in some way.

    Once we began to move up the slope, I had the advantage of height. The wounded warrior was wary of my staff and he kept behind his companion. I lunged with the staff at the eye of the second man at arms and as he raised his shield to protect his sight, I brought my sword down hard upon his helmet. It stunned and stopped him. I had dented it and his head protector had done its job but, temporarily at least, he stopped, and I swung the staff at the side of his head. Already dizzy and unbalanced he tumbled to the side and then began to roll down the slope. The wounded man saw his chance and swung his sword at my hips which were obligingly at sword height due to the slope. I used the spinning technique which Ridley the Giant had taught to all of the squires when first we were trained. He always took great amusement when he did it and was able to slap the flat of his sword across our backsides. My blow was deadlier, and the sword hacked through the mail and aketon to slice into flesh. As the stunned man rose, I went on the offensive for I was now on the same level as he was, but he was looking up the slope. I swung my blackthorn staff at the man's knee. The crack told me that I had hit him hard and when the knee dropped to the ground, I showed him no mercy and rammed the sword into his screaming mouth.

    Turning, the wounded man at arms lumbered back to the other men at arms and archers except that they had either fled or been killed and one of the knight's servants rode up to the man and brought his sword across the side of his head. Unlikely as it had seemed when I had shouted my warning, I was alive, and we had won.

    The voice was one I knew! "Sir William! Your nephew and your men are looking for you! Yet you rise like a wraith and give me a warning of an attack! Are you a wizard?"

    I looked up and saw Sir Robert Pounderling sheathing his sword. I shook my head as I sheathed my own. "I did not recognise you for the sun was behind you. Well met."

He turned and shouted, "Ralph, fetch one of those captured horses for Sir William." As his armed servant fetched a horse he said, "We have no time to tarry. We can talk in my castle. The valley has risen. Mold has fallen and other castles are under siege. Even as we speak Dyserth may have fallen. Things are not going well for King Henry!"

My mind was filled with an agitated beehive of questions not least was, *'where was my son?'* but he was right. We would need our wits about us.

The sun was setting behind us and Sir Robert sent his squire to ride twenty paces ahead of us in case there were more men waiting to ambush us. We passed through St Asaph without incident and then headed the three miles to Dyserth. We neared it well after dark and as the skies were filled with threatening rain clouds it felt like riding through a dark tunnel.

The campfires which ringed it told us that it was under siege! We reined in just a mile from the fires and Sir Robert turned to me. "Perhaps you want to take your chances and get to the King and your nephew, Sir William?"

I shook my head, "As much as I want that I think I have used up whatever luck I was given. Besides, the King may win in the west and then head here." As I said it the first drops of rain began to fall.

"I would not count on that." He turned to the others. "We walk in leading our horses. Rhys, you speak Welsh, you lead and if they ask who we are, say we have come from Deganwy with news of the battle." He waved him closer and spoke in his ear. I could hear nothing. Rhys grinned and began to walk towards the castle. "Sir William, the blood on your tunic is enough to make them believe that you are a refugee from the battle, you go second. We will try bluff to get through and if we are discovered then we mount and ride as though the Devil himself is behind us!"

"Aye, sir."

"Are you with me?"

We all said, "Yes, Sir Robert."

I dismounted from the borrowed horse and drew my sword. The rain was falling heavier now, and I knew that would help us for the Welsh would take cover in whatever tents and hovels they had. We began to walk towards the camp. I saw that the camp was at the bottom of a steep slope which led to the castle. I kept my head down as we neared the Welsh. I had not had time to tell Sir Robert of Lord Maredudd's involvement in all of this and we were close enough to his home for him or some of his men to be present. In fact, the more I thought about it the more I believed this was part of his mysterious plan. Rhys had stopped and he rattled off some Welsh. The man who had spoken directed him somewhere to our left and then scurried back into the tent he was using. It had been a long time since I had been to Dyserth. The castle was far from finished but it was defensible, and I saw the curtain wall and the three towered gatehouse was finished. Rhys walked in the direction we had been given but only for a few steps and then he turned to head for the castle walls. The rain was bouncing now and was so heavy that it was hard to hear anything.

We reached the top of the slope and the Welsh defences. I knew that there was a ditch and I guessed that the drawbridge had been raised and I wondered how we would gain entry. That would be up to Sir Robert. He had come up with this plan and I assumed that he had thought it through. It was when we reached the front line of defences that we were stopped. Two Welsh men at arms stepped forward and Rhys spoke to them again. He pointed to Sir Robert and spoke again. The two Welsh men at arms laughed and waved us forward. I wondered what had been said. We reached the ditch and the new stone of the castle stood ominously before us. I wondered why we were not showered with arrows and then realised that the torrential rain would render them less effective and if there was a siege then they would need every arrow they could get.

Sir Robert stepped forward and he gestured for me to turn around. I saw that his squire and the other servants had turned also, and they had their swords held down. Sir Robert shouted, "Open the gate, Gerald, it is I, Sir Robert!"

I know not what Rhys had told the two Welsh men at arms, but it was not that and they suddenly shouted something in Welsh and ran at us. Both were hewn down by Sir Robert's servants. I saw from the way they handled their swords they were warriors and it explained how they had dealt with the ambush so effectively. The other men on guard at the siege works had to grab weapons and don armour.

Sir Robert shouted, "Open the gate now and get crossbows on the battlements!"

I heard the creak of the windlass as the drawbridge was lowered. Like the rest of the castle, it was all new. A Welsh spearman lunged at me and I barely managed to deflect it with the blackthorn staff. The man then obligingly impaled himself on my sword and I pushed his body from me. More Welshmen were coming but I heard Rhys shout, "Get inside quickly!"

We moved back as one. I held my horse's reins in my left hand along with the blackthorn staff. I was loath to lose it. I trusted that I was heading for the wooden bridge and not the ditch. It was with great relief that my horse's hooves clattered on the wood. I heard the crack of crossbows from the walls as Sir Robert's orders were obeyed and, as arrows were sent from the dark to fall at our feet the drawbridge was slowly raised. I heard objects hitting it, but we were all safe. We were surrounded by our Welsh enemies, but we had stone walls around us, and I felt happier than I had for some days!

Henry Samuel

Chapter 9

It seemed to take Idraf and the others an inordinate length of time to reach us down the steep scree filled slope. As soon as they did Dick leapt from the back of Idraf's horse and ran to my arms. "Where is my father?"

I kept hold of him as I said, quietly, "We have yet to find him, cuz, but we shall."

I looked at Geoffrey and he looked to be whole. "There are spare horses for you, Geoffrey and Dick. We will ride to Penmaenmawr and await Sir Richard and the others. That shall be our camp tonight and while we ride, we will hear this tale. Geoffrey, Dick, Idraf, ride close to me."

The three of them told me the tale over the next couple of miles. As Penmaenmawr was a tiny place we did not have to fight for it and we simply rode in for the people fled. The tale continued while my men prepared food in the abandoned houses but I just listened to the story.

Geoffrey and Dick had been separated from my uncle as soon as they reached the hall of Lord Iago and that was the last they had seen of him. When they had been escorted to what they thought was the dining hall two huge thugs had grabbed, tied and gagged them. Thrown into the stable they had been closely guarded. It had been late when they were joined by Lord and Lady Iago. When the account of Lord Iago's murder was told I saw the effect on Dick.

"Cousin, it was the Lady Angharad who did the deed! She kissed her husband and as she did so, she slid the blade, it was my father's rondel dagger, across his throat. She laughed as she did so and then they buried him! And that steward, Rhodri, he was more than just a servant. I saw that! The two of them were close and I feared for my life so long as I was in their presence."

The terror which was in his eyes was one which would take a long time to leave him. It was the horror of the cold-blooded nature of the deed.

Geoffrey nodded, "I have been a prisoner of the Turks, Sir Henry, and I felt safer when I was their captive. It was as if you did not know what the two would do. They were unpredictable. When we reached the Welsh camp we were taken to their Prince. Lady Angharad spoke to him but we did not understand their words. Thereafter we were kept apart!" I saw the flaw in their plan. They were not using Geoffrey and Dick to corroborate the story that my uncle had been the murderer. They could not speak Welsh and they would just use their presence as evidence! Had Prince Dafydd questioned them himself he might have discovered the truth.

Geoffrey had kept his wits about him and as they were loaded into a wagon, he saw a body being thrown into another. As they did not see the wagon again, I deduced it was the one which went east and that my uncle was in that wagon. He told me that the two murderous looking men who had gagged them had gone with the wagon. Much of the rest of the tale was told by Geoffrey. They were taken, as we had thought to the Welsh camp, where their bonds were cut, and they were allowed to walk. They were given a drink and a little bread, but they understood little of what was said, and Geoffrey had to piece it together from what he saw. He deduced that Lady Angharad was playing the grieving widow for when she spoke to the Prince she wept and kept pointing at Geoffrey and Dick. The Prince had come over and said, in French, that when he was caught, my uncle would be executed for the murder of Lord Iago."

"Caught, Geoffrey?"

"Aye, lord, but I do not think that was true. I do not think he was free for Lady Angharad," he shuddered, "Lord, she is a witch! Lady Angharad had a sly look on her face as though she had deceived the King and besides, we know that my father did not kill Lord Iago."

"Did you not think to put the Prince right?"

He shook his head, "Lord, I feared for master Dick, and if I am to be honest, myself. The Lady…" He shuddered.

I nodded for him to continue with his tale. This puzzle was not getting any easier to solve! They were keeping my uncle somewhere separate and it lay to the east of the Conwy. We no longer had enough men to search that land and to fight the Welsh.

The two of them were taken away the day before the ambush. While they were in camp, they had their hands bound and they were guarded although they were fed and given water. Geoffrey had recognised the preparations for the ambush and I could now see just how clever a foe was Prince Dafydd. The information gathered by Geoffrey was useful. He said that fifty knights and men at arms accompanied the King when he crossed the Conwy in boats. Lady Angharad accompanied the King as well as the steward. That meant that there could not be as many knights facing the King as he thought. We had a chance, albeit a slim one, of emerging with some sort of honour from this western debacle.

Geoffrey also confirmed Dick's opinion of the relationship between the steward and the lady, "Lord, that Lady and her steward were close!"

"Close?"

"I saw them touch fingers and steal a kiss on the way from the hall to the Prince. I think they are lovers."

The waters were becoming murkier rather than clearer.

Geoffrey told how, when they reached the other side of the river, he determined to escape for he knew that if they crossed the water then they were lost. "We had not tried to escape, and our legs were unbound also Dick still had his dirk in his boot and I told Master Richard that when the chance came, we would take to our heels." He pointed further along the road towards Llanfairfechan. "It was along there where the mountain is as close to the sea as it is here that I chose my moment. Perhaps they thought we were terrified. We were tied to the stump of a tree and fed. There was a sentry who watched but he was not very good. I had learned that the man who watched us did not speak English and so I told Dick the plan. While the sentry was distracted by a call from another sentry, he raised his buskin and I slipped the dirk out. I cut our bonds, but we held them so that when he returned, he thought that they were still tied. We waited until it was dark and he went to make water; when we heard the noise we slipped out of the camp and headed up the slope."

"They came after you?"

"They tried to, lord, but we had been caught once and I was determined that we would not be caught again. We had a head start and I used it and the dark to our advantage. We ran up that slope until our legs burned and our chests heaved. We made as little noise as possible and even though we hurt we did not stop until we reached the top. We did not take a direct route and we zigged and zagged our way there. We heard them searching the slopes below us. We kept going until we could not hear the sounds of their boots on the rocks."

I remembered the slope and it was high. It was no wonder they had escaped. I was just amazed that they had done that. "You did well, Dick."

He nodded, "They said my father murdered a man and I wanted to get back so that we could tell the world that he did not!"

"And then, Geoffrey?"

"We climbed until we found large rocks. I remembered such rocks from the Holy Land and how men could not be tracked over them. We crossed them until we came to a stream. We drank from the stream and then walked up it until I found a cave and there we slept. We woke at noon and I left Dick asleep while I went to see if there were hunters. There were not and so I woke Dick, we drank more water and I headed north and east to get back to the Conwy. It was not as easy as I thought, and we made but a mile or so before darkness fell. Dick was hungry and although we had had water and there was plenty to be had, I knew we needed real food. The next morning, I went scavenging and I found more berries on bushes. I collected as many as I could, and we ate them. It was after the sun had reached its zenith that we left and then Idraf found us and we were saved."

Even though he was recalling from the past I heard the relief in his voice.

Idraf took up the story and told us that they had seen the Welsh in the camp and had got close enough to see that Geoffrey and Dick were still alive but they were in the part of the camp which was too close to the King to allow them to affect an escape. He shook his head, "Nor could we warn you and the King of the ambush for they had a line of their scouts along your line of march. They knew you were coming. Had we tried to get through we might not have been able to rescue the two of them. It was as though the Prince knew what the King would do. I am sorry, Sir Henry."

"De Clare walked into the ambush! You did the right thing." I saw now that removing my uncle from the army had given the Welsh an advantage. Had Lord Maredudd and the Welsh Prince acted together?

"When the Welsh left to cross the river, we had a problem for we had no boats. We rode upstream to find a ford. Then I made a mistake, lord, for it took us too far to the south and was a dangerous one. We nearly lost men and horses. When we reached the west bank, I decided to cut across country. I knew that the road was narrow and if we followed there would be no place to hide and so I headed for Bangor, thinking that we could get ahead of them. It was when we were above Llanfairfechan that we saw the men whom we now know were seeking Geoffrey and Master Richard. We ambushed them and one of the dying men told us that the two had escaped and they had been sent by the Lady Angharad to find them. We spent a day looking for them, but they had hidden their trail well. When we did find them poor Master Richard was in a bad way. He had the shits. We made a camp and fed them with the supplies we had brought. In total, we rested for a night and a day. I then took the decision to risk the coast road. We were on our way down it when we heard the sounds of fighting. We hid above the road and I scouted out the road. When I saw that it was our men, I decided to bring us down and then we found you."

By the time he had finished Sir Richard and our men arrived. There was joy amongst our whole host that the two had been found. We had managed to do that which the King had wished, and we had rescued our people. Now the problem we had was to get back across the river. I assigned Erik Red Hair to be the personal bodyguard of the two former captives. He had already done more than enough and if we had to battle our way through the Welsh then I wanted Geoffrey and Dick safe.

"Idraf, could we take the route through the mountains?"

He shook his head, "Had Geoffrey carried on the way he was going then he would have reached a dead end. There is either this road or the one we took to get towards Bangor and, as you discovered, lord, the Welsh are there."

I nodded, I realised that we had just missed Prince Dafydd and Lady Angharad. Had we not delayed at the start while looking for my uncle we might have caught them about to embark and ended the war! There was little point in bemoaning our fate. We had rescued Geoffrey and Dick. More importantly, we now had a better idea of where my uncle was to be found. He was many miles east of the river, and he was alone. When we crossed the Conwy, I would send Idraf to find him.

I sent for Dywi, "Before dawn I want you to take your men and scout out the river. We will be coming along the road. I need to know their dispositions."

"Aye lord."

I also sent for Harry Longbow, "I want you and five archers as a rearguard. Wait here until we have been gone for an hour and then follow slowly. News must have reached Anglesey of our raid and Prince Dafydd will not be slow to react. He will follow and I need warning of any pursuit."

Finally, I spoke with Idraf, "This crossing you made over the Conwy, could we make it?"

"I would not recommend it, Sir Henry."

I nodded, "But if we had to?"

"Aye, it is the best place to cross close to the mouth of the river. It will depend on when we try it. If it is high tide then we will not be able to cross."

"Then let us hope that God is on our side when we do so." Just then it began to rain. We did not know it then but it would rain for three more days.

I had to ride at the fore with my knights and trust that Erik and the servants would keep our charges safe. We were still far from safety and I knew that we had to risk an attack on the men at the mouth of the Conwy. It was Dywi himself who met us a mile from the river. "Lord, they have many men at the river and boats to cross and attack Deganwy."

"Could we take the boats and cross?"

He shook his head, "There are too many and they have dug ditches and planted stakes to protect them from attack."

I sighed; my plans were in tatters. "And could we pass them without being seen?"

"Perhaps but it would have to be in the dark. Men can get by for there is an open area a mile wide, but they have horsemen in the camp, and they could mount and catch us. There are camps all the way to the river. It looks to me as though they are expecting reinforcements."

I knew not what to do and so I gathered my knights and captains for a council of war. "I had planned on attacking their camp and easing the pressure on the King. Dywi tells me that we cannot do this. I am loath to risk Geoffrey and Dick and so I have decided to wait until dark to sneak past the camp and cross the river."

Idraf shook his head, "A night crossing would mean men would die, lord."

I saw that none of my knights had any better suggestion and I was about to order that we wait when one of Harry Longbow's men rode in, "Lord, it is Prince Dafydd and he is heading along the road. Harry has men waiting further west to keep an eye on them. He says that they are five miles away."

That made the decision for me; we could not afford to wait. As I looked at the others, I saw that they were watching me for a decision. "Then we attack the defenders at the river crossing and force our way through. Idraf, you will take your scouts and lead Erik, the servants, horses and the others to the crossing. Use the safe ground as far away from the river as you can manage it. John, have the squires go with them as added protection but I want you and the horn with me! The archers will rain their arrows on the Welsh camp, and we charge them. The archers will then head down the river and follow Idraf. When John sounds the horn three times then we break off and ride along the river. I want the archers to cover our crossing of the Conwy. The knights will be the rearguard!"

As plans go it was not the best, but I could see no alternative. I was pleased when Sir Richard smiled and nodded. Dywi's description had given me a rough idea of what to expect. Conwy was a small fishing port with narrow streets. There were smallholdings around the houses, and we would use those. I intended to hit the smaller camps on the outside and hope that my archers could reach the crossing and protect us as we crossed the river. This time the archers would not use horse holders. They would dismount as close as they could get, tether their horses and send as many arrows into the enemy camp as possible.

As we neared the camp I saw that there was more room here than there had been when we had passed Penmaenmawr. We had a frontage of eight men, the knights and men at arms. The archers had plenty of room to the flanks. I did not see Idraf as he led the captives, squires, servants and spare horses but he and his riders were seen first, and I heard the cries of alarm from ahead. As we burst around a bend in the road, I saw the town and the camps. We were helped by the fact that the west was not the direction they expected an attack, and their defences were on the river side facing south and east. The archers were dismounting even as I pulled back my spear to skewer the Welshman who aimed his bow at me. It was not a good strike and I just speared him in the shoulder. Our horses began to trample through tents as Dywi and the archers sent showers of arrows into the Welsh camp. Some men, still in their tents would be crushed by the horses' hooves. It did not matter how many men were hit by our arrows just so long as they made the Welsh look to their defence and the skies. The last thing we needed was for them to mount their horses and charge after us; if they did not then we had a chance. I withdrew the spear and plunged it almost immediately into the chest of a mailed man at arms who turned at the sound of the hooves. It was not a mortal blow and he wrested the spear from my hands. Guy knocked him to the ground, and I drew my sword.

I saw the river just forty paces from me, "John, sound the horn three times."

As the horn sounded, I reined in and surveyed the camp. We had caused damage and we had shocked the Welsh, but they were beginning to react. Horses were being saddled. I whirled my sword around my head, "Knights to me! We make a fighting retreat! Alan, take the men at arms."

The archers had mounted their horses and were whipping their mounts' rumps with their bow staves. The men at arms would be slower as they were mailed but Alan was already forcing them along the river road. John was the only squire with us, and he had a spear. I waited until Alan and the men at arms were a hundred paces from us before I gave the command to fall back. We had the best horses and our mail gave us the best protection. My intention was to ride along the road but to be prepared to turn and discourage pursuit. We made half a mile before I heard hooves behind us. We had kept the same gap with the men at arms before us and so I was confident that Idraf would have made the crossing. I glanced over my shoulder and saw that the Welsh had mounted twenty hobelars. I shouted, "John, wait here! Knights, turn and charge the hobelars!"

Hobelars had short spears, a sword and a round buckler. Most had a helmet of some type as well as a leather jerkin or brigandine but the horses they rode were small and sturdy horses which could ride all day. They were perfect for pursuit; unless of course, they were pursuing knights. We wheeled and rode back down the road. We filled it and I was able to ascertain the danger we faced. Their knights and mounted men at arms were more than half a mile away. If we could keep that sort of lead, then we might make the river.

We ploughed into the hobelars. The wet ground suited our heavier horses for the ground was not yet muddy enough to make them sink and the nimbler hobelar mounts tended to skid on the slick soil. Our horses towered over their smaller horses and the small spearheads, whilst they could and did penetrate mail were not long enough to cut through an aketon. They were intended to stab into the unprotected backs of fleeing men. My sword hacked through the chest of the first Welshman whose spear pricked my knee. My shield broke the spear of a second and I stood in my saddle to bring my sword down across his shoulder. Even as the next spear came at me, I swiped my sword into the side of a Welshman's head.

We might have carried on and killed them all, but Sir Richard shouted, "Sir Geoffrey is hurt!"

"Fall back!"

We had taken out more than half of the hobelars and the rest were a little nervous. I encouraged them to flee by riding at them diagonally. I swung my sword to the left and right. I connected with each blow, but I had no idea of the effect for I was wheeling Guy to bring him around. He was cut by spear thrusts, but he was a courser and they merely angered him, he was a good horse! After emerging from the mêlée, I looked behind me and saw that my attack had, indeed, discouraged the hobelars but it had allowed the men at arms and knights to close with us. Ahead I saw that Sir Geoffrey was slumped over his saddle and John was leading the horse. The rain made the rivulets of blood seem worse than they were. The others had slowed to wait for me. They said nothing for words would not help the situation. Blood flew from my mount's wounds. They would need to be tended when time allowed. Idraf had told me that the crossing was almost five miles from Conwy at a place called Caer Rhun. It was the site of an old Roman fort and when I saw it on the bluffs above the river then I knew we were close but, behind us, the Welsh had closed to within a hundred paces. I was just pleased that they had none of the horse archers we had met in the Holy Land! My uncle and I had been pursued there when we had fled across a river. The difference had been that then the Turks had used horse archers and men had died! I saw that Alan was urging his men at arms across the river. Tom of Rydal was organising the men on the west bank. Although it was not high tide the water, in places, came to just below the horses' heads and they were already tired. The weight of mail upon their backs also slowed them. The Welsh would catch us in the water. Their horses would have ridden just five miles and ours had done more than twice that.

I spied the archers across the river. Dywi had dismounted them and they were nocking arrows. The ford had been made by mud banks which split the river up into a number of channels. In all, it was more than two hundred paces wide and explained why it was taking the men at arms so long to cross. I watched as John led Sir Geoffrey's mount into the water. I saw Alan Longsword turn his horse to help my squire. The rain was now falling so heavily that it was hard to see where the sky ended and the river began.

Sheathing my sword, I shouted to the others, "Put your shields across your backs. You may need two hands to negotiate the river."

As Sir Mark stepped into the river, I saw that some of the Welsh were less than fifty paces behind us. I followed Sir Robert of Redmarshal, and I was the last one in the chilly river. As luck would have it the first channel was also one of the deepest and the water flowed over the back of my horse's rump. It washed the blood away and its icy coldness would have sealed the wounds. The water chilled my legs and feet immediately. I concentrated on moving quickly through the water. As we reached a mudbank we emerged, dripping from the river. I saw arrows ahead as my archers sent them at our pursuers. The rain had made the bows less effective, but they were still causing damage. Our bowmen could not afford to let the arrows fall too close to us for there was no way for them to accurately gauge our progress. There was a crack and a sudden pain in my back. Drawing my sword, I turned. A man at arms had tried to spear me in the back but my shield and mail had saved me. He was still clambering from the deep channel and my sword swept across his open helmet, tearing through his flesh. He reeled back and, as he did so, pulled his reins too far and he and his horse were thrown into the water which took the horse away. The mailed man disappeared beneath the foaming river. Sir Robert had come back to aid me, and he managed to hack his sword into the side of a hobelar who had come close to my left side. Idraf had been right, the ford was a dangerous one. There were deep channels and shallower channels. I watched another hobelar, trying to get at Sir Robert, sink into a deeper channel and he was swept away. Sir Robert and I were having to fight the river as well as the Welsh. It was a battle we could not win.

The nearest warrior was twenty paces from me, but an arrow plunged from on high and hit his horse. It did not kill it, but it made the horse veer. I turned and headed towards the next channel. I was weary beyond words and I knew that Guy was weakening. The archers, however, were winning the day. The Welsh were fighting the river for the tide was on the way in and was rising. Sir Robert and I might struggle to reach the other side but the Welsh knights and men at arms were struggling just as much as we were. I began to hope we might escape when Sir Robert's horse sank into a deep channel and, as he rose from the water, a bodkin arrow slammed into his shoulder. He slumped over his saddle and I urged a weary Guy to his side. Luckily both horses found purchase and as I grabbed the reins, we began to make progress. The wound had encouraged the Welsh but it had also angered my archers and when a man at arms was hit in the helmet by a bodkin arrow and his body whisked away then the Welsh horns sounded and they withdrew. We had survived but it had not been without a cost.

I shouted, "Sir Robert is hurt!" His squire and Tom of Rydal ran to his side as I surveyed the scene,

Sir Geoffrey was on the ground and Leofric, who acted as our healer, was with him, "It is a bad wound, lord. The spear has torn through his cheek and taken his eye. I have packed it with river moss to slow the bleeding, but he needs a real healer."

"You and the squires ride as fast as you can with him and Sir Robert to Deganwy. Tell the King that we will follow."

I dismounted and took my shield from my back. The spear thrust had split it. I did not mention it to the others but I suspected mail links had been broken. Then I took the vinegar sack from Edward's saddle and began to clean Guy's wounds.

Sir Richard dismounted and came over to me, "You did well, Henry Samuel, but you take too many risks."

I nodded, "It is the blood which courses through my veins. Sir Robert showed no less courage too! Are you telling me that my uncle would not have done the same?"

He laughed, "To speak truly, it could have been Sir William I saw today."

"And we have bad news to report to the King!"

"Bad news? We have recovered the captives!"

"Aye, but we have an army following us. If we can use the crossing, then so can they. When daylight comes they will follow and we will be trapped at Deganwy!" I looked at the sky, "Of course, if they are in the least bit tardy in crossing then the river may flood, and we will be saved."

Erik Red Hair had been listening and he laughed, "Sir Henry, do you not know yet that there are powers here, close to this mountain, which determine who shall live and who shall die! This adventure in the west is not yet over! We should just be thankful that we are above ground and not below water!"

My uncle's Viking was right. A knight who planned for a future while he was still embattled was a fool. We had two of the captives and we had hurt the Welsh. Now we had to find my uncle and a way of extracting ourselves from this Welsh trap.

Chapter 10

"Your Majesty, here is proof that my uncle did not kill Lord Iago! We have witnesses!" I brought forward Geoffrey and my cousin, Dick. "These were there when Lady Angharad slit the throat of her husband. My uncle was misjudged." The rain was bouncing off the tent and, perhaps, I had spoken more loudly than I ought.

The King then angered me for he turned to Geoffrey and said, "Is this true?" I clenched my fists in rage but tried to keep a neutral expression on my face. My grandfather had told me of the ways of kings.

"It is, Your Majesty, she is a cruel woman and she treated Master Dick here worse than a whipped dog."

The passion of his words seemed to convince the King. "Then all is forgiven, Sir Henry, and what news of the Welsh?" My uncle's fate was dismissed as though irrelevant.

"Prince Dafydd is coming, King Henry, and he has a large army. He will cross the river and then cut us off from an escape."

The King gave me a sad smile, "The truth is, Sir Henry, that we are cut off already. Sir Robert left yesterday for his castle. Mold has fallen to Lord Maredudd. I have been outwitted. Lady Angharad is his daughter and this is a spider's web of a conspiracy." I frowned for I did not understand. The King explained, "Dafydd ap Gruffyd does not, as yet, have the support of all the people of Wales. Lord Maredudd has a daughter and by allying himself with Prince Dafydd makes her an attractive proposition for any young Welsh lord with aspirations to rule this rocky land. Lord Maredudd supports the King and ensures that Prince Dafydd, in the absence of any children with his wife, will be named ruler!"

"But they could have children!"

"They have not as yet. Their rivals for the crown are Llewellyn and Owain. They have children and, hitherto, have sat and watched. This may decide them to throw their support behind Dafydd and unite Wales. Of course, it would not be a united Wales and might fall apart in a civil war but that would not matter for by then we would have lost Flintshire and Denbighshire. So, you see, we cannot leave. We have to make a castle here and then fight our way to Sir Robert. We may be able to retake Mold." He smiled, "I thank you for what you have done."

As soon as I left him, I went to see the healers. Sir Geoffrey had looked a mess when we had brought him in, but I had seen other wounds which looked as horrendous and they had been healed. However, when I went to the tent the other knights had expressions on their faces which suggested another outcome. "Well?"

"He has lost one eye and the doctor fears for the other." Sir Richard saw my look and shook his head, "Do not despair yet. The doctor is the King's own. If aught can be done, then we will do it." I nodded; he was right.

"And Sir Robert?"

"Not life-threatening but he cannot use his sword hand." That was another knight lost to us. "And what did the King say when you told him we were cut off?"

I told them all the cold, bald truth and they did not react one way or another. They would follow my standard for it was my grandfather's and that was what we did. It was not over yet and, if we had to, then we would fight our way out of the situation. The doctor worked on Sir Geoffrey for many hours, but we did not have the luxury of waiting.

I spoke with Sir Robert, "The wound will heal, Henry Samuel. I may be out of action for a few days, but you will need all the knights that you can muster."

I shook my head, "You would be a liability and we do not have a few days. Sir Geoffrey is badly hurt, and I need him taken home. He is family. If the doctor says he can travel, then I will send him and his squire back to Stockton. If I do then you will be his escort and you will tell my grandfather that his son is lost." I shook my head. "My first command may be my last and I would like someone to tell the tale."

"I will see that Sir Geoffrey gets home safely."

Before that could be organised the Welsh arrived, and we had to help organise the defences. I was called upon by the King to make suggestions. I insisted that he keep a strong force to guard the road to the east. We needed mounted men there to prevent the Welsh from cutting the road. Naturally, he chose me and my men for the task. We shifted our camp there and none of us took any food or drink until we had the defences in place. We had taken advantage of weak Welsh defences and we would not make the same mistakes!

It was very late when we ate, and I was aware that supplies would be an issue. We had taken many sheep which we had slaughtered and salted. We would have to eke them out, but I also intended to raid the

Welsh. I would not simply sit back and allow the Welsh to make all the moves. I would be aggressive. Like the Scots at Elsdon, I had not seen any warriors who frightened me. The men I led were superior. We might not have the quantity, but we had the quality.

The next morning, I was summoned to the doctor's tent. I rushed there through a torrential downpour. I left Sir Richard in charge of our men. He met me outside the tent. "I have saved one eye, but Sir Geoffrey is terribly disfigured. More than that the wound has badly affected him," He shrugged, "Wounds affect some men that way. If you were to ask my opinion, Sir Henry, then I would say he would be a hindrance rather than a help in this campaign. His heart would not be in it."

"You are suggesting that I send him home?"

He smiled, "I could not say that, my lord, for the King would not wish to lose any men."

I saw his dilemma, "You are a good man. And he can ride?"

"I have stitched the wound and it has been well cleansed. I spoke with his squire and he has a sleeping draught for the night-time."

The healer had done all that he could. "Then I will speak to him and send him home." I held his gaze. "Do not tell the King of this. He will discover it from me but by then Sir Geoffrey will be at Chester."

After telling Sir Robert that he was to leave I entered the tent. Sir Geoffrey's squire was there, and I said, "Go and prepare your master's belongings and your servants. Choose four good men at arms and two archers. Then return with them and take Sir Geoffrey to our new camp at the eastern end of the defences. Sir Robert will command."

"You will send him home, lord?"

"I will for he needs my aunt's care not to mention my grandmother's." He left and I looked at Sir Geoffrey whose head was swathed in bandages. If he had sight in one eye then, at the moment, the bandages prevented him from using it. "Sir Geoffrey, it is Henry Samuel."

"Why did we come to this God-forsaken hole? There is nothing here for us!"

The healer was right. "And that is why I am sending you back to your home and your wife."

"Bring the men with us, Henry Samuel, for all is lost here."

"You know the history of our family, Sir Geoffrey, and that cannot be. I will have to stay here and fight for the King."

"Even though he is as incompetent as his father?"

"Hush, for men might hear. Now rest, your men will take you to our camp. The doctor says that you can ride but I will have him adjust the bandages so that you can see. The world is always better when you can view the sky and not the darkness that lies within a man. Do not fear, Sir Robert, who has also been wounded, will be with you!"

He laughed, "So young and yet so wise. Leadership does not run in your family, it gallops!"

I passed Sir Geoffrey's men as I headed back to our camp. "Be not tardy for I wish you to leave before the Welsh have a stranglehold on us."

"Yes, my lord!"

Once I was back in our camp, I wasted no time. "John, I want every knight and man at arms mounted and ready to ride. Send Idraf to me."

When Idraf arrived he said, "You wish me to find Sir William, my lord?"

I shook my head, "I want you to but that must wait and Sir William, wherever he is, will understand that." I still expected him to walk back into our camp! "Sir Geoffrey, Sir Robert and some of Sir Geoffrey's men are being sent back to the north. I wish to attack the Welsh and distract them. They are still building their defences?" He nodded. "Then we kill two birds with one stone. We attack them and wreck what they have built. We hurt them so that they are too busy fighting us to notice a small group of men slipping away to the east."

"What would you have of us?"

"I intend to charge the building work. When we do, I want the archers to be close behind and to rain death when they counter-attack. I will draw them on to your bows. Whatever you can steal from their camp and works will aid us and hurt them. I will leave it to you to make the decision to leave. Judge it well!"

He nodded, "Until I find Sir William then I shall not die!"

When my men at arms and knights arrived, I told them what I intended. My squire, Geoffrey, was there and after the others had left to don their mail he asked, "My lord, can I join you?"

"I will not say no but I want you to ask yourself if you are ready." I looked at Dick, "And before you ask, cuz, you will be staying with the servants!" Dick nodded.

Geoffrey said, "I am ready, my lord. I have vengeance to wreak; that bitch took my family sword!"

I was mailed and ready by the time Sir Robert rode up and reported that they were ready. "You have chosen good men?" He nodded. "Wait until we are in the Welsh earthworks and then ride east as fast as you can. I would say head to Dyserth but that may be under attack. It is forty miles to Chester and a hard ride. Make for there and then you will be safe. You can rest before heading home." I clasped his arm. "God be with you and tell my grandfather what has happened. Sir Geoffrey's view will be coloured by the loss of the eye."

"He is a good knight, my lord."

"I never thought otherwise. Now hurry for I want you to have all the daylight that you can!"

John had Guy ready and I mounted. We rode to the edge of our defences. I knew that I was taking a risk. The very men who should be defending against the Welsh were now going to attack but it was a calculated one. The Welsh had not even begun to dig their trenches. They had neither brought nor even made the fascines they would need. As they had only recently arrived, they were busy erecting tents and expecting us to sit and tremble in fear. My knights lined up with me and the men at arms flanked us. Erik Red Hair and Alan Longsword made sure that they were at the fore and Tom of Rydal took the place of Sir Robert. Our squires, as well as Geoffrey, rode behind us. They would not bring us horses and they had no horses to lead. They would fight alongside us.

The Welsh were so busy building that they did not even notice our approach. I used no trumpets and we carried no banners. The muddy ground and the rain masked the sound of our hooves and our approach. The rain was like the veils worn in the Holy Land; it hid detail. Our horses began to increase speed. Soon the Welsh would have ditches and a charge like this would be impossible but, for the moment, we had clear ground over which to ride. I held my spear vertically. There were no clear targets yet. As we neared to within a hundred paces then the Welsh realised that we were attacking, and men ran from the ditches they were digging to their stacked weapons. Guy had stretched out his legs and Sir Richard and I were slightly ahead of Sir Mark and Sir Gerard. That was as it should be. The first Welshman to die was a spearman. He turned and tried to spear Guy. I pulled back and rammed my spear into his chest and, as Guy passed him, tossed the body aside. Idraf and our archers were running like deer behind us and when they reached the ditches, they would begin to loose at any target they saw. The wet bow strings limited their range, but they were accurate. Welsh men at arms and knights had armed, for they were already armoured, and they were hurriedly forming a shield wall, but they were too late. Sir Richard and I hit the first knight and the man at arms who were still trying to lock their shields. Their attention was not on us but each other. My spear found the mail of the man at arms and drove the links hard into his body. The spearhead penetrated its full length and I allowed my arm to drop so that his bodyweight would pull the corpse from the spearhead.

Throughout the Welsh camp, horns were sounding. If nothing else I was delaying the ability of the Welsh to enclose us and that meant the King could improve the defences of his castle. We were drawing men to us and I turned to John, "Be prepared to sound the retreat!" I noticed that the rain was lessening. I was not sure if that was a boon or a curse.

"Aye, lord!"

I hoped that my two knights had managed to use our diversion to put as much daylight between them and the Welsh. If nothing else, we would save at least two knights of the valley!

Idraf and our archers were now sending arrows to shower down on the Welsh and as the hurriedly organised Welsh held up shields; I took our chance. "John, sound the horn!"

My men at arms were in their element and I saw that some had managed to not only kill and wound the enemy but also to take horses and, in one case, a sword. Now they turned and began to fall back in good order. We did not turn our backs on the Welsh but walked our horses backwards. Prince Dafydd had sent more men from other parts of the siege works and if we turned our backs and they rushed us then they could hurt us. As it was, we were able to move forward and discourage any who came too close to us. We reached my archers and I saw that the ditches the Welsh had dug were now largely filled in with a mixture of soil, dead men and broken equipment. The wooden shovels they had brought were now ruined.

As we reached our own lines I shouted, "Dismount! Prepare to fight on foot! Take the horses to the rear!"

Our horses had done their work. My men formed two lines and, as many still had spears, we presented a hedgehog of weapons. Our archers stood behind us and they were ready to shower the enemy if they were foolish enough to advance over a land which was muddy, wet and now covered in debris. The Welsh moved forward and I wondered if I had accidentally precipitated a battle. There were still some wise heads amongst the Welsh, however, and although a handful of reckless knights raced at us, the rest stayed where they were. Only two of the eight knights made our lines and one was hewn in two by Erik Red Hair and his mighty axe whilst the other was wounded and disarmed by Sir Mark. We had a prisoner! We faced off until noon by which time King Henry and his brother had arrived. I was not sure if he was angry or not. He had a bemused look upon his face as he surveyed the serried Welsh ranks.

"What were you thinking, Sir Henry?"

I lied. I pointed to the wrecked ditches, "I thought, King Henry, to slow down their progress. If they have no ditches, then they cannot begin to attack the work on your castle."

"This part of the earthworks is not close to the castle."

I smiled, "Then, Your Majesty, why do they bother to dig ditches here? They mean to surround us and starve us out. I have kept the road open and I can send my men to raid the land for food. We have some supplies but soon they will run out. What is it that we shall eat then?"

I could see that King Henry had not thought that far ahead. "It will take us two more months, at least, to make this castle defensible."

Richard of Cornwall said, "And we have but a three-week supply of food."

I nodded, "And what about arrows?" I pointed to my men who were busy foraging for the arrows the Welsh had sent at us. When it was dark, they would risk going back to where we had fought to recover missiles.

"Then we shall have to work more quickly."

His brother had been surveying the scene of the skirmish, "Brother, what happens when the Welsh finish their ditches and begin to attack us?" Richard had fought in the Holy Land, albeit briefly, and he had seen sieges. The King looked at him blankly. "When they attack, the men who are building the walls will have to stop to fight."

The realisation set in and he nodded, "Come, brother, let us return to the works and see how we can speed up the process. Thank you, Sir Henry."

When he had gone, Sir Richard came up to me and said, "This will not end well, Henry Samuel. You have the right of it and the King cannot finish his castle before winter sets in."

"I know. We will have to be aggressive. Let us divide the men into three groups. One watches the Welsh, one will raid for food and the other is a strategic reserve to be used if the Welsh become overly aggressive." I waved over Idraf. "How are we for arrows?"

"We have few bodkins left, lord. We can re-use the arrows the Welsh send at us, but they are just war arrows." He smiled sadly at me, "The ones with mail should be safe."

I told him of my plan and the three of us divided up the men into three groups. I placed Sir Gerard with Sir Richard for Sir Mark, although young, had fought in the Holy Land and knew more about fighting. I gave Alan Longsword the task of watching over Sir Mark.

We began our new regime the next day. I led my raiders along the road east while Sir Richard and his men stood to and his archers sent arrows at the men who were digging the ditches. We hoped to hurt them but if we merely slowed them then that would be a good thing. Along the rest of the perimeter King Henry was having to defend for the ditches were in place and, using their fascines, Welsh archers sent arrows at the men who were building the castle walls.

As I rode east, I was looking not only at opportunities to scavenge food but also at the route we would have to take when we fled. That we would have to leave, ignominiously, was now obvious to me. To the north of us was a largely empty rocky peninsula with a huge bird population on the cliff tops just a couple of miles from Deganwy. Idraf had told me that there were opportunities, albeit dangerous ones, to harvest sea bird eggs. That was the last resort. We headed east towards the tiny hamlet of Colwyn. The Welsh had no defences along the coast road and, as we approached, I saw the fishing ships leave the beach laden with their families. They would wait offshore until we had left. When we reached the houses, I saw that the people who lived there had been drying and salting fish. My men took all that were drying whilst others took every scrap of food and ale from inside the dwellings. Every animal which could be taken was. We would not burn the houses. If they returned, then we would have a source of food. I suspected they would not return until the siege was over. We headed back laden.

We sent half of what we had collected to the King. We had taken the risk and my men deserved to be well fed. We would be the ones who would have to fight our way from this trap. Sir Mark would be the one raiding the next day while my men and I annoyed the ditch makers! I told Sir Mark what to do. "Head for Llandulas, it is just a few miles from Colwyn. Take what you can but do not fire the buildings. We may need them when we retreat. Sir Richard, when you raid, do not take the coast road but ride south and east towards Dolwen. That is sheep country and they may not have taken the sheep to safer pastures. Prince Dafydd will realise, eventually, what we are about so let us make hay while this Welsh sun shines!" The rains of the last few days had stopped and the sun made the boggy camp seem a little less inhospitable.

It was three days into the raids when Sir Mark brought back the unwelcome news that Dyserth was under siege too. When I told the King, he looked as though I had struck him a blow. Our route home was now, effectively, barred and we had reached the limit of the land we could raid.

By the time September arrived, we had taken all that there was to take from the land around Deganwy. Men had even braced the cliffs of the Orme to take eggs. Worse, the castle was not progressing as many would wish. The Welsh sent arrows at the workers so that every archer was needed to duel with the Welsh while the workers each needed a man with a shield to protect them. It was only on our left flank, where we guarded, that the Welsh were kept at bay. Every few days we would launch a night attack, or sometimes a dawn attack to disrupt their ditches. By the end of August, they had stopped trying to dig ditches and were just waiting for us to attack. It meant they did not have as many men to attack the rest of King Henry's army. At the end of the first week in September, I was summoned to a council of war. The meeting was held at the end of a day which had seen a determined Welsh attack on the castle earthworks. Ten men at arms and four archers had died.

The King did not look well. It was the toll the siege had taken. He was a builder by nature; Westminster and Windsor showed that, but this was different. He was trying to make an old castle into something new and the Welsh were making life hard. When he spoke, it was in a tired and weary voice, "We are running out of arrows. Despite Sir Henry's valiant efforts, we are running out of food and my doctor tells me that we have many cases of dysentery in the camp. I fear that God has not answered our prayers and we must abandon the siege. The question is, how do we manage that with the men of Gwynedd watching our every move?"

In truth, this had been the topic of conversation around our campfires each night. No one else answered and the way that the heads of the other lords hung down told me that the siege had sapped every positive thought from their bodies. We had come west to win a war, and nothing had gone right since the King had made the fatal and fateful decision to send my uncle on a secret mission.

"King Henry, I have a plan, but it involves risk."

Richard of Cornwall nodded, "But we are already risking all. Speak on Sir Henry."

"We need to leave sooner rather than later. I suggest that we keep working during the day. Thus far the knights have been responsible for the defence of our lines. I would have every knight under my command. Tomorrow morning, I think that they should ride east with me. The Welsh near to us are used to men riding to forage. We will ride around the rear of their lines and, at dusk, when the work on the walls ceases, we will attack their camp and try to get to Prince Dafydd. It is then that the rest of the army simply breaks camp and heads east. It is fourteen miles to Dyserth. When the knights and I have drawn the Welsh to us we do not head down the coast road but head across the fields towards Dolwen. My men and I have ridden this part of Gwynedd and horsemen can travel across it. It should allow you and the army to escape. We do not stop until we reach Sir Robert and his castle at Dyserth."

"But Dyserth is under siege! What is the point of heading there? We shall be trapped between two armies."

"No, King Henry, we will not. When Sir Mark scouted it out the army which was besieging Dyserth was smaller than ours. I cannot believe that Sir Robert Pounderling will not join us to drive those besieging us from its walls and Dyserth has walls which can be defended. We exchange one siege for another but the one at Dyserth is one we have a chance of winning."

Richard of Cornwall grasped the idea behind my plan, "And then we send men to Chester for help."

"Aye, all that we need is to ensure that the King and yourself, along with the other senior leaders escape. Winter is coming and we do not need our King trapped in Wales."

King Henry's shoulders slumped, "But that means we have lost!"

I looked at Richard of Cornwall for it was not up to me to state the obvious. He said, quietly, "Brother, we have lost already but let us not make a defeat into a disaster. Come the Spring we start again."

The King nodded, "Then let us adopt Sir Henry's plan and pray that God does not abandon us again!"

Sir William

Chapter 11

Once inside the castle Sir Robert ran to the fighting platform. His squire took me to the Great Hall. As we went, I questioned him, "Do you know anything about my son and squire?"

He shook his head, "Not as much as Sir Robert. I am sure that he will join you just as soon as he has spoken with his castellan, Gerald, and checked the defences. I will get you food and drink. I know that you need it!"

That was an understatement!

The castle had its defences in place, while the accommodation was still being built and, as I ate hot food for the first time in days and drank wine, I studied the castle and realised that, if help was forthcoming, then we could hold out. Sir Robert, when he had spoken with his people, would have a better idea of the likely outcome. It was some hours before he returned and despite the joy of having survived the ambush and having gained entry to the castle, his slumped shoulders told their own story. "It still rains and that is good news for it will fill the ditches and make the Welsh existence even more miserable and that is all the good that I can bring to you."

"No chance of relief then?"

He shook his head, "Mold and the other castles fell quickly. The only force which could do anything is based at Chester and I cannot see Robert of Chester leaving to come to the aid of Mold. King Henry at Deganwy might be able to relieve us but when I left, he was hard pushed anyway. He had sent your nephew on a chevauchée. My castellan told me that he sent two riders to Deganwy. As they did not reach there then we must be, effectively, cut off. I am afraid that you have exchanged one cell for another. Now, tell me all for I am intrigued by your tale."

I told him all and when I had finished, he nodded. "I had heard that Lady Angharad was a beauty and wondered why she had made the marriage with Lord Iago for she could have had any knight in the land.

The men who are besieging us are the men who follow Lord Maredudd. I can see that he has used Lord Iago's coin to pay for the men. When we fall, he will hold the whole of Flintshire and Denbighshire. He can bargain with Prince Dafydd for power."

I poured myself some wine and shook my head, "Forget the politics of the situation, Sir Robert. That is for the future. For now, we need to work out how to hold on. Let us assume that we will receive no relief and plan for that outcome."

"Then we lose!"

"Why?"

"There are just one hundred and twenty men in the castle. We are lucky that there are no women but twenty of those men are builders."

"Builders who can use a crossbow and hurl a stone!"

He nodded, "We have enough supplies for a month at the most and that would mean short rations."

"Then we tighten our belts. The sumpter I rode in can be butchered. That will feed us all for two or three extra days. We can extend our food supply by working our way through the horses."

I saw him pale, "Eat my horse?"

"Yours and the other knights would be the last we would eat but, aye, Sir Robert, we fight, and we make the enemy bleed." I waved a hand down my ragged, bloody clothes. "Have you mail for me?"

He nodded, "We lost men in the initial attack."

"That shows the cunning of the Welsh. They knew you were not here and took advantage. Then I will retire now, not because I wish to but because if I do not then I will collapse. I will not ask to bathe for all of the water must be kept for drinking, but I would ask for cloths to wipe the worst of the dirt and blood from my body." A sudden thought occurred to me. "And while God has sent this bounty to protect us from the Welsh let us not let it go to waste. I would have the rain collected while it pours.

He nodded, "I will have Rhys escort you to the chamber you shall use, and he will bring cloth, clothes and mail." I stood, "For what it is worth I am glad that you are here."

I nodded and followed Rhys up the steps in the semi-circular keep which lay on the wall which was the furthest from the gate. Unlike most castles, the steps were so new that they had not worn. It felt strange to walk up such stairs.

"Will that be all, my lord?"

"Where is the door to the fighting platform, Rhys?"

"This way lord," he led me into the corridor and pointed to a stone flight of stairs, "but there will be no need to fight this night."

I nodded and began to strip, "Aye, but I shall let the rain wash the worst of the dirt from me and use these cloths to clean and dry myself."

If the two sentries on the top were surprised to see a naked man emerge from the door to take an impromptu bath, they said nothing. I did not care. The rain was cold, but it was hard, plentiful and cleansed me. By the time I returned to the room I was shivering but I dried myself and when I was wrapped in the sheets, I soon warmed up and I allowed my mind to wander. I was pleased that my nephew was doing so well but I still worried about Geoffrey and Dick. Idraf was their best chance for he was a good archer but what if they had been murdered in the same manner as Lord Iago? I slept but that was because I was exhausted. When I woke, I ached all over for it had been a hard few days. I rose and, mindful of my own words refrained from washing. I dressed in the clothes which Rhys had brought with the mail and then donned the borrowed mail. I saw the broken links where the previous owned had been killed. There was a coif and a helmet too, but I did not think that I would need the helmet yet. The rain was still thundering down. This was a typical late summer storm. If the wheat in Anglesey had not been harvested already, then it would be ruined and that might help King Henry.

It was a frugal breakfast. There were oats aplenty and we ate a porridge. Sir Robert smiled, "You almost terrified the night guards in the keep, Sir Henry."

I shrugged, "I feel cleaner and this rain keeps the wolf from the door, does it not?"

"It does. My men tell me that there are less than five hundred men around the walls but that is still sufficient to keep us here. We cannot sortie although the thought crossed my mind." I nodded and scraped the last of the porridge from the wooden bowl. "Have you endured a siege before?"

"Not as such. I was trapped in a castle when the Scots attacked but it was brief. I have fought on the fighting platform of a castle and it is not easy but, unless they have a tower then the advantage lies with us. If they attempt to use ladders it will cost them men."

"Good, then let us put our minds together and come up with a plan. There are but four knights in the castle and twenty men at arms."

"How many archers do we have?"

"Not enough, just thirty of them. We have fifteen crossbows but only four crossbowmen. I have set them to training the builders to use them, but they will not come today and unless the rain ceases soon then not for a couple of days!"

We went to the central tower of the gatehouse and surveyed the siege lines. The natural ditch had been extended and the high domed hill before us sloped down to the stream. The Welsh had built ditches, as we had seen, and embedded stakes to prevent a sortie. The hill meant we could not see down into the Welsh camp although we knew where it was from the smoke from the fires. The nearest Welshmen were a hundred and fifty paces from the walls and were behind fascines and pavise.

In the end, we had three days of grace when the rain fell. Admittedly, after the first day, it was not as heavy but there were showers each day. The fourth day saw bright sunshine and there was a mist as the rain began to evaporate. Perhaps Sir Robert had angered the Welsh by his cunning trick to get inside the castle but whatever the reason by noon the Welsh were massing to attack. They had ladders and small wooden bridges to cross the ditch. We had not been idle in those three days. The builders could now use crossbows, after a fashion, and we had used the wooden scaffolding from the new towers to brace the main gate and the smaller gate. We had also used the stone for the new tower to build a temporary wall behind the gates. If they did manage to gain entry, then it would be with ladders and over the walls. Sir Robert's men had made darts and they were in buckets along the fighting platform along with the small stones which were the infill for the bridging wall from the keep to the main gate. As soon as the Welsh were spotted then the walls were manned. The largest number of men were on the gate wall for it was where their main camp was to be found. The river running down one side afforded protection and the ground was rough on the other sides. When Sir Robert had built the castle, it was to direct the enemy to this one gate.

As we stood on the gatehouse, he turned to me, "Are you well enough to fight?"

"There are two dead Welshmen who would attest to that fact. I have eaten horse and drunk wine. I am ready. I even had your weaponsmith repair this hauberk. The sword I have may just be a bastard sword, but I am content." A bastard sword was an ordinary one used by men at arms and not as long as my own. It would serve on the walls of Dyserth.

The archers and crossbows were ready. The inexperience of the builders meant that they would only release their bolts when the Welsh were by the ditch but the archers would target the archers and the men carrying the ladders and the wooden bridges as soon as they came within range. Releasing arrows from the fighting platform gave our archers a greater range than the Welsh. I held my borrowed shield loosely for I was not sure I would need it and I wore no helmet. Instead,

I had an arming cap and coif. If a warrior was able to bring down a weapon upon my head, then we would have lost for they would have made the fighting platform.

As the enemy advanced the archers hit men and, more importantly, hit Welsh archers. Men carrying ladders could be replaced but not archers. A wounded archer was, effectively, out of the fight. They had knights and men at arms encouraging the ladder carriers. The men who carried the ladders and wooden bridges were largely without armour. Some had a leather or hide jerkin. A few had a helmet, some metal but most wore a leather cap. None had a long sword. They relied on hatchets, short swords and spears. Their shields were the round buckler type. What saved them was the sheer weight of numbers. We did not have enough archers to slay them all. It was as they neared the walls that we began to win. As Edward, Sir Robert's squire gave the order then the builders sent their crossbow bolts at the advancing warriors. It may have been that they did not think we had any for it made them pause and that allowed our archers to kill more and the crossbowmen had more time to reload their cumbersome weapons. A Welsh voice urged them to keep advancing and they did. As soon as they put the ladders against the walls and men began to climb, then the wooden ladders started to sink into the muddy ground. Worse, they did not sink evenly and as they lurched and rocked, the ladders and their climbers fell. Ladders struck others and some men were thrown into the water-filled ditch. The stakes and spikes placed there by Sir Robert's men when the castle had first been built were now covered in water, but they still wounded and killed. None of us on the fighting platform had had to draw our weapons but the Welsh attack broke and, leaving their ladders where they fell, they fled.

Sir Robert shouted to his men to fetch ropes and grappling hooks. Despite the Welsh efforts to recover them, we managed to pull three ladders inside the castle and the others were pulled into the water. It would not be an easy task to recover them. What the failed attack did do was to raise the spirits of all those within. The builders had killed men and were now more confident. They had loosed their weapons from the slits in the walls and they had been relatively safe. They had not known that until they had won. Now they would be less afraid of using every inch of the arrow slits.

"Will they come again, Sir Henry?"

"Probably but not today. They have ladders to build. There is little timber hereabouts. I believe we have bought a few days. We will now need to consider slaughtering another horse."

"But the King may come!"

"That rain has fallen all along the coast. I fear he will have had it harder than we have. No, my lord, if relief does come, it is a week away, at least. We slaughter another sumpter. A man fights better with a full belly!"

I was proved right and they did not come for a couple of days. When they did attack, they brought pavise which they carried before them. It was during the attack that I saw Lord Maredudd and my theory was confirmed. He stayed well beyond the range of bows and crossbows, but I knew him. It did little to help us, but it gave me satisfaction. The attack began just after dawn and moved far more slowly than during the first one. The ground had dried considerably but it was still too soft, in my opinion at least. Our archers had recovered some of the Welsh arrows sent at us and as we had a weaponsmith we were able to forge bodkins and war arrows. I do not think that they expected bodkin arrows. When they were one hundred and fifty paces from the walls, I saw a knight raise a sword and, from behind the pavise, the Welsh sent their arrows. They were loosed blindly, and we had shields. Arrows thudded into them but hit none of us. We simply ripped them from our shields so that they could be re-used. The Welsh archers had to wait to loose their other arrows for the pavise were creeping forward. The Captain of the Dyserth archers was a Cheshire archer called Gerald and he did not release with the others. He waited and when the knight raised his sword, he sent a bodkin into his chest. It was just one man, but it was a mailed man and the whole line seemed to judder to a halt.

This single arrow slowed their attack even more and they inched forward. It took them until the fifth hour of the day to reach the ditch. It was clear to me and, I think, every knight, that they intended to put their bridges across the ditch which was still a half moat. Whilst most of the water had drained away the fact that Sir Robert had used clay in the bottom had retained enough for it to be an obstacle.

Sir Robert turned to me, "We will have to fight today!"

I nodded, "And we will now need to use the fat we rendered from the horses and the pig fat. We will have to use fire to defeat them."

He shook his head, "That is dangerous. What if the gate catches fire?"

I waved my hand to the left and right, "It is simple, we use fire as far from the gates as we can. I am confident that they will not breach the gate." I laughed, "In fact, I wonder why they have not tried fire themselves. I think they are overconfident and that fills me with dread."

"Why so?"

"It means they think they have King Henry defeated!"

He looked appalled. When he had left the King had had the largest army in the area. What could have happened in the time since he had left?

The crossbows took a toll as did the archers when the wooden boards were laid across the ditch. It was impossible to do so and not be visible to eagle-eyed archers. Twelve men fell but six boards were placed across. Another four slid into the watery ditch and they could not be retrieved easily. The men with the ladders ran all the way from the Welsh lines and they were protected by men with shields. Another dozen or so were hit but enough made it to plant the ladders against the wall. They had men at arms with shields and they ran to the ladders to place their weight on the bottom. That meant we could not push them from the wall. They would begin to ascend.

"Prepare the rocks!"

Sir Robert and I had discussed this possibility and we were prepared. A man could ascend with a shield, but he could only use one arm to defend himself while he did so. A heavy rock could hit the shield and either shatter the shield or, perhaps, break the arm. The stones we used were the ones for the infill in the castle walls. We could always recover them and reuse them to build the castle while the enemy could not. Besides, we were armed with darts. They took little skill to use and if they hit, they hurt and could kill. Four ladders made the walls and the men at arms started to climb. The builders killed two by sending bolts at such close range that they appeared from the dead men at arms' backs. The archers, too, had a good chance of killing but still the Welsh climbed. Then we began with the stones and the darts. Often it was a combination of a stone hitting a shield making a man move it and a dart sent into an open target which worked but none of the men made the top and when fifteen or so men had fallen the horn sounded and they fell back. We used the grapnels to retrieve the ladders.

I pointed to the knight who was sat on his horse with three other knights. They had approached towards the end of the attack. "That is Lord Maredudd. I did not see him at the start of the attack. I wonder where he has been?"

"The man is a plotter. He will have had underlings prosecute the siege. Perhaps he thought it would be ended by now."

"Then we can expect a different approach from this moment on!"

"And now what?"

I nodded to the six wooden bridges, "Tonight we use fire and burn those bridges. We can use the Welsh ladders to return. They will rebuild but that will take days and King Henry might still come."

"You are right."

"Their next attack will be at night!"

Sir Robert's shoulders sank for he knew I was right. A night attack reduced the efficacy of our archers and, in the dark, they could attack anywhere. It would not be for a few days but when they were ready it would mean sleepless nights.

Using the Welsh ladders, men at arms clambered down the ladders and set the wood bridges alight. The Welsh, of course, tried to stop them and I think they had planned on retrieving them. Our archers won the duel and the men climbed successfully back into the castle. The sight of their hard work being incinerated must have been demoralising for the Welsh.

The castle had a good view of the surrounding land; it was why it had been chosen and we saw their foraging parties as they travelled further afield to hew the trees they would need for the ladders. The best timber had been taken by Sir Robert's builders and our destruction of the bridges and ladders had taxed them. It was another four days before the sentries at the top of the keep reported that they had finished their work. The rain which had heralded our arrival had long gone and the September sun had dried out the land. More importantly, for us, it meant clear skies at night. The sun had begun its journey to the west when we spied the ladders and bridges being piled close to their lines. They were not coming yet.

"If the Welsh come at night, we will see them a little easier."

"True, Sir Robert, but by the time we do see them our crossbows will only be able to manage one bolt and our archers three arrows." He nodded, glumly, "And they will be able to attack in more places."

Sir Robert shook his head, "The rough ground on two sides would make an attack difficult and we would hear it. They will come to the same place as they did before. Now that the water has drained from the ditch, they can see the stakes and avoid them. I will keep watch all night."

"And I will join you." I knew that I would not be able to sleep and I could nap during the afternoon. Being horizontal with my eyes closed would rest my body and clear my mind which was ever wandering to my son and my squire.

Sir Robert had fat prepared and it was carried to the gatehouse. This was a new castle and there were two metal rings to secure it to the walls and iron gullies to carry the boiling fat below to the ditch. A stone fire pit was below it and a gentle fire kept the fat hot. If we needed it then levers would raise the rear and the fat would pour from the stone gargoyles to the ditch below. We did not have the whole garrison stood to. That was a waste for if the Welsh did not come, we would have many more tired men. The Welsh had the upper hand and we had to follow their moves. The Welsh camp looked peaceful but that was deceptive for if they were coming then they would be armed and mailed already. The fires which burned would be to lull us. It was a quarter moon and it bathed the land around the castle in blue light. We could see some two hundred paces but the nature of the ground, which was domed and rose towards the castle meant that men could approach that two hundred paces unseen. The ones who would come first would not be mailed and they would be hard to see. They would cover those two hundred paces quickly, even carrying boards and ladders. As we had discovered during their first attack the bridge boards could be used as a shield. Rhys was on watch with us. I had discovered that although he was Sir Robert's servant, he was more than that. he acted as a bodyguard to the knight. He had been a man at arms who had served Sir Robert's father, and it had been pure luck that Sir Robert had been sent to build a castle in the land of his birth. It was Rhys who spotted the movement.

"Sir Robert, there to your right. Shadows are moving."

We both looked to where he pointed. He had good eyes and he was right; with no wind then shadows do not move. It was like a wave rolling over the ground. The Welsh were cowled and cloaked and they insinuated themselves over the ground like a snake.

I saw that the men moved too slowly to be encumbered with anything. "The ones we can see do not have bridges, Sir Robert."

"Then they will be archers! Rhys, rouse our men but do so silently. Let us make them believe that we only have night guards." He hurried off. "Edward, spread the word to remain silent." Edward went one way and I went to the next man on the other side and passed the message on to him.

The whisper which was passed sounded like a sigh travelling the walls. I did not draw my sword but, holding my shield in my left hand, picked up three of the weighted darts. I slipped two of the darts into my left hand which supported my shield. The Welsh did not rush towards our walls and I deduced that they must have been crawling beneath their cloaks. It allowed our men to begin to fill the walls. As they arrived Sir Robert spoke to the archers and pointed to the shadows. I pointed as I watched men leaving the Welsh camp and these did carry the boards and the ladders. Sir Robert ordered the archers to loose just as the Welsh archers rose and, from a range of less than one hundred paces, sent their arrows at us. I flicked my shield up quickly and arrows thudded into it. The warrior next to me was not quick enough and an arrow drove through his shield and into his chest. He crumpled to the ground. We were one defender down and we could ill afford any such losses.

I could not see the battle of the archers but I knew it would be a deadly duel. The range was close enough for each archer to choose a target. This was almost personal. I risked moving my shield a little and I looked under it and peered over the crenulations. The men with the boards had almost reached the ditch. I saw the bodies of dead and wounded archers on the ground. The builders below us were now sending their bolts and I saw two men carrying a ladder fall, but the bridges were quickly thrown across. I pulled my arm back and hurled a dart at one of the men carrying the first ladder. There were three of them, but my dart hit the first man in the head and as he fell screaming into the ditch the other two tumbled to the ground and they were easy targets for the builders' crossbows. Even as I slipped another dart into my hand, I heard the thud as ladders were placed against the walls. As I leaned over to hurl the dart an arrow slammed into my shield and showed me how close I was to death for it penetrated. Had it hit square on then like the defender next to me I could have been badly injured. My dart hit one of the men ascending the ladder, but he was protected by his round shield. Unlike an arrow the bulbous dart was heavy and when he came to use the shield, he would struggle to use it effectively.

I drew my sword as I heard Sir Robert shout, "Now Edward, light the brand. Rhys!"

"Aye, my lord." His sing song voice sounded quite calm, but he had the task of using the lever to pour the boiling liquid. The mechanism had never been tested. If there had been a fault in its manufacture, then Rhys would be the one to discover it!

I went to the wall and peered over. The Welshman whose shield I had hit was just five feet from the top. I reckoned I was safe from archers as the warrior was close enough to be struck by an arrow. I brought my sword over and smashed it into the top rungs of the ladder. The edge rang off the stone walls as it cut through them. The ladder was weakened and, even more importantly, the warrior would have to hold on to the sides and not the rungs. He held his shield above his head.

"Now, Rhys!" There was a hiss as the fat began to race down the metal gutters.

I swashed my sword before me and connected with the shield of the climbing man. He was already unbalanced for he was holding the right side of the ladder and he tumbled, screaming to the ground. Miraculously he landed on his back and seemed to survive.

"Edward!" The burning brand arced over the walls. I watched in fascinated horror as the man who had fallen struggled to his feet. He must have landed in some of the fat for as the brand hit the ground, flames leapt along the rendered fat and ignited the cloak on his back. It must have been terrifying for instead of simply taking the cloak from his back, he ran towards the bridge. His injuries allowed him to make just three steps before his burning body landed on the bridge. The ladders closest to the gatehouse were now on fire and other Welshmen were burning. Most of those who had survived turned and ran. Before we could celebrate disaster struck.

"Sir Robert, they have taken the far end of this wall!"

We turned as Sir Walter's squire, Raymond, ran to us. We had a knight at each end of the main wall. There they had no fire to help them. I followed Sir Robert and we ran with a handful of men to where we saw Sir Walter fighting off the six Welshmen who had managed to get to the fighting platform. It was heroic but doomed to failure. The men of Gwynedd hacked the knight to the ground and then wasted time hacking into his body. The three dead men Sir Walter had already killed must have angered them. The delay proved fatal to them. I brought my sword over my head to hack into the neck of one Welshman while I punched another with my shield. Unbalanced he tumbled over the crenulations. Sir Robert and Edward laid into the other men and Sir Walter's squire seemed like Erik Red Hair as he hacked and chopped at the others. The Welsh soon lay dead and we saw that there were more than a dozen Welsh bodies. We had, however, paid a price. We had lost a knight and four warriors. We could ill afford such losses. Leaving the squires to dispose of the Welsh dead over the walls we returned to the gatehouse. The attack was over. The smell of burning wood and human flesh filled the air.

Sir Robert nodded towards the empty cauldron which had carried the fat, "We have enough rendered fat for one more attack."

I pointed to the dead below us. "They will not risk that again. I think, Sir Robert, that they will now try to starve us into submission."

I saw the sadness in his eyes as he looked at our dead who were now being carried down to the outer bailey. "And we have lost more than a third of our defenders, not to mention the ones who are wounded. I fear that unless the King comes soon his castle at Dyserth will fall!" He shook his head, "However, if nothing else I have learned much about the defences we had built. The ditch needs to be deeper and wider. I will build a defensive wall and a tower on the river side of the ditch and keep any attacker from the heart of the castle. I fear I should have built the keep closer to the gatehouse and I cannot remedy that but I am pleased with the steep position and aspect. We have kept them at bay and done all that we could with an unfinished castle."

He was right, of course, but we had also been lucky. The weather had helped us and that was the work of God!

Henry Samuel

Chapter 12

I do not think that Roger de Clare was happy about taking orders from such a youthful lord, but he had little choice. Since he had led the archers into the disastrous ambush, he had been a bystander and every success had come from my men. He insisted, however, on riding in the van and I did not discourage him. He would learn that it was not as easy as my men had made it look. My knights and I knew the road well and as we headed east, I saw that the Welsh appeared not to react. We reached Colwyn and then I took the small road we had seen south. It climbed into the hills and I followed it until we reached Dolwen. We had raided it a number of times and it was now deserted. We waited there for a while. It was just six miles to the Welsh camp, and we had plenty of time to reach it. While we waited I explained the plan again to the other knights. I now understood the problems my grandfather had had when leading knights who served other lords. They viewed me with suspicion. I put their looks and comments from my mind.

"We will ride on the small roads which lead to the Welsh camp. I want us to arrive there in the late afternoon. The workers will have stopped for the day and the Welsh will, as is their habit, return to their camps. I intend to attack when we smell their food being cooked for by then they will have taken off their mail and laid down their weapons. Our aim is to make them believe we are trying to kill or capture their Prince."

De Clare shook his head, "There is no honour in this!"

I became angry, "And was there honour when my uncle and his son were kidnapped? Do not speak to me of honour, my lord. If you have no stomach for this, then wait here for we shall return this way. I doubt that we shall miss you!"

I knew that I had made an enemy. He glared at me with pure hatred in his eyes, "And if I stay here then so do my knights!"

I laughed, "And that suits me for I would rather have knights I can rely upon rather than fools who walk into an ambush that even a squire could spot!"

It was a crucial moment and I wondered if I had gone too far. My purpose was to spur them into action. Sir Gilbert de Bois was one of de Clare's closest confederates and he snapped, "My men and I will ride with you, pup, if only to show you that the men of the Marches know how to fight!"

De Clare was defeated for the rest of his retinue began to mount and he had no choice other than to follow us.

We passed the hillock which hid the road and it twisted and turned through small farms and tiny hamlets. We had not raided these and the people just hid as we passed through. When we reached the river, it was getting on to late afternoon and we could smell the woodfires as they prepared their food. We stopped just a mile from their camp. I was confident that they would not have guards on that side of the camp, and we took the time to don helmets and prepare our weapons. John had the horn and the knights knew that three blasts meant we turned and headed east. Sir Mark would lead. When we were ready, I raised my spear and we formed a long column of knights four wide. I had my knights at the fore and I noticed that Sir Gilbert was behind me. He wanted to make a point. We trotted up the river road towards the banners, tents and horse lines of the Gwynedd army.

We were seen but not until we were just three hundred paces from their camp. The Welsh horns would be the signal for King Henry and the army to head east. I concentrated on causing as much damage as we could. The Welsh had cleared the land on either side of the road, and we spread out. De Bois and his men trampled over and through tents. They speared the horse guards and drove away the horses of the Welsh. I rode with my men towards the tent of Prince Dafydd. His bodyguards had grabbed weapons and armour, and they were half-dressed and unprepared, but they were brave. They formed a line before us as the Prince was whisked away to the river. The Welsh had boats there which kept them supplied from Conwy. I pulled back my arm and rammed the head of the spear into the chest of the bodyguard whose shield came up just a heartbeat too late.

Sir Gerard was now a skilled knight and as a Welsh warrior swung a poleaxe at him, he jerked his horse's reins to the side and brought his own sword into the back of the man's neck. Sir Mark and Sir Richard used their horses to trample two men whilst hacking and cutting at two others. Chaos and mayhem were the order of the day and our few knights caused such confusion that the Welsh must have thought our whole army had descended upon them. Their deadliest weapon, their archers, were at a disadvantage for they normally sent their arrows at us from a safe distance and serried ranks. Wherever we saw an archer pulling back on his bow we rode at them and speared them. It was easy and it would hurt the Welsh. Enough of the Welsh knights were protecting their Prince so that we had more time than I had expected. The Welsh horses added to the disorder by galloping in panic through the camp. We just followed so that men who had managed to avoid being trampled by their own horses were then speared and stabbed by us. When we had passed through their camp, we reached their earthworks and I reined in as the last defenders were slain. I saw the rear of King Henry's column as they hurried east towards a darkening sky. Sunset was less than an hour away.

I wheeled and shouted, "One more attack!"

I saw that all of my knights were there, but I recognised two empty saddles. We had not had it all our own way. The Welsh had seen our numbers and they were reorganising. More arrows came at us, but we had slain enough archers to minimise the risk. Their men at arms tried to make a shield wall and I saw that they misunderstood our intent. They were trying to stop us from reaching the river and the boats which lay there. Our raid on Bangor had had an effect.

We no longer had order and knights were fighting in their familia. De Clare's men were with him and they protected his person. As they were the largest familia they had the greatest effect and they were herding archers, spearmen and men at arms towards the river. I saw a chance to hurt the men of Gwynedd even more and I wheeled the knights I was leading into the flank of the mass of men who were trying to get some sort of order. I rammed my spear so hard into the shoulder of the man at arms that the head shattered in his flesh. I hurled the stump into the air. When it fell, it would hurt another. Drawing my sword, I brought it down on an archer who was drawing back on his bowstring. My blade severed the bowstave and slashed deep into the muscles of his right arm. He would live but he would never draw a bow again. The Welsh were so packed that they could not use their weapons and so they just made a hedgehog of spears. When I saw one of de Clare's knights unhorsed and butchered when his mount came too close to a spear, I knew it was time.

"John, three blasts if you please!"

As soon as they sounded Sir Mark wheeled his horse and shouted, "On me!" We both knew that in the heat of battle it was easy to forget commands.

I was grateful when Sir Gilbert shouted, "Fall back!"

We managed to disengage far more easily than I had expected. I reined in Guy for I wanted to be the rearguard. It was as I turned that I saw darkness ahead. The sun was setting behind us and, with luck, the Welsh would not realise that our camp had been abandoned. I hoped that they would try to second guess us and head north and east to cut us off. When I was sure that we were the last knights I spurred Guy. We caught up with the knights who had been wounded and those riding wounded horses. Sir Mark would halt in Dolwen where we could tend to their hurts and allow our horses to have a short rest. Sir Richard, Sir Gerard and I halted a mile before Dolwen to look for a pursuit.

I hung my helmet on my cantle and took my coif from my head. It would help me to hear better and make me cooler. Sir Gerard said as he slipped his coif on to his shoulders, "Perhaps we should have tried that earlier on in the siege."

Sir Richard said, "And had we done so then we would not have been able to escape. As it is, we have broken away from the Welsh and if there is a pursuit it will be a day behind us. Of course, we will have the problem of relieving the siege at Dyserth, but that bridge is in the future and we will cross it then. We take one step at a time!"

I had noticed that Prince Dafydd had not wasted time in fleeing. He was a pragmatic man. "Prince Dafydd is a careful man. Did you notice that he fled rather than standing? Had he stood then who knows what the outcome might have been."

"I think, Henry Samuel, that we have learned much about our opponent. He has a good sense of self-preservation and, from what I have heard, with good reason. His relatives seek to wrest the crown from him any way that they can."

I stroked Guy's neck and his breathing was more regular, "I cannot hear pursuit. Perhaps they fear an ambush. We will rejoin the others."

De Clare had dismounted the knights and the wounds of the injured knights were being tended. Sir Mark looked relieved when he saw us. Sir Gilbert came over to me, "I was less than happy with your insults before we began this raid, but I can see that you are a brave man and a good leader." He lowered his voice, "A word of warning, however, it does not do to antagonise de Clare. He is a powerful man with friends in high places."

"Thank you for the warning but my family tends to be stiff-necked. I live in the north and there it is my grandfather who is the powerful man."

He smiled, "So I have heard. And now what? We meet up with the King and ride to Dyserth? What awaits us there? Another army to fight?

Our horses are weary now and after another ten miles of riding they will be in no condition to fight another battle."

"I am hoping that it will be dawn when we arrive and as the sun lights up the west, they will see King Henry and his army arrayed across the river. No riders can reach them from Prince Dafydd as the King is on one road and we are on the other. They will think we have defeated their Prince." I shrugged, "To be honest, Sir Gilbert, it was the only plan I had and whilst not perfect can you see another way to extricate the King from that trap?"

He shook his head, "This is, however, another defeat!"

There was nothing more to be said for he was quite right. We rested for an hour and then mounted our horses to walk them down the road to the coast and the deserted village of Llandulas. It had not been deserted until we had raided it. The baggage train and the men at arms who escorted it were still there. I was relieved that they had got this far and the knights formed the rearguard. I dismounted, as did my knights and we walked to save our horses. The baggage train and the men who marched on foot were going at the same pace. Some of the other knights followed our example. I noticed that not only was de Clare not one of them, but he also did not stay with us but rode to the front and King Henry. He would give the King his version of events! Dick and Geoffrey were riding with the wagons and they dismounted so that they could walk with us. Sir Mark told them all that had happened.

Dick then said, "Cousin, what of my father?"

"When we reach Dyserth I will beg permission from the King to seek him. I cannot believe that he has perished, and your survival gives me hope. You have shown great fortitude, Dick, and I can see you becoming a squire, sooner rather than later." I knew it was the right thing to say for it drove all sad thoughts from his mind and replaced them with hope.

The plan had been for the King to stop on the east bank of the River Clwyd and that meant another six miles before we could halt. We would then have to march south to ford the river south of Rhuddlan. The road upon which we rode was not a paved one and sand had blown in from the sea to cover it in places. This was an empty part of Wales. The knights with whom we had fought and who also walked spoke to us as we trudged along the tussocky sand. The attack on the Welsh camp had been the only success they had enjoyed. The men who followed de Clare were with de Bois and so the knights around us were those from Cheshire and Shrewsbury. They had more reason to wish for success. De Clare's land was far to the south and not threatened by Prince Dafydd.

"We need more castles, my lord!"

"Aye," said another, "but ones which can be supplied and reinforced by the river. Dyserth has a good position but if it is besieged then there is no way to resupply it. That is why I liked the idea of Deganwy! It is a shame we had to abandon it."

The first knight who had spoken said, "There was little choice. We needed more men!"

I spoke, "And men cost money. The war in France cost the King's treasury too much. Parliament would refuse him the money. In the north, we do not ask the King to come and fight the Scots for us. We know the wisdom of strong castles."

"Aye, we should do the same although the Welsh are poor and there is little ransom to be had."

Sir Richard laughed, "I was Lord of Otterburn and, believe me, that was poorer than any Welsh manor. We still made the manor viable."

We spoke at length of the similarities and differences between fighting in the west and the north. We found that we had much in common.

The King awaited us by the Clwyd. "The plan worked, Sir Henry!"

"Aye, King Henry, and with a little luck this part might too." I waved forward Idraf. "This archer knows the land well. He will lead us to a ford, and we can approach the castle from the south and west. It is the direction they will least look for danger. There is a small river and my men tell me that the Welsh are camped on this side of it. If we ride to the ridge then, when the sun comes up, the Welsh camp will wake to see a line of knights, men at arms and archers under the command of King Henry. With luck, they will break camp rather than risk a battle."

"You are gambling, Sir Henry."

"Perhaps, but even if they do not flee what can they do? They will have enemies on both sides of them. Your archers have shown themselves to be skilful. They will win the castle for you."

My confidence won the King over and we followed Idraf and his twenty chosen archers down the river. We would leave the baggage, healers, priests and servants with the squires while we rode the short distance to the siege works. The ford was not as deep as I had expected and barely troubled our horses. I thought the rains would have swollen it but that had been many days ago now. Idraf kept all from the ridge until the King and I arrived. I saw that de Clare was less than happy to be given orders by an archer. Tom, one of his scouts returned. He spoke to the King, but his eyes kept glancing at me.

"The castle still stands, Your Majesty, and there must have been fighting for the moonlight showed burning on the limestone walls."

"And how many Welsh do we face?"

"Slightly less than we have, King Henry!"

Even in the dark, I could see his face light up and he said, "You may have been right, Sir Henry, and I spy a kind of hope."

We walked our horses to the top of the ridge and waited for false dawn before we mounted. The fires of the Welsh camp were like pinpricks below us and we could see the castle across the shallow valley. As I had said when I had first seen it, the hill was a good site for a castle. The rock upon which it was built was a natural mound. I think that had it been completed and fully garrisoned then this would have been a hard castle to take. The King gave the order to mount but he looked at me first. Behind us were the archers and they each had an arrow nocked. We watched the first hint of light as the sun peered from behind the towers of Dyserth.

Idraf said, "Nock!"

There was no reason the Welsh should have seen us for we were in darkness. We were two hundred paces from the camp and their horses were on the far side of their camp. It was as the sun first flared and the King shouted, "Loose!" that the Welsh realised we were there. The range meant that most of the arrows fell on our side of the camp. Some warriors were hurt and killed but the effect of the arrows was to make the Welsh panic. I heard horns from inside Dyserth which told me that Sir Robert had seen us too. The Welsh, quite simply, ran. They headed the only way that was open to them, south. If they had had their wits about them then they might have asked themselves why we did not pursue them. I was just glad that they went. Our horses were exhausted, and we were in no condition for a battle. As we moved through the camp the men at arms were sent to escort the baggage to the castle. The archers began to loot the camp and we headed for the soot-covered castle. It was no longer in perfect condition; it bore the scars of war. Dyserth had ceased to be a virgin! The Welsh had violated her!

Sir William

Chapter 13

When I heard the shouts of panic from the Welsh camp I knew, I know not how, that by some miracle King Henry had arrived. The cries told me that an attack was taking place but as they were distant then it was not our alarm and as it was still dark it was unlikely that the Welsh would herald a surprise attack with horns. This was not like King Henry who was, at best, a cautious general. A dawn attack was both bold and risky and neither traits seemed to fit the King. Perhaps one of his Marcher Lords had taken charge. I threw on my mail hauberk

I reached the gatehouse towers and peered to the west. The sun was rising behind us and the low ridge was bathed in darkness, but we could hear the attack. Sir Robert was already there, and Edward was helping him to put on his mail. He looked at me, "King Henry?"

"Who else could it be? Whoever it is they are fighting our enemies."

"It could be infighting amongst the Welsh. You said this was Maredudd you saw. This could be either Llewellyn or Owain. However, if it is our King then he may need help. Sir William, if you would remove the timber and stones from behind the gate, we can be ready to add our weight to this fight."

"Sound the horns, my lord!" He turned and gave the command. The horns sounded defiant.

As I led some men to obey Sir Robert, I realised that he was right. I knew the politics of the north far better than here. I knew Maredudd for I had been his prisoner, but the others were a mystery to me. It took some time to remove our defences and the thick walls hid the events from the other side. Then Sir Robert said, "It is King Henry, open the gate, lower the bridge and let us add our swords to the King's"

I did not even have my arming cap, but I drew my sword and said, "Open the gate and man the windlass to lower the bridge!"

I saw that it was Rhys who was already lowering the bridge. The gates were hauled open and the bridge slowly lowered. I hoped that there were no obstacles in the way. As soon as it thudded on the other side of the ditch then I ran across it with half a dozen of the Dyserth's defenders. The Welsh were abandoning their camp and they were fleeing down the valley towards the shallow stream which ran south. Knights and men at arms were laying into them. This was the same camp through which Sir Robert and I had sneaked during that rainstorm. Some of the Welsh were trying to salvage valuables. Like us they had been caught out at night and abed. A knight, his squire and a man at arms emerged from a tent with a small chest and weapons. I still had two men and Rhys with me. They all wore mail and the knight had a hand and a half sword. He was older than I was and slightly larger. One of the men I led was too eager and he lunged with his spear at the man at arms who threw his chest at the man and in one motion drew his sword to slay the unfortunate and hasty warrior.

The knight shouted something to his squire who ducked beneath the spear thrust at him by the other who had followed us and grabbed the chest. At the same time, the man at arms chopped into the arm of the spearman and would have slain him there and then had not Rhys used his own sword to block the blow. The knight now saw a man with a hauberk but neither helmet nor spurs and he must have thought that the two of them could deal with us for Rhys sported grey hairs. The hand and a half sword came down towards my unprotected head. His sword was longer than mine and I had to hit it just right or I would die. I blocked with my sword and the blades rang and sparked together. I saw the surprise in his eyes for he had expected to kill me with that one blow. I riposted and swung my sword at his side. I hit his mail and hurt him. Like me, he had not had time to don his aketon. I could hear Rhys and the man at arms behind me as they exchanged blows, but my concentration was such that all else was masked from me. There was a battle ahead of me, but I only had eyes for this Welsh knight. I saw his eyes flicker to the south. He wanted this to end so that he could follow his squire. He stepped back to allow him to swing his longer sword at me. As he swung, I ducked beneath its arc and lunged at his middle with the tip of my sword. I felt the blade whistle across the top of my head but by some miracle, it did not even take a hair. The tip of my sword touched his mail, but he stepped backwards. He was now heading down the slope and the advantages of height and length he had enjoyed were now gone and we were even. When I whipped my hand to swing my sword at his head, he barely blocked the blow and I took the opportunity, as he stepped backwards, to take the rondel dagger from my belt. His eyes were drawn to the second weapon. He had a choice; he could continue to use his sword two handed and risk my dagger or fight one handed and draw his own. He chose the latter and that was a mistake for the longer sword was harder to wield one handed and the advantage of length was offset by his slower movements.

"Yield Welshman for I have you!"

"Yield? To a man at arms!"

"I am Sir William of Hartlepool and your master, Maredudd the treacherous will pay for his actions."

Sometimes it is minor things which decide a combat, and this was one such occasion. I saw his eyes swivel, obviously Maredudd's tent had been close to his, and that distraction enabled me to swing my dagger up and under his flailing sword. It was a lucky blow, but I caught him under the chin and the dagger drove into his skull.

As he fell I heard Rhys laugh, "As neat a strike as I have seen. Few knights know how to use daggers!"

I nodded and said, "Lord Maredudd's tent is close by. See if he is still here. I would know what he did with my son and squire!"

As we ran to the two nearest tents, I realised that Lord Maredudd was one of life's survivors. He would have been the first to flee. When King Henry came, I would ask him for permission to take some of his men and pursue my abductor!

I found the tent straight away. He had a spare surcoat on the cot he was using. I had missed him. I searched for clues as to his whereabouts and then I heard hooves outside. I stepped out and was almost skewered by the spear which came at my head. I looked up at the knight who wielded it and saw that it was my old friend, Sir Richard. I smiled, "A warm welcome, old friend."

Throwing the spear to the ground he leapt from his horse and embraced me. "William, how came you here; we thought you were a prisoner still?"

I shook my head, "I have been here with Sir Robert for some time. Now that you are here, we can seek my son and Geoffrey!"

He laughed and pointed to the west, "They are here; Idraf found them and they are safe as is your nephew."

Sir Robert and the rest of the garrison had poured out while I had searched the tent and I saw that the battle was over. There were no Welsh left for us to fight. The rest of the knights led by the King were making their way to the castle.

Just then Henry Samuel rode up and when he saw me, he too leapt down to embrace me. "God has answered my prayers."

"And you have answered mine. However, the architect of this plot, Lord Maredudd, has just fled. Give me some men and I will follow him."

Henry Samuel shook his head, "I am sorry, uncle, these horses are dead on their feet. They will need at least two days rest before they can ride again. We have fought Prince Dafydd and ridden all night to get here."

Hope rose within me, "You have defeated him?"

Sir Richard laughed, "We gave him a bloody nose. This is as close to a victory as we have come." He might have said more but I saw Lord de Clare and King Henry riding towards us.

I bowed, "King Henry, you have relieved the siege!" I saw Sir Robert striding over to us.

The King nodded and dismounted. I do not think that he was used to riding so far and for so long. He looked at Sir Robert and smiled, "And I thank you for holding on until we could reach you. Who was it besieging you?"

Sir Robert said, "Lord Maredudd of Llangollen."

The King said, "The list of enemies grows. I fear we shall be your guests for a while, Sir Robert."

"I have room in my castle for the senior lords, but the rest will have to camp here."

My nephew showed how far he had come by smiling and saying, "Well, King Henry, the Welsh have obligingly left the camp for us and, I have no doubt, food. We shall manage. For my part, I am just relieved that I can hand over the leadership of our knights to a worthier warrior, my uncle."

The King seemed distracted and, leaving his horse for his squire, headed towards the castle. De Clare followed him and I saw Sir Robert shrug as he headed after them.

"Sir Robert, send my belongings here. I will camp with my men. I do not doubt that either de Clare or the King will have my chamber."

"You know that we could not have held on without you."

"Pure self-interest. I have a journey to take, the vengeance trail!"

Nodding Sir Robert sheathed his sword and hurried after the King.

"Where are Dick and Geoffrey?"

"They are with the wagons, but they are safe!"

At that moment John, my nephew's squire, rode up. I saw that he had the chest the man at arms had thrown. "Where did you get that?"

"A squire hurled it to the ground as he raced to get across the river."

"It is a pity you did not bring him. He might have known where Lord Maredudd has fled. He is the one behind this."

Henry Samuel nodded, and he told me what Geoffrey and Dick had learned.

"So, they thought to paint me a murderer. Lord Maredudd told me that but I did not think the King would give it credence."

"A clever plan and I can see why they kept you alive. Had Prince Dafydd defeated King Henry, then it would have been the English who were seen to be treacherous and Lord Maredudd would have publicly executed you." My nephew was right. It was a carefully crafted plan.

Sir Richard said, "Let us be honest, Henry Samuel, he did defeat the King."

"Perhaps but if it had been a complete victory then they would have had an important English figure killed for all to see. It would have compounded the defeat and they thought to take away the leader who might have defeated the Welsh Prince."

I saw Erik Red Hair, Alan Longsword and my archers walking their weary horses through the camp. "Nephew let us choose the better tents. You and I shall share Lord Maredudd's for it is large enough and I would have all of my family with me."

It was noon by the time the wagons finally reached Dyserth. By that time, I had thanked Idraf and the others who had found my son and we were cooking food. Geoffrey and Dick must have seen me when the wagons started to cross the stream and rather than travel on a slow-moving wagon, they both leapt from it and ran up the hill to me. Dick threw himself in my arms and I almost unmanned myself when he began to weep. He said, huskily in my ear, "Father, I thought you dead. That witch told me that you were killed too, and I thought to believe her."

"Shush, my son, that is behind us. She will pay for her crimes, you can count on that but for now, we thank God that we have survived, and we plan our vengeance." I looked at Geoffrey and held out my arm. He clasped it, "And I owe you much, Geoffrey of Lyons."

He shook his head, "It was you saved me in the Holy Land. The debt I owe you is still there."

The evening in the company of my men was denied me when Henry Samuel and I were summoned back into Dyserth Castle. The King commanded us and as we walked into the castle, I saw the difference the extra men made. Those who had defended Dyserth were now forced to move to the stables although there they would have to share the accommodation with the King's horses.

I shook my head and said quietly to Henry Samuel, "These men fought bravely, and it isn't right that they are evicted."

Henry Samuel nodded, "Especially as knights like de Clare have done little to help the King's cause." I gave him a questioning look. "I will tell you on the way back to Hartlepool, Uncle. This is not the place for such words but let us just say that Welshmen are not the only ones who wish me hurt!"

I laughed, "It seems to be a family tradition!"

When we reached the hall where we would dine poor Sir Robert looked to be at his wits' end, and, indeed, looked relieved that we had arrived. The King waved the two of us over to him and I saw that he had left two seats for us. Such honour did not bode well. He smiled at me as I sat down. "We are pleased that you have managed to survive, Sir William. Your nephew did well in your absence, but it is good to have you back in the saddle again, so to speak."

"Lord Maredudd was my captor and it was he prosecuted this siege. Will he and his daughter be brought to justice?"

There was a pause during which all conversation around the table seemed to cease. Once again, I was given the political smile, "When this land bows the knee once more to England, then we shall see that Lord Maredudd pays the price."

De Clare put his goblet down heavily on the table and said, "What you need is a Marcher Lord here, King Henry. We keep the lands in the south free from rebellion."

"And you, no doubt, have the perfect lord for such a task. No doubt one of your own lords." The earl coloured. King Henry gave a sardonic laugh, "We will have no Marcher Lord for it seems to me that Marcher Lords are a law unto themselves and we receive little in the way of tax from them."

"Yes, King Henry, but there is no cost to the crown for policing the border is there?"

It was clear to all that this was an ongoing conversation and I wondered why Henry Samuel and I had been summoned. I would far rather be in the camp with my own, honest men than here with political lords.

The King waved an irritated hand, "Tomorrow the knights of Cheshire will escort me to Chester. Sir William, I leave you in command here for the earl has decided that he and his retinue are needed further south!" I saw the smile on de Clare's face. We were being abandoned and it was clear to me that he thought that we would lose. When we did, no doubt, he would bring his knights north again but there would be a price to pay!

"But King Henry, winter will be upon us shortly and this is not the land to overwinter."

"Do not worry, Sir William. I will send reinforcements to fight under your banner in the spring, but I would have you recover the lost castles and protect Dyserth!"

"With less than a hundred men?"

"I do not say that you shall succeed but annoying the Welsh and keeping Prince Dafydd occupied will hurt his cause." I was about to refuse for we would have given him the forty days service he was due by the end of September when he said, "And you will, of course, be paid. Your knights will be paid £200 each for the year you will spend here. Your men at arms and archers £10 each. That is generous is it not?"

I saw the incredulous look on de Clare's face. If he had thought that he could have earned that amount of money for his men, then he might have accepted the King's offer. "The treasury will pay for losses? Animals and the like as well as arrows and grain?" He nodded. "And we would serve until...?"

"This time next year or until the Welsh sue for peace."

That was the incentive for me to work miracles. I knew that I had little choice for he could simply make it a command. I nodded. I knew that the men at arms and archers would be happy at the pay. It left me with the problem of Dick as I was loath to keep my son here over winter. While we ate the King went through what he wished me to do in detail. In essence, it was to make the Clwyd Valley, English. Such was my mind that I was already making my own plans even while the King spoke of his own. If he was in London, then I would have free rein. I would do it my way!

As soon as I had the details sorted Henry Samuel and I left. Sir Robert walked us to the gate, "A hard task Sir William."

"No harder than yours."

"Our guests will be leaving on the morrow." He could not keep the sarcasm from his voice. "You and your men will be welcome to stay in the castle."

I nodded, "I think that we will have to. The first thing we shall need to do, once the dead are burned, is to raid the Welsh for food. We had little enough before we began."

Henry Samuel added his agreement, "Although I thought otherwise when we came here the knights from Cheshire told us that they thought it a poor site for a castle."

Sir Robert shook his head, "We need to improve it, I grant you, and your uncle and I have discussed it but when it is finished then the Welsh will not take it."

Henry Samuel had grown, "And how will you resupply it, Sir Robert? Unless the rest of the valley is in English hands then it can be surrounded, and help cannot easily reach it. It should be on the River Clwyd. Rhuddlan?"

"Perhaps, but it is a little late now. You are right Sir William. We have the well and the stream, but we need food."

As the two of us headed to our camp I said, "There are plenty of sheep for us to raid."

"Not so, Uncle, my men and I raided the land between Deganwy and here. There is nothing left to take. We will have to go further afield. Those knights I spoke to were right. Mold is another castle which cannot be easily supplied. Chester is laid open to an attack from the Welsh!"

"You have shown what can be done with a handful of men and, besides, I do not think that Prince Dafydd has the full support of his people. This victory over King Henry will have given him more power but there are knives waiting to plunge in his back. If I was the Welsh Prince, then I would not have Angharad so close to me."

We were nearing the camp and Henry Samuel slowed and said, "Geoffrey told me that Dick has been badly affected by the witch! The women in his life have been the very antithesis of her and seeing her murder her husband so callously… well, he is young."

"And now I cannot do as I would wish and send him home. With Sir Geoffrey and Sir Robert gone we need every sword that we can get. Was it a bad wound?"

"It was but his heart was not in the fight before then. He is grown too comfortable and I cannot blame him. I have yet to find a bride and who knows, that may well change me."

"I doubt it," I put my arm around his shoulders, "You have your father's blood, your grandfather and that of the Warlord. He came from hardy stock who fought with King Harold. You cannot help yourself, Henry Samuel. You would fight even though you knew that you would fail!"

As soon as we entered the camp then we were assailed by questions. I held up my hands, "Listen and I shall tell you all that I know." When I had silence I continued, "We are to stay here for up to a year." I saw the look of disappointment on Sir Richard's face. He had, like me, a family but I also knew that he would do his duty. "The knights and their retinue will be paid a single sum of £200 each. The archers and men at arms, £10. Horses will be replaced, and arrows provided when they are available."

To the men at arms and archers, this was a welcome sum of money. They were each paid by their lord and replacement horses was a bonus. Sir Mark and Sir Gerard would be rich men. Already the dead had been stripped and that would also be shared out. Henry Samuel would be rich for he had the ransom from Sir Rhodri. Even as the men were spending money they had yet to receive, a plan was forming in my mind. Before the weather worsened and while the Welsh thought we would be licking our wounds I would raid Llangollen. If nothing else, it would punish Lord Maredudd. It was thirty miles away and had not been raided. There would be sheep there. The first thing I had to do, however, was to speak with Dick and Geoffrey.

I took them to one side where we could talk away from the bustle of warriors speaking of the coming campaign. The nights were becoming autumnal and I gestured to the two of them to fetch their cloaks. I donned mine. "I hear that you both had a difficult time after you were taken."

They nodded and Geoffrey said, "Not as hard as you, lord. Master Richard did well, and he stood up to all that they could throw at us."

"We are here for a year." They both nodded. "If you wish, Dick, I can have some men at arms escort you back to Stockton for…"

He burst out, "Have I let you down yet, father? Are you ashamed of me?"

"No, Dick, what a ridiculous thing to say! I am thinking of your safety for this will not be easy. We will be spending long days in the saddle and you will be stuck in the castle of Dyserth."

"I am your page and I can ride abroad with you. I admit that when we came here, to Wales, I did not know what to expect but I have endured much, and I wish to get some revenge on the Welsh."

I looked at Geoffrey who also nodded, "I am of the same opinion. There is a sword which the witch took, and I would have it back."

"You are both of a mind, I can see that but if at any time you do not wish to ride forth then there is no shame in staying with Sir Robert. When the snow comes in December, we may all be confided to Dyserth."

Geoffrey asked, "But we hunt Lady Angharad?"

"There may be a time for that, but we are warriors and we have other tasks to do. Vengeance is a dish best served cold. She and her father will be hiding somewhere while we serve the King, we seek that hiding place, but it is not our priority. As for a sword, take one from the dead. I slew a knight, take his."

"We did take it, lord, but for you. Your sword will be with mine." He brightened, "At least your mail, spurs and helmet are with Leofric."

That cheered me too, "Aye, they are."

Chapter 14

The King and de Clare left without any farewells. They would both travel down the valley to Shrewsbury. It was a token gesture to make the Welsh think that the King had achieved something. He had not! We burned the bodies the next day and all of us were glad to move into the castle away from the smell of burning flesh. Geoffrey, Dick and I were given the chamber I had occupied during the siege. For the next few days, we saw little of Sir Robert as there was much to be repaired and he had to continue the building work. We had more defenders, but the Welsh would return in the Spring for they would be emboldened by their success. I spent two days with my knights, Idraf and Alan Longsword. Their horses needed the rest for we would be working them hard. Walking the walls of Dyserth during the siege had allowed me to think. This was not the hot blood of vengeance; this was the cold and calculating planning to finish what we had come here to do! Make this part of Wales English!

"We will ride in two days to Llangollen. It is thirty miles and we will stay there to scour the land of all that they have once we have raided them. We need their animals, their grain and their food. If we can take Lord Maredudd then we will have gone a long way to fulfilling our orders as well as making up, in some way, for the abductions, but I think he will be far from that home. I want prisoners from the people at the hall. My plan is simple. Idraf and the archers will ride ahead of us and surround the town. They can do that journey in six hours, but it will take mailed men eight, at least. When we ride in the archers prevent flight and also rain death upon their warriors. We will not be taking our servants nor our healers. I want to be as fast as a sudden summer thunderstorm and just as deadly!"

"And the townsfolk?"

"We spare them, but I need them to know why we do this. Lord Maredudd has brought it on his people." I was thinking of Davy ap Hywel when I spoke.

Wearing my own aketon, mail and surcoat made me feel, somehow, better. I still missed the sword which had been taken from me but, as with Geoffrey's, that would be something we would get back. Unlike the other horses, Lion was fresh and ready to go. No one had ridden him since I had been abducted and I had to fight him as we headed south to Llangollen. Idraf and the archers were soon lost to sight as they obeyed my orders. They would avoid all towns and ride across country and through woods whenever possible. I did not mind if my knights and men at arms were seen but I wanted the archers to be a shock! They might prepare for men at arms but the surprise of a shower of arrows might make this an easy victory.

The only towns of any size which we would have to negotiate were Denbigh and Ruthin. There was no castle close to either of them. Denbigh was the nearest and the knight who was lord of the manor had been part of the force besieging Dyserth for Sir Robert had recognised his livery. We thundered into the small town and people fled. The fact that we were not attacked showed me that the lord of the manor and his armed men were with Lord Maredudd still. My plan was still working. There was a bakery and we rested the horses briefly, taking still warm bread from it. My men at arms found the alehouse and we drank that too. After a short rest, we moved on and struck Ruthin with the same speed. This time we burned the hall of the Welsh lord for it was in the centre of the small town. He too had been at Dyserth!

Henry Samuel rode next to me and he was curious about my strategy, "Will this not warn the Welsh at Llangollen and make the people who live in the Clwyd Valley resentful?"

"They resent us anyway and when we have castles along this valley then King Henry can show them a more enlightened rule. Our task is to wrest the valley from them. The King hoped that Dyserth would do so but it is not enough. As for warning the men of Llangollen that we are coming, I hope that they are warned. I would destroy their ability to fight. If they are not there and with Prince Dafydd then when we do fight them it will be a greater number who face us."

He nodded, "I do not ask to question you but to learn. I have a long journey ahead of me."

"And as the King said, you have made a good start. All men spoke well of you."

"All men?"

I laughed, "De Clare apart!"

Llangollen had no castle either but there was an ancient hill fort. Idraf had told me that it was not fortified. The manor of Lord Maredudd, as I well knew, lay on the edge of the prosperous town and was across the River Dee. If men were waiting to fight us, then I assumed that they would guard the bridge for that would be the easiest place to stop us. It was late afternoon when we galloped into the town which seemed deserted and I knew that riders had come from either Ruthin or Denbigh to warn them. We would have our fight. Idraf and my archers would have forded the river. Their horses would be tethered, and they would be advancing with nocked arrows and the town would be cut off from the rest of Maredudd's lands. I rode at the fore, flanked by my knights, Alan Longbow and Erik Red Hair. I had my shield held tightly and a spear across Lion's neck. I headed for the bridge and saw, to my surprise, that it was undefended. We simply galloped across. I saw why. The gate to the manor was closed and there were men on the fighting platform. Had my prayers been answered and was Lord Maredudd going to place himself within a sword length?

Arrows were sent at us as we approached. One stuck in my shield and I turned the shield to identify the arrow. It was a war arrow. I shouted, "Use your horses as ladders! Mount the walls."

It sounded dangerous but it was not. Idraf and my archers would be making the reverse of the journey I had made when I escaped, and they would be climbing the rear walls. By making the defenders come to this wall it allowed my archers the chance to attack from the rear. Some of the Welsh archers were using bodkins and some men at arms fell but fewer than the Welsh would have hoped. I rode towards the gate and pulled my arm back. I had learned to throw a spear in the Holy Land. I sent it at the Welshman who was drawing back on his bow. It struck him in the chest and threw him from the walls. Hanging my shield from my cantle I rode Lion to the wall. Grabbing the mortared stones, I pulled myself up so that I grasped the top of the crenulated wall. The defenders had been spread out and my spear throw had cleared my section of the wall. As I pulled myself up and through the gap, a spearman ran down the fighting platform to spear me. I balanced myself and as he lunged used my gloved left hand to drag the spear to my side and I punched him in the side of the head. He pitched from the fighting platform to land in the courtyard. Drawing my sword, I ran towards the steps. The few men who were on the wall were trying to keep my men from climbing up and I slew two of them before reaching the steps.

I ran to the gate and I was just about to lay down my sword to enable me to lift the bar when a Welsh man at arms ran from the other side. He swept his sword at my left side and I managed, albeit awkwardly, to counter his blow. Neither of us had a shield and it would take guile to win the contest for I saw by his grey hairs that this man was experienced, and you had to be good to get grey hairs! We were both balanced and on the balls of our feet. I was watching his eyes for the tell-tale flicker which would tell me he was about to strike. There was nothing. His eyes were dead. When the blow did come it was so fast that it took me by surprise, and it rasped along the side of my coif. I dared not underestimate this man and, more importantly, I needed to win quickly. I tried a trick. The top of the platform and the gate restricted my choice of blows while he had no such restrictions. I pulled back my arm quickly and feinted a strike at his eyes. It was the only move I could make, and he had to bring his sword across in an awkward block which placed his sword across his face and chest. I swung my left hand in a wide arc. I had metal strips along the backs of the fingers and when I connected, I knocked him to crash into the gate. He had blocked the sword blow, but I was able to punch at his head with the hilt of my sword and he reeled once more. Two hits to the head had disorientated him and he flailed his sword almost blindly. I pulled back and rammed the tip of my sword into his face. I gave him a quick death.

Erik Red Hair appeared at my side and I shouted, "Get the gate open!"

I ran to the hall and saw that the door was open. Idraf and my archers were flooding across the courtyard. We had won but I hoped they had heeded my orders and taken prisoners. I ran into the hall. I had seen nothing of the interior save the kitchen and the cellar. I saw a couple of bodies and heard footsteps on the upper floor.

"Who is there?"

"Sir Mark and Ned!"

I could leave them to search and I ran through the hall. I found Sir Gerard and his squire in what I remembered as the dining area. Two men were fighting them but as neither had mail it would be a one-sided fight. "Put down your weapons and you shall live! Fight and you die, I swear!"

They might have recognised my face, or they may have had a death wish but whatever the reason they hurled themselves at Sir Gerard and his squire. It was a reckless attack, but Sir Gerard and his squire knew how to fight and there was only one outcome. You fight to win and any who fights to wound is doomed. The two men lay dead within a few strokes.

I heard more footsteps and saw Idraf and my knights. I nodded, "Well done! Idraf, take your archers and begin to collect tribute from this town. I want wagons filled and not an animal left to Lord Maredudd's people."

"Aye lord. We lost not a man!" He left and I berated myself for I should have asked.

I turned to Alan Longsword, "Did we lose any?"

"One of Sir Gerard's men is dead and there are five with wounds. None are serious, lord. I cannot work out why they fought with so few men."

That thought had crossed my mind. "Search the house. It is unlikely but my sword may be here. Henry Samuel, Sir Richard come with me to the cellar. I would look for the place I was incarcerated." I had not seen my sword when I had been a prisoner but then I had been pre-occupied with escape. I took a lighted brand and descended the stairs to the cellar. The bed was still there, and the wall was spattered with the blood of the men I had killed but that was all.

Sir Richard said, "This is where you were held?"

I nodded. "Before we leave tomorrow, we burn this hall to the ground."

Geoffrey and Dick were in the dining hall when I arrived. They had obeyed my orders and waited until the hall was taken before entering. "We will stay here this night. Find food. You and the other squires will be cooks."

Sir Mark entered and he held in his hands a sheepskin. He laid it on the table and opened it. There lay my sword and scabbard. "We found it upstairs in what must have been Lord Maredudd's bed-chamber. It was in a chest at the foot of the bed."

I took the sword and examined it as though it had been soiled. I took off the borrowed sword and strapped on my own. "Why leave it here where it could be easily found?"

"Uncle?"

"Lord Maredudd would know that I wanted my sword back. When he left why not take it with him? Why leave it here? Was it bait?"

Henry Samuel shrugged, "Perhaps he was in a hurry and forgot it. He may have feared we would come for him."

"And that is why he would have taken it and why leave men guarding the walls? There were not enough to stop a determined enemy and more than caretakers."

Sir Richard smacked one fist into the palm of the other, "It is a trap and he wants us in the hall."

"Stand to! Man the walls!" I had sent Idraf and my archers away, most of the men had taken off helmets and coifs. We had won so why remain vigilant? I drew my own sword. I prayed it was sharp.

Even as we ran outside Walter of Stillington fell with an arrow in his chest as Welsh archers poured over the same walls that Idraf had just used. They must have watched Idraf and his men as they climbed them. Our horses had been brought within the walls by our squires and my shield hung there. I saw a dead Welshman from our attack and grabbed his buckler. I barely managed to whip it up before a bodkin tipped arrow slammed into it. The fading light was our only saviour. The archers were on the west wall and we were in the shadows of the east but without our archers, they held the upper hand. Of course, there would be men at arms with them. I suddenly realised, as I ran towards the Welsh, why Denbigh and Ruthin had been devoid of warriors. They were with Lord Maredudd. There would have been spies at Dyserth and a chevauchée such as ours would have been clear to any who were watching. He was a clever and cunning foe.

Alan and Erik shouted orders to the men at arms. Mine would need no such commands but Sir Gerard's and Sir Mark's would. Henry Samuel and Sir Richard were both with me. They had also managed to acquire shields.

"We need the walls back in our hands. Idraf and his archers will hear the commotion and come to our aid. The gate side of the manor should be safe." Raising my sword, I shouted, "Take the walls!"

I had last run across this ground when I was seeking an escape. I knew that the wall could be climbed and that the height of the wall while not a real obstacle would give the Welsh who knew the hall an advantage. They could rain bodkin arrows on us. Tam Dickson was the next man at arms to fall to a bodkin. Using horses to scale the walls had meant that few of my men had shields with them. I forced myself to run harder towards the men at arms led by knights who had descended the walls. The closer we were to them the less chance we had of being hit by an arrow. I was confident that my best friend and my nephew would guard my sides. The three of us smashed into the knight and four men at arms. It may have been that they thought we would slow and wait for help and we took them by surprise.

The small shield had few defensive qualities but as an offensive weapon it was quite handy and I smashed it into the face of the man at arms before me and, as he fell, lunged with my sword at the knight next to him. He blocked the blow, but the speed of my charge made him step back. Darkness had now fallen and that meant the arrows no longer fell from the walls, but I knew that the Welsh archers would add their deadly knives to the battle in the dark. The knight recovered quickly and brought his sword down to split my skull. My helmet was hanging from my cantle! My own sword felt like part of me and I deftly blocked the strike and, stepping forward, hooked my right leg around the back of the knight's left. When I pushed, he tumbled backwards but he had the wit to slash at my leg as he did so. I jumped and as I still had momentum, my jump made me land on his face. I did not mean to kill him but a mailed man crashing onto an unprotected face can only have one outcome.

I had no time to even think as a spear came towards my side and the buckler was too small to stop it. The head rammed into my hauberk. The shield had deflected it slightly and so, whilst it hurt and tore through links and my aketon, it did not penetrate flesh. I would know I had been hit when I tried to rest. The spearman paid for his success when my sword hacked into his neck, his blood spraying out like a fountain.

Behind me, I heard Idraf as he shouted, "To Sir William! Kill the bastards!"

It was the deciding factor in the attempted ambush. The sneak attack had almost succeeded but the appearance from the dark of my deadly archers, made the survivors of the attack fall back to the walls. They must have had horses on the far side for as we climbed the stairs, we heard horses galloping. I shouted, "I want prisoners! Idraf, mount your men and get after them. Their archers will be on foot!"

"Aye, lord!" I heard the anger in his voice. They would hunt down the archers. The men at arms and knights who had survived might escape for they were mounted but not their archers.

"Fetch lights and search for survivors! Alan Longsword, I want sentries watching the walls and the gate barred." I suddenly turned as there was movement behind me. I had my sword raised but I halted it when I saw that it was Geoffrey and Dick. I sheathed my sword and shook my head, "Call out when next you attempt anything so foolish!" There was little point in reprimanding them for leaving the hall. It was what I would have done. "Now return to the hall and begin preparing food for the men will be hungry."

I turned to Sir Richard, "We were nearly caught there. Thank you for the warning."

"You are welcome!" He nodded, "A clever plan. The Welsh must have been watching for Idraf and his archers. When they left to ascend the walls they merely followed. We did what everyone does when they are successful, we relax. Had we not realised then…"

I looked at my sword, "And this was the bait. This and Lord Maredudd himself."

Henry Samuel said, "He may be amongst the dead!"

I shook my head, "He will not have been part of the attack. He is too clever for that. He will have others to lead his men and put themselves in danger. That snake will be hiding in some hole somewhere, but we will find him and his spawn. Erik, see to the wounded and then fetch the prisoners to me. I will be in the hall!"

I was angry as I returned to Maredudd's hall, but it was anger with myself for I should have anticipated something like this. At the back of my mind was this thought that Lord Maredudd was plotting and planning for something far grander than a share of power. He wanted it all. I saw that Idraf and his men had already begun to collect what they could from the town, but I knew that when the fighting began, they would have gathered whatever treasures were left to them and fled. We would catch them when we left for they would not move far and Idraf and my Welshmen would know where to find them. I went to the kitchen and washed my face which was spattered with blood and the chilly water helped to cool me down. Geoffrey and Dick were busy with a stew they were making. It was the safest thing to make as more water could be added to make it go further.

Geoffrey said, "There is wine on the table, Sir William!"

I nodded and went to pour a goblet. I was distracted and I knew why. Since I had arrived in Wales, I had been reacting to whatever our enemies decided. If I was to do what King Henry wanted, I had to fight in a different way. This raid had been a mistake for I had wanted vengeance and it was predictable. When I returned to Dyserth I would have my men help Sir Roger to improve his castle. The men of Cleveland would hunt and raid close to the castle and make the valley of Clwyd fear the English. That would give me some months to plan something which would take the Welsh by surprise.

The wounded were brought in first. We had men who could act as healers and the hall had enough rooms to use one as a hospital. My knights returned and joined me. "How many?"

Sir Richard knew what I meant, "Six men at arms are dead and eight wounded, four seriously. I know not how many amongst the archers."

"Then we do not have enough men to do the job we were sent here to do."

Sir Richard shook his head, "Do not blame yourself. You could not have known this was a trap."

I snorted, "Had this been Elsdon I would have seen it. Perhaps I should go back there, The Viking longship, Lady Angharad, the ambush at Deganwy; all of those could have been avoided."

Sir Mark said, "My lord, hindsight is always perfect, and we are mortals. We have yet to suffer a disaster."

I heard a noise and Erik Red Hair and Alan Longsword dragged in six prisoners. Four of them were bleeding. They would get little sympathy from me. I stood as Erik and the other men at arms forced the six to their knees. There was one man at arms and the rest were spearmen. I spoke in English. "Where is Lord Maredudd and where is his murderous daughter?"

There was silence. Henry Samuel said, "Perhaps they do not speak English, uncle."

I noticed that the man at arms' eyes were following the conversation. I nodded, "That may be true of some but this man at arms speaks English. Who knows he may even be English?" The man at arms had an arm which bled. I said to Erik. "It might be that his wound needs to be tended to. Erik, fetch a brand from the fire and seal it for him. It will prevent him from bleeding all over Lord Maredudd's rugs."

The flicker of the man at arms' eyes told me that he understood English and I watched the faces of the others. Three others reacted to my words. While Alan ripped the cloth from the wounded arm Erik went for a burning band. He blew on it to make it hotter. I nodded to John son of Johannes and he helped Alan Longsword keep the arm still. The man at arms knew what was coming and he gritted his teeth, Erik held the brand to the wound and there was the smell of burning hair and flesh. The man passed out and Erik took the brand back to the fire. Catching Alan's eye and winking surreptitiously I said, "If the others cannot speak English then they are of no use to us. We have a prisoner to question. Take the others out and hang them!"

That worked and two of them dropped to the floor. One said, "My lord, Lord Maredudd is at Llanwryst."

His companion added, anxious to garner favour and to save his life, "But he will not be there long. He and the Lady Angharad were heading to Anglesey to spend the winter at the royal palace of Aberffraw with Prince Dafydd."

"You are trying to tell me that he sent men to attack here and did not intend to stay and see the results of his raid?"

The first one shook his head. "All we know is that as we were being sent here his lordship, daughter and Lady Angharad's steward were heading for Conwy to take a ship. Prince Dafydd was already there."

The other added, "Aye, lord, he feared treachery from his nephews, Llewellyn and Owain."

I now had more information than before and some of it was gold dust. If we could subvert the two nephews, we might use them to our advantage. "Bind them and put them in the cellar. We will take them to Dyserth with us. They can labour."

Sir Richard said, "This is a new enemy for us, William. He fights from a distance and he is so confident that he does not even wait to see the results of his actions."

"I am learning about Lord Maredudd. He is overconfident, and he cares not for the men he leads. If his men had won, then he would be happy. That they failed will not worry him for he will feel safe on Anglesey and can continue his plotting. The man seeks a crown!"

We had eaten by the time Idraf returned. He had some good news and some not so good, "We lost no men, my lord, but thirty or so of the enemy managed to evade us and escaped. They were so desperate that they dropped their bows and their arrows. We took them but I am sorry we were tricked."

"Tricked?"

"Aye lord, I should have known that something was amiss for the people did not try to hide their animals from us and even told us the fields where they were to be found. It kept us to the east of the town. They will pay!"

"That is for the morrow. Eat and let your men rest. We will spend the morning hunting them down and taking everything. We leave for home on the day after for I want this hall and the town burning to the ground! We send a message to our foes!"

When we left, a few days later, we all had mixed feelings. As a raid, we had managed to collect many animals and Dyserth would be supplied until November at least. The town was ruined, and the hall burned down but we had lost men. They were buried in the churchyard and Lord Maredudd was still at large. When we passed through Ruthin and Denbigh, we burned them also and took from them. They had been complicit and there were no innocents in this war. These were not farmers like Davy and his wife trying to get by; these had known that we were heading for a trap and so they paid! By the time we reached Dyserth, it was the middle of September and the days and nights would be of equal length. In another month or so the farmers would begin to bring their sheep down from the high pastures and we would raid them as they did so. While we had travelled north to Dyserth we had devised a plan to divide the archers and men at arms into five equal conroi. Each day two would raid. When I told Henry Samuel that I had taken the idea from him he grew by two feet. By doing so our horses would not become exhausted and every conroi would have at least one period of two days of rest.

We reached Dyserth and saw that Sir Robert had begun work on the defensive work for the gatehouse. We had discussed it during the latter days of the siege. It was, quite simply, a square enclosure with a tower over the gatehouse. With a fighting platform, it could be easily defended for there was a rock like the one upon which the main castle was built and a steep slope all the way around. When we had been attacked there had been dead ground for the Welsh to use. All the stone which had been gathered to add new buildings inside the castle would now go on the new building. It meant that we now approached the castle through a building site. The foundations were hacked from the solid rock which would, in turn, be used as infill for the walls.

Sir Robert, stripped to the waist., was helping the builders and he stopped to quench his thirst from an ale skin as we passed. "Well?"

"We were tricked and ambushed. We have lost men and our ability to fight has been diminished." I pointed behind where Idraf and the archers drove the captured animals. "We have food for a month or two and my men and I will raid."

He laughed, "And that means you will not have to labour on the walls! I like the way you think!" He pointed down the Clwyd Valley, "And in case you had not thought of it, there is plenty of game in the valley. Let us deny the Welsh our bounty eh?"

And so we spent two months and more filling our larder!

Chapter 15

It was All Saints Day, which was a particularly short one when riders were spotted coming from the east. We had returned from our daily raid not long after noon. We had managed to scavenge much less in the last week, but we were better supplied than we might have expected. As soon as the bell sounded the workers left the half-finished outer defences and men manned the walls. The only time my men took off their mail was to sleep. To alleviate the stink, we each took a bath in the icy stream once a week. Not only was All Saints Day short, but it was also a foggy day and the men who approached Dyserth were shadows. This column of men who rode towards us were our first visitors since the King's messengers in late September. He had informed us that we would have to wait for our money until the Spring. Parliament was being awkward!

Sir Robert's Captain of Archers, Dai, shouted, "Nock!"

From the mist came a familiar voice, "Hold your arrows! We are friends and come from Stockton!"

Sir Robert took nothing at face value, "Approach the walls; the gatehouse is around a bend and follows a steep climb. Keep your hands from your weapons. Any treachery will be dealt with harshly." We had improved our defences since the siege.

I smiled at my friend, "Fear not. I recognise the voice. It is David of Wales."

He cocked an eye, "The friend of Lord Maredudd?"

"And that news was told to us by our enemies. Let us wait until we speak with him!" I confess I was anxious to know the truth of it and I hurried down to the main gate to wait for him.

He had grown old in my father's service, but he still looked as though he could draw a bow. I recognised other archers and men at arms as well as Alfred, my nephew and Sir Geoffrey's son. He was wearing spurs. I had intended greeting David of Wales first, but I knew that I had to speak with Alfred now.

"So, nephew, you are a knight! Congratulations!"

He smiled, shyly, "When my father returned with his wound Grandfather said that another of the family had to return in his place and he knighted me there and then!"

I laughed for that sounded like my father all over. "You are welcome. Henry Samuel, take your cuz and the others to their chambers while I speak with our captain of archers!"

He dismounted with some difficulty and said, as he faced me, "I am no Captain of Archers these days, but your father thought I ought to come as my name was the cause of your incarceration." His eyes narrowed, "I do not like my name being used by others." I nodded. "Your father was relieved when he heard you had been rescued!"

"It was the King who was duped, and I was suspicious. I pray do not harbour feelings of guilt. We are dealing with an evil, corrupt and cunning man."

"Lord Maredudd?"

"The same!"

"And that is another reason for my presence. I know him better than this unfortunate Lord Iago." As they had ridden past the archers and men at arms had all waved and nodded to me. David said, "When Sir Geoffrey returned and told us what had happened, he said that you needed reinforcements."

"But how did he know that we were ordered to stay here for a year?"

"When Robert of Chester sent the ransom won from Rhodri of Abergele he sent a message to your father explaining what the King had told him. He did not wish to commit it to parchment. As soon as he heard then Sir Thomas sent you these twenty men at arms and twenty archers. They should make up for the men you have lost."

"Aye, it means we can raid." The gates slammed shut and I heard the drawbridge being raised. David and I were alone. "This is as good a place to speak without being overheard. Lord Iago?"

"It is true, I served his father… for one month! It was not the work for a warrior. I tried to teach young Iago how to use a bow, but he had no interest and wished only to read! There is nothing wrong with that, but I did not wish that life and I left."

"I thought as much."

"And Lord Maredudd?"

"I knew him better for after I left Lord Hardd I found employment with Lord Maredudd. He was a young and ambitious lord then. His daughter had yet to be born but his wife was a beauty. There were rumours that she was a witch, but they were stories spread by women. Often, they are jealous of beauties, but I confess that she frightened me. I stayed for just three months. This time there was work with a bow, but he wanted us to be killers of men. At first, I was not asked to do anything untoward, but I was the best of the archers and he asked me to join men and to ambush and kill an enemy. I refused and left. I think that was why my name was used. It was to have vengeance on me for we left on poor terms. He drove me from Wales and said that if I ever returned, I would be hanged. I joined your father a little later."

I put my arm around David of Wales who now looked his age, "I knew there was an explanation. Now, come, you shall be an honoured guest!"

He nodded and then said, "There is more."

His voice was not sad but resigned and it did not sound like the David of Wales I had known since I had been a boy.

"This is for your ears alone, my lord, for I wish no sympathy nor sad looks." He sighed, "I am dying. The doctors your father found for me explained it as a worm which eats from within. They tried to purge it from my body and failed. I fear to go to the garderobe for fear I see more of the blood. I am losing weight and losing strength. The doctors said it could be a month or it could be six months that I have left on God's earth and they told me that almost two months since. I should have died in battle, but I did not. When I had the verdict from the doctors I asked your father for permission to come here to die and I put my affairs in order. This is the land of my birth and … well, I feel I should die here."

"Of course, and I will not say a word."

"Before I become too weak, I would try to find my niece."

"Your niece?"

He laughed, "Aye, lord, I had a family, or did you think that the men who serve you were made from yew and ash?"

"You are right, David of Wales, of course you could have a family."

"There were twelve of us at one time and I was the eldest. Four of my brothers died in wars and battles. Five sisters died of illnesses before they saw five summers. One brother broke his leg falling from a rock and died when badness set in. My last sister was my favourite and she was the reason I stayed at home. When she died in childbirth it broke my heart. I stayed until Myfanwy, her daughter, was a year old and I determined to go to war and make enough coins to help her and her father. Dai was a sad man. When my sister Morgana died, he went into himself." He was silent for a moment as he recalled the past and then shook himself. I have made a great deal of money serving your father. I gave some to the men with whom I served and the church, but I still have a chest and I would find Myfanwy and give it to her and her family. Who knows, she may be a grandmother by now."

"After all these years that would be hard. She might have married, moved on…"

He gave me the reproving look I had seen as a child when I had made an error, "My lord, do you not understand the men you lead? All of us follow and we help you fulfil your quests. Do you not think that it is possible for ordinary men who are not lords to have such dreams and the desire to fulfil them?"

I felt awful. My grandfather and grandmother understood that and if they had heard my arrogance, they would have chastised me. "Forgive me, David, you are right it is just that I wondered where you would begin?"

He smiled, "We Welsh do not move far from the place we were born." He shrugged, "Unless, of course, you are an archer who needs to fill a purse. We lived southwest of Llangollen. The farms and villages there are where the family will be found… if she is still alive but," he patted his chest, "in here I believe that she is still alive and if she is then I will find her for the mountain will guide me."

"That is the land of Maredudd."

"He will not be seeking an old man. I will be safe."

"When you go you shall not go alone. I will send men to protect you."

"There is no need, my lord!"

"There is every need. You have, quite rightly, chastised me and we both know that there is a bond between warriors. My grandfather, my father and I owe a great deal to you. This is my opportunity to repay the debt. Now come or they will all be wondering what it is we speak of! Our men are worse than gossiping women."

He laughed, "Aye, lord, and, in the time I have left to me I would spend it in the company of archers. The men you lead were trained by me. I have no children of my own and, Myfanwy apart, they are as close to family as I have."

My mind was a maelstrom as I entered the keep. The news, both personal and military was so much that I thought that my mind might erupt from my skull! I was lucky for the arrival of so many men, mostly old friends, meant that I was left alone with my thoughts. I had known that Lord Maredudd was a clever plotter and now all made perfect sense. I even knew where he would be: Aberffraw which was the royal palace of Gwynedd and he would stay as close to the Prince as he could. Prince Dafydd had no children and Lady Angharad was young and looked to my eye to be fecund. I wondered if Lord Maredudd would try to be like the cuckoo and rid the world of Prince Dafydd's wife and replace her with his own daughter. In that way, he could ensure that his family ruled a united Wales! I looked at David of Wales as he and Idraf laughed at some memory. I could not allow him to travel through Gwynedd in winter and alone nor could I go for I had a task to complete. I would send Henry Samuel with him. My nephew had shown that he had grown. I would have gone for I owed David much for it had been his arrival which had saved Elsdon, but I had a responsibility to the King.

The arrival of so many men meant we had to rearrange the accommodation. The building work in the warrior halls inside the castle had been halted while we built our external defences. While my men chattered about the past, I sought Sir Robert who was looking on, somewhat bemused. "Your men are more like a family than most families I know!"

I laughed, "Blame my father for that, he has made them that way. Sir Robert, we have been lucky with the weather but soon it will become colder and tents will not suffice."

"I know and my new building has taken all of the labour. What do you suggest?"

"We erect, using the new men and my men who are not on patrol, a temporary warrior hall. We use timber, lath and turf. Erik Red Hair has told me of such buildings in the land of the Norse. If they keep them warm, then they should suffice here. Being temporary they can soon be removed to make your stone buildings." I smiled, "When we are gone!"

"I think that is an excellent idea and there is enough empty land. You can use the plot we had planned for the chapel. That will be the last building I erect in any case!"

And so the next day, under the supervision of Erik Red Hair, my men erected what was, to all intents and purposes, a Viking longhouse. The building only lasted three years and was eventually demolished but it kept my men warm, warmer in fact than we in the castle, for that long cold winter in Wales.

The house took just seven nights to build. During that time, we continued to patrol, and it was I who led the patrol which headed, for the first time in many days, west, towards Deganwy. We had avoided the area mainly because we knew there was little to be had on that stretch of the road. The mountain was so close to the sea that none could farm. However, I chose to ride it because the sea kept the road free from snow and ice. Before both came and trapped us in Dyserth I was anxious to see if the Welsh had prepared defences at Bangor. We had wrecked the port but just as we had been busy as bees so, I assumed, would the Welsh. I led my ten men at arms and twenty archers across the Clwyd and north to the coast. Dick had become bigger in the months since we had left Hartlepool. I wondered if his mother would even recognise him. His diet had consisted mainly of sheep and fish. He seemed to respond well to it. Working each day with Geoffrey he had become stronger. In the absence of other knights and with Erik and Alan still busy with the longhouse, Geoffrey and Dick flanked me. Idraf and his archers were the scouts. We forded the Conwy and I saw that the Welsh had yet to invest Deganwy. That was not a surprise. King Henry had been some months away from making the castle habitable. One of the purposes of this ride was to see if they had done any work and they had not. When February was passed, I would bring all of my men and destroy the defences. The last thing we needed was a castle at the mouth of the Conwy and it was unlikely that the King would be given the funds to finish it this year. My intention was for us to reach Llanfairfechan while Idraf scouted the outskirts of Bangor.

The child I had brought south was now grown. His abduction had hastened his maturity and rubbing shoulders with real soldiers had given him a military mind. He saw the road as a military problem rather than a winter ride! People had returned to the houses we had passed by in August and we saw their menfolk in the icy straits, fishing. That would be their diet now until the spring when their hardy plots would yield their first greens and beans. We had taken their grain. They would not have bread. They kept indoors as we trotted down the semi-frozen road. The wind-blown sand gave us a good surface for our hooves.
"How far do we go this day, father?"

Geoffrey said, "When we are abroad it is my lord or Sir William."

"Sorry, I am still learning."

"I did the same when I rode with my father. It is good to learn but there is no harm in the occasional lapse. We ride to Llanfairfechan and Idraf will tell us what they have done at Bangor. When the warm weather arrives, we will need to be ready to raid. We are paid for the year regardless of how long it actually takes us."

Geoffrey laughed, "My lord, with just Dyserth in our hands and being surrounded by enemies do you think that it is likely we will be home before September?"

"Let us be positive and assume that we will succeed. We could not have foreseen David of Wales and the reinforcements, could we? Who knows what the future will hold?"

Geoffrey nodded and then said what Idraf and some of his old comrades had said, "David of Wales has suddenly become old and thin, my lord!"

I nodded. I would not reveal his secret. "All men grow old, Geoffrey. My father is old too."

"Yet he does not look as thin as David of Wales."

I did not answer him.

Dick had an endless supply of questions. His curiosity was insatiable. "And will we fight this day?"

"A good question, Dick, and one which deserves a thoughtful answer. We are ready to fight and if we have to then we can acquit ourselves well, but I would hope not for we are relatively few to fight and we will need every man once the weather begins to improve. The Welsh will come and try to drive us from Dyserth. It is our last toe hold in the north of their land. Prince Dafydd has enemies and driving us from Dyserth will ensure that he holds on to power. Then he can start to reclaim the south but that, I fear, will be a harder task as the Marcher Lords have very strong castles which can be resupplied by sea."

As we approached Llanfairfechan I saw that the boats were drawn up on the beach. They must have been fishing earlier. We had passed boats and the first couple of houses and the coastal strip upon which we rode widened sufficiently for me to put two men at arms to the south of us to keep watch. The ground was slightly higher and firm. Idraf and his archers would have forced any Welsh scouts to hide. They might emerge when they had passed. As a precaution, we had our shields on our arms and as we were travelling west, we were protected. It was noon and I intended to rest when we found water. We found it just eight hundred paces from the village. It was the stream, Afon Llanfairfechan, and we dismounted to allow our horses to drink. Matty and Edgar were the sentries who were keeping watch. Geoffrey and Dick watered the horses while I studied the land. A castle here would tax the Welsh and slow down incursions from Anglesey but the castle would, perforce, be too small. We needed somewhere closer to the straits. Geoffrey and Dick were just bringing our food when we saw, riding slowly down the road, Idraf and his archers. Their mission was complete, and we could return home. The last mile would be in darkness and Henry Samuel and the others would fret.

The cry when it came, was from the small hillock upon which Matty and Edgar stood. I saw Matty clutching his shoulder and there was an arrow in it. "Geoffrey, Dick, take the other horses to the beach. The rest of you, to arms!" Lion was a well-trained warhorse and he stood patiently waiting despite the shouts and cries of pain as men were hit. I put my coif on my head and grabbed my shield. I was just in time for an arrow slammed into it. I saw that Ethelbert of Loidis was down with an arrow in his leg. His shield brother was protecting him as he took the arrow from his leg. I mounted Lion and, drawing my sword galloped up to where Matty and Edgar were fighting off too many Welshmen. I knew that Idraf and the archers would be galloping down the road but it was doubtful that they would reach us before the Welsh could hurt us more and then flee up the rocks which were too steep for a horse. I rode towards the hillock and held my shield before me. As usual, the Welsh archers were aiming at me for I was a knight and they saw me as the greater threat. Had I been the Welshman holding the bow I would have sent an arrow into Lion!

Matty, already wounded, was felled by a blow to the head leaving Edgar to fight on alone. He would not leave his brother in arms. Lion appeared to be angered by the buzzing arrows which flew over his head and along his flanks. The arrows hit my cuisse and hurt although they did not penetrate. The Welsh were not using bodkins. Lion's speed took him up the slope quickly. My dismounted men at arms were following me and Idraf was bringing the archers but Edgar and Matty would die before they could be reached. As Lion slipped a little scrambling up the rocks which lay scattered below the crown of the hillock, he snapped his teeth and snorted. A small thing but the three Welshmen who had their backs to him turned in fear. The Welsh are not horse people. The slight delay allowed Matty to swing his sword from a prone position and slice into a crudely made buskin and Edgar to slice into the arm of another Welshman. I slashed my sword in a downward strike and split the skull of one Welshman. The other two had turned to face Lion and I wheeled his head around and used my sword to swing in an arc. One Welsh swordsman fell down the slope and the other was hacked in the neck by my sword. I whipped Lion's head to the right and, now that he was on flatter ground, he had more purchase and he leapt at the Welshmen. His hooves broke the leg of one of them and my sword took a second. When Edgar slew a third the other two took to the heels.

I heard Idraf give the order, "Nock!" I saw the arrows descend into the rocks behind which the Welsh were hiding. A dozen men rose and fled.

Dismounting I said, "Edgar, put Matty on Lion and take him to the beach. I will follow."

My men at arms had reached us and before I could order otherwise, they had killed the remaining Welshmen including the wounded. Matty was one of their own and they wanted vengeance. Idraf and his archers did the same for the archers. While his men collected weapons and arrows, he ran over to me. "I am sorry my lord. They were hidden higher than we looked."

I nodded, "It is a lesson learned. Matty is hurt so let the rest flee." I pointed to the boats drawn up on the narrow beach. "I want every boat destroyed and the houses burned. The men who attacked us had to come from the village."

"Aye lord."

I walked back with my men. Most of the weapons were too poor to salvage and after bending to make them useless as weapons we would throw them into the sea. I went directly to Matty who was being tended to by Geoffrey and Dick. He was sitting up and Dick was bandaging the honey-covered arrow wound. Geoffrey was wiping away the blood from the head wound.

Matty said, "It is good that my helmet was well-made lord. That cudgel blow was a powerful one."

I nodded, "You are fit to ride?"

"Aye, lord!"

"When you are done the three of you mount. We have work to do."

As I expected the village was empty for having seen the failure of the ambush, they had realised they would face our wrath and had fled. We took their pots, dried fish, everything we could carry and threw on the fires their crudely made furniture. Soon the houses were ablaze, and my men carried the boats to feed the flames. It was two hours after high noon before we left. The villagers would come down and try to salvage what they could. Most would end up in Bangor where belts would need to be tightened even more.

"They have repaired Bangor, my lord, and there are ships at the quay, but they have yet to build defences."

"Then what is Prince Dafydd up to?" Idraf had no answer.

It taxed me on the road back to Dyserth and then it came to me, as the newly built outer gatehouse hove into view. He had spies who had told him that the King had no funding and his only enemies were the men of my conroi. Why build when you could take a ready-made castle? He was coming back for Dyserth!

Henry Samuel

Chapter 16

After my uncle returned from his scouting expedition the weather changed. It was not the full onslaught of winter, but it was a warning and we were far enough from the sea and close enough to Wyddfa to feel the full force of its icy blast. It was during that week of icy storms that David of Wales fell ill. My uncle did not seem surprised and the castle doctor was called to him. Two days after he was summoned then Idraf and the archers were allowed to see him. My uncle spent a whole afternoon closeted with him and that evening, after we had eaten, he took me to the south wall. I wondered why for although the snow and sleet had stopped falling the icy wind still roared from the east. We wrapped in cloaks and when we reached the tower, he sent the guards into the guard room for a warm.

I laughed as we stood and stared out, "This is strange, my lord, two knights taking a watch when they could be before a fire in the warm."

He smiled, "There is nothing wrong with standing a watch now and then but that is not the reason I brought you here. I have something to ask you and I wanted to give you time to think where you would not have distractions!"

My humour left me for he sounded serious, "You do not have to ask. I will do whatever you tell me."

"And that is not the way our family do this." I saw him sigh and then he began, "David of Wales is dying. Part of the reason he came here was that he wished to die in his own land."

Suddenly things made sense, "And when he was ill the other day?"

"That will happen increasingly often for he has a worm which consumes him from within. He has a chest with his life savings, and he wishes to give them to the daughter of his sister."

"That is kind and where does she live?"

My uncle gave a sad smile "And that is the problem. he does not know exactly. We had both hoped that he could have waited until spring to search for her. By then we should have enough men to go on the offensive and roads are easier to travel. We have debated all afternoon and he is adamant. When this storm abates, he will take to the road and seek his niece."

"You cannot allow him to travel alone!"

"As if I would! I am asking if you would take some volunteers to help him find his niece."

There was but one answer I could give, "Of course. You could have asked me outright."

"No, for you were entitled to know the truth. You may not find the girl and David may die on the road. You need to decide what you would do in such circumstances."

I had not thought of that. I looked to Wyddfa which dominated this land. Its brooding presence was supposed to be supernatural. Perhaps it was for this strange collection of events could not have been predicted. If David gives me enough clues then if he died on the road I would continue to search for this child. How old will she be?"

"From what David has told me a little older than me and certainly younger than him. He said she has distinctive hair and his sister, her mother, was considered a beauty."

"That helps but we do not know if she is even alive." He said nothing for I was now stating the obvious. When do we ask for volunteers?"

"Remember only you and I know that the illness is fatal. All that the volunteers will know is that they seek David's niece."

"That is not fair on the men."

"Nevertheless, that is what David wishes and a dying man has priority over all others."

"Then let us go and tell him," I pointed to the eastern sky. A shaft of moonlight shone on the slopes of the mountain, "The weather is changing!"

At first, David was adamant that he needed no one else to accompany us, but my uncle pointed out that if he became ill on the road then it would be bandits who took his treasure and not his niece. That convinced him. Almost everyone volunteered and that gave us a problem. In the end, we chose six men to come with us. Fewer would not have been able to protect him and his treasure and more would, quite simply, have attracted too much attention. The next day while my uncle chose the horses and equipment we would need, I chose the volunteers. Some were easy; Idraf and Erik Red Hair were amongst the first volunteers and they stayed with John and me to choose the rest. Wilfred son of John was the only other man at arms we took. The journey meant that archers would be more useful. We took the two brothers, Peter and Paul son of Dafydd of Towyn and another Welsh archer, from the south of the land this time, Rhiwallon ap Rhodri. The ones we did not choose, most of the conroi, were disappointed. I told the six a version of the truth, that we sought David's niece and it was possible that we might be away for a month or more. They were all happy to take part although their reasons were all different. The four archers all felt that they owed David something. Erik was intrigued by the threads which bound us all together. The fact that Vikings had made an attempt on my uncle's life and Maredudd had done the same in the west brought out the pagan side of the Viking. The fact that we would be close to a sacred mountain also helped. Wilfred son of John also had an unusual reason for coming. His sister had been taken by Welsh slave traders and was always keen to see places she might have been sold. Every town we had raided he had inspected the women who would have been an age with his sister. When they knew the details, they went to choose the equipment and weapons they thought they would need. I allowed John to back out, but he would have none of it. He was coming. I knew that Sir Richard, my cousin Alfred, and the others were all more than curious. None of them were fools and the errand seemed wrong. It was hard not to give them a hint for if things went wrong then they might never see David again and he was such an important figure that all would wish to say goodbye.

As we prepared to mount the embrace which my uncle gave David of Wales was one of two men who believe they will never see the other again. My uncle had no words for me, and I saw that he was close to unmanning himself as he clasped my forearm.

I spoke for him, "I will fetch him home!" He nodded but I could see he did not believe it.

He said huskily, "Bring yourself home safe, Henry Samuel!"

The snow had stopped two days earlier and the road south was hard, virgin snow. Idraf swore that it would melt before too long, but I was not convinced. Erik Red Hair was the best prepared for the cold and the snow. He had a bearskin and a sealskin cape. He joked, "When you return home, Sir Henry, ask your uncle if you can hunt on the sands where we caught the pirates. Seals are easy to hunt and their skin keeps you drier than anything else."

The men then debated how to keep dry if a seal skin was not available. I let them banter and studied David of Wales. He was not only in discomfort but outright pain. He was hiding it, but I saw the signs. He tried to stand in the saddle as frequently as possible often disguising the action as though he was surveying the horizon. I said quietly, "We can stop whenever you like, David of Wales."

He gave a sardonic laugh, "All the riding is painful, but I will endure it. We have thirty odd miles until our first stop and after that, it will be short rides where I can dismount or even walk my horse."

"Tell me more about your sister and her family."

He nodded, "Aye, for if I die you will need as much information as you can get if you are to fulfil my wishes."

He was resigned to death and I wondered if I could be that calm in the face of my impending doom. We all knew that we could die in battle but there you had some control. You chose a good horse, good weapons and the right combination of blows. No matter what David did he would die and soon. Even worse none of us could do anything to stop it or to help him.

David knew me well. I had been my grandfather's squire and lived in Stockton Castle. The old Welshman seemed to read my thoughts, "I have had a good life and would not have chosen another. All that I do, Henry Samuel, is what I would have done years ago but for Lord Maredudd. He is a powerful man and if your uncle can do nothing else then I hope he puts an end to his life."

Shaking my head, I said, "The King, I think, still sees the political importance of having him as an ally."

"Your grandfather is a great man who is above such things. When I first served him in the Holy Land, I was little older than Geoffrey here and yet I saw in the young knight a man who had honour and valued life. I served him when he slew the Bishop of Durham and that needed to be done. Even though he knew it meant banishment it was the right thing to do. Your uncle is cut from the same cloth and he will end Lord Maredudd's life and not care about the consequences." He lowered his voice, "It is a sad fact of life, Henry Samuel, that I have served three Kings and none of them has been worth one drop of blood. You and your family have the right attitude. I suppose that one day we will have a king who is worth following." He looked at me, "You wish to know about my sister's child?" I nodded. "She may not be alive, but I hope that there is someone from her family who lives. This money I bring is blood money and I would have my blood benefit. We were poor and the lords, like Maredudd, who ruled us ensured that we stayed that way."

"My uncle said that she had distinctive coloured hair."

He nodded and smiled, "Mine is grey now but when I was younger it was as my sister's and my mothers. We all had red hair but Morgana's was not just red it seemed like a sunset. My younger brothers used to tease her that the fairies had left her in our home. She took it all in good part for she was not as full of herself as might have been expected by someone who looked like a princess. I will not be duped out of my money. I will know my niece or her child. I care not if it is a babe in arms, I will know it."

He knew his own mind. "Then tonight we camp at Llandrillo and hope that someone remembers a red-haired beauty called Myfanwy." To me, it seemed an impossible quest, but we would go on.

Idraf had chosen a route which avoided potential danger. Ruthin and Llangollen were far enough from Dyserth for the Welsh to control the land. Denbigh had been raided by us so often that they now offered tribute to us just to stop the raids. We would head through Denbigh and then take the high road through Derwen and Llandrillo. The road might be harder, but we would be invisible, and it would take us to the land David hoped would be his niece's home.

Llandrillo was a speck on the road. There were three houses and that was all. The doors were barred, and it was dark when we reached it. Erik Red Hair was all for banging on doors and demanding entry. I looked at the Viking giant and knew that would simply terrify them. I shook my head, "Idraf, let us try Welsh and persuasion. Tell them we seek a barn or a stable for the night and that we will pay in Welsh silver!" We had coins we had taken from the Welsh dead and I had a purse full of it. He did as I asked and after a short conversation, the door opened a fraction. I handed the purse to Idraf. I knew that our archer would pay the minimum we had to. After a short discussion, he handed over five silver pennies. It was probably more silver than the family saw in a six months. Idraf led us around to the rear where there was a dry-stone wall and a lean-to barn. To be fair to the farmer the barn was designed well and kept out the worst of the wind, but it was clear that we had overpaid. The men were all for going to the farm and demanding food.

David of Wales shook his head, "We have food and we can cook. Information is more important than a meal. I have to find my family as soon as I can!"

The men read much into that and all looked at one another. I set the men to cooking and took out the phial the doctor at the castle had given to me. There was no cure for the worm, but the phial contained a potion which alleviated the pain and enabled sleep. I had plenty in my bags. I would put some in his beaker when he was not looking. He had told the doctor that he wanted to be sharp and did not wish drugs. My uncle had told me differently and I would lie to David of Wales for that was what you did when it was necessary. The potion worked and David was asleep the first. He had gone some way to empty his bowels and I knew why. He wished to hide his illness from the others, but they were sharp.

As soon as we heard David's regular breathing, Idraf asked, "What is wrong with David, lord?"

"Wrong?"

"My lord, he is ill. The blood in the snow told me where he had emptied his bowels and he has the smell of death about him. We have a right to know."

I nodded, "Would you have me break my word?" They all shook their heads. "And if you asked David, would he tell you?" Again, they shook their heads. "When I can I will tell you all until then…"

Erik Red Hair said, "It matters not what the reason is. We are honour bound to protect such a great warrior. In Norway, men would have happily died protecting one such as David of Wales. To serve is enough!"

And with that, they were silenced.

When we woke David gave me a knowing look, "You do not need to give me a sleeping draught in future. Soon I will have eternal sleep when the pain which wracks my body will be gone. All I need to do at night is rest my eyes. I have a good past to think on and when I am dead then I shall not be able to do so."

I nodded, dumbly. He was reading my mind and I could keep no secrets from him.

"I will go with Idraf to the house and speak to the farmer. Perhaps two Welshmen can loosen his tongue. I will eat when we return."

We prepared the horses. The silence amongst the men told me that they were thinking of David and the fact that his life was ending for they were not fools and had worked that out for themselves. Blood in the snow was not natural. We were all young men and such thoughts rarely found anywhere in our mind where they could grow. David and his predicament had given us a different perspective. For me, that was his need for family. My grandfather and the men with whom he had fought had been his family but, at the end of his life, that was not enough. I knew that I was guilty of assuming my family would be there forever, but David and my grandfather were close in age. My grandfather was not immortal!

All the horses were saddled and the supplies balanced and arranged on the sumpter. We had our cloaks wrapped about us for while the snow and rain had stopped the wind whipped through us. We stood in the centre of the cluster of huts and waited for the two Welshmen to appear. It seemed to take an age. When they did both had a serious expression. Using our horses for a windbreak we leaned in to hear Idraf's words for David of Wales seemed to be somewhere else.

"We have good news and bad. The farmer knows of a red-haired beauty, but she cannot be David's niece for she has seen just twenty summers. She lives in the village of Llanarmon which is not far from here. As this place is on the road to Llangollen then he knows all of the farmers who live within thirty miles of here."

Rhiwallon said, "Then this will be a simple task!"

"I said there was bad news. The man who is the husband of this woman gave shelter to an Englishman." Idraf looked at me, "From his description, it sounds like your Uncle, Geoffrey and Dick!"

Erik Red Hair had a strange looking amulet beneath his tunic. He suddenly grabbed it and said a word I had never heard before, "*Wyrd*!"

Idraf nodded and continued, "Lord Maredudd sent men and there was a fight. This farmer does not know exactly what happened, but he believes that hostages were taken."

I put my foot in my stirrup and hauled myself into the saddle, "Then let us ride there now! Any speculation would be useless and whether this is David's family or not we owe them for they suffered as a result of my family!"

David of Wales grinned, "Your family's blood is strong, Henry Samuel. That could have been your grandfather speaking!" He hauled himself painfully into the saddle and said, "You are right and Wyddfa lives up to its name. There is powerful magic in this land."

Erik Red Hair mounted too, "And the threads of the sisters are indeed long!"

As we followed Idraf down the white road to the east and south I was too concerned with the news of my uncle to pay much attention to Erik but John asked, "These sisters, are they the same ones my father spoke about when he returned from the Baltic Crusade? Are they witches?"

Although I was distracted, I saw some of the others clutch at their crosses. Erik nodded, "Sort of. There is a legend in my homeland of three women who live in a cave at the top of the world and they spin. Their threads are men's lives. Sir Henry's uncle is one thread, David of Wales another and this flame-haired beauty a third. They were all brought together here in this corner of Wales and then our threads were connected." He shook his head, "I should have known they were spinning when the pirates came! I had forgotten my past!"

David of Wales shifted uncomfortably in his saddle and said, "We do that at our peril, Viking!"

We saw the hamlet below us a couple of hours later. There were just four houses although there were another four farms within four hundred paces of it. The farmer Idraf and David had spoken to had told them that the house we sought was the largest. One house had a second story to it and an ice-covered water trough told us which one it was. Idraf was taking no chances for if Lord Maredudd had attacked the place then he might have left men to watch. Idraf sent the brothers Paul and Peter around the hamlet to watch the far side.

I said, "I will fetch you myself if all is well!" They rode off.

We reined in outside the house and Idraf banged on the door. There was relief on the face of David as he dismounted. There was no answer from within. Idraf spoke in Welsh as he banged again. The door opened a crack. I could not see anything except for a maimed hand which grasped the frame. Idraf spoke urgently and for some time. Then the door opened and the farmer, or so I took him to be, peered out. His face showed the marks of a beating and he stared at first me and then David.

He said, "You two Welshmen and you, the young knight, may enter. The rest can go in the barn at the rear!"

I handed my reins to John. Erik Red Hair said, "Fear not, lord, I will command. Do not worry about us. This was all meant to be."

Idraf and David were the first ones inside and David carried his chest. I was the last one in. There were two women and they were huddled together as far from us as they could get. It was hard to get a good look at them but I saw plaited chestnut hair flowing down the back of one of them. Idraf, David and the farmer spoke in Welsh for a while. The smile told me that David of Wales had recognised the hair. The two women looked up during the conversation and when they did, I saw that one of them was indeed beautiful with red hair but the other, while dark-haired and younger appeared, to me, to be no less beautiful. I could not help myself and I smiled at her. To my surprise, she gave me a shy smile back.

"My lord?"

I was aware that the three men were looking at me, "Yes?"

"This is Davy ap Hywel and he is happy to speak in our tongue to make it easier for you, but he will have to translate for his wife Myfanwy and his sister Eirwen."

I nodded, "I thank you, Davy ap Hywel."

David of Wales began with his story. I had heard it, but it still touched me. When he spoke of his sister and his niece, I saw Myfanwy clutch at her cross. She rattled out so much Welsh that I barely understood one word. The three Welshmen's reaction told me that what she had said was profound. David laid down his chest and walking over to her embraced his sister's granddaughter. As they both wept Idraf said, softly, "This is the girl he sought. His sister's daughter did not die in childbirth, but she did not see Myfanwy here, married. Erik Red Hair was right, Sir Henry, we were meant to come here."

Davy spoke, "That may be true, but my sons and my servant have paid the price for our kindness."

"What?"

"There are men who serve Lord Maredudd and try to ingratiate themselves into his favour. Someone told him that I had given shelter to a William of Hartlepool. He sent men here to punish us. Idwal was hanged and I was beaten and the fingers of my left hand broken. Then my two sons were taken as hostages so that if Englishmen came again, I would tell Lord Maredudd! I fear that one of my neighbours may be a spy."

It was Idraf who joined all the pieces up the quickest. He suddenly ran from the house. I saw the look of surprise on the faces of Davy and his family. I smiled, "Idraf knows what he is doing. He will return." I turned to David, "You have found your home?" He nodded. "Then while Idraf is gone you must tell them the rest for you have not long on this earth and I do not think that your family will wish to miss a minute!"

"You are right, lord, and you have your grandfather's wisdom!"

He let go of his great-niece and opened the box of treasure. It was enough to buy a manor in England! He then began to speak. I knew when he told of his illness for Myfanwy began to weep and kiss his hand. Eirwen looked at me and smiled.

Davy nodded and said to me, "And this, our kinsman is just a warrior who serves your family?"

"The word '*serves*' is not the right one, but you have the right of it."

He shook his head, "I can think of no Welsh lord who would do this for there is naught in it for you!"

"You are wrong, Davy ap Hywel, there is a lifetime of service I am repaying."

Eirwen spoke Welsh and Davy translated.

We were interrupted when Idraf re-entered, "The man you think might be Lord Maredudd's spy is he a lean man with a hook nose and a scar down his cheek?"

Davy nodded, "Aye, Ieuef ap Rhodri is a mean-spirited man whose wife and family left him ten years since. He is a poor farmer and likes to make life hard for others. He drinks!"

"Then he is a spy no longer." He looked at me, "Peter and Paul were keeping watch and he tried to escape. They captured him and were bringing him here when he pulled a knife and stabbed Paul. Peter slew him."

"And Paul?"

"He is not badly hurt, and Erik is tending his wound."

Myfanwy spoke again and when Davy translated, she stood and said, in halting English, "I will prepare food!"

David spoke Welsh and turning to me said, "I will help her. I might as well make myself useful."

"Idraf, it is a pity that the brothers did not question him."

He smiled, "But they did. They told him he was dying and unless he answered their questions, they would leave his body on the hillside for the wolves. He said he was heading for Bala and then he died."

Davy suddenly shouted, "I am a fool! Of course, that is where they would take my sons! The man who rules there is Maredudd's bastard! Iago ap Maredudd is a nasty little man with delusions of grandeur. His father gave him the manor to guard that edge of his land."

I nodded, "Then, Davy ap Hywel, my men and I will travel there and fetch back your boys. My family pays its debt and as Erik Red Hair might say, this is meant to be!"

Chapter 17

Of course, David wished to come but I forbade it as I did when Davy said he would ride with us. I was brutally honest with both of them. "David, we need speed and you will slow us down." I hated to be brutal with an old comrade but there was little choice. "Davy, you have been injured and you are not a warrior. You, too, would be a liability and I will not put one of my men in jeopardy because he is keeping his eye out for you. We will fetch back your sons. I am leaving Paul here because he, too, is unfit to fight."

Davy looked from me to David of Wales. David nodded and said, "He is right, Davy, and I was not thinking like a warrior."

"But that means there will just be seven of you! What if they have more men?"

I laughed, "They would need five times our number for me to worry! Will Iago ap Maredudd have thirty odd men?"

Davy shook his head, "It is likely to be fewer than ten for as well as being evil, like his father, he is also tight-fisted and will not spend the coin on warriors."

"Good, now we will leave tomorrow before dawn. Idraf has told me that if we follow the Dee, we will avoid settlements and the bridge which they will no doubt watch. What will we find there?"

I think Davy was still in shock that we were so readily willing to put ourselves in danger for children we had never seen. We were but the more important reason was that we were doing it for David of Wales. "You will follow the river?"

"The ground is still frozen, and it guarantees that we find Bala and the lake. Now, what will we find?"

"His home is built like his father's and Lord Iago ap Nefydd Hardd's. There is a hall which is surrounded by a wall and a water-filled ditch. The river and the lake supply it. There is one main gatehouse along with a secondary gate. They have a single tower attached to the hall and it is used in times of danger."

"Your boys, what are their names and ages?"

"Dai is four, almost five, and Davy is three, coming up to four."

That surprised me for they were younger than I expected. "How will they react to this ordeal?"

Instead of answering he turned to Myfanwy and rattled off questions. It was Eirwen who answered, and her voice was so melodious as to be like that of a fairy; it enchanted me.

He nodded and said, "They will be upset for they are close to Eirwen and my wife, but Davy, my son, is clever and uses his mind. He likes to play pretend games. I think he will have told his brother that this is a game."

I nodded, Idraf, Peter and Rhiwallon would have to speak to them and convince them that we were friends. To them, we would be strangers. "Have you a token to show them that we come from you?"

When Davy asked the question Eirwen dashed off and returned with a wooden poppet. It had scraps of clothing and the raw wool from a sheep as hair. He smiled when Eirwen handed it to me. As she did so our fingers briefly touched, and I felt a shock race up my arm. Davy said, "Of course, Bleddyn the sheep. The two boys find it hard to sleep without it in the bed with them."

I handed it to Idraf who nodded.

"The boys are too young to ride and so we will fetch them back riding double with one of us. Have you a cloak for them? I doubt that Iago ap Maredudd would have bothered about such things, but I would bring them back safely!"

Davy nodded, "We have two sheepskins we were going to use for something else, but we have time this night to make them into cloaks."

"Good."

He looked me in the eye, "My lord, this puts me in your debt. Even if you fail, I am in your debt for you will have tried."

"There is no debt and we will not fail!"

That night I spent time with my men and slept in the barn with them. David stayed in the farmhouse. I would have to tell Davy and Myfanwy about the potion but that could wait until we returned. Idraf had not been to Bala but Rhiwallon had and between us, we managed to create a picture of the place.

"We cannot afford a pursuit. We break in and have two tasks, to save the boys and then slay every man who could wield a weapon! This will be hard enough as it is."

Wilfred son of John said, "Lord, I know we do not need spare horses for the boys, but we should take David and Paul's mounts, not to mention the sumpter, as we dare not be afoot. Thirty miles is how far we shall have to travel without rest and in this type of weather we are asking for trouble if we do not take spare horses."

Idraf shook his head, "The extra horses will make it easier for them to see us when we head west. There must be horses in the hall, better that we steal them and that, too, will prevent us from being followed. We may manage to slay every man in the hall but what of those in Bala who seek to win favour with Lord Maredudd?" Wilfred grudgingly nodded his agreement.

"Then get some sleep for I want us at the river just after dawn!"

I had intended just to ride away without bothering David of Wales and his new family but as we led our horses from the barn light shone from the farmhouse door and we were greeted by the smell of freshly griddled bread and biscuits. Davy handed to us fresh slices of bara brith, the yeasty bread made with dried fruit and smothered in butter. Eirwen handed me a cloth-covered parcel and Myfanwy did the same for Idraf.

David of Wales smiled, "There is food for the day. They could not bear the thought of you riding without hot food in your bellies and the bairns will be hungry." I smiled at the use of bairns. He had been at Stockton so long that he used the northern word for child.

I took the parcel, although I confess that I only had eyes for Eirwen. "Thank you!" I put the parcel in the leather saddlebag and then took the piece of bara brith. I began to eat once they had gone back inside the house. It was so cold that the air seemed to freeze before our faces. The hot bread warmed us, and I followed Idraf towards the river which lay six miles away. Davy had told us to follow the tiny stream, Afon Llynor, until we met the Dee. Idraf was right and this was a desolate land. Once we were a mile away from the hamlet, we could no longer smell woodsmoke and the frozen icicles and snowdrifts made the land look nothing like ours. Only Erik seemed comfortable and I listened to the conversation between Erik and John, the son of the warrior, who had first joined my grandfather in the Baltic.

"And my father fought in these conditions?"

Erik laughed, "This type of weather is perfect for raiding; not from a drekar you understand but you can cross rivers easily. They become like roads. Here the ice is not yet thick enough but in Sweden and Estonia the lakes and rivers are so thick you can drive a horse and wagon across them. We wear seal skin boots so that our feet are warm, and the frozen snow means that a man does not sink. Sir Henry is clever. The last thing this Welsh lord will expect is an attempt by Franks to attack him. I can think of few other lords who would attempt this."

It was just after dawn when we reached the River Dee. Here it could be easily forded although none of us relished the prospect. Dawn had not brought with it any warmth and I was grateful for my leather, metal-backed gauntlets! We rode in a single file once we reached the Dee and rode along its southern bank. Idraf would cross it once we found a shallow point. It would, no doubt be a wide crossing but that did not matter. We intended to hide up until dark once we reached a place from which we could spy out the town. We knew that the lake afforded the opportunity for fishing and there were forests where men could hunt. All of those were to the south of us and the harsh, uncompromising land through which we travelled was largely empty as few could make a living and that suited us. We stopped once to water our horses for Idraf had seen that we could cross the river which had many small islands at that point. We allowed the horses to drink as they crossed, and they were not as stressed as they might have been. I wondered at the wisdom of bringing my warhorse, Guy, but it was now too late to change.

Once we reached the north shore we dismounted and Idraf and I distributed most of the food. We would keep some for the two boys. We did not know what condition they would be in. The food, although no longer warm, was delicious. There was also dried mutton as well as more bara brith, cheese and a few apples. Before we mounted, we tightened our girths and checked our weapons. We had sharpened them in the barn. Idraf and his archers would not need bodkins and, in all likelihood, once they had killed any sentries would be using their short swords or daggers. John was still less than happy that he was designated as horse holder but the last thing we needed was to be left to make our way home on foot.

The last four miles of travel was a tricky section as we travelled through thickly wooded land which spilt down into the river. We were forced to ride, for part of the way, in icy water. Idraf and the ones at the fore kept a sharp ear out for any hunters but the weather was so cold that it appeared none had ventured forth. We stopped when we saw the vast expanse of Llyn Tegid ahead of us. We could see the small town and the smoke rising in the late afternoon. There was little movement but then again why should there have been? Any hunting or fishing would have taken place earlier in the day. All the buildings we could see were mean and wooden buildings. The folk who lived here would be poor. They would eke a living from fishing and hunting, but they would be hardy men. Apart from Iago ap Maredudd's warriors, there would be a town levy. These would be men who would be mustered to fight in times of war. I did not doubt that some had fought against us already but now they would be in their homes. Davy had been uncertain if they would hunt us once our attack had been discovered. While Iago ap Maredudd was not a popular lord the fact was that he was the lord and some men would obey him. For that reason, I decided to leave John and the horses on the opposite side of the river from the town. The tiny river which fed the Dee and then the lake was shallow enough to be waded. Indeed, in places, it was frozen. We avoided walking on the ice for fear of the noise the breaking ice would make.

We waited until darkness had fallen completely before we moved. None of us wore helmets and I was the only one who wore an arming cap and coif. Idraf was confident that he could find the hall from the description Davy had given. As the nearest town to his farm, he was familiar with it. Our small numbers meant we could move more easily and remain unseen. Idraf would move first and when he was safe then he would wave for Rhiwallon to follow. Erik, with his familiar axe, followed then me and Wilfred and Peter brought up the rear. I knew that I was the one we could most afford to leave behind. This was not knightly combat but a deadly fight to the death with whoever we found. Others were better suited to lead. There had been enough land to leave a good twenty paces between the walls and the houses. The dung and piss pots which stood outside the houses we passed told us that they would have men who would collect the night soil and urine. The fact that none had been collected was a warning. We would be passing back this way later on and if we came across the men then the alarm would be given.

Idraf halted in the narrow space between two buildings, one of which, from the smell, could have been somewhere they smoked fish. Peter had an arrow nocked and Wilfred had his short sword in his right hand. No one moved or spoke as Idraf scanned the walls and the gate which lay thirty paces from us. There was little movement for it was winter and leaving a home meant opening the door and losing all the heat. People would only venture forth if they had no choice. We knew that there was a second gate at the lake side of the hall but, if we could, we would use this one. We all heard a noise and pressed back into the gap. My sword was in my hand and Idraf and Rhiwallon had an arrow nocked but only Idraf had eyes on the open area. The noise became a conversation which Idraf and Rhiwallon would understand. I was feeling increasingly irrelevant in this venture and then I reminded myself that we were not doing this for me but for David of Wales. Despite the cold, I found myself sweating. This could be over before it had begun. The conversation seemed to last an age but Idraf did not look to be agitated. Then the noise faded.

Idraf turned to Rhiwallon and whispered in his ear. Nodding, the Welshman from Towyn ran. Erik stepped up and Idraf whispered to him. When I stepped up Idraf waved Peter forward and whispered in his ear. It was so quiet that although I was close, I heard nothing. Peter ran and Idraf waved the last of us forward. He said to the two of us, "The gate is fifty paces down this piece of land. There are houses opposite and there are two sentries. They just changed the guard and the other two have gone into an alehouse to buy a jug of beer. They have poor ale in the hall for the Lord drinks wine. Erik and Peter are waiting for them to return. They will take their place. I will join Rhiwallon. There are two guards on the towers towards the end of the wall. I will take this one and Rhiwallon will slay the other. When you see Erik and Peter with the jug of beer then follow but use the shadows. Hopefully, Erik and Peter will manage to gain entry but if they fail then you two shall complete the task."

Idraf disappeared in the blink of an eye and I stepped up to peer around the edge of the building. I saw the gate and in the gloom of the misty night saw the breath of the two sentries. They had a brazier to keep them warm. I could not believe that they would stand outside all night and I assumed this was just until they closed and barred the gates. When I saw two women admitted then I began to understand this Lord Maredudd. He was sending for doxies and whores. Once he had what he wanted then the gates would be barred. We had to act quickly, and I fretted at the delay. This all hinged on Erik and Peter getting close enough to the two guards to silence them! I had nodded my agreement to the plan for this was not the place for a debate but I wondered at the wisdom of this for Erik Red Hair was a giant and unless the man he was replacing had a similar height then we were doomed. Suddenly there was movement just down from where Wilfred and I stood. Peter and Erik appeared and they both held a jug in their left hands. As they stepped out of the alley I moved, and Wilfred followed me. Erik was clever and he had his right hand on Peter's shoulder. I could see his axe hanging down from his right hand by a thong, but the effect was to make Erik shorter. The mist helped. As we moved closer to them, I was aware of a movement from my left and I saw Idraf ghosting next to the wall. His bow had an arrow nocked. I assumed that Rhiwallon was even closer to his target as he had left first. One of the Welsh guards shouted something when Erik and Peter were just twenty paces from them. In answer, Erik raised the jug to drink from it and Peter began to laugh. That did not please the two guards and they stepped from the shadows, I assumed, to confront the two men. The two arrows which slew them were sent just a heartbeat apart and showed the skill of my two bowmen for they hit the smallest of targets, the guards' heads. Erik and Peter ran to the two dead men and had their bodies inside the gateway before Wilfred and I could react. We stepped out into the open and followed the other four into the walled manor house.

Time was no longer on our side. Two girls had just entered and if anyone else did so then they would notice the lack of guards. The two bodies were unceremoniously dumped in the ditch. The mist and the dark would hide them until dawn. We closed but did not bar the gate. As Davy had told us the hall was crenulated and had a strong door. There was a fighting platform close to the roof but the sentries had been slain by my archers. Peering into the misty courtyard the glow from the gate showed us that it was ajar. The two whores had not closed it properly and we ran towards it. Wilfred and I were now at the fore and it was Wilfred who pushed the door gently open and peered inside. He drew his long sword and nodded to me as he entered. We knew what we would do: first, kill all the warriors and then find the boys!

As soon as we were inside, we were hit by the heat and a wall of noise which was an indication of the numbers we might expect. There was a staircase leading to the upper floor and I waved Wilfred and Peter to it. Erik and I ran to the light which came from the hall itself. I stood to the side and peered in. There were ten men seated around a table and the two doxies we had seen were at the head of the table with their arms around a man who, I assumed, was Lord Iago ap Maredudd. Rhiwallon and Idraf joined me. I held up my left and splayed the fingers of my left hand twice. They nodded and, without further ado, Idraf and Rhiwallon stepped out and sent two arrows into the room. Erik and I followed. I think that Erik must have terrified them for he had the blood of the dead sentry he had carried all over his face. I had my sword drawn behind me as Idraf sent an arrow into the chest of Lord Maredudd's bastard son. Rhiwallon slew a second as I slashed my sword into the stomach of the man who had just risen and drawn his sword. The greatest damage, however, was done by Erik Red Hair whose axe took two heads in successive swings. He then ran like a berserker towards two men who had drawn their swords and before they could even raise them had hacked into their bodies. The last man was hit by two arrows. It had taken moments and there was little noise. In fact, I feared that anyone else in the hall might wonder at the sudden silence. Idraf said something and the girls nodded and, pointing, one answered him.

"The boys are locked in the cellar, lord, and there are others!"

"You two go and release them. Erik, see if there are stables. I will join the others."

All had gone well until then but the fates conspired and as Erik and Idraf ran from the hall into the kitchen there was a cry. I should have known that they would have servants. They ran from the building and the alarm was given. Wilfred and Peter ran down the stairs to join me. They both had bloody swords.

"There are none left alive above us."

"Wilfred, go with Erik and find us some horses. The town will soon know we are here!" With a drawn sword I ran after Idraf and found him in the kitchen. Two men lay slain and one was obviously just someone who worked in the kitchen while the other was a warrior.

"Lord, I am sorry. He came at me with a meat cleaver!"

I nodded for we did not have time for this, "Tell the servants to run. The noise will tell them we are here and put this death from your mind." I ran past him and hurtled down the stairs. It was lucky that I had fast reactions for, at the bottom of the stairs a sword was suddenly thrust at me. I had retained my metal-backed gauntlets and I flicked the sword aside with my left hand as I rammed my own into the man's chest. A second man came from the dark but the first dying sentry blocked his blow and I headbutted him. The arming cap protected me, and the mail coif made him reel. This was no time for honour, and I pushed the sword up through his throat and into his skull.

Idraf arrived and shook his head, "Had I been first then I would be dead."

We had no time for these recriminations, "Find the key, open the door and identify the boys." He gave me a blank look. "Remember that the whores said that there were others!" I turned to Rhiwallon, "Go and see if the doxies are still there. We may need them!"

I stood back and watched the stairs while Idraf entered the cellar with a lighted torch. He had the poppet in his tunic. "Davy and Dai, I come from your father." There was silence and then I heard a shout. Idraf said, "The poppet worked!"

I turned and looked. There were six children, three boys and a girl in addition to Dai and Davy. "Get them out!"

I ran up the stairs and found the two girls and Rhiwallon. He said, "They say that this is where Lord Maredudd keeps his hostages." He shrugged, "They know not where they come from." I nodded.

Idraf had the two terrified looking boys with him. One had the poppet. "Take the two of them to the horses and we will join you." He picked them both up and ran. The other hostages looked pale and shocked for they had been freed but into what kind of creatures. "Rhiwallon, ask the hostages where they come from."

As he began to speak one of the whores spoke and Rhiwallon grinned, "Lord, they say we can leave them with them. Now that Lord Iago ap Maredudd is dead, they will no longer have to endure his advances."

I spied Lord Iago's purse and picking it up I threw it to them, "Here is for your pains." One squealed as she caught it and the other grabbed me and kissed me. I had no time to waste and I smiled and waved a farewell. Rhiwallon and I ran out and found that Erik had acquired eight horses. That was more than enough.

I saw that Idraf had one child and Peter the other. That was good for they were with Welsh speakers. "Wilfred and Rhiwallon, guard the rear. Erik, at the fore with me!"

I mounted the hackney and dug in my heels. The mare leapt towards the open gate. When we had entered, I had been the follower, but this was my world and I led. I held my sword behind me as we burst through the gate. Already men with weapons had gathered and Erik and I charged at them. As much as I did not want to kill these men, I could not allow them to hurt my men or stop us from completing our quest. I swung the flat of my sword at the man with the spear. It smashed into the spear, throwing it from his hands and then struck his head, rendering him unconscious. Eric was a Viking and they do not know how to be considerate. With them, it is kill or be killed and his axe head split the skull of the man who foolishly tried to spear him. That simple action had a greater effect than my stunning blow. As blood, brains and bone splattered those around the dead man the rest ran away from the charging horses.

We splashed through the stream and headed for the woods. We could not see John but that was a good thing as it showed he had remained hidden. I had good men and I did not make the mistake of looking over my shoulder. They would be behind me. I reined up when we reached the place we had left John. With his sword drawn, he emerged from the woods. "We have won?"

"Do not tempt fate, John, we are winning and that is all!" I wheeled my horse and dismounted. I would ride Guy. "Are any hurt?"

"No lord!"

"Then feed the boys and put on the cloaks that were made for them. Idraf and Peter, you will lead us back. Rhiwallon and John you ride close to them. Wilfred, Erik and I will be the rearguard."

The sweat we had accumulated in the fight now began to cool making me, certainly, feel uncomfortable. With food in their hands and sheepskin cloaks around them, the boys were mounted and we headed away from Bala. We rode in silence partly because we were listening for pursuit but also because men reflect after a battle. If there is the opportunity, they talk of it with the other warriors but when that is not possible, they have a conversation in their heads with themselves. They run over every blow they struck, wondering if they could have done it differently. Every warrior knows that he will have to fight again and learning from what you did could save you the next time. After an hour of steady riding, we stopped. At least Idraf at the fore stopped and we joined them.

Erik said, "There is no pursuit. I was listening. I do not think they had horses and I know they did not relish a fight with us."

John who was always anxious to learn asked, "Why? How do you now?"

Erik laughed, "A handful of men break in and slay every warrior who has terrorised Bala since," he waved a hand, "I know not when and then charge all the men of the village. Few men would venture at night after them and for what? The men of Bala do not care that we have taken two boys." He looked at me. "Now Lord Maredudd will be different. We have slain his bastard son and taken his hostages. I cannot see him being pleased."

I looked at the two sheep wrapped boys who patently did not understand a word of what was being said. "You may be right, Erik, but let us get these to their family and then make a decision. We still have many miles to go and while the enemies behind may fear us, we will be travelling through Welsh held land and we have two fewer men to fight as they have the boys on their horses!"

As we rode on that chilly December morning we spoke of David of Wales. All of the men now knew that he was dying. It was an open secret and I had not needed to betray a confidence. They were warriors and spoke of death as inevitable. They spoke of how they would like to meet their end. Not one of them wished an end through illness or old age. They wanted to die with a weapon in their hand amongst friends.

We reached the farm just before noon. We had changed horses once and eaten the last of the food we had brought. My mind had run through all the choices we had and there was but one that I could see.

Chapter 18

"David, we need to leave this place and do so as soon as possible."

In all honesty, David looked worse than when we had left the farm. It had only been a day or two that we had been away but perhaps the worry for the boys or a combination of that and his illness had fed the worm.

He shook his head, "This will be my home. While you were away, I spoke with Davy. He is a good man. My sister would be happy that her granddaughter chose so wisely and that their lives will be better."

"And when Lord Maredudd finds his dead son, what then? Will he just accept the loss of the hostages and forget Davy and the English?" I was looking at Davy as I spoke. David was dying and just wanted to spend as much time with his family as he could before the end. The worm had taken over his mind as well as his body and he was not thinking straight. Davy, in contrast, could see the point that I was making.

"This is our home! I am the headman of the village. To uproot and move to…" he looked at me, "where would we move to, my lord? Where is safe? From what you say Prince Dafydd has won and King Henry holds on to a tiny piece of Wales by his fingertips. Where do we go?"

I shook my head, "I will not lie to you, the only place I can think is Dyserth and you are right, we have been beaten but I also know my uncle and Sir Robert Pounderling. They will find a way to defeat this Prince Dafydd. It may not be this year, but it will happen. Bring your family to Dyserth. Lord Maredudd will be hunted down and his evil reign will end and then you can return here. You cannot stay here and that is clear."

I had planted the seed and as with all such things it needs time to begin to grow and bear fruit. He nodded, "What you say makes sense but there is no hurry. From what I have been told by Idraf, Lord Maredudd is across the sea in Anglesey and he will not hear the news until Christmas at the earliest. He then has to return here. We have until

Michaelmas! By then I will make my decision and besides, the roads might be easier to travel."

I knew that it was unlikely that David would last that long. I looked into the faces of my handful of men for this was not my decision only. I saw nods and I sighed, "Of course Lord Maredudd himself need not stir. He could send others to do his bidding and they might come sooner rather than later."

Idraf said, cheerfully, "We can keep watch and hunt, my lord. When we passed through the forests, I saw game trails!"

Erik added, "Aye, and we can improve the barn. We can make it quite cosy!"

I was still not convinced but I could not abandon David and this family. However, the decision was taken for me when Eirwen, who must have taken some lessons from David, said in English, as she touched my hand, "Please stay!"

I looked up as Erik Red Hair shrugged and said, almost to himself, "*Wyrd*!"

I nodded and said, "We stay but we will be vigilant!"

There was a look of joy on Eirwen's face and, I confess, that I felt a warm glow too. Looking back what I should have done was to send Peter and Paul back to Dyserth to tell my uncle of our plans but I was aware that Paul had been wounded and that we needed both archers with us for we had much work to do. The extra horses we had brought would be invaluable when we made our way back to Dyserth but they needed to be fed and so we had to clear ice and snow from one of the fields so that they could graze. In addition to the improvements we had to make to the barn Davy was forced to slaughter some of his sheep for food. He chose the older animals, but his livelihood would be affected.

It was David of Wales who pointed out the most obvious answer to Davy's dilemma, "With my gold, you could buy every sheep in the whole of the Clwyd Valley! You are a rich man!" I could see that Davy had not thought through David's presence. He had seen a man seeking a family. The chest of gold had been, until then, almost an irrelevance.

David, despite his illness, for he deteriorated day by day, was as happy a man as I had ever seen. The two boys and he spent every waking moment together along with Myfanwy. He was teaching them English and he did so with the same patience he had taught me to draw a bow. He did it by telling the story of his life and that of my grandfather. As I passed them, I often saw the boys looking up at me and, as their English improved, they would speak to me and ask me questions about my family and how I had become a warrior.

Of course, all of this meant that Eirwen had more work to do and as my men and Davy were often outdoors, labouring, I was the one who helped her, along with John, to prepare the food. My men thought that their lord should not soil his hands labouring or that was what they told me but the looks they exchanged made me wonder if there was another motive. I spoke no Welsh and so Eirwen had to learn English. She learned it far quicker than either John or I would have learned Welsh! By the time that Christmas Eve approached we could hold conversations about matters other than beans, cabbage or the inevitable mutton. John, for some reason, found more times to be absent from the kitchen. I suspect he was enjoying Myfanwy's ale with the others, but I cared not for those times alone, in the humble kitchen of Davy's home, were special to me.

Looking back our conversations were not particularly romantic; I told her of my father and my family. I spoke of the crusade in the Holy Land and the deaths of those who had been close to me. She, in turn, spoke of her own life where she was little more than a servant and yet how she did not regret one moment of it. It was clear to me that her two nephews were her life, or until I had arrived, they had been her life. Each night, as I lay in the barn and tried to sleep, I found my thoughts wandering to Eirwen. Erik was right about the threads which bound us. It was like a Gordian knot and trying to unpick it to see where the thread had begun was a pointless task. I had to resign myself to the fact that Eirwen and I had some connection and if it was broken then more lives than our own would be affected.

Christmas Eve should have been joyous, anticipating the birth of Christ, but it was not for it was marred by a sudden deterioration in David's condition. He even asked for the potion. The two boys were distraught at the pain they saw and Eirwen had to whisk them away. We all believed that he was dying and, with no priest in the village and none for more than twenty miles, we would have to shrive him. As a knight, they all delegated that task to me. I was uncomfortable, to say the least, but I did my duty and heard his confession which we all thought would be his last. When he recovered and greeted Christmas Day, I was the most relieved man on the farm! I think his brush with death made the day extra special.

Myfanwy had used the last of the dried and the fruit too poor to eat to make the pudding which would be served after the meal. Peter had had the foresight, when we had been in the kitchen in Bala, to grab flour, oats and a pot of honey. Myfanwy had added them to the pudding, and it had helped to make a special version of Bara Brith. Idraf and Rhiwallon had managed to hunt and they had killed a deer. The stew, fortified by some of the ale, made the meal a real feast. All of us crowded into the farm to eat. There were not enough chairs and we had to use the tree trunks which were being seasoned. It was almost laughable to watch Erik Red Hair trying to make himself smaller. He failed but we admired his efforts. David rarely ate. He told us he did not wish to feed the worm any more than he had to and so he drank ale and encouraged the two boys to eat. They had no wooden chairs, but David's two knees were more than adequate as replacements. Eirwen was seated next to me. It was not our doing although it suited us both, the rest of the diners left two spaces for us and we sat so close that our legs touched and each time I used my spoon our elbows collided. It was bliss.

After we had eaten the pudding, David filled his beaker and placing the two boys on his chair he stood, "I thought last night that my time had come. I confessed all to Sir Henry, but God has spared me another day. I fear there will not be many more such days, but I do not wish grief when I am gone. Had I not come here to this piece of heaven then I would never have known the joy of family. I am indebted to you all for each of you has been part of this, my last journey on earth." I saw Erik Red Hair clutch at his amulet. "The warriors who kept me safe and the great-niece and great-nephews who have made me smile and to Davy who has opened his home to an old warrior. When I die do not mourn but celebrate!" He raised his beaker, "To our Lord, on the day of his birth."

We all stood and did the same. When the words had echoed around the small room in which we ate there was silence. No one sat and each of us looked at someone they deemed special. David looked at Dai and Davy. The farmer and his wife looked at each other. The brothers clasped arms and I looked into Eirwen's face as she stared up at me. Her green eyes looked like inviting pools into which I could dive. I had seen such pools when we had sailed to the Holy Land around the islands of the Middle Sea. All that I wanted to do was to kiss her, but I dared not. She was a maiden and I was a guest in the house. We just stood and silent words passed between us.

Then the moment was broken as Erik Red Hair began to sing or rather chant one of his Norse sagas. We sat enthralled and listened.

The Great Sea called and men set sail
To voyage to the west with sword and mail
Across the void where no man went
Erik and his crew were different
They rowed through seas deep and black

War in the West

They knew they could not go back
The blood feud made them sail away
From snow and ice to a brand new day
Men made strong by ice and snow
Men with no place else to go
They found a land of deer and bear
With all they wished, with food and sun
They thought a new life had begun
They made a home but briefly there
When the Skraeling came they fought and bled
They sailed back east and left their dead
Men made strong by ice and snow
Men with no place else to go
They sailed back to the wolf's wildland
A small and determined Viking band
One day the folk will sail again
And find a home fit for great men
Men made strong by ice and snow
Men with no place else to go
Men made strong by ice and snow
Men with no place else to go

When he had finished John said, "Where does that tale come from, Erik?"

He quaffed his ale, "It is from my clan." He shook his head, "Sorry, my family, and we were the clan of the fox. It is the story of one of my ancestors after whom I am named. He and the rest of his family lived in the land of ice. There was a feud and they fled. It is said they sailed west and found a bountiful land, but some tragedy happened, and they had to return to this land. The stories passed down from generation to generation describe somewhere north of here." He shrugged. "I was born over in Norway, but we value the stories for they keep the dead and the past alive."

David nodded, "Perhaps men will tell tales about me and that will keep my memory alive."

Silence fell until Wilfred said, "It cannot be true! Men would fall off the edge of the world!"

Erik smiled; he was in too good a mood to fight but I saw the glint in his eye. No one called a Viking a liar. "In which case, my friend, there would be no seas for they would have also fallen off the edge of the world and we would be able to walk to Anglesey!" His logic silenced Wilfred.

When we retired that night, I noticed water dripping from the roof of the barn. Idraf said, "A thaw!"

I nodded, "And that does not bode well. With the land frozen word might struggle to reach Lord Maredudd but if there is a thaw then the roads will be open."

"But it does not matter, Sir Henry. We cannot leave for David is too ill to move."

"I know. We will have to scout the land to the east as well as the west from now on. Men might come from Bala but, equally, they could come from Conwy. I fear we should have left as soon as we rescued the boys for we might be trapped here."

Erik seemed to be asleep, but he showed he was not when he said, from his bed, "What will be, will be. We were meant to be here if only so Sir Henry could meet the love of his life!"

When all laughed, I knew that protestations were pointless.

The warmer weather seemed to make David of Wales worsen and three days after Christmas we began a watch over David. Idraf, Myfanwy and I took it in turns to watch each night. None of us wanted him to die alone. I was the third to have the watch and I thought him asleep. His voice made me start. "You know, Sir Henry, I have put this off for many years. When Sir Thomas ceased going to war, I thought I would find my family then. But something always arose, and I put it off. Had I come four years or more I would have had as much treasure and four more years with Myfanwy. I would have seen the two boys as babes and enjoyed that." I said nothing for there appeared to be no words which I could say to make him feel better. He was right. He coughed and said, "I would have a drop of the potion, lord. Not enough to make me sleep but enough to silence this worm."

I took a wooden spoon and poured a little on it. He swallowed it. "Better?"

He laughed, "The doctor must be a wizard for it works as soon as it leaves my throat." He sighed. "Do not put off that which you wish to do."

I smiled in the dimly lit room, "I have nothing that I wish to do."

"You do not lie to a dying man, Sir Henry, we all see the lightning between you and Eirwen. Speak to her!"

"She is a maid and…"

"Then speak to Davy. He is a good man, as are you!" He became silent and I thought he was asleep. He almost was for his voice was sleepy as he said, "If you do not ask then you will never know!"

When we rose, the next day, the snow had gone. As Idraf said, it would return again but, for a brief period of time, we were vulnerable. I put off speaking to either Eirwen or Davy for I feared for our safety. I had all my men mount and divided us into two. "We will ride as far as we can until noon. Avoid being seen and look for signs of movement. We need to know if the Welsh warriors of Maredudd seek us."

I took the road to Llangollen. I had Rhiwallon with me and he rode just ahead of Erik, John and I. With just four of us we were a relatively small target and I hoped that we would escape observation. The roads appeared empty but, already, there were patches of flooding as the snowmelt gathered. That gave me the hope that any travel along these poor roads would prevent the Welsh from moving. Of course, as soon as we reached the Roman Road, my hopes were dashed. The Romans had built a road with a good surface and two drainage ditches which still worked a thousand years after they had been built. They had made the road to go from London to Anglesey. If Maredudd chose he could easily send men down the road to retake his hostages and to punish Davy. As we peered along an empty road, I was fairly confident that they would not know the identity of the abductors. Indeed, why should they even suspect? They did not know that the hostages were David of Wales' family. We had seen no one by noon and headed back.

Idraf was already in the farmhouse when we reached it and was watching for us. "We saw no one, Sir Henry. We may be lucky."

Erik had become even more superstitious since we had begun this quest and he said, brightly, "If we are meant to fight then it will be so! We are playthings!"

Idraf shook his head, "And you are getting on my nerves, Viking!"

Erik was not to be provoked, "And as you are just an archer you are safe from my wrath." He put a huge arm around the archer's shoulder. "Come, I am ready for a beer and they brew good ale here!"

Even before I had got into the house Davy came to speak with me. "David is in a bad way, Sir Henry. He is struggling to breathe, and he is in great pain."

"I gave Myfanwy the potion."

"He refuses to take it. He says that he does not wish to waste one moment more asleep."

I shook my head and pushed past him, "This is a nonsense." I found David on the bed they had made for him before the fire. "David of Wales what is this about you not wanting to take the potion and alleviate the pain?"

He smiled, "It is my life, lord, and I can bear the discomfort. I would not sleep while these two are awake." Dai and Davy looked up at me. They could understand almost everything that was said now.

"I will give you just enough to dull the pain." He did not answer. "I will command you, David of Wales and bring in Erik and Idraf to hold you! Trust to me. I am determined."

He laughed and it hurt him so much that a tendril of blood dripped from the corner of his mouth, "Aye, you have grown. Swear that it will be just enough to dull the pain."

I shook my head, "If you cannot trust the grandson of Sir Thomas then…"

He nodded and I took the spoon and put in just slightly more than I had given him the night before. The relief was immediate, and I saw the grateful smile on Myfanwy's face. It was Myfanwy's turn to watch that night and I joined my men in the barn.

"Idraf, tomorrow take Peter and patrol towards Llangollen. Fresh eyes may see what we may have missed. Rhiwallon, take Paul and do the same for the road towards Bala."

"We saw no sign today, lord."

"It has been long enough for a message to reach Lord Maredudd and I was foolish. They could still use the Roman Road even when it was frozen. The Romans built well. It is not just warriors we are concerned about. There are two children and two women who need our protection." I lowered my voice, "We have to force them to come with us to Dyserth, even if they do not want to. They have the hostages back but there will be a reckoning."

Idraf nodded, "You are right, lord!"

I was woken in the middle of the night by Eirwen. She shook me awake, "Come, Sir Henry, David needs you. Myfanwy sent me to fetch you."

Rising I ran after her. When we reached David, I could see that he was barely breathing. "Sir Henry, the potion!" Myfanwy was on the edge of tears.

I put my ear to his mouth and then opened his eye. I shook my head, "He is not in pain and the potion will not help. He is dying." A sob broke from her lips. "Speak to him for I believe he can hear your words although he cannot speak to you. He came a long way to find you. Tell him all that you wish him to hear before he makes the long journey. Eirwen and I will make sure that you are not disturbed."

"But can he hear me?"

"I know not but it cannot hurt, and I know that if I was slipping into that long and dark tunnel then I should like to hear the voice of one whom I loved!"

She nodded and put her lips to his ear. Eirwen slipped her arm into mine and squeezed as we moved out of earshot. She looked up at me and I saw that she was weeping. "You are a good man, Sir Henry."

I shook my head, "It is Henry Samuel, or, if you will, just Sam. My grandfather and mother call me that. Sir Henry is for battle and here there is no battle."

"I have spoken with David of Wales and he speaks highly of you. We share things in common. Neither of us has a father and we are of an age."

I smiled, "You flatter me for I am much older than you."

"A little older. My brother has the same age difference to Myfanwy. It is good. I am young and I will bear children easily."

I was taken aback a little and I smiled, "Is this a proposal, Eirwen?"

"I know it is presumptuous as you come from a noble family but David told me that you are shy and if I waited for you to make the first move then I would be an old lady! From the moment I saw you I wished to be your wife. If you would not have me then tell me so that I can put you from my mind." I was stunned. "But I have looked into your eyes and believe that you love me too! Am I right?"

I held her in my arms, "Of course I do but you are a maid and your brother…"

"My brother is happy!"

I took her in my arms and kissed her. Unlike many young lords who had sowed seeds far and wide, Eirwen was the first girl or woman that I had kissed, and I did not know what to expect. It was like riding into battle for the first time. My heart soared and all thoughts went from my head. When she stepped back and I looked at her I wondered if I had gone too far but I saw, in her eyes, such love as I had only seen in my mother's eyes.

Before I could say anything, I was aware that Myfanwy was standing and she said, with a sad smile, "David of Wales is gone. I heard your words and I believe that he did. He chose his time to die. The two of you have his blessing."

It was as though this was a tableau of life itself. I felt joy and such despair at the same time that I did not know what I ought to feel. The three of us hugged and tears washed each of our faces. A great man had died, and the world was a poorer place for it.

We buried him the next day in the village graveyard. It was a simple ceremony and the two young boys wept as did their mother. All of us were affected by the death and the funeral. As a result, I did not send men on patrol. Myfanwy insisted that we celebrate his life and she and Eirwen cooked a feast for us. I had remained at the grave when they left us. I think my men wished to mourn David of Wales in their own way. Davy's voice, when it came, made me start. "Sir Henry! I am sorry to disturb you, but Myfanwy asked me to. You wish to marry Eirwen?"

"We wish to marry each other."

He smiled, "Then that is even better. From the moment you two met I hoped for this outcome." His face became serious. "Your family will not object? She has no fortune!"

I laughed, "You do not know my family. That is the least of our considerations. They will want me to be happy and they will adore Eirwen. I am just sad that I will take her from your boys."

"It is the price we have to pay for the time David of Wales spent with us. This is good."

"While we talk, I should tell you that I believe we have to leave before Michaelmas."

He nodded, "I know but this is my home!"

"We stay away until Maredudd is no longer a threat to your family. You do not want your sons taken again!"

"You are right. It will take a couple of days to gather what we need."

"We will be riding horses from here. There will be no wagons. The others in the village can watch over your house and chattels."

He nodded, "I will make the most of the next two days."

I sent out my archers and the three of us helped Davy to gather what they needed. We had to improvise bags for they had none. We used the sheepskins they had stored. If it rained, then there might be a problem, but it was all we had. The measure of a man is often the way others view him and I saw that Davy was held in high regard by the other villagers and farmers who were genuinely sad to see him go. They promised to watch over his flocks and refused to take any as payment. Davy was the true headman. We all worked so hard that it was cold food for our meal. Rhiwallon and Paul arrived back first with the good news that there were no enemies coming from that direction. I was not worried about Idraf until darkness fell and they had not arrived. I stood with Erik and Wilfred to watch the road from the east. When the two arrived, it was with bad news.

"My lord, there is a column of men coming here. We spied them four miles along the road where they have camped. They did not take the road we expected but a small trail." They were coming for us and we were not ready!

War in the West

Chapter 19

"How many men?"

"Only one knight; I did not recognise him or his livery." That meant we had not fought him at Deganwy. "There are eight mounted men at arms and fifty dismounted archers. I saw a few with ponies. Had we ridden forth yesterday we would have seen them at Llangollen."

"Aye, and by now we would be away from here. As it is, they will catch us if we leave in daylight! We need to pack now and get away as soon as we can."

"They will follow, lord, and Welsh archers can run almost as fast as mailed horsemen can ride!"

I gave him a wry smile, "We have very little choice, Idraf. If we stay and fight, we lose. We will ride as soon as they are all ready. I fear the boys will have another night adventure! Tell the others and I will tell the family."

I walked into the room in which we all ate. I said nothing but Davy said, "Bad news?"

"Maredudd's men are four miles away. We need to leave now. They will follow us, and they will catch us. Our only hope is to be as far north by morning as we can. All is ready, wrap up well and mount your horses. Davy, tell the others in the village to cooperate and tell the hunters where we have gone. If they try to deceive them then it will go ill for them."

He left.

Myfanwy said, "Eirwen, get their cloaks." I saw that she was near to tears. The last two days had been emotional for her.

"John will ride with Dai and Davy can ride with his father. I am afraid that you and Eirwen will have to manage as best you can."

She wiped away the tears and forced a smile, "And we will hold you up." She shook her head, "Just when things look up, we have money, Eirwen has a man and life looks hopeful, we are to have it all dashed from our hands!"

"David of Wales would not have said so and I believe that his spirit is looking down on us. If we avoid Llangollen, then we have a thirty-eight-mile ride to reach the safety of Dyserth. Normally I would make that into two journeys, but we will try to do it in one long night and even longer day!"

I watched as she stiffened her back, "We will not let you down!"

It became clear, within a mile of leaving the farm that we were travelling too slowly. That was partly the terrain as well as the fact that it was night. We were not on a smooth road. The other factor was that the two women, although they were desperately making the effort to keep up did not have control over the horses. I had to use myself and Wilfred to lead their mounts and that left just two archers as scouts. As Peter and Paul were leading the horses with the family's belongings, we were left with Idraf and Rhiwallon as the scouts and Erik as the rearguard. I had forbidden any conversation and I saw Eirwen apologising with her eyes. Since I had spoken with her brother events had overtaken us both and we had not had the chance to be alone and speak of our future.

By the time dawn came, we were just ten miles from the farm. The only advantage we had was that we could now see the better road which led northeast, and we could talk. That was offset by the fact that half a mile to the south-west was the village of Bryneglwys. We would be seen and while the villagers would not do anything to hinder us, they would tell our pursuers. We would have left a clear trail. The thaw had made the ground muddy and we had so many horses that their clear swathe and piles of dung were like markers for an enemy to follow. Erik dropped back forty paces once we reached the road. He could turn and look for enemies. Idraf and Rhiwallon did the same at the fore so that we were spread out even more. It was necessary but it made us a clearer target. When we dropped down into dead ground or behind a hill, we were invisible but, all too often, we could be spied from as much as a mile behind.

I always found it easier to talk problems through, "Wilfred, how long do you think it would take the hunters to reach the farm?"

He looked up in the sky. It had been daylight for about an hour. "I would say about now."

I nodded, miserably, because his assessment matched mine and I had hoped I was being pessimistic. "So, a short time to discover we had gone and a little while longer to question the other villagers."

He shook his head, "They might do that, but their horsemen would see the trail we left and simply follow. They could make almost three times the speed which we managed."

I also realised that this road took us through Ruthin. The Welsh were there. If Wilfred was right their horsemen would catch us just a mile or so from Ruthin. We would be trapped between two sets of Welsh warriors. There was little else for us to do but carry on. The inviting empty fields to the north offered us a short cut which could save five miles or more and bypass Ruthin, but we could not travel fast over that ground and we would be seen. The words of Erik's Christmas song came to me. His ancestor had sailed not knowing what lay ahead but, having set the course, they had to follow it. We were in the same position. I smiled, not quite, for we knew what lay ahead and knew that twenty odd miles away lay my uncle and safety.

Eirwen saw my smile, for I had looked north, and said, "You spy hope, Henry Samuel?"

My name sounded like a song when she said it, "We are alive and I see a glimmer, no more. With stout hearts and strong swords, we will survive this ordeal and, mayhap, one day will regale our children with the story of our flight!"

It was as we approached the hamlet of Llanfair Dyffryn Clwyd that Idraf took matters into his own hands. Instead of carrying on north, towards Ruthin and whatever awaited us there, he headed due west towards the river. I trusted my men, but he was adding miles to our journey. I had to trust him. The villagers would tell our pursuers which road we had taken and the higher ground on the other side of the river did not bode well for our progress. One advantage of this route was that it was tree-covered and as we headed for the ford across the Clwyd we were hidden from view. Idraf waited on the other side. Of Rhiwallon there was no sight.

Idraf dismounted and allowed his horse to drink. "Lord, the horses need some rest. They can drink here. I have sent Rhiwallon to scout out the road ahead."

I nodded, "Dismount and let the horses drink!" I helped Eirwen down from her horse. She went to fetch Dai. I knew that Idraf would explain his decision to me.

Idraf waved me to one side and spoke quietly. "Lord, they will catch us. Had we tried to pass by Ruthin we would be captured or dead already." I nodded. "It is sixteen miles from here to Dyserth. Denbigh is easily passed. I think that we can delay them here." He pointed as he spoke, "Erik, Wilfred, the brothers, you and me, we ambush them. Three archers can hurt them. As you can see, once they cross the river the road rises and three men at arms who are well mounted can slow them down. We need to buy three hours."

"And the baggage?"

"Lord, what is more important? A few pots and pans or the lives of David of Wales' family? We tether them in the woods on the other side and take them with us if we are able... or leave them here."

He was right and I took the decision. I turned and spoke to the others, "We will ford the river. Once we are on the other side Rhiwallon will lead you north to Dyserth." I smiled at Eirwen, "You ladies have had your riding lesson."

She looked at me, "And what of you?"

"We will dispute this crossing." I saw Davy about to argue and I said, "There will be no discussion. I command and this is my wish. John and Rhiwallon will be your guards until Dyserth!"

It took far longer to ford the river than I expected but as Erik said when I began to become frustrated, "Sir Henry if it takes us this time to cross then that means those who follow will not have an easy time. With arrows falling they will struggle!"

The rest had been enough for the horses and when Rhiwallon returned with news that the road ahead was clear we bade them farewell. As I hoisted her into the saddle, Eirwen kissed me. We had no time for long words of farewell. We would either meet again or... She and her sister in law rode in the middle of the tiny group of riders. Once they had gone the brothers went with the baggage and tethered the horses in the woods. The rest of us set to making an ambush. We cut and sharpened stakes from the woods and embedded some below the water. Others we placed at the side of the road, hidden in the bushes so that if they tried to rush us, they would have a shock. When Peter and Paul returned, they took Idraf's horse and theirs and hid them a little way up the road. The three of them then went to a large flat rock which lay behind a tangle of ivy-covered brambles and scrubby trees. I could not see them, and I was thirty paces from them.

The three of us held our horses' reins and waited just thirty paces from the river amongst the trees. When we had forded the river, I had studied the ground and knew that it would be hard to see any who waited there. Our cloaks helped to mask us. I was nervous and I knew why. Before Christmas, I would just have seen the problem as an opportunity to use my skills. Now I feared to lose my life for I now had Eirwen. I had changed.

Erik had skills and powers which no other of my men had. He was a Viking. He wore the same mail as the rest of my men, but it always looked like borrowed raiments. He must have sensed what was in my head, "The advantage is with us, lord. They have nine or ten men in mail and a few who are mounted. If their archers have kept up with them then they will be so tired that they will be able to do little. We forded the river on horses. Their dismounted men will struggle to cross the river for it came up to our horses' bellies. I trust in the archers and I know that the three of us will be the equal of those we fight."

Wilfred, like me, held a spear and he nodded, "If they make this shore then we charge from these woods, lord. The slope is with us and, as we discovered, the slippery riverbank gives no purchase."

They gave me confidence, "I thank you both for all that you have done."

Wilfred said, "We did it, lord, for David of Wales."

Erik laughed, "That may be the reason you told yourself, Wilfred, but I know that none of us had any choice in this matter. It was meant to be!"

The Welsh were eager, and we heard them less than an hour after we had finished our preparations. Idraf had been right. I doubted that Rhiwallon and the others were more than five miles up the road and had we not delayed them then they would have caught us in the open. This would be a test of my six men against more than twice their number. Idraf and his archers would begin the fight and we would only be involved when the Welsh crossed the river and attempted to charge the hidden archers. The nature of the road from the south meant that while we could hear them, they only came into sight thirty paces from the ford and my heart sank. They had more horses and then it came to me. The villagers in Llanarmon had had eight horses. They had mounted some archers. Along with the ponies they now had a dozen mailed men and a dozen archers. The odds were no longer two to one but four to one! I should have been ruthless and taken all the horses! This was not a time for regrets. You fought with what you had, where you had to fight!

The Welsh halted and I saw the knight, who wore no helmet, survey the ford and he turned to his squire. The Welshman wore a good brigandine and he entered the water and made his way cautiously across. I saw the Welsh archers dismount and string their bows while the men at arms hefted their shields to protect their arms. They were suspicious. The squire reached the halfway point and was seemingly satisfied that he could see no ambush. He waved the knight and men at arms forward. I noticed that they came in a broad line and that showed they knew their business for it was a wide ford. Idraf and his two companions would have a short time to pick and hit a target. The timing was everything. If they released too soon and they were further away the archers would risk missing. Besides, as soon as they released, even though my archers were hidden the Welsh archers would send their more numerous arrows at them! My failure to be ruthless might cause some of my men to die. Had I confiscated all the horses from the village then there would only be four archers for us to face!

The ford was only sixty paces wide and when the horsemen were twenty paces in Idraf launched the first flight of arrows. A second and a third were sent before the Welsh archers could react. Two horsemen fell into the river. One horse was struck and galloped off down the river throwing its rider. Another horseman had an arrow sticking from his leg. The remaining eight spurred their horses as arrows rained on Idraf and the hidden archers. The range was closer, and the horsemen and archers could not see each other. Two men at arms and the squire were plucked from their saddles. The knight shouted something, and the riders switched from merely crossing the ford to attacking the hidden archers. That meant their own archers could no longer use their bows and as the Welsh were now side on to us and just forty paces from us, I deemed the moment was right, and I spurred Guy.

The other two had been waiting for my move and they followed me. The Welsh archers saw us and switched targets. It was incentive to close as quickly as we could with the mailed men. The three of us hit the two men on their left. My spear struck one of their shields and the man reeled. As he raised his arm for balance Wilfred's spear went under his arm and ended his life. Erik's axe smashed and crashed through the shield of the closest man at arms. It struck his shoulder and the man fell screaming into the water. I heard a cry from Wilfred and saw that he had been hit in the back by an arrow!

"Get to shore!"

It was now two of us against three of them and I wondered why the arrows had ceased flying and then an arrow came from our side of the bank and hit the knight's horse. I felt something hit my back, but I ignored it as I galloped at the nearest man at arms. He tried to turn to face me but failed and my spear struck his face as he attempted to block my spear with his shield. In his death throes, he grasped the end of the spear and pulled it from me. Leaving Erik to deal with the last man at arms I rode at the knight. As I did so I saw Paul lying in the river with three arrows in him and his brother, draped over his body, a spear in his chest. The knight's horse was bleeding from a wound while Guy was still full of fight. I felt something else hit my back. I deduced that it had to be a second arrow but unlike the first, this one hurt. It had penetrated the mail and aketon. There was no question in my mind; I would not seek surrender. The knight would die and pay for the deaths of the two brothers! I think that having his squire killed and his horse wounded had the same effect on the Welsh knight for he rode furiously at me.

Our swords clashed with a ringing of steel. Guy snapped at the wounded horse and it reeled. Sometimes it is a small almost insignificant action that wins the day. As the knight adjusted his seat to compensate for the animal's slip I punched with my shield and smacked him in the face. Blood spurted and it angered him. I was cold and intent on vengeance. He was hot and angry with the world! He stood in his saddle and attempted to split open my head. Guy was still agile, and I dug in my spurs and he leapt forward allowing me a free swing at the knight's back. He wore good mail, but I was young, powerful and with a well-made sword. The edge sliced through the mail and aketon to rip into his spine. It was a mortal blow. I wheeled around and saw the Welsh archers had entered the ford.

Erik shouted, "My lord! You are hurt!"

I shook my head, "It is nothing. Idraf!"

My archer emerged from the trees where he had taken shelter. He was leading three horses. He shook his head, "I will not leave them here, Sir Henry!"

I nodded, "Erik, let us go a little berserk!"

Laughing my Viking said, "Of course, my lord!"

Pulling up our shields we galloped at the Welshmen now stranded in the middle of the river. They had no mail and had thought we would flee. Instead, we charged them on mounts covered with the blood of their own men. A panicky man is a poor marksman. Their arrows flew over us as we smashed sword and axe into unprotected heads. They ran.

Idraf's voice halted us. "I have them, lord!"

We turned and galloped back across the ford. We kept going until we found Wilfred slumped over his saddle. Idraf led the two brothers' horses with their bodies draped over them.

"Erik, see to Wilfred. Idraf, fasten the bodies to the horses and I will go and watch the Welsh."

The wounded Welsh men at arms and archers were having their wounds tended on the other side of the river while three of the archers were recovering the horses. I saw, to my dismay, the rest of the archers as they appeared to the south. They had caught up. I wheeled Guy and rode to the others. "They will be after us within the hour. Idraf, I will lead the brothers' horses, you fetch Davy's." As he handed me the reins of the two horses and rode off, I said, "Erik, how is Wilfred?"

It was Wilfred who answered, "Hurt, my lord, for it was a bodkin and hit my shoulder. I cannot fight but I can ride, and I will not slow you down!"

"Then let us ride and see if we can outrun these persistent pursuers!"

Erik said, "Hold, Sir Henry." He rode up to me and I felt him touching my back. There was a double snap and he rode next to me showing me the two broken shafts of the arrows. "The bodkin is in your back, but it is not bleeding badly. Better that we leave it in. You are lucky, if that had been a war arrow then you would be bleeding like a stuck pig."

I did not argue but he was wrong. Had it been a war arrow it would not have penetrated the mail, but he was right in one respect, I was lucky!

It was slow going for we led many horses and two of us were wounded but we kept going. I began to hope that we might escape but, as we approached Denbigh, I saw that John, Davy and Rhiwallon had halted before the small town. Why had they disobeyed me? When we reined in and Eirwen saw the dead bodies draped over the saddles and the blood on our surcoats her hand went to her mouth.

"Rhiwallon, why have you halted?" He pointed to the houses. There was a barrier across the road and behind it were armed men and archers. "Idraf, with me. The rest be ready to charge when I give the word."

Davy said, "We should fall back!"

I shook my head, "There are forty and more Welshmen behind us!" I spurred Guy. I held up my right hand to show I meant to talk and not to fight. I saw Idraf nock an arrow and lay his bow across his saddle.

When I was forty paces from the barrier a Welsh voice shouted, in English, "Halt, Englishman, you go no further. Lord Maredudd has offered a reward for you. Surrender or you will die."

I nodded and smiled and said with a confidence I did not feel, "I was just going to offer you the same terms." I stood in the saddle and pointed north, "At Dyserth is my uncle and knights of my familia. Surrender and we will not destroy your village." We had attacked it once, but we had not destroyed the buildings. "Lord Maredudd is in Anglesey. We are your neighbours, who do you fear the most?"

I saw that my words had worried him. I think they might have allowed us through had not Erik shouted, "They are here!"

The Welshman heard the words and shouted, "Get them!"

It was the last thing he said as Idraf's arrow smacked into his head and then we turned and fled. Arrows came after us, but they were hurriedly drawn and released. They missed. I reined in.

"John give the child to his mother. Idraf, Rhiwallon, you need to keep our pursuers at bay."

Davy said, "What about the men of Denbigh?"

I laughed, "Mercers and farmers will not leave the barricade. It is these twenty men we must defeat and with just two archers and two men at arms and a squire…"

Wilfred said, "I can fight!"

"No, you cannot." I drew my sword, "Are you ready?"

Erik had the joy of battle in his eyes, "We will show them, my lord! Another berserker charge?"

I nodded, "If Idraf and Rhiwallon cannot hold them then, aye!"

I saw that the men coming up the road had dismounted and were marching with nocked arrows towards us. This would be our last stand. Just then I heard a commotion and I feared that I had been wrong, and the men of Denbigh were coming at us. I saw them running, but it was not towards us, it was into the fields and I saw why, Sir Gerard and Sir Alfred were leading a column of men at arms. It was a patrol and we had been saved. We moved to the side as they thundered down the road. The Welsh archers saw them just too late to do anything and it took the work of moments to slaughter them. We were saved!

Sir William

Chapter 20

When Christmas approached and my nephew had not returned, I feared the worst. The poor weather meant we had not had any patrols out and, even had I wanted to, I could not have reached ... wherever David of Wales had taken him! Sir Gerard, Sir Richard, Sir Mark and Sir Alfred were all keen to ride south and to search for him. It was not until almost Christmas that their frustration boiled over. They came to me on Christmas Eve and it was Alfred who acted as spokesman.

"Sir William, uncle, give us leave to ride forth and find my cousin and his men. It has been some time since they left!"

I heard the anguish in his voice. Henry Samuel was the most popular of my father's grandchildren. Perhaps it was because his father had been so treacherously slain, and I understood his concern. I had thought much the same as Alfred over the last month, but I had also analysed the situation and realised the futility of randomly sending men out in such harsh conditions. I waved them to seats around the table. Sir Robert Pounderling stood diplomatically by the fireplace with his knights. We all shared the same hall and the same dangers, but this was a problem for my retinue, the men of the north. "Sir Richard, pour some wine and let us see if that will cool the blood!"

Sir Gerard, who had taken Sir Alfred under his wing, said, "Your nephew is right, lord, it has been too long."

"Really, Sir Gerard?"

"He should have been back by now!" He said, somewhat lamely for that was obvious.

"Did David of Wales know exactly where his family was to be found?" There was silence but Alfred felt obliged to shake his head. "So, for all we know they are still seeking the family. We have no idea where he will be except that it is south-west of Llangollen. Our best Welsh speakers are with Henry Samuel so how could we find them? I expect he is still looking for David of Wales gave himself a monumental task."

"In this weather?"

"Sir Mark, if this was your family that you sought would you give up because it was cold?" He shook his head. I went on the offensive. "Let us imagine, if you will, that they have been captured or killed do you not think that the Welsh would either ask for ransom or crow about the deed?"

Sir Gerard said, "They asked no ransom for you, my lord!"

"And that was a trap!"

Sir Richard said, "What I cannot understand is why the old man chose to do this in the depths of winter! It was not like David to be so foolish!"

I had kept my word but, in my heart, I knew that I would never see David of Wales again. Each day he had spent with us had seen a daily deterioration in his condition and they had been away so long that I feared he was dead already. "He was, perhaps, foolish but he had no choice." I paused, "David of Wales is dying, and he has but months to live. It may well be that he cannot return because of his illness."

That stunned them into silence. It was broken by Sir Richard, "I am sorry I called him foolish. I should have known better. Did Henry Samuel know?"

"Of course, and he also knew how unlikely it was that they would find the family, but he still went."

Alfred nodded, "He would, and you think that they are still alive, Henry Samuel and his men, I mean."

That was the real question and I asked it of myself a hundred times a day, "I pray so and in my heart, I believe he is still alive." I saw Sir Robert looking at me with a bemused expression on his face. Suddenly many of my actions and words would make sense for I had kept my word until then. It was Christmas Eve and I thought it right that they all know. "What I will say is that when this snow dissipates, and the weather improves then you can go out and seek them. By then it will be time to begin our offensive against Prince Dafydd. We can kill two birds with one stone; seek those who are lost and make the Welsh pay for their summer campaign!"

My words meant that although Christmas was not quite as joyous as one would have wished, there was an air of hope in the castle and as word spread about David of Wales and his illness so the men at arms and archers we had brought went to the newly finished and, as yet, unconsecrated chapel, to pray for the senior warrior whom they had all served under in Stockton Castle.

The weather changed at the end of December and I knew that the knights, not to mention the archers and men at arms were keen to begin but this was a misleading land. The weather where our castle was situated might be more benign than further south or closer to the mountain. Sir Robert and I were not convinced that it had broken until the first days of January and even then, neither of us was certain how long it would last. I divided my command into three. Sir Gerard and Sir Alfred would take men and scout out the Denbigh Road. Sir Richard would head for Mold and scout out their defences. I would take a third of our men and see if they had occupied Deganwy. I know that I annoyed all but Sir Richard with my caution but I insisted that the day before we left on patrol, we each sent a handful of archers to ensure that the roads were clear. When they returned my caution was justified. The roads east and west were clear but Denbigh, which was the nearest Welsh town to Dyserth, looked to have armed men within. I debated switching conroi, but I knew that would damage Alfred's confidence.

He wished to be the one to hunt for his cousin. As we waited in the false light of pre-dawn, I gave my instructions one more time. "I want every knight, man at arms and archer within these walls before it is dark, not a moment later! Is that clear?"

They nodded, albeit reluctantly and I led Sir Mark and our men along the coast road. Apart from my archer scouts no one had been down this road since we had scouted Llanfairfechan. As we rode along it, I saw little sign of snow. The pockets of white which we had had close to Dyserth were now melted and I had a bad feeling about the situation. Even Rhuddlan at the mouth of the Clwyd looked as though it had enjoyed a milder time than we had. I was increasingly of the opinion that Dyserth was not the best site for a castle. We had just fifteen miles to travel and yet I was aware that we were being watched. The archers who had scouted the road were not native Welshmen. Idraf would have sniffed out the enemy. I just knew that on the slopes to the south of us were Welshmen. Birds would take to the sky before we reached them and yet close to us there was neither beast nor fowl.

"Harry Longbow, take ten archers and ride up into the foothills. Let me know if we are being watched."

"Aye, my lord."

Geoffrey and Dick flanked me. The winter had seen Dick grow four inches and he had begun to broaden out. He now rode a small palfrey and looked like a young squire these days. His incarceration had changed him. Geoffrey rubbed the back of his neck. "There are Welshmen out there, lord!"

"You feel it too?"

He nodded, "I can neither see nor smell anything untoward, but they are there."

"They may be just watching us but that does not mean we are not in danger."

As we headed away from the coast we had to pass through a wood, and it was there that Harry Longbow flushed out the watchers. He was not Welsh, but Harry was cunning. He later told me that he had seen signs of men watching us and knew that they were listening for the horses' approach. He sent half his men ahead in a long loop. As we travelled through the woods with raised shields, we heard the shouts as Harry's scouts clashed with the Welsh ones. When two men burst from the woods riding ponies, I did not hesitate but spurred my horse and led my men to apprehend them. As we burst from the woods and descended towards the River Conwy, I saw that there was an army there. They were camped and they were not expecting us, but they did outnumber us!

I reined in and shouted, "Archers dismount! Horse holders!"

This was not a time for reckless action. I had less than fifty men with me and we could ill afford to lose any. The Welsh horns sounded as the camp stirred to life.

"Do we fight, Sir William?"

"Only if we have to! Let us gauge what it is we face. Count them!"

It was clear that they did not have many mounted men. I saw the banners of a dozen knights. Each would have a horse and possibly a second while their squires would also have a horse. The Welsh did not tend to use men at arms but I saw at least ten and their horses. Their greatest threat lay in their archers and spearmen. This land was perfect for both. There were few places for a charge of mailed heavy cavalry. I looked at the campfires and used the normally reliable equation of ten men to each fire. The Welshmen's spears were stacked together and that identified them. The Welsh bowmen had their precious staves in cases. I estimated two hundred archers and two hundred spearmen.

Harry Longbow and his scouts arrived. "We slew four but two escaped."

I pointed to the camp, "And they fled there. My guess is that they would have ridden to the camp as soon as they thought we might see it. Join the other archers!"

What stopped them just charging us was the number of our horses. They outnumbered us but not in horses. This was a stalemate. We had time until it was broken, and I took out some ham from my saddlebag and chewed it. I washed it down with ale from my skin. Some men dismounted to make water and we waited. The impasse was finally ended when whoever led them, I did not recognise the banner for the Welsh all tended to fight under the Welsh dragon, pointed his sword at us. They were half a mile away and any words he might have shouted were in Welsh and lost to me. The archers scurried forward while the spearmen formed ranks and began to march behind their locked shields. Their horsemen formed up on their left.

"Do we charge, Sir William?"

"No, Sir Mark. We will bloody them a little and then fall back in good order. Do not fear, we will return and demolish this little camp, but we will do so with every man we have. If I fight, then I want to win! We have not enough men for a glorious defeat!"

We had the small advantage of a slight incline which gave our men a greater range, but our fifty archers were outnumbered by four to one. I nudged Lion down the slope. "Harry Longbow, I would just hurt them and then retire. Five flights and then mount and fall back. We will cover your retreat!"

"Aye, Sir William."

I went back to the men at arms and watched as this game of archery chess was played out. Harry would wait until he thought the Welsh were ready to stop and release. An archer cannot march and pull a bow. As soon as they stopped then five arrows would be sent in rapid succession. Archers wear neither mail nor helmets and two hundred and fifty arrows would find flesh. It was also hard to concentrate on sending a well-flighted arrow when fletched death was descending. The leader of the archers told us when they were about to stop, for he stopped and raised his bow. The first fifty arrows killed him and twelve others. The next four flights added to the carnage and then, as a ragged volley was sent in our direction Harry and his men ran up the slope and mounted their horses. Four of our archers were hit but, as I saw them mounting their horses, I knew that they were not badly hurt. The Welsh spearmen began to run up the slope towards us, but the leader galloped before them and slapped them into line with the flat of his sword.

"Now we can go home!"

It had been a worthwhile journey. We had found enemies and they did not frighten me. There might be more at Deganwy and they might, indeed, be working on the castle but we could defeat this outpost and then decide how to take the other. The wait for the Welsh to attack delayed our return and it was after dark when we reached Dyserth and we approached the new outer defences. I wondered if the other patrols had returned and I was distracted. I did not notice the cheery faces for I was looking down. It was as we entered the gatehouse to the bailey that I was aware of all the people who were there. I heard children's laughter and when I looked up, as I dismounted, I saw Henry Samuel running towards me. There are times when you act as a lord and others when you forget such nonsense, and this was one. I simply ran to him and hugged him. "You are safe!"

We held each other there for what seemed a lifetime and then pulled apart. I did not say a word, but the question was in my eyes. He nodded, "We found his family and therein lies a tale, but I will answer the question in your eyes. David of Wales died a few days after Christmas. He was happy at the end and he had enough time with his family to etch their memories into his heart."

I nodded, I was both sad and relieved. "Any losses?"

"The brothers, Peter and Paul, fell south of Denbigh. They died well. Wilfred is wounded but other than that we survived."

I was pleased for it could have been much worse. I would send money to Peter and Paul's mother. Her loss would be hard to bear. "Then tonight we will feast."

I saw him smile, "First there is someone you must meet."

I was suddenly aware of people standing in the doorway to the keep. There were two young boys as well as a man with a scarred face and two attractive young women. One was a stunning redhead and I knew immediately that it had to be David of Wales relative, but she looked to be too young to be his niece. My nephew was right. Here was a tale. It was clear the two women were not related but the younger one looked beautiful too.

Henry Samuel said, "This is Myfanwy who was David of Wales' great-niece and these are her children, Davy and Dai and her husband Davy."

I smiled, "I know who they are and I am just pleased that all of you are well. What I did not know was that David of Wales' family was the one which gave me shelter!"

Myfanwy knelt and kissed my hand, "My lord, thank you for letting David of Wales come to us. We did not have him for long, but it has changed our lives."

I nodded, "I owed Captain David much as do all of my family and we pay our debts. I did little except allow this young man to have an adventure."

I turned to a grinning Henry Samuel who took the young green-eyed beauty by the hand and, kissing it, said, "And this is Eirwen, the woman I shall wed!"

It was when Sir Richard and the rest of my knights burst out laughing that I knew I had stood in silence for an excessive amount of time. I took her hand and kissed it, "Forgive me, Eirwen, for my nephew left a bachelor and now…"

She smiled and the world seemed a happier place, "There is nothing to forgive, uncle."

Sir Robert said, "Why we carry on a conversation in this cold, wind-blasted bailey is beyond me. Come inside for all of us wish to hear this tale!"

There was no longer enough room for all to dine together but those who had endured this quest, Erik, Idraf and the others were invited along with all the knights and senior captains. The others would eat in the newly finished warrior hall. My nephew had changed. As he told the story I saw and heard a young man who had grown up in the time he had been away. Even had he not been my nephew the story would still have gripped me as it did all of the others. I was there with him, at Bala, as he told me of the rescue of the two boys. They were seated on their parents' knees awed by the number of knights around us. When I had been told he was to wed I was shocked, but it was clear, as he spoke and Eirwen stared lovingly up at him, that they were in love. I did not doubt that she would be adored when she went to meet our family in Stockton. but I also knew that Henry Samuel would be in trouble with the matriarch of our family, my mother!

The archers and warriors who were present were all touched by the tale of David of Wales. I knew that it affected all of them for I saw it in their eyes. They were seeing the alternative to a death in battle. Henry Samuel was eloquent in his description of the joy of finding a family after so many years without one. That, too, made the older, unmarried warriors think. They could still fight and while they might be away from their family for some time there would be a home to which they could return and there was a prospect of children and grandchildren for their old age. Erik Red Hair was quite right, we had been meant to come here and to stay over the winter. All of us were changed.

When the tale had finished there was a gentle buzz in the hall as those seated close to each other spoke. I was next to Henry Samuel but he and Eirwen only had eyes and words for each other. I turned to Sir Robert, "This news of Maredudd is disturbing. He is a dangerous man for this keeping of hostages tells us much about him."

Sir Robert nodded, "I confess that I had underestimated the man. Even after he abducted you and your family, I thought he was an opportunist. Now he is close to the Prince." He sipped his wine, "Does Dafydd know the danger he is in?"

"It was you, I believe, who told me that he is not close to the crown. Owain and Llewellyn are. If you were Prince Dafydd who would you fear had designs on the crown? Maredudd is not young like Owain and Llewellyn he might be seen as an advisor, and a kindly one at that." He gave me a surprised look. "Where did he keep his hostages? About as far away from Anglesey and the Prince as he could. That is another reason for him to hate Henry Samuel."

We ate in silence for a while. Sir Robert said, "This force you found today, you believe it is just part of a larger one?"

"They were far enough from the Conwy to make me believe so. I will take all of my men next time and try to bring them to battle. As soon as March arrives, we will have to go on the offensive anyway and this way we can disrupt their preparations until King Henry sends us more men. Do you need my men for the building work?"

"No, now that the outer defences are done and the warrior hall it is just a case of the masons polishing up the work and making it look like the King's Castle. The chapel will need time, but it will need care too. Indeed, I had planned on riding to Mold to view the possibility of recapturing that castle."

"You command here but I would advise you to wait until we have scouted out the River Conwy. We cannot fight on two fronts. If we can slow down the work on Deganwy then we have time to take Mold." There was a sudden burst of laughter from Davy and his family and I said, "What do we do with David of Wales' family? My nephew did the right thing by bringing them here but we both know that it might be years until they can return to their home. So long as Maredudd lives and stays on Anglesey they must stay here."

"I have already given that some thought. There are four farms close to the castle. The Welsh there fled when we came. They have lain empty ever since then. The houses are in good repair for we used them to house the builders. Now there are only two which are occupied. They can have one. Indeed, when our men go raiding, they can even bring sheep and cattle back for them to farm. They have endured much, and we owe Davy of Llanarmon. He gave you shelter and that has made him a refugee. I will go and speak with Davy now."

Henry Samuel saw Sir Robert head for Davy, and he turned to me. I explained why. "He goes to offer him a farm close to the castle. Davy and his family will have just one night to live in this cramped castle." I saw disappointment on his face. "Nephew, I am delighted with your news but Eirwen is a maiden and you are a young man. It is better to remove temptation eh?"

He looked outraged, "Her honour is safe!"

I smiled, "Of that, I have no doubt, but you are now back with this conroi and I will need you to be focussed. For Davy and his family's sake, we not only have to defeat Prince Dafydd but also rid this land of Maredudd and Angharad."

"You are right, Uncle, but this will be hard."

"Our duty is almost half over. In six months, we shall ride north and there you can be wed... after you have asked my father for permission. You are his knight and while I do not doubt that he will give permission, you must ask!"

In the end, it was a week before we rode. A storm filled with snow, sleet and rain hit us and we endured four days of it. We managed to move the family to the farm and even found a small number of sheep to be the nucleus of their flock. When the storm ceased the archer scouts reported that the coast road was inundated with sand and weed. We gave it another day and then I took the largest force I had led since we came to Wales on a raid to hurt the Welsh. My father had replaced Sir Geoffrey and Sir Robert's men and our losses with more than twice the number of replacements. Alfred, after his success at Denbigh, was keen to get to grips with a larger enemy which would be a truer test of his skills. Perhaps he thought his father had failed, I do not know but as we rode along a road which looked, in places, like a beach I took the opportunity to offer him counsel.

"Alfred, the men we go to fight will be a different prospect to the ones you chased along the road to Denbigh. Henry Samuel had killed their knight and the couple of men at arms you had to fight were as nothing. When we reach the camp guarding Deganwy they will have archers in greater numbers than you have ever seen. You saw the wound in Henry Samuel's back?" He nodded. "He was lucky, and he knows it. Wilfred son of John was not as lucky, and he is in Dyserth for he is not yet fit for war. Use your shield and keep your head down, quite literally. Men who look up often see the arrow which kills them. Your helmet will protect you."

He nodded, "I know, Uncle, and this is the same conversation I had two days ago with Henry Samuel and that giant of a Viking!" He lowered his voice, "I wish my father had taken me to war more but he did not for he thought to protect me. I am not much younger than Henry Samuel and yet he led the knights when you were captured. I have much to learn but I was named after the Warlord and I would honour his name by living up to it."

"From the stories my father told me the Warlord who regained the throne for the son of the Empress began life as a lowly knight who had to learn to become a warrior. You have time!"

As much as I respected Harry Longbow and the other English archers, I always felt happier with the Welsh ones at the fore. Idraf and Rhiwallon rode four miles ahead of the rest of us and were our hunting dogs sniffing out the Welsh. We were close to Colwyn when we saw them descend from a wood to the south of us.

He pointed south and west, "Sir William, the Welsh are camped yonder. I spoke with Harry Longbow before we left, and I believe it is the same camp they had when you scouted. The storm has hurt them. You can see the wrecked tents and they do not seem to have a large number of horses."

"Then we have a chance to begin to win back this land! Is there cover enough for you and the archers to flank them from the south?"

Idraf looked west. He was not looking at what was there but beyond the horizon and picturing the terrain. "Aye, lord."

I looked up at the sky. "Soon it will be noon. I will attack just after noon."

"And we will be ready!" He whistled and waved his arm. Mounting his horse, he headed up into the trees to ride around the enemy camp.

"Dismount and check girths. Let the horses drink. We attack just after the sun begins its journey west." I turned to Dick and Geoffrey. "I want the squires and pages under your command, Geoffrey. When we sweep into their camp, I hope to drive them towards the river. I believe there is another camp there. I want somewhere we can defend when we return. You and the squires will turn the Welsh camp into an English bastion. Idraf and the archers will join you, but it is you will command."

"Am I ready?"

I smiled, "When we return north to Stockton then I will ask my father to give you your spurs, Richard here, is ready to become my squire." I knew I had said and done the right thing for both looked pleased. They did not see that this was my way of keeping them safe!

We headed for the trees overlooking the Welsh camp. Idraf's news had pleased me and I had my battle plan in place. The knights and those men at arms who were better mounted would ride in the front rank. The rest would form two lines behind. I hoped that the sudden appearance of so many mounted and mailed men at the same time as they were showered with arrows might make the Welsh break. If they stopped to count, then they might decide to fight. I wanted a broken enemy.

You cannot form three lines less than half a mile from an enemy without them being aware and even though we did it quickly the Welsh horns sounded, and the enemy prepared to receive us. I lowered my spear and we descended the slope. We kept a steady pace for I wished to maintain the integrity of our lines. I was also allowing Idraf and our hidden archers to choose their moment well. We were just three hundred paces and cantering when the arrows descended from the right into the Welsh. The effect was devastating. We had had time in the winter to make many arrows and Idraf's archers showered more than a thousand in the time it took for us to come into range of the Welsh arrows except that there were none returned. The Welsh archers turned to loose at the invisible enemy as our horses reached their maximum speed and, pulling back my arm we ploughed into shocked and disordered knights, archers, spearmen and men at arms. Those who were able simply turned and ran to the horse lines. Idraf and his archers could loose at those without fear of hitting us. My spear was pulled back and struck down so often that my forearm muscles burned with the effort. Our speed slowed as we negotiated tents and dead bodies. It meant that those on foot who fled were going at the same speed as we were. I saw that they were heading for Deganwy and, in the distance, I saw the standards and tents of their camp. They had come to continue King Henry's work and build their own defence at the mouth of the Conwy.

This was the reverse of the situation in the autumn. Now the Welsh builders were having to down their tools and grab their weapons. Their archers would be unable to use their bows effectively for fear of hitting their own men who were fleeing towards them. The land between the defensive camp and the castle was filled with our men on horses slaying all around them and the Welsh trying to get into the unfinished castle. I knew that I had to judge the moment to withdraw well. I wanted to inflict as much damage as I could and yet lose as few men as possible. It was a mailed warrior who broke my spear as I thrust down at his back. The spearhead caught in his surcoat and the mail links; it was dragged from my hand and as the man fell, I drew my sword. I now had to lean from my saddle.

When I reached the ditch they had dug I saw that they had built a small wooden bridge to aid their passage and I led the men at arms who had followed me over it. They had a crane in place and, as I reined in to give Lion a rest, I slashed at the ropes which held a large rock in place. We had obviously interrupted their work. The Welsh were too busy trying to get inside the gatehouse which King Henry had finished to worry about us and as the rope was severed the rock crashed not only into the crane itself but rolled into the ditch. The gate slammed shut and the first arrows flew from the wall. Glancing around I saw that I only had thirty men with me. The rest were spread out on the flat ground and enjoying the sport of skewering Welshmen. Some of the enemy were racing to the river to try to escape that way.

We had done enough and turning in my saddle I shouted, "Back and drive the rest of the Welsh into the river!"

Even as we turned an arrow struck Edward of Wiske in the back. Edgar, his friend, grabbed his reins and led him to safety. We rode away from the arrows and towards the remnants of the Welsh camp. Some surrendered. They hoped that a knight would accept their surrender. We had few knights and the men at arms I led were ruthless. Barely a dozen managed to successfully surrender. Another forty or so who braved the mouth of the Conwy also survived and dragged themselves ashore. I watched as more bodies were washed out to sea.

It was late afternoon by the time we returned to the Welsh camp we had destroyed just after noon. Geoffrey and the squires had done a good job, aided, no doubt, by Idraf. The Welsh had obligingly brought a small flock of sheep to feed their builders. We would eat some and take the rest back. I had Alan Longsword assess the damage and, as I tasted some of the food the squires had cooked, he came back to me.

"Three men dead, lord, Alan the Grey tumbled from his horse and broke his neck. Eight men are wounded but all will live and are not maimed."

"Good. And the Welsh?"

He shook his head, "Too many to count, my lord. Let us say that I do not think they will be able to continue their building works."

Idraf came over to me to report that none of his archers had been hurt. "When we leave, Idraf, leave a couple of men in the woods to watch them. I would like to know if we have to come back and attack again or if they will leave."

"Aye, lord. If you were to ask my opinion, then I believe that they will leave. Unlike King Henry, Welshmen are not natural builders. They have managed little since we were here."

"Good."

My knights gathered around the tent Geoffrey had commandeered for me. They were in high spirits, especially Alfred. I listened to them as they described their battles, blow by blow. In truth, it had been easy, almost too easy. When King Henry had led us east the previous year, we could not have dreamed of such a victory and I knew why, Prince Dafydd was a better commander. He was obviously still on Anglesey and did not realise that there were still English warriors close to Wyddfa. As I smelled the food being cooked, I worked out that the men who had crossed the river would go to Conwy to fetch boats. They would either sail back to Deganwy or, more likely, sail to Anglesey to tell the King. I watched Idraf approach.

"I have the men who will watch, and we have managed to salvage more than two thousand arrows. The Welsh had a good store of them, and our attack was so swift that they just abandoned them."

I waved him to the seat next to me, "I have spoken to Henry Samuel about David of Wales but I would hear about his end from the likes of you who were archers and served with him for a long time."

I poured him some of the ale we had liberated.

"He was happy, my lord. I had known him since I came as a young archer to serve Sir Thomas and I never heard him laugh as much in all those years as he did in those last days. If I had not known that he had a worm devouring him from within I would have sworn that he was going to live forever. He did not eat while we were away, and I am not sure I saw him eat when we were at Dyserth and yet he seemed not to need it. Those two boys were the best of medicine for him and he loved them."

"When did the end come?"

"He was really ill on Christmas Eve but recovered on Christmas Day and then he deteriorated hour by hour over the next days." My face must have shown my thoughts. "Why do you ask, lord?"

"My knights came to me on Christmas Eve and asked me to search for David and the rest of you. Had I heeded their request then we might have found you."

Idraf shook his head, "You would not, lord. We found the farm, but it took some days and we had to use Welsh speakers. With the bad weather we had, you might have fallen victim to Lord Maredudd's men. He almost trapped us and but for Sir Henry they would have done."

"He did well then?"

Idraf smiled, "Lord, it was like serving with you or your father. I would follow him anywhere and there are few others I would say that about."

We left the next day and drove not only the sheep we had found but we also gathered others from the fell sides as we headed home. The archers we had left reached Dyserth a day later. The Welsh had abandoned Dyserth and the builders and survivors were taken off by ship. We assumed to Anglesey. It was a small victory but a victory nonetheless and that gave us hope!

Chapter 21

Our losses had not been severe, but I decided that we would wait for our attack on Mold until the men were fully recovered, and the weather had improved. That proved to be a fortuitous accident. We had not been totally isolated from our neighbours and both Sir Robert and I had frequently visited the monastery of St. Kentigern in the town of St. Asaph. It was the nearest church to us and until our own chapel had been built it was the only place of worship. We got on well with Bishop Dywi who was a practical man and he quickly realised that if we were welcomed then we would leave his monastery and town alone.

I visited the monastery the week after we had returned from the raid on Deganwy. I wished to pray for David of Wales and to light a candle for him. Henry Samuel had told me how the only confession he had been able to make had been to him. I prayed so that God might overlook the fact there had been no priest there at his end. Bishop Dywi waited until I had finished and he, quite naturally, asked me the purpose of my visit for I had been alone, Geoffrey and Dick waited without, watching the horses. I was honest with him and told him the tale, all of it, including the abduction of the boys. I thought he would just nod and bid me farewell, but he did not.

"Come with me, Sir William. We will share a glass of wine and I will tell you some news which you might find disturbing."

Intrigued I followed him. He made certain that we were alone and, after closing the door put his chair so close to mine that we were practically touching. "News came to me about this a week since, that Prince Dafydd is seriously ill, dying it is said."

That shocked me for he was not old. "Dying?"

"I have many friends at the court of Prince Dafydd and the priest who brought me the news was one of those friends. He left the court for he feared for his life. He believed that the Prince had been poisoned."

I closed my eyes, "Lord Maredudd!"

"More likely his evil daughter Angharad." He shivered and quaffed the wine in one. "I knew her when she was growing up and she was the embodiment of evil. I confess that I gave no credence to the story that you had murdered Lord Iago. When they married, I found it a most unlikely union except that he was the richest man in Gwynedd."

"But, even so, to murder the Prince…"

"They are ambitious, and their timing could not be better. The brothers Owain and Llewellyn have fallen out and wage war on one another. Lord Maredudd now controls the army of Gwynedd. He will choose one of the brothers and when they marry Angharad, he will have the crown. I confess that is why many people have fled the court. One arrived yesterday with news which leads me to believe that the Prince is actually not just dying but dead!"

I poured myself some more wine and said, "And why do you tell me this?"

He smiled, "You are English, and I do not wish the English to rule my land, but you are also honourable and fair. I would rather have a Welsh ruler but not Maredudd or one controlled by him. You can stop this evil creature. Llewellyn and Owain rule the land south of Wyddfa. This is Maredudd country. He will come here to reclaim it."

"Thank you for your honesty and you have given me much to think on."

I rode back to Dyserth as fast as my hackney would carry me. Geoffrey and Dick, who had come with me were more than intrigued but I needed to speak with Sir Robert, Sir Richard and Henry Samuel first. When they heard the news, like me they were pleased that our greatest military threat was gone but dismayed that Lord Maredudd could seize power. It took Henry Samuel to point out the obvious. "Lord Maredudd wishes the crown but he does not have a ruler. The Welsh do not follow women and he is too old. He has to marry Angharad to a suitable candidate. That is either Owain or Llewellyn. As the Bishop said, they are south of here and winter ends later there. We have a chance now, uncle."

"A chance?"

"A chance to win the peace. We ride to Mold and demand that they surrender. They will have heard the news and if we had that in our hands then the route to Chester is secure. We could send there for help and reinforcements. If Maredudd succeeds in marrying his daughter to one of the rulers then we shall certainly need them."

Sir Robert pounded his left fist into his right palm. "You are right, Sir Henry! And I will write to King Henry. Now is his chance for a bloodless victory! With the brothers fighting he can bring whatever troops he can from Chester and Shrewsbury, that will be enough to cow two fighting brothers."

War in the West

They were both right but there was something else, even more draconian we needed to do. I nodded, "And while we do that, we find some ships."

"Ships?"

I saw that I had mystified them both although Sir Richard, who knew me well gave a knowing smile. I nodded, "We shall need ships to sail to Anglesey and to end the lives of Maredudd and Lady Angharad. We cannot allow them to become the new rulers of Wales."

I saw Henry Samuel nod, but Sir Robert shook his head, "That is against all the rules of war! You cannot do this thing!"

"Do not speak to me of rules. I was the one they kidnapped and planned to murder. My son and squire were abducted and what of the families whose sons were held hostage? Anyway, Sir Robert, I do not ask you to soil your hands. The knights and men at arms who have followed me from the north will do! I will not need a large force. I need trusted men who can be stealthy and...kill!"

I saw Sir Robert clutch at the cross around his neck. He feared for his soul, but he could not know that my family made a habit of such reckless behaviour. I turned from him, "Henry Samuel take Erik and Idraf. Find us enough ships to carry knights, twenty men at arms and twenty archers. Erik has something of the pirate in him and Idraf will know the places to seek such captains. Sir Richard, choose the men we shall need! I will go with Sir Robert to take Mold."

I felt energised not least because I saw a chance to end the war before the full year was up. Why had Maredudd killed the Prince now? Was it that the Prince suspected him and his motives? From what I had heard and experienced at first hand Prince Dafydd was a clever and resourceful leader. He would have seen through Maredudd. Perhaps his daughter had been too obvious in her attempts to seduce the Prince. This was pure speculation and would avail me little. We had to take advantage of the situation!

We left a week later and took almost all of the garrison with us. Mold Castle was just sixteen miles from us and we had constantly raided the land around it. We knew from our observations that the garrison had been on short rations for some time. As we rode towards the castle, we put all of our knights and men at arms, with polished helms and armour, at the fore. We surrounded the castle with archers and then we waited. We waited until the castellan, Dai of Flintshire, could wait no longer and he shouted, in English, which told me much, "What is it that you wish?"

Sir Robert shouted, "Surrender the castle to us and you and your men can walk from here and keep your arms. If you do not, we will reduce the castle and hang every living person we find!"

The pause told me that he was considering it and so I spoke, "In the last two weeks we have defeated the men who were building Deganwy castle and the building works are abandoned." I paused, "And I have heard, as, no doubt, have you, that Prince Dafydd is dead or if not he soon will be. Who will lead your armies then?"

Sir Robert waited a heartbeat and lied, "King Henry and an army are coming from Chester. I do not think we will need them for the four hundred archers we have will rain death upon your walls!" He put enough venom in his words to convince me.

The castellan nodded in resignation, "I have your word?"

"You have my word!"

And with that we retook Mold. I daresay we could have done so at any time in the past month, but hindsight is always perfect. We placed Sir Gerard in command with a hundred archers and twenty men at arms. We could afford to be generous for I would not need every man at arms with me. Sir Richard had already identified the best men to take

As we rode back Sir Robert said, "The King will be pleased with this. Will you not reconsider your rash decision?"

"It is neither rash nor reckless. I am cold and I have calculated. I take the best of men with me and I know my enemy. He fights through others and from behind men's backs. That sort of leader does not inspire loyalty. I cannot believe that men will fight for him."

The rest of the way back to Dyserth we rode in silence. I was mentally picking men to sail with me from the names Sir Richard had given, and Sir Robert, no doubt, was trying to find a way to distance himself from me so that he would not be tainted by my actions. It took three days for Erik to secure the two boats. They were small coastal traders and they did not come cheap. I did not mind for I hoped that King Henry would pay me back when he had peace and did not have to pay for knights. Even if he did not, I had hopes of treasure from the royal palace. While my archers and men at arms travelled to the coast to board, I sought out Henry Samuel.

"You need not go, Henry Samuel. You now have a bride to be and another family. I have knights and men at arms enough. There is no dishonour in staying here. Your rescue of the two boys is action enough."

He looked at me almost contemptuously, "Do you know so little of me, uncle? I am not Sir Geoffrey. I do not run when life becomes hard. I will come with you for it is the right thing to do. I have seen, as you have, the cruelty of Lord Maredudd. He must be killed then my new family, Davy and Myfanwy, will be able to return to their home and know that they will not be hunted. I know there is a risk, but I am of the Warlord's blood as are you. True, Eirwen may be sad when I leave but she knows my purpose. I am going and do not make that suggestion again, my lord!"

He was right and I was not embarrassed at bringing up the matter. If I had not, then I might have worried that he wished to be with Eirwen and not risking his life with me. We did not take squires and pages, much to the annoyance and frustration of my son. I had no time to explain and I was short with them. "You will stay here and the two of you will serve Sir Robert. I will return and there is an end to it."

We had sent the archers and men at arms first to begin loading the vessels and when we arrived, we were ready to board. We had no horses to load and we were soon able to sail. The two ships were not large and were overcrowded. I might have feared we would capsize before we even saw Anglesey but then I realised the captains knew what they were about. They would wish to enjoy the coins they had robbed us of and despite the terrifying motion they would not sink. We took no shields nor helmets. This would be a raid, pure and simple. We had men who had been to Aberffraw and we knew that we had less than three quarters of a mile to travel up a small stream to reach the royal palace. It was not a fortress for Anglesey itself was a fortress and when we landed, we should attain complete surprise. There was a motte and bailey castle in the centre of the royal enclosure, but it was not large. To that end, we intended the day and night voyage to end in the middle of the night. Of course, it would depend upon the tides. Sir Richard advised me to leave men on the boats to ensure that they were still there when we returned but we had too few men for such a precaution. Either we would succeed and be able to make our own way back or our bones would bleach the beach! I was convinced it would be the former.

Before we embarked, I had explained to all the men exactly what we would be doing. "In a perfect world we would capture both Lord Maredudd and Lady Angharad and take them back to Dyserth to stand trial but I am not a fool and I know that we live in a world which we have made imperfect. If the two surrender, then we take them but if they do not then they die. Priests and those who do not fight will be spared but all else will be put to the sword." I knew by looking in their eyes which of my men would baulk at killing a woman. There were enough of us who would kill her without losing a moment's sleep. Dick had woken in the night screaming for the first week after his return from her clutches and Geoffrey had told me of her evil. There were enough people to whom we could speak who had been to the royal palace for us to have an idea of what we would be facing. It was a palace rather than a stronghold. It lay almost on the beach and the river up which we would walk would give us a silent approach. I went through all of this in great detail with everyone before we boarded the two ships.

I had Alfred and Henry Samuel with me. Sir Richard had Sir Mark. I also let Sir Richard have Alan Longsword to command his men at arms. We had no squires with us, and Alan knew Sir Richard well. In a battle that could make all the difference. The two ships were not speedy. Erik Red Hair was contemptuous of their lack of lines and sailing qualities. He was right and if we had had more time then I would have chosen something swifter. We had left at night and dawn saw us still north of the island and heading for the channel between Ireland and the island. The deck stank of vomit for even though the seas had been relatively calm not all men were good sailors and Erik set them to cleaning the deck when we saw what they had done. It kept them occupied.

Alfred and Henry Samuel were with me at the bow while men hauled buckets of water to sluice the decks clean. "How many men will there be, uncle?"

"I know not. Prince Dafydd would have had his oathsworn but who knows if they were willing to follow Maredudd. Lord Maredudd had, perhaps, twenty bodyguards. We know this from the warrior hall we found but we are in the dark, Alfred. There could be as few as forty or as many as four hundred. When I spoke with the Bishop, he said there was accommodation for such a number, not in the castle but in the old warrior halls. My only fear is that Lady Angharad and Lord Maredudd secrete themselves away in the castle for I believe the two will cling on to whatever hope they have. They want power and they have gambled. So far they have not lost. Llewellyn and Owain are playing into their hands."

Henry Samuel was thoughtful, "Do you think, uncle, that our raid on the camp at Deganwy had something to do with Prince Dafydd's poisoning?"

"What do you mean?"

"We hurt the Welsh and inflicted a defeat. It may have seemed a good time to replace the Prince."

"It may have done but as Erik Red Hair will tell you when you throw a stone into a pool the ripples keep travelling long after the stone has settled on the bottom. We are mortals and cannot control much beyond the edge of a sword. If you are asking if I regret my actions, then I say no. I would do it all again! King Henry has paid us to defeat the Welsh and when that is done, we can go home. That is incentive enough. I pray that he comes north from London soon, for God has given us an opportunity now to end this war!"

We turned around the island at the tip of Anglesey, Holy Island, an hour before dark and tacked our way up the coast to Aberffraw. I was not confident that the two captains would wait for us and as they pulled onto the beach a mile or so from the palace, I confronted our captain. He held out his hand for the promised coins. I gave him one gold piece.

"What is this Sir William? We were promised ten!"

"And when we return then you shall have the other, and perhaps, more."

"What if you do not return?"

"You shall have to pray we do."

The captain looked behind me and saw Erik Red Hair and some of my other men at arms. The murderous looks let him know what he was in for if he abandoned us.

"Then I will pray for you, but we shall not wait close to the shore. Light a signal fire and we will come in if the tide is right!"

Erik leaned in, "Listen you miserable excuse for a sea captain, there is a river here and this tub will float in it. You will come when I signal you with my axe or I shall swim out and fetch the ships myself!" I knew it was sound and fury but even I felt fear at Erik's words. The sea captain nodded, and I knew that the boats would be waiting for us in the river.

The ship's crew ran a gangplank from the side of the bobbing ship. I led the way down it. Thankfully, I did not fall in, but I had to wade through waist-deep water to reach the beach. Others were not so lucky and splashes behind me told me that some men had fallen. It was just pride which was hurt. As soon as Idraf joined me I waved him and his archers forward. They ran up the beach which lined the twisting estuary. When we had all landed I left Sir Mark with the rearguard. He had with him four archers and four men at arms. He was to secure our escape. I hoped we would not need him, but a reserve was always handy.

We passed houses on the way to the palace, but the folk inside did not venture out. They were fishermen and those who eked out a living collecting shellfish and seaweed. Harry Longbow held up a hand to stop me. He was standing close by the sand dunes and he pointed at the low wooden wall which surrounded the ancient wooden buildings. I could just see, in the middle, the stone walls of the recently finished castle. It was smaller than Elsdon and I knew that the accommodation would not suit Lord Maredudd. He would stay in the royal palace itself. The castle was there in case of attack. I hoped that they would not know they were in danger.

Turning I pointed to the three knights I had with me. Each would lead their own men at arms and archers. They nodded and waved to the men they would lead so that we had four small columns. Sir Mark and his men waited at a discreet distance. Once Idraf had secured the gates then we would rush in and split up. Each of us would seek Lord Maredudd and his murderous daughter. John the Archer appeared and waved us. I slid my sword from its sheath and followed him. Idraf was wiping his dagger on the tunic of the dead sentry at the now open gate. There were two other bodies close by. Idraf and his killers had done well.

I could hear noise from a feasting hall some distance away. I also heard the sound of horses; there were stables nearby. As well as fires in the halls there were also open fires and I could smell food being cooked. The enclosure was overcrowded with buildings. The Bishop had told me that successive rulers of Gwynedd had added more and more. This suited us for it hid us from view and we could move silently in the shadows, unseen. I headed for the castle. When the alarm was sounded then it would be seen as a place of sanctuary and everyone would try to get there. I would be waiting for I guessed that Maredudd and his daughter would lead the charge!

The bridge was lowered, and the gate was invitingly open. I had Idraf and John the Archer with me. Idraf put his hand across my chest and shook his head. He nocked an arrow and edged forward. He had seen something I had not. There was a guard lounging against the stone of the gatehouse. As he appeared the arrow was released, and the sentry pinned to the wooden frame of the gate; the arrow had hit his throat and silenced him! I hurried forward. The stone keep was not large and I saw that it was even smaller than I had expected. A wooden stair led to a first-floor entrance and I raced up. The door was relatively new and did not creak as I opened it. I heard voices; they would be the guards. I risked widening it and saw that there was a table and four men were seated around it. They were throwing dice. I waved the rest of my men into the guard room. The six of us were almost all in when one of the guards turned around and saw us. Idraf and John had arrows nocked and they pointed the bows at the men while Idraf rattled out some Welsh. They nodded and, standing, placed their weapons on the table. We outnumbered them but there was more to it than that. I had been right and Lord Maredudd was not worth fighting for.

I asked, "How many are in the castle?"

I asked the question of Idraf but one of the guards answered. "We are the guards and there is a prisoner below." He pointed to a trapdoor in the floor.

War in the West

"John, Martin Longsword, see who is there." Just then I heard the distinctive sound of steel on steel. It was dulled for it came from the royal enclosure, but it told me that the battle had begun. "Idraf and Walter, secure the prisoners. Erik, come with me." Leaving the other men I had brought to watch the prisoners I ran with Erik to the gate. I nodded to the dead sentry and Erik pulled the corpse from the gateway and hurled it into the ditch.

"Lord, do we raise the bridge and close the gate?"

I shook my head. "No, we leave the rat trap open." It was frustrating for us to wait not knowing how my nephews and knights were faring, but my plan appeared to be working. I turned as I heard a noise from behind. I saw John the archer and Martin Longsword. They were half carrying a man who had obviously been tortured. "My lord, this is the man we found. He is one of Prince Dafydd's advisors. He is weak but he wished to speak to you." They laid the man on the ground and I knelt next to him. "Lord, he is close to death!"

"John, get on the fighting platform. Martin, you and Erik watch the path from the enclosure." I was aware of shouts and screams as men fought in the royal palace. "What is your name?"

"Maelgwn, the Prince Dafydd's keeper of the treasury. The Prince was murdered, lord. I tell you this because I know that the witch who did the deed fears you and my master and myself shall have vengeance."

"We will get you help!" I needed this man as a witness that the Prince had, indeed, been murdered.

He shook his head, "They have done for me and I shall not see the dawn. Let me speak. They sought to replace the Prince's wife with Angharad and did all in their power to make it happen."

"Lord, men are coming from the enclosure."

"Hold them!"

I looked down and saw that his eyes were closed. He was dead. I was about to stand when a claw-like hand grabbed my wrist. "The Prince began to suspect their motives. He sent away his wife and then…" This time he did die; I heard his death sigh. I stood with drawn sword and joined the others at the gate. Twenty or so men were rushing towards us. They were led by Rhodri, the so-called steward and I saw behind them, protected by three men with shields, were Lord Maredudd and his daughter.

There were just three of us and we barely filled the gatehouse. I recognised the sword in Rhodri's hand, it was the one I had seen him wear when I was taken. Martin shouted, "To Sir William!" There was no way that three of us in the gate and two on the fighting platform could hold off twenty odd men. Where were my knights and the rest of my men?

Erik ran at the advancing men. I had known that he would for that was his way, but it exposed my left side and I moved closer to the gatepost with the dead sentry's blood still on it. Rhodri was no coward and he came directly at me. As I raised my sword to block the swinging sword, I drew my dagger from behind me. Rhodri was a powerful man and his blow partially turned me. Although Martin managed to slay one man at arms my movement exposed his left side and he was run through by a spear. The spearman had little opportunity to celebrate his success for Idraf sent an arrow at him, from the steps of the keep, and it slammed into his head.

John, on the fighting platform, had slain four men while Erik Red Hair was bathed in the blood of the men he had slain but the gateway was now open and if Lord Maredudd and his daughter made it they could free their sentries and bar the keep! I had to force such distractions from my head as Rhodri rammed his own bodkin dagger at my eye. My ballock dagger saved my life as the bulbous cross piece held the needle pointed blade.

Rhodri laughed, "My lady put a spell on this sword, Englishman! You will die by magic. You might be the most skilled swordsman in the land, but you cannot fight my lady's magic. You will die!"

For some reason that strengthened my resolve. I said nothing but I twisted my dagger to expose his left shoulder and then sliced at his neck with my dagger. I did not break flesh, but the edge tore some links from his coif. It was a small victory. With Martin now dead, Lord Maredudd and his protectors ran past me. As I brought my sword from on high, I shouted, "Erik Red Hair, get Lord Maredudd!" My sword was blocked by Rhodri who no longer seemed as confident as a moment or two ago. From the corner of my eye, I saw Erik swing his axe around his head before hurrying after Lord Maredudd. I heard, in the distance, the sound of Henry Samuel's voice as he urged my men on. They would reach us, but would it be too late? There were two men still outside the castle and I saw one slain by John the archer before the other dropped his sword and raised his hands. Rhodri now saw his dilemma and he tried to back into the castle. As we turned a little, I saw Erik Red Hair fighting three men who were attempting to close the gate. Erik was wounded. He was like a cornered animal and he fought for his life. Rhodri rammed the bodkin at me again but this time I did not use my dagger to block the blow. He would go for my eyes again and there was a simpler defence. I ducked and the narrow bodkin sliced across the top of my coif. At the same time, I lunged upwards towards his throat with my sword and he blocked it but in doing so he raised his right arm and I drove my dagger under his armpit and into his neck. He dropped his weapon, and, sheathing the one I held I grasped the one the witch had put a spell upon. Rhodri's dead body slid to the ground, pumping his lifeblood across it.

Henry Samuel and my knights were a mere forty paces from us, but I simply turned and ran into the bailey. I was just in time for although Erik had slain one of his attackers he had been wounded again. I hurled myself at the two attackers and hacked and slashed with dagger and sword. I saw Lady Angharad turn and begin to curse me. Suddenly an arrow slammed into her back and she fell at her father's feet. Another arrow from John slew the last of Lord Maredudd's defenders and I slew the two who had been attacking Erik.

I shouted, "Hold! This snake is mine!" The rest of the men had been slain by my archers who would have emptied their arrow bags.

Lord Maredudd threw his sword to the ground. I saw that it was Geoffrey's, his family sword, "I surrender, and I will take King Henry's justice."

"Pick it up and fight for your life. I am King Henry's justice!"

"You would not kill an unarmed man! You are a knight and bound by the laws of chivalry!"

"When you abducted my son and squire and murdered Prince Dafydd, you put yourself beyond the law! Now pick up the sword for, believe me, I will take your head if you do not."

He picked it up and I put my dagger back into my belt. I would need no second weapon to deal with this apology for a man. I knew he would not make the first blow and so I swung from on high. He blocked it but not well and the edge of my sword rasped against his mail. He stepped back and swung at me. I blocked it and then pirouetted and brought my sword into the top of his leg. I broke mail and sliced into his leg. The blade was bloody, and he squealed.

"Enough, you have drawn first blood!"

I shook my head, "It is not as simple as that. You are going to die. Piece by piece. Drop of blood by drop of blood." I swung again and my sword smashed into the side of his knee. He screamed and dropped to the ground.

"Please, Sir William, I beg you!"

"What did I ever do to you that you sent murderers to my river, abducted my son and made me to be a murderer?"

"It was the Prince. He said that the only man he feared in battle was you! I had never heard of you, but I saw a way to get close to power.

You cannot know what it is like to be so close to the crown and yet know it will never be yours."

I put the tip of my sword to his throat, "The Prince knew that you sent killers after me?" I pushed so that a little blood trickled down his neck.

"No, no! He had too much honour. And then we thought to make him marry my daughter, but he was immune to her charms and had to die. If I am to die, then fetch a priest to hear my last confession!"

Pushing down on the sword I said, "You have just given it! Rot in hell!"

There was a laugh behind me, and I whipped around. The witch was not dead! "You are cursed, William son of Thomas the Bishop killer. I am dead but you and your spawn will be cursed I..." She got no further. I brought down my sword and severed her head from her body! I turned and saw my knights, all whole looking on in horror as the lifeblood of Lady Angharad ran down the cobbles of the bailey. It was over and we had won but was I now cursed?

Epilogue

Erik Red Hair was a tough man and he survived but he would not go to war again for some time; he had four wounds which needed to be stitched and seared. We reached Dyserth four days after we had ended Lord Maredudd's life. We had lost men but the treasure we had taken would be compensation. King Henry had sent his brother, the Earl of Cornwall, to begin the conquest of Wales. That the King and his brother were delighted was clear. With the brothers, Owain and Llewellyn fighting each other the King did not need to summon an army. He could make demands.

"My brother intends to have the Welsh cede the land east of the River Conwy to us and to acknowledge that King Henry is lord of Wales. You have done well, and you and your men are now released from your duty. The scutage you are owed will be forthcoming for we will take it from the Welsh. I shall deal with the brothers!"

Others might have been resentful that he and King Henry would garner the glory for our victory, but I did not care. I could go home. It would be a few months later that the Treaty of Woodstock confirmed that we had won. By then we would be back home, and Wales just a painful memory.

Davy and his family had a tearful parting from Eirwen. Ever since Christmas, or so Henry Samuel said, they had known the day would come but it had come a little quicker than they had expected. As Eirwen mounted the wagon, for we had booty to take back, I said, "And you will be welcome to visit in Stockton any time that you wish!"

Myfanwy nodded and said, "That is kind Sir William, but we all know that we will not stir from our home again. We will pray for Eirwen and my sons will never forget her. It is enough that we are all safe and can live our lives as David of Wales hoped. We will put his gold to good use. Our home will become stronger and we will reward our neighbours. All is well."

Henry Samuel rode next to the wagon all the way to Stockton. I rode with Geoffrey and Dick. "So, Geoffrey, now that you have your family sword back, I can have my father dub you and make you a knight."

"If it is all the same to you, Sir William, I would that you were the one to give me that honour. It is you I owe all to."

As we approached the ferry and I saw my father's standard flying over Stockton, Sir Richard said, "And do you think Sir Gerard will stay in Wales?"

I nodded. "The King has peace, but it will not last without better and stronger castles. I am confident that Sir Robert and Sir Gerard will cope but they will have to fight."

"And you, William, what of you? Are you content?"

I lowered my voice, "I do not believe in the supernatural, but I wonder if the witch did curse me. I shall visit the Bishop in Durham and seek his counsel."

Richard laughed, "I think she was just an evil woman and had no powers at all."

Was he right?

My mother and father strode down to the ferry. I was the first one off and after embracing both of them my mother said, "Who is that pretty young thing in the wagon, William?"

I smiled, "That, mother, is the girl Henry Samuel will marry!"

She looked at me with a shocked look, "What?"

My father laughed and put his arm around her, "You should know, my love, that when this family goes to war, sometimes the treasures we bring back are worth more than gold!" He turned to me, "I look forward to this tale and King Henry's involvement!" He then became serious. "And to hear of David of Wales and his fate."

I nodded, "He died content and King Henry is well pleased with us. We fought in his war in the west and, remarkably, we won. We are at peace."

My father put his arm through mine as we headed to the castle, "Until the next time he needs us!"

The End

Glossary

Buskins-boots
Chevauchée- a raid by mounted men
Courts baron-a court which dealt with the tenants' rights and duties, changes of occupancy, and disputes between tenants.
Crowd- crwth or rote. A Celtic musical instrument similar to a lyre
Fusil - A lozenge shape on a shield
Garth- a garth was a church-owned farm. Not to be confused with the name Garth
Groat- An English coin worth four silver pennies
Hautwesel- Haltwhistle
Hovel- a makeshift shelter used by warriors on a campaign- similar to a '*bivvy*' tent
Marlyon- Merlin (hunting bird)
Mêlée- a medieval fight between knights
Pursuivant – the rank below a herald
Reeve- An official who ran a manor for a lord
Rote- An English version of a lyre (also called a crowd or crwth)
Vair- a heraldic term
Wessington- Washington (Durham)
Wulfestun- Wolviston (Durham)

Historical Background and References

Henry III did embark on a failed war with France to support his Lusignan family and lost to King Louis at the Battle of Taillebourg where King Louis' 4,000 knights defeated King Henry's 1,600 and effectively ended King Henry's French ambitions. He was lucky that the Welsh and the Scottish borders were relatively quiet, but that peace did take many nobles to the continent to fight for their king and that allowed others to prosper at home. This was when Simon de Montfort began to increase his powers and those powers would eventually bring him into conflict with King Henry.

Scutage was a sort of tax. Some knights and lords of the manor did not wish to obey the King's command for service. They paid scutage which was used to reward those knights who gave more service than they owed. The amount varied but there were increasing numbers of knights, especially in the south and the midlands, who had a comfortable life and did not bother to supply their own men. They were more like men of commerce than warriors. The King would take his cut and then give the rest to the men who fought for him. Eventually, this would lead to the Free Companies. (See the Struggle for a Crown series. Book 1, Blood on the Crown.) The King would then pay the scutage to knights who were willing to do so.

The only fictitious characters amongst the Welsh are Lord Maredudd and his daughter. I needed a couple of villains. However, Dafydd did die in February 1246, which was almost six months after Mold Castle fell, Dyserth was besieged and the King lost the battle of Deganwy. Owain and Llewellyn fought each other and King Henry took advantage. The Treaty of Woodstock in 1247 ceded all of Wales east of the Conwy river to England. It was not to last. Unlike his son, Edward 1st, Henry III was not a very good soldier and had a tendency to make poor decisions.

When I begin the next book in the series (yet to be titled) I will be in a strange country for I have already written about this period in Lord Edward's Archer. I fear it will be a tricky one to write!

- Norman Stone Castles- Gravett
- English Castles 1200-1300 -Gravett
- The Normans- David Nicolle
- Norman Knight AD 950-1204- Christopher Gravett
- The Norman Conquest of the North- William A Kappelle

- The Knight in History- Francis Gies
- The Norman Achievement- Richard F Cassady
- Knights- Constance Brittain Bouchard
- Knight Templar 1120-1312 -Helen Nicholson
- Feudal England: Historical Studies on the Eleventh and Twelfth Centuries- J. H. Round
- English Medieval Knight 1200-1300 Christopher Gravett
- The Scandinavian Baltic Crusades 1100-1500 Lindholm and Nicolle
- The Scottish and Welsh Wars 1250-1400- Rothero
- Chronicles of the age of chivalry ed Hallam
- Lewes and Evesham- 1264-65- Richard Brooks
- British Kings and Queens- Mike Ashley
- Ordnance Survey Kelso and Coldstream Landranger map #74
- The Tower of London-Lapper and Parnell
- Knight Hospitaller 1100-1306 Nicolle and Hook
- Old Series Ordnance Survey map 1864-1869 Alnwick and Morpeth
- Old Series Ordnance Survey map 1868-1869 Cheviot Hills and Kielder Water
- Old Series Ordnance Survey maps 1863-1869 Hexham and Haltwhistle

Griff Hosker
June 2020

Other books by Griff Hosker

If you enjoyed reading this book, then why not read another one by the author?

Ancient History

The Sword of Cartimandua Series
(Germania and Britannia 50 A.D. – 128 A.D.)
Ulpius Felix- Roman Warrior (prequel)
The Sword of Cartimandua
The Horse Warriors
Invasion Caledonia
Roman Retreat
Revolt of the Red Witch
Druid's Gold
Trajan's Hunters
The Last Frontier
Hero of Rome
Roman Hawk
Roman Treachery
Roman Wall
Roman Courage

The Wolf Warrior series
(Britain in the late 6th Century)
Saxon Dawn
Saxon Revenge
Saxon England
Saxon Blood
Saxon Slayer
Saxon Slaughter
Saxon Bane
Saxon Fall: Rise of the Warlord
Saxon Throne
Saxon Sword

Medieval History

The Dragon Heart Series

War in the West

Viking Slave
Viking Warrior
Viking Jarl
Viking Kingdom
Viking Wolf
Viking War
Viking Sword
Viking Wrath
Viking Raid
Viking Legend
Viking Vengeance
Viking Dragon
Viking Treasure
Viking Enemy
Viking Witch
Viking Blood
Viking Weregeld
Viking Storm
Viking Warband
Viking Shadow
Viking Legacy
Viking Clan
Viking Bravery

The Norman Genesis Series
Hrolf the Viking
Horseman
The Battle for a Home
Revenge of the Franks
The Land of the Northmen
Ragnvald Hrolfsson
Brothers in Blood
Lord of Rouen
Drekar in the Seine
Duke of Normandy
The Duke and the King

New World Series
Blood on the Blade
Across the Seas
The Savage Wilderness
The Bear and the Wolf

The Reconquista Chronicles
Castilian Knight
El Campeador

The Aelfraed Series
(Britain and Byzantium 1050 A.D. - 1085 A.D.)
Housecarl
Outlaw
Varangian

The Anarchy Series England 1120-1180
English Knight
Knight of the Empress
Northern Knight
Baron of the North
Earl
King Henry's Champion
The King is Dead
Warlord of the North
Enemy at the Gate
The Fallen Crown
Warlord's War
Kingmaker
Henry II
Crusader
The Welsh Marches
Irish War
Poisonous Plots
The Princes' Revolt
Earl Marshal

Border Knight 1182-1300
Sword for Hire
Return of the Knight
Baron's War
Magna Carta
Welsh Wars
Henry III
The Bloody Border

War in the West

Baron's Crusade
Sentinel of the North
War in the West

Sir John Hawkwood Series
France and Italy 1339- 1387
Crécy: The Age of the Archer

Lord Edward's Archer
Lord Edward's Archer
King in Waiting
The Archer's Crusade (Due out in November 2020)

Struggle for a Crown
1360- 1485
Blood on the Crown
To Murder A King
The Throne
King Henry IV
The Road to Agincourt
St Crispin's Day

Short Stories
Tales of the Sword

Modern History

The Napoleonic Horseman Series
Chasseur à Cheval
Napoleon's Guard
British Light Dragoon
Soldier Spy
1808: The Road to Coruña
Talavera
The Lines of Torres Vedras
Bloody Badajoz

The Lucky Jack American Civil War series
Rebel Raiders
Confederate Rangers
The Road to Gettysburg

The British Ace Series
1914
1915 Fokker Scourge
1916 Angels over the Somme
1917 Eagles Fall
1918 We will remember them
From Arctic Snow to Desert Sand
Wings over Persia

Combined Operations series
1940-1945
Commando
Raider
Behind Enemy Lines
Dieppe
Toehold in Europe
Sword Beach
Breakout
The Battle for Antwerp
King Tiger
Beyond the Rhine
Korea
Korean Winter

Other Books
Great Granny's Ghost (Aimed at 9-14-year-old young people)

For more information on all of the books then please visit the author's web site at www.griffhosker.com where there is a link to contact him or visit his Facebook page: GriffHosker at Sword Books

Printed in Great Britain
by Amazon